INDRA ACADEMY: REBORN

Nurit Noik

Book Cover by Rena Violet

Map by Cartographybird Maps

Illustrations by Nurit Noik

First edition February 2024

ISBN 979-8-9896826-0-7 (paperback)

ISBN 979-8-9896826-2-1 (hardcover)

ISBN 979-8-9896826-1-4 (ebook)

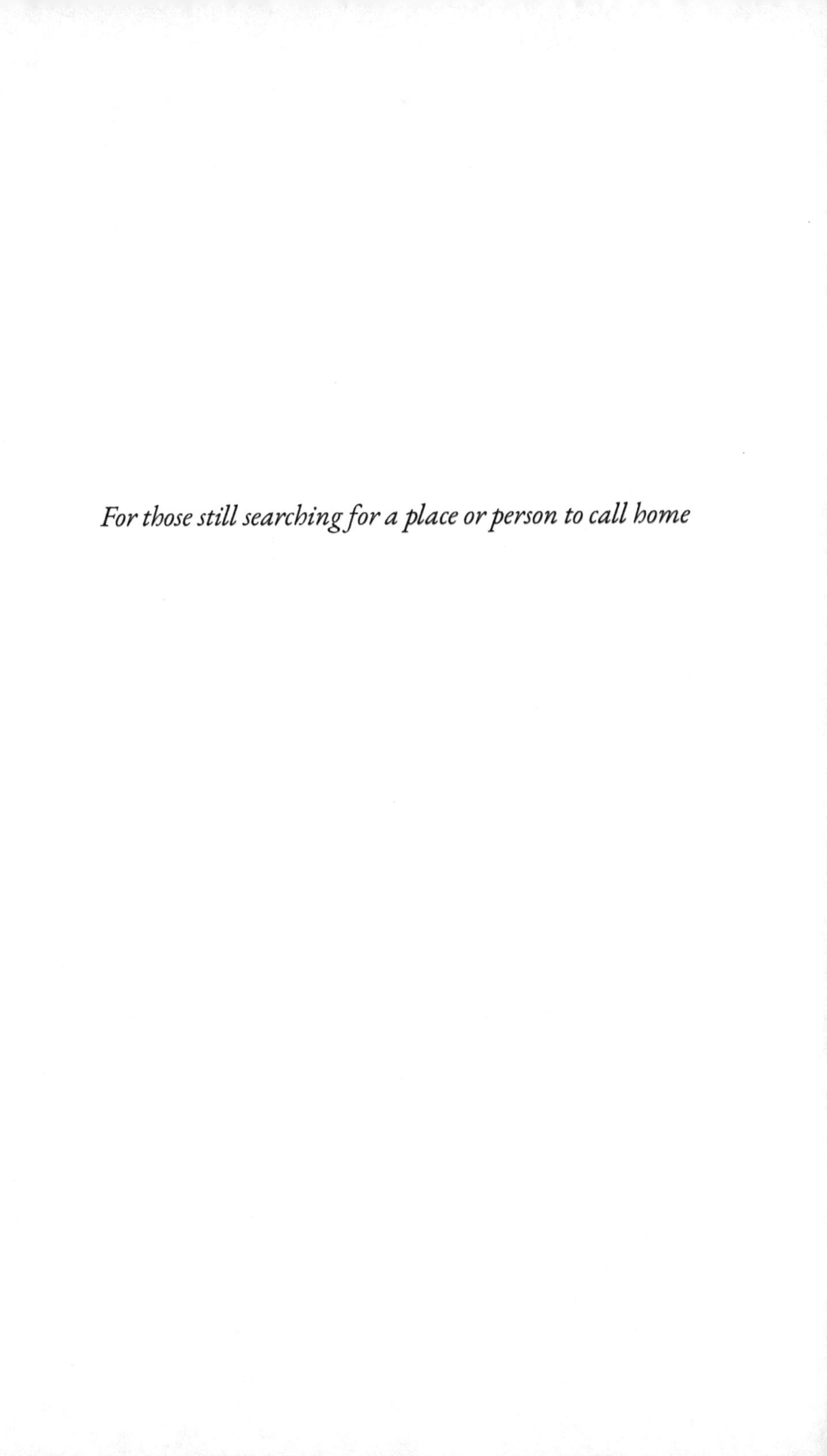

For those still searching for a place or person to call home

AUTHOR'S NOTE & FOREWARNING

THIS IS A BOOK about the unknown. It's about love, loss, greed, friendship, and more. *Indra Academy* followed me all throughout my teenage years, growing and evolving the same way I have. It's seen my victories and failures. My writing manifested these events and emotions in different ways, with different faces.

Because of this, it's my responsibility to say the content in *Indra Academy: Reborn* may not be suitable for all audiences. This book deals with themes such as physical and mental abuse, manipulation, fantasy violence, child neglect, and references family death, homophobia, and the contemplation of suicide. Should you need to put this book down at any point, please do so.

Indra Academy: Reborn was worked on from when I was eleven to seventeen years old. I went from being a year younger than one protagonist to a year older than the other. This is a book about teenagers written by a teenager. A book about queer kids looking for a place to belong and broken kids looking for a purpose in life. A book about how far acts of kindness can go. And for these reasons, I hope Tyler and Oliver's story finds a way into your heart the way it has for mine.

APOLLON OCEAN
KALAMA PEAK
IDALIA
ROYAL CASTLE
WHAGER LAKE
THE DEAD VALLEY
IKREL
MYSTRAL'S CAVERN
THE TIMBER COAST
ERJUN SEA

DERNGATE
VANORAN OCEAN
AUDUN
MARLIN'S COVE
THE BANDIT SLOPES

PROLOGUE

"We shouldn't be doing this."

Isabel Aysun whipped her head around to face McKenzie Evans, her lips curled in a pout. Long strands of navy-blue hair bounced over Isabel's shoulders. "I don't see anything wrong!"

McKenzie pointed a stiff finger in front of them. "Are you blind? There's a hole in the wall!"

Their other friend, Camila Alvi, was busy poking her head inside. It being late in the afternoon, the school library was deserted, silent other than the crackling tension in the air. So when Camila called "Hello?" inside, her voice echoed and bounced back at them.

What were three teenage girls expected to do if they found a secret door in the wall of their school library? Follow it, of course.

Dropping their backpacks by the entrance, they slipped inside. Indra Academy was bound to be full of mystery, considering how it was centuries old. Ancient buildings were cool, yes, but they were nothing compared to the tunnel of dirt and stone the girls found themselves in. Fresh air billowed around them, ruffling McKenzie's and Isabel's hair and Camila's hijab. It was a treat to the lungs as it mingled with the scent of rainwater, cleansing their insides.

"Wait, you want to go in all the way?" Camila squeaked as Isabel ventured a few steps deeper. "Isn't this far enough?"

Isabel turned around to face her. She sighed upon seeing that Camila had looped her arm around McKenzie's. "You guys don't have to come with me if you don't want to. Stay here and make sure we don't get caught." With that, Isabel spun around and kept going. Her flats clacked against the stone ground, bioluminescent moss and mushrooms on the walls leading the way.

She didn't have to look to know they'd followed her. To confirm it, McKenzie exhaled from beside her. "We're not letting you die without witnesses."

Camila and Isabel laughed, and it echoed all around as if ghosts were mimicking them.

As they walked, the passage widened, and the glowing moss thinned out. Their footsteps grew uncertain, hands brushing against damp walls and each other as they navigated along. With every turn, Isabel's excitement waned. They were either going nowhere, or in circles.

She was about to admit defeat when Camila pushed her way to the front and called, "I see a light!"

She was right; a bright blue glow shone from behind the next bend, illuminating the dust that welcomed them. With sighs of relief, they quickened their pace and approached the gleam.

The passage opened into a large, cave-like room with jagged walls and corners. Moss hung from the ceiling, lit up by the sight standing in the center. The ground dipped into a pool of crystal-blue water.

"Great, so it's a…puddle." Isabel frowned, peering over it to see if there was more beneath the surface. Only her disappointed reflection looked back.

"This can't be it." McKenzie flanked her side, crouching down to brush her finger against the water.

At her simple touch, blinding light erupted from the pool. Camila, McKenzie, and Isabel jumped back, covering their eyes with their arms and cowering under the shine.

"Why did you do that?" Isabel fired at McKenzie as soon as the light faded.

"Guys—" Camila tried butting in.

McKenzie cut her off. "You're giving *me* shit? You're the one that opened the hole leading here!"

"Guys—"

"You could've stopped me!" Isabel whined.

"There's no stopping you, Isabella Aysun," McKenzie quickly fired back. All three girls knew it was serious when Isabel's nickname was disregarded.

Camila grabbed their shoulders and shook them. "*Guys.*" She tilted her head toward the pond. "We've got company."

The squabble was immediately discarded, and they looked at the strange pool. Standing on the other side of it were six translucent figures. They stared back at them with pale eyes that seemed to see both nothing and everything. What caught Isabel's attention were their ears; they were pointy and branched away from their heads like the elves she'd read about in fantasy books.

"Well, would you look at this?" one of them, a woman with a short afro and billowing cloak, finally rumbled. Her gaze swept over the girls' rattled figures. "We've been waiting for you, Isabella, Camila, and—"

"*McKenzie*," the three teenagers corrected, cutting the ghost off before she could deadname the tall girl.

The spirit blinked in surprise before dipping her head. "My apologies. Isabella, Camila, and McKenzie." She walked forward, right over the water until she stood in front of them. "Do not be alarmed. I was once an Indra Academy student, too." Gesturing to her companions, she added, "We *all* were."

Camila searched the ghost with wide eyes. "Who are you guys? What even *are* you? What is this place?"

"Patience." The spirit lifted one hand to silence her. "My friends and I, we were the Assembly of Six." Her smile faded, her elongated ears drooping. "Trouble is brewing beyond the border, I'm afraid." She looked to the pool solemnly. "It's at times like this I regret the naivety of simple humans. You only know of your own world. That's why you must retrieve our successors. Aid and guide them here. The fate of all life depends on it."

Isabel clenched her hands into fists. "Slow down! You aren't making any sense. Are...are you not human? What's the Assembly of Six? Is the pool the border? How are we supposed to know?"

McKenzie mirrored Isabel's distress. "We don't speak riddles. Who are we looking for and why?"

All six ghosts started to fade, but before they were gone, the spirit in front of them whispered, "They'll come to you when the time is right."

"Wait! Don't leave us! We need answers!" Camila lashed out, trying to catch the spirit before them. Her fingers closed around mist.

They faced the pool in stunned silence, alone with their neglected questions.

The Assembly of Six only spoke the truth; it was years before their so-called successors were identified, but they appeared in their own time.

Only the sixth wasn't found, his unanswered fate left to choke.

PART 1

Twelve Years Later

CHAPTER ONE

A BROKEN BEAT

TYLER

THIS WORLD IS A dance floor, a party that never ends. You must be quick on your feet to survive. You have to keep a rhythm while your mind focuses on a hundred other things. If you lose your balance, it's over. The towering legs will stomp over you until you're a faint, forgotten stain. You must be strong. You must have a voice.

If that's the case, I'm a stain so smudged you'd never believe it existed.

Or maybe I'm a ghost. That thought plagued my mind every time I trudged through Times Square. Even early in the morning, the place was bustling with people shoving past me as if I didn't exist. Who'd notice a twelve-year-old boy here by himself, anyway? Everyone was so occupied with their own things; they couldn't even stop and admire the gray clouds. I was the only one who paid attention to them. *It's like we're in a painting.*

At that moment, I wished I was a bird, so I could fly up there and marvel at the details.

Everyone's shoes clacked along the sidewalks with confidence, briefcases and purses swinging, coats flowing behind them. My worn, red sneakers weaved around the sea of people, not one sparing me a second glance. The crowd thickened as I carried on, bringing my pace to a stagger. My hands lifted to cover my ears from the booming speakers and overwhelming blend of voices. Strands of brown hair fell over my eyes as I watched the ground roll by, right before my foot slipped on the curb and the whole world rocked.

The dirty snow on the side of the road caught me as I thudded on my back. For a moment, I just lay there, staring at the dark sky decorated with neon billboards, until an unfamiliar young woman peered over me. She held her hand out and asked, "You alright?"

An uneasy tingling washed over me, and I scooted backward. Only when a car honked behind me did I remember I was on the road. I ducked away from the lady's fingers, scrambling to my feet and walking away.

From behind me, the lady shouted, "You're welcome!"

Guilt formed a lump in my throat, as did my words.

I swallowed, the pounding of my heart too loud as I veered toward the side street I always used as an exit. Though the path was still crowded, I could escape the flashing billboards and torturous sounds. It also meant abandoning the smell of food vendors and cigarettes.

A few blocks later, the crisp November air finally cleared up, and I drew in a quiet breath. Almost out of pure instinct, I glanced over my shoulder and opened my mouth, but no words came out when I remembered I was alone. I was supposed to be turning to face my older brother, to laugh about how my back ached from the fall and how surprising it was that the car noticed me. Disappointment kept my mouth shut. *You would've liked that story, Dominic.*

My broken sneakers kicked the pavement when I stopped at a red light. The dance would now continue the way it usually did, with me sitting in Central Park before going home to an empty apartment. *Mia is bound to be hanging out with friends and Mom is working late again.* With a huff, I thought of how Dominic always chose me over school friends. He'd sit with me in the park for hours as we watched ducks swim up and down the lake.

And he was a popular kid! When he used to pick me up from school, friends always flanked his sides. Even parents smiled and waved to him. He could've been doing so much more, but he chose being with me instead. To him, it didn't matter that I was failing my classes or coming home with wet pants because I couldn't ask for a bathroom pass.

No, no, don't be sappy. Today, you're supposed to try changing the rhythm. Isn't that what you told yourself earlier? It's what I'd been telling myself for a week now, actually, that I needed to try breaking the loop. The emphasis was on the word "try." No matter how much I hyped the idea, I never got around to it. There was comfort in repetition.

The light turned green, and I stepped onto the crosswalk with my head hung low. *Just make it across. It's so simple.* But the headlights of waiting cars stared at me, seeming all irritated. They watched, willing for me to hurry up so the next green light would appear. What if they thought "fuck it" and ran me over? I picked up my pace, and my heart dropped in relief when I reached the approaching block.

It was a short-lived moment, though, as the sound of high-pitched yapping dragged my eyes away from the ground. A small, white poodle barreled toward me, its pink leash flapping uselessly in the air as it ran. I watched, dumbfounded, as it raced around the corner and continued flying down the street. An elderly woman stumbled after it, shouting, "Fluffy! Fluffy, get back here!"

That's when Fluffy veered toward the road.

My stomach lurched, and I bolted toward the dog. I gasped as I grabbed the leash, and with my other hand, I scooped the poodle up. The car heading toward us came to a slamming halt before honking like crazy. Fluffy responded with more ear-splitting barks.

I hope this thing has an "off" switch. Cowering under the driver's glare, I hurried back to the sidewalk, out of breath from the sudden exertion. *Now what?* I stared at the poodle squirming in my arms and frowned.

As if my thought had summoned her, the elderly woman appeared from around the corner, and in a heartbeat, we were face-to-face.

"Oh, my precious!" She scooped Fluffy out of my grip, bouncing the pooch in her arms like a baby. "It's okay. It's okay. Mommy's here." Continuing to cradle Fluffy, she started to walk past me as if nothing had happened. But at the last minute, she turned around and said, "Thank you, young man!"

My mouth went drier than the pavement.

When I didn't respond, the lady's smile vanished, and her eyebrows knitted together. It was an expression of disgust, and while I was beyond used to it, my stomach still folded in on itself. Another blow rained down on me as she spun around, muttered "stupid kid," and proceeded to stomp away.

I saved your damn dog! But it was pointless. She was gone, another ghost to haunt me at night.

A sigh escaped my mouth as a cloud, and the wind tossed it to one side. In that direction, the steam from a subway grate evaporated to reveal a restaurant. The sounds of chatter and glasses clinking drifted out of the building. There were smiling faces and warmth, and what was that great smell? My stomach panged, but my legs refused to move. I was left staring like an idiot. Thunder rumbled in the distance, unless that was my hunger.

There must be some food at home. Still, I subconsciously searched both my hoodie and jeans pockets as if money could've magically appeared. All I found was fuzz and the apartment keys.

I tossed away the useless fuzz and started to leave. The noise disappeared behind me, and the air went cold once more. Shadowlike, the chill followed as I started the course for Central Park. Today was about changing the rhythm, yes, but I was a kid with nothing else to do. Looking up at the heavy, gray sky, I let that thought teeter in my mind.

Rain clouds.

Maybe the first step was to not get caught in the rain. I pictured Mom's angry expression and shuddered. It had nothing to do with the biting air.

Miraculously, the sky controlled itself, holding back its tears and only letting the occasional gale sweep through the streets. Afraid I wouldn't make it home before the rain started, I sped to the nearest checkpoint I knew.

It was a tiny convenience store on the corner of the block, where my mom worked for hours on end. As predicted, she was behind the counter when I slid inside.

Her eyes lit up at first to think she was dealing with a customer, but once she saw it was only me, her expression fell. She didn't bother to hide it. "Oh. Are you looking for Mia?" Her tone matched her expression: blank.

"Is she here?"

"In the back." Mom grabbed a pile of granola bars from the counter and organized them on a nearby stand. Unlike me, her hair was blond and neatly cut short with kitchen scissors, as neat as it gets. Her eyes were a deep blue, as unforgiving as the ocean. All we shared was the same pale skin.

I mumbled my thanks and passed her. There was giggling from within the storage room, and the culprits were revealed when I peeked inside.

Mia and two of her classmates were sitting on cardboard boxes, one of them using a phone for a flashlight. Homework papers sat on their laps, but I could tell it was the last thing on their minds.

When the store's light poured over them, they immediately quieted down. The way they death-stared me down reminded me of how terrifying high school freshmen were. I didn't even know their names, but I still wanted to run away.

"What is it?" Mia gave me a defeated look.

They must've been playing "How Long Can We Go Before Tyler Ruins It?" because her classmates started to clean up and gather their belongings.

"We can finish this tomorrow instead," one of them said rapidly, standing up. The second one nodded vigorously, and both hurried past me and into the store. I heard my mom wishing them a warmhearted goodbye, and my lungs squeezed at the irony. How could she regard them with excitement and not her own son?

Mia and I waited in silence until the front door opened and closed. She sighed and collected her homework, stuffing it into her backpack. Like mine, the bag was roughed up and full of holes and loose threads. At least she used hers.

"What?" My sister demanded again, this time with a sharp edge to it. "Didn't you see I was busy?" She was a younger, copy-and-paste version of our mom, with the same blond hair curling around her shoulders.

"Mom didn't mention it," I peeped in my defense. "Sorry."

Mia slung her bag over her shoulder, twirling her umbrella on her wrist. "Whatever. I'm going home."

She pushed past me, back into the store, and I followed. While it was gray and dark outside, the streets remained dry. I gave Mom a questioning look when Mia left the shop. "Will it not rain?"

Mom leaned over the counter, giving the sky a bored glance. "No. Go home with her, though. I'll close up in a little bit."

"Thanks." With that, I raced out of the store, chasing down the path I knew by heart. I would be home before five in the afternoon for the first time in...how long? Smiling, I asked Dominic, *Does that count as changing the rhythm?*

Next time, I'd keep that thought to myself. If the universe couldn't tell what I wanted, it wouldn't go out of its way to destroy it. The sky decided to open the gates and let rain wreak havoc on Manhattan. The dark clouds turned the whole world to nighttime, and like mice, everyone scattered to find shelter. Umbrellas popped up like pigeon heads spotting bread. I was the unfortunate rat, the last one to scurry into the building.

It was the first time in ages that I actually wanted to unlock the apartment door and get inside. I stood in the passageway with puddles of water trailing behind me, teeth chattering and body shaking so much I had to lean against the door to open it.

"Looks like someone didn't get lucky." Mia was already in the kitchen, heating up instant ramen in the microwave.

It made me so hungry, I felt nauseous. "Will you save some for me?"

Mia pursed her lips as she scanned me up and down. She grabbed a hand towel and tossed it at me. "Not if you're soaked." Of course, *she* was lucky enough to make it home dry.

"I know." Water and shame dripped down my hair, feeling cold and sticky against my forehead as I pulled the towel over me. It was hard to push past Mia to find the bathroom; the apartment was hardly big enough for the two of us. And if Mom was included, there wasn't even room for air.

The bathroom was neat, mainly because we didn't have anything other than three toothbrushes and one tube of toothpaste. When my brother's old friend, Noah, used to visit, he'd laugh. "You guys are so organized!" he'd say, when in reality, I wished it were messy.

I stood in front of the sink, rubbing the towel over my hair to make myself look less like a drowned poodle. Once satisfied, I hopped onto the sink counter and started to wring out the drenched hoodie I still wore. It dripped and splattered onto the counter as well as the floor, joining the wet footsteps I already left behind. Realizing my mistake, I stiffened.

Before I could hop off the counter, the front door slammed open and my mom called, "Tyler, have you seen the mess you left?"

A rough sensation burned in my stomach, like bird talons scraping along my inner lining. I dropped to the floor, my wet shoes squeaking on the hardwood as I frantically wiped the puddles with the damp towel. It only left more mess. "I'm cleaning it now!" *Her shift wasn't supposed to end so soon!*

Mom appeared in the doorway, her face red with anger. Like Mia, her hair was dry thanks to an umbrella. "You're making it worse. Haven't I taught you better?"

"I'm not—"

"I'll fix it myself, like I always do." Mom bent down, snatching up the towel. She did it so quickly, I flinched, which only soured her expression even more. "Well, don't just sit there. Do I have to bring the shed into this?"

I scrambled to my feet. The mention of the shed made my stomach twist. "I don't—" It was a weak attempt to defend myself, but I tried nonetheless. "It was raining hard, and I didn't have an umbrella! Mia didn't wait for me. It wasn't my fault!"

Mom tilted her head to one side, her expression cold. "Oh?" She stood slowly.

"Don't punish me for something I didn't do! *You* said it wouldn't rain!"

Then came the part I knew like the back of my hand.

Blunt pain spread just below my collarbone. It rippled through my body like a pebble thrown in a lake. I stumbled back, gripping the old shower curtain so I didn't fall in the tub.

Mom clenched and unclenched her reddened fist with a scowl. "Go. Now."

"It was an accident!" This time, it came out shrill.

"Don't blame me or your sister for your irresponsibility." She grabbed my shoulders and yanked me out of the bathroom.

My back hit the wall with a thud, and suddenly, I was more scared of leaving a dent than getting hurt. I spun around to make sure I hadn't, but the relief faded as a foot kicked my back.

"Do you need help getting upstairs?" Her voice seethed and hissed like a dragon.

All that mattered was getting out of her sight. "No," I whimpered, before scrambling to the entrance. The towel whipped my shoulder blades as I turned.

Mia was still in the kitchen, staring at her bowl of ramen noodles. I knew she'd been listening from the way her eyes narrowed, but she didn't speak.

Unable to take either umbrella, I opened the front door and left. The puddles and my footprints still shone in the dim hallway light, seeming to taunt me as I stormed past them. I paused at the fire escape, considering the path leading up and the one leading down. The shed was on the roof, and I'd taken the stairs there as part of a ritual for years.

But I didn't make the sky rain. Why was I taking the blame when it was something else's fault? Rubbing my hand over my bruised chest, I started my way down the fire escape.

The rain outside had strengthened, blasting me with a wave of icy water. If I went back now, I'd only track more of it into the building. So I tossed my useless hood back on and staggered down the street. The world outside was empty and dim, lit up by streetlights. I was the only human in sight if the occasional car didn't count.

Again, I wished I was a bird. Birds were untouchable to the average hand.

My feet moved on their own, taking me down the road and around all the familiar corners. I wondered if the pigeons had enough shelter.

Why did changing the rhythm have to hurt so bad?

Thanks to Dominic having taught me the art of pickpocketing years ago, I easily grabbed some tourist's Metro Card and found myself in a crowded subway an hour later. People kept scooching away from me, the kid who looked like he went swimming in November. All I heard, though, was the roaring of tracks with hints of conversations I picked up on from other passengers. It was peaceful. I didn't care where the subway took me, as long as it was somewhere new.

Night had fallen by the time I surfaced from underground, mingling with the dark clouds. According to the signs, this was Long Island. I knew my brother once attended school here, so maybe that's what drew me to the place. The rain hardened ever so slightly, which I was numb to as I wandered the unfamiliar roads. Or at least, I explored as best as I could in the dark.

By the time my legs started to ache, I'd found my way to a cute, suburban neighborhood. Cookie-cutter brick houses lined the roads, the yellow lights from their windows glowing, taunting me with the warmth they promised. The bare trees were black in the dark. Cars drove by every so often, spraying puddles at me as they passed.

It was so quiet.

I leaned against a brick wall, sliding to the ground. A streetlight nearby granted me some sort of company, and I appreciated its efforts. Thinking that it would protect me, I brought my knees to my chest and closed my eyes. I couldn't bring myself to worry about Mom and Mia, because then, I'd have to go home. Logic would bring panic.

In Dominic's voice, I asked myself, *Where does it hurt?* Slowly, I put my hand to my chest. It ached as if I'd run three miles.

I was just starting to relax when the rain suddenly stopped hitting me. *So why can I still hear it?* My eyes fluttered open, my whole body stiffening when I saw an umbrella over my head.

It was held by a young woman standing in front of me, her eyebrows knitted together in a worried expression. Her hair was magnificently navy blue, steadily darkening as rain pelted her head. It clung to the shoulders of her trench coat. "You're a little young to be out here by yourself. What's your name?"

My throat closed, my lips refusing to part.

She tried again with a different approach. "Where are your parents?" Her hair reminded me of a mountain bluebird.

I couldn't explain this to her without someone getting mad at me. Working some saliva into my mouth, I finally whispered, "M-my mom will–will tell me when I can go–go–go back inside." The words sounded so broken coming from my mouth. So hoarse. So disgusting.

"She sent you out here?" The lady tightened her grip on the umbrella.

Guilt crawled up my spine. She was getting wet in the rain. I was already soaked, so it didn't matter if I was under the umbrella or not. The quicker I got rid of her, the quicker she'd take her umbrella back. "I-I came by–by myself. I'm fine."

"No parent should leave their kid in the freezing rain. You'll catch a cold out here." She held her other hand toward me, an invitation in her stormy eyes. "Let me call your mom and see to it that you make it home."

My hands rested on my knees, a clear refusal of her offered hand and help. "She won't like that." It wasn't necessarily a lie. Mom would kill me if she heard I went all the way to Long Island without reason. The real issue was that she didn't have a phone. She relied on the one at her job.

"I work at a boarding high school just across the street. You see the window over there?" She nodded to the tall sets of old-fashioned buildings across from us. Bright windows dotted the campus like stars. "One of those is my office. I'd rather deal with an angry mother than have a front row seat to a child in the rain by themselves." Noting my reluctance, she crouched down and pulled out a small ID card. Under the dim streetlight, it read "ISABELLA AYSUN, PRINCIPAL OF INDRA ACADEMY."

This is the principal? Embarrassment clawed at my stomach, and I doubled over as it mingled with hunger. "Sorry."

"What are you apologizing for?"

I focused on the rain hitting the sidewalk, unable to meet her gaze.

"If I can get your name, I can search some school databases for your mom's information." Ms. Aysun gave me a weak smile. Insistent, she still hadn't put her extended hand away. "At least come inside while I do that."

Mia won't want to share a room with you if you catch a cold. My mom's voice was harsh in my mind, and the thought of returning home made me shiver. I was supposed to be on the roof, in the shed. I had never disobeyed Mom's rule before. Whether I stayed or returned, she'd kill me. That was the motivation I needed. Ignoring the lady's hand, I stood up by myself and nodded weakly.

Let this be quick and painless.

Chapter Two
A Tough Crowd
Oliver

I hadn't expected my Sunday evening to be sacrificed for a lost cause. But here I was, sneaking into the library because of my two best friends. They'd spent all week crafting this devious plan to hunt for the truth about Indra Academy's many rumors. I'd been so busy trying to tune out their ridiculous scheming that I'd missed the chance to bail out.

The rain made it ten times worse. We were drenched to the bone. All this to avoid security guards in the hallway, huh?

"Oliver, are you spacing out up there? Hurry up and get the window open!" Bryce Colliss hissed from beneath me.

I gripped his brown, side-swept hair from where I was sitting on his shoulders. "You have to stop squirming, first!"

With the way he rocked and swayed, I couldn't reach forward and widen the bay window. I was half tempted to ask Bryce to put me down and start searching for a rock to throw. To keep my ginger hair out of my eyes, I'd put it into the tightest ponytail imaginable.

Now, I couldn't tell if it was that giving me a headache or this wild expedition.

Luke Ferris, hovering behind us, finally stepped forward and planted his hands on my back to steady both Bryce and me. Being Bryce's height, he could reach more easily. "Does that help at all?"

"A little." Relying on Luke to catch me if I tipped backwards, I reached over and grabbed the dainty edge of the bay window. I held my breath as I slowly pulled it back, creating an opening.

Rumors spread around Indra Academy like a wildfire. The desire to uncover the truth wasn't uncommon. All it takes is one person to mutter, "The hallway ghosts enjoy loud sounds," and then the next night, you'll have a group of kids sneaking out to shout nonsense into the corridors. The previous school year, some kid convinced everyone that a beautiful spirit saved him when he fell into the lake. Jumping into the dirty water to find pretty, ghostly girls became a short-lived trend, one that I never understood.

Bryce inched closer to the wall, giving me something else to lean on as I shakily stood up on his shoulders. Ignoring how he hissed at the added pressure, I hauled myself over the windowsill.

I was greeted by the pleasant sound of silence. Whatever the navy-blue sky's light didn't reach was coated in comforting darkness. Once assured I hadn't set off any alarms, I opened the window all the way and offered Bryce and Luke my hands for assistance in scaling the wall.

Of course, you also have outsiders muttering about how the school used to practice witchcraft and other supernatural activities, but it was never confirmed to be true. Or maybe their snooty looks came from thinking, "Oh, here come the boarding high schoolers again! Hah, look at them flaunting their fancy asses around." They hadn't seen how quickly a student would jump into the lake for a myth.

Because Luke and Bryce were both powerhouses at six feet tall, they made my exertion seem pathetic. Landing next to me with ease, they ignored my dumbfounded expression and grinned at me. As the building's warmth started thawing me out, I shuddered. It made my returning smile look as awkward as I felt.

Most of the rumors came and went with the news. We would laugh over it for a week before something else came along. The only gossip that truly stayed was the one about Indra Academy's past, and it kept everyone asking the same question: Was Indra Academy really haunted or tied to something supernatural?

My friends and I wanted to see how deeply rooted these stories were for ourselves. Although my idea of research hadn't involved thievery, I was outnumbered.

"I overheard that they might keep old texts about the school in the far back," Luke explained as he fumbled in his pockets. He pulled out his phone and switched the flashlight on, illuminating our surroundings with brilliant light. His warm brown skin glowed under the flashlight's radiance, as did the little cluster of bleached blond atop his coily black hair. It was the result of an experiment from over the summer.

Finally, we could see where we stood. The library was easily one of my favorite spots on campus. Wooden pillars stretched up to the high ceiling, adorned with massive bay windows that let natural light flood in during the day. Usually, in the sun, it turned every polished, dark decoration a wonderful golden color. Ornate windows and paintings circled the walls undisturbed by shelving. Tables, chairs, and cushions provided an abundance of spots to chill out, study, or get lost in all the books.

I'd never seen it so void of life before. The room was drenched in cold darkness. It felt as though ghostly fingers were tracing up and down my spine. I wanted to protest the idea once more, but Bryce and Luke were already navigating their way through the corridors. Unwilling to risk being caught by myself, I scurried after them.

"For someone who traveled all the way from ritzy California to attend a boarding high school, your sense of adventure is lacking." Bryce draped his arm over my shoulders. When he pushed his weight onto me, we both stumbled like drunk sailors. "Three years here hasn't done much for you!"

"Shut up!" I fought to wrestle him off.

Luke gave us a disapproving look. "Stop yelping, or you'll get us caught." He sounded more tired than angry. A furious Luke was an impossible concept.

"You don't want us to get caught?" I feigned a wide-eyed, innocent look. "It isn't too late to turn around."

Bryce dug his elbow into my neck with one arm and ruffled my hair with the other. "We aren't *that* scared!"

I shoved him off with a playful huff. "I'm also not scared! I just don't want to get busted, especially since first semester's almost over. It's been a good year so far." As I spoke, I tugged my hair out of its ponytail and wrung it out in sections.

"Fraidy-cat," Bryce hissed to Luke. His amber eyes gleamed in the dark.

I swatted him upside the head, and he burst into laughter. We both knew I could never dent his thick skull.

The air penetrated by Luke's flashlight swam with dust particles. This tiny nook of the library had been long forgotten about by everyone but the spiders. Their webs hung delicately across every corner, and a lone rat scurried out of sight as Luke, Bryce, and I ventured into its territory. My stomach did a slow roll as I took the scene in.

Unsure of how much time we could risk spending here, we swiftly got to work. I tackled the bottom shelves while Bryce and Luke scanned the upper levels.

All I found were yearbooks dating back to the start of the twentieth century. However, as I inspected the final one, a weathered envelope fluttered from inside the cover and to the floor. I lifted it carefully, admiring the wax seal before guiltily ripping it open.

My eyes were treated to rushed, cursive text. The ink scribbles were faded and chipped at. It was a letter to "My dearest Crystal," telling her to meet the sender somewhere on campus.

Lovebirds, I assumed with a scoff. Deciding it wouldn't be awful to dissect it later, I carefully folded the letter and slipped it back into the yearbook.

Before I could mention any of it to my friends, a blunt force hit the top of my head. I doubled over with a strangled sound, watching as a book bounced to the floor beside me. "Seriously?" I hissed to Luke, who stood over me.

"Sorry, are you okay?" He crouched down next to me but didn't stand again after retrieving the book. Instead, he held it on his lap to show it to me. "I was just starting to flip through this and got startled."

"Startled?" I raised an eyebrow at the book. This artifact must've been older than those yearbooks with how the leather cover was falling apart. Its spine was ripping at the seams, loose threads and chunks sticking into the open. What truly caught my eye was the lack of a title or author.

"Yeah! Hey, Bryce, check this out, too." Luke waited for him to join us on the floor before slowly opening the book. "It's all about the origins of Indra Academy."

Bryce gave him an unwavering look. "I already found it all. The school dates back to the early twentieth century."

Luke gave him a stupid grin. "No, it doesn't! Look!" He shoved the book in his face before rubbing it into mine. "It was built on Long Island soil in the late 1800s. It was a school for magic. A sort of magic called your Mageia."

"Mageia what?" I gasped, right as Bryce laughed a little too loudly. We frantically shushed him.

"You're joking. Right?" Bryce's smile was strained. "Right?"

"Nope." Luke continued to flip through it.

I stopped him on a page near the beginning, scanning the faded text. Quietly, I read it out loud. "Originally, this school was dedicated to the practice of elemental magic, Mageia, for all ages. Those who wielded this power were known as the Meraki."

Resting on the bottom of the page was a taped image of several schoolgirls playing in a fountain. Their ears were long and pointy, reminding me of an elf in a fantasy book. Floating around them were blobs of water, with their fluid motion frozen in time.

"Decades after the opening of Indra Academy, the number of Meraki began to dwindle," Bryce read carefully from the text, soaking in every word. "Fighting broke out. There was unrest in the country. The final straw snapped when all the Meraki disappeared, taking their magic with them. Indra Academy remained, however, and it was turned into a regular boarding high school."

Nausea pressed against my throat. "I hate to say it, but nobody is gonna believe us."

"Why wouldn't they, if we got proof?"

"That's the thing. This doesn't prove anything. For all we know, we might've been scammed. People are gonna think we're wild conspiracy theorists!"

Luke cackled, "Because of a library book?"

"Kids mess with school property all the time! It doesn't even have a title," I said. This probably meant the letter I found was forged, but there wasn't time to worry about it now. "Or, if this was real, it's covered in middle school, and they don't teach it in California."

I looked to my friends in hopes they'd prove my point. Luke grew up here in New York City, whereas Bryce was born in Tokyo, Japan.

Bryce looked down at the book again, chewing his bottom lip. "My school didn't talk about this, either."

"Exactly." It killed me to see the hope drain from his face, but I couldn't stand the thought of publicly humiliating ourselves by presenting this. "If magic was real, wouldn't it be widely known? People would teach it! Other history books would confirm it! This is just another stupid rumor. One book doesn't prove anything."

"It's real." Luke's voice held a frightening amount of certainty to it. "The book was hidden in a place it wasn't meant to be found in. This was meant to stay a secret."

I rubbed the top of my bruised head. "Didn't you find it really quickly? How was it not meant to be found?"

Either it was deliberately left in the open, or someone had beat us to discovering Indra Academy's past. My muscles cramped at the idea, and from the way Luke tensed beside me, he was thinking the same thing.

"So...now what?" Bryce risked asking.

I glanced over my shoulder, scanning our dim surroundings. "Let's leave it and never speak of it again." *Clearly, we shouldn't have gotten involved.* There was no way this stuff could be real...right? Even if it was, people would just say we were mischievous sixteen-year-olds wanting to cause chaos. *In that case, we'll have a safety net if the story ever gets out.*

"We should dig into it more." Luke nodded to the shelves looming over us. "One book can't confirm everything, after all."

"Besides, if you're so certain it's just a rumor, you won't mind learning more about it!" Bryce grinned at me.

I scowled at him in return. "Fine. Now then, can we get out of here? Dinner is about to start, and people are gonna notice we're missing."

Bryce snatched the book from Luke and tucked it into the large, inner pocket of his coat. He shot to his feet and raced down the corridor, shouting behind him, "Last one there owes the other two dessert!"

Luke muttered under his breath about how all meals were included. He offered me a smile before barreling after Bryce. That left me to follow.

Making me the last to abandon the library was a poor move on Bryce and Luke's part, since I wasn't tall enough to close the open window without assistance. To make things worse, hail had started to fall alongside the torrential rain. I had no choice but to ditch the open window. The library might've already been inside the Main Building, but it was locked from the inside, meaning we had to circle half the structure and endure the torturous weather. In the corner of my eye, the clouds flashed white. Rumbling thunder followed suit. It made for a perfect and spooky atmosphere with the ancient campus and our stealthy mission. We were making our escape under the cover of a storm.

Despite it only being around six in the evening, it was pitch black as I raced across campus in hopes of catching up to Luke and Bryce. Gravel, sand, and cobblestone crunched under my boots, the main pathways turning into mush as I ran. Heavy gusts of wind slapped my hair into my face, threatening to knock me down. Like I was on a battlefield, hail fired at my skull as I dashed for cover.

With its glowing, yellow windows, the Main Building was a glorious sight. It reminded me of a hospitable ship in a stormy sea. My rain-blurred eyes soaked it up with eagerness.

That's why when the entire school flickered and lost power, my vision blackened with it. I stumbled to a halt, catching my balance as screams and shouts echoed in the distance. It was a chain reaction of every student on campus.

"Over here!" Bryce's voice called. He was hiding in the archway of the large staircase leading inside the Main Building, lit up by another flash of lightning.

I jogged up the stairs to meet him. Luke must've been inside already. My wet hair clung to the back of my neck, gravel threatening to trip me from below. For a moment, the strain made me wonder if the whole ocean would rain down.

As I approached, sounds of murmurs and laughter bubbled around me. The majority of kids had gotten over their shock and took this as a chance to shine flashlights in each other's eyes and horse around in the dark. I did, however, catch snippets of people expressing concern over the strength of the storm. Some whimpered at the thunder, and others nervously kept away from the windows.

Teachers and staff weaved through the clusters, telling students to return to the dining hall as planned. The lanterns they held overhead, combined with the eerie echoes and architecture around, gave the whole scene a medieval vibe. We were like soggy street boys about to be handed a roll of bread.

Students were already filing into the dining hall, the kitchen attached to it lit up by the emergency lights. Teachers snapped for everyone to stop fooling around and continue as if nothing was wrong. They placed their lanterns along the stretched-out tables and made it clear that nobody should touch them. Of course, as soon as they turned their backs, kids tapped the lanterns, held them, and swung them in the air.

It might've been a boarding academy, yes, but we were still high school students. And okay, maybe it *was* a bit of an adventure, despite feeling trapped in the wrong era. At least it was the weekend, and nobody was in uniform. That would have been the cherry on top of the old-school cake.

The orange glow from the lanterns crept up the massive pillars lining the hall, with ornate illustrations carved into their stone bases. Students' voices echoed in the high ceiling, which was crafted of mosaic stained glass. As I separated my mind from the chaos around me, I gazed upward, wondering if that roof had been around long enough to see this magical era my friends and I were trying to prove real—or not. My shivers came from more than being soaked to the bone.

Eventually, the excitement level grew tolerable as dinner continued. Heaters hummed lazily, warming the air and soothing my icy skin. Luke and Bryce huddled close together, flipping through the nameless book we'd stolen. They held it on their laps, leaning over to guard the precious item. Too nauseous to even think about joining them, I observed their facial expressions and how they shifted from shocked to horrified to amazed and back again.

We had all this incredible knowledge sitting in front of us and nobody to confide in. Everyone around us was peacefully ignorant of Indra Academy's potential big secret. For the first time in a while, I felt utterly alone.

As I took a slow sip from my glass, the water inside trembled with the vibrations of approaching footsteps. I looked up to see none other than the blue-haired principal approaching our table. Her expression brightened once our eyes met.

"Oliver, I need you for an important job," was all she said after giving Bryce and Luke a wave hello. Her trench coat was damp, but her smile was warm against the chilly night.

I stared at Isabel, fighting the urge to straighten up. What did she want from me, of all people? Maybe it was her first name–basis rule that made it easier to relax despite my racing heart. "Sure, what do you need?"

Before Isabel could respond, the sound of glass shattering and kids shrieking turned all heads, including ours, to the center of the hall. A chunk of hail, the size of a golf ball, had pierced the ceiling and was now surrounded by glass and shocked students. Rain and smaller bits of ice relentlessly pounded through the new opening. As wind howled outside, more hail smashed one of the side windows open.

"Back away from there!" Isabel barked to the forming crowd. She turned to the nearest teacher and hissed, "Get everyone to someplace with better shelter. We can't risk anyone getting hurt."

"Of course." Frazzled, the teacher dispersed into the sea of kids.

Isabel beckoned me with her hand, and I followed her to the exit. Only when we were in the emergency light-powered hallway and the chatter died behind us did she speak again. "I'm sorry about that. Anyways, we have a visitor, and I want you to show him around. Get him settled, you know? I feel like you two will get along." As she spoke of this mysterious person, her expression turned...serious. Like this was something important.

Her words raised the hairs along my neck. "A new student?"

"Not exactly."

What else could it be? I chewed the inside of my cheek, running scenarios through my head as we trailed the dark corridors.

But before I could think too deeply about it, we turned down the familiar bend that led to the main office. When we entered, the receptionist was sitting at her desk, using her phone as a light. She smiled at us. For once, she wasn't typing at her computer, instead reading an emergency manual. My tongue tied at the sight.

"Before you freak out, just know I'm in the process of finding his parents," Isabel said to me, stopping in front of the wooden door to her office. "The power outage has led to a few complications, of course. I must talk to the technicians about that, so will you keep an eye on him in the meantime? If you two want to leave the office and go elsewhere, you're free to do so. Just email me so I don't panic and think he ran off or was stolen."

You're talking to me like I'm a babysitter and you have a date night! I smoothed the wrinkles of my damp coat and mumbled, "Alright."

Isabel opened the door to her office, which was lit by a weak electric lantern on her desk. Sitting in her chair was a giant lump of blankets, but as my eyes adjusted to the gloom, I realized a body was snuggled within it. A small boy sat wrapped in the cocoon of blankets, watching us with wide eyes.

The principal smiled at the kid despite his worried expression and said, "I'm leaving you in good hands! He'll take over from here." And with that, she waved and walked away, muttering something along the lines of, "That hail is gonna cause so much damage."

I fumbled with a loose thread on my sleeve and forced myself to walk closer. Sliding into the chair across Isabel's desk, I nodded at the kid. "Hey! I'm, uh...Oliver. Quite the twist with the power outage, huh?"

He stared at me like a disoriented owl. The silence stretched on until he looked as uncomfortable as I felt. I was about to say something else to fill the emptiness, but he just whispered, "T—"

More silence. Facing the lantern, he tried again. "T-T...Ty-T. Tyler." His widened eyes showed off the unique coloring of them. His right eye was blue, and his left eye was brown, reminding me of a puppy. Shaggy brown hair framed his narrow face.

"It's nice to meet you, Tyler," I said.

The poor kid looked like he wanted to cry, disappear, or throw up. Maybe all three.

Outside Isabel's window, the hailstorm strengthened. It pounded against the glass pane until I feared it would break. Lightning flashed in the distance, and then came a roar of thunder. Tyler flinched at the noise.

A familiar, protective urge flooded me. I was an only child, but I had a cousin around Tyler's age. The difference between the two was startling. If they were put in a room together, I could already imagine it ending with Tyler keeled over from the pressure of being around someone so excitable. My cousin would hate him for being so, as he'd put it, "boring."

For that reason, I relaxed my voice and expression as I continued. "How did you end up at Indra?" I averted my eyes from his face, watching his reflection in the desk instead. "Do you have a sibling here?"

Tyler hesitated again, like this was a test. "No—not—not a...a-anymore." He glanced at the door. "Ms. A...Aysun said—said I should stay. While she calls my m-mom."

It was hard to ignore his stutter. I smiled, hoping he would take it as an apology for my earlier stiffness. "You can just call her Isabel. She says she feels old when people call her by her last name!"

"S-sorry."

I shook my head. "You're okay. Everyone takes a while to get used to it."

Tyler gave me a skeptical look, his face scrunching up. But before he spoke, a massive sneeze racked his body. Mumbling another apology, he reached for a tissue on the desk. Two more congested sneezes followed.

Curiosity got the better of me. I finally lifted my eyes to face him again. The boy was in a blanket burrito with soaked hair, for crying out loud! How had I not caught on? "Are you cold? Come on, Isabel said it's okay for us to leave, so why don't we get you warmed up for real? Those damp blankets don't seem to be doing much." *Bryce and Luke won't mind if I ditch them for the evening.*

"I–I can't. My mom..." His voice trailed off.

"You'll get sick." I stood, taking the lantern with one hand and offering the other to Tyler. He eyed me warily before getting up without assistance. When he left the blankets piled on Isabel's chair, I finally saw the rest of him for real. He was tiny, hardly taller than my shoulders. His jeans clung to skinny, bird-like legs, his black hoodie making half of his body disappear.

Wrenching my gaze away, I set the lantern back down and pulled my coat off. "A little extra warmth," was all I offered as I handed it to Tyler.

Taking it, he looked like he had a million things he wanted to say.

CHAPTER THREE
OWL-EYED KID
OLIVER

BABYSITTING HADN'T BEEN ON my agenda that day, but here I was, leading some kid through the dormitory building hallway. Tyler trailed behind me, with skittish footsteps that scratched on the wooden floors. His pace continuously picked up and fell as if he didn't know how much distance to put between us. As if any sudden movement would send him bolting.

He kept looking at me with those round eyes, like a little bird about to be led into a trap. I didn't know how to reassure him without coming across as suspicious. Not a word had left me since we'd first entered the dorm building, and Tyler had ripped my coat off, handing it back to me. I'd been left to awkwardly lug it around since.

"Here we are," I sighed when we finally reached the dorm I shared with Bryce. Handing the lantern to Tyler, I fished around for our key.

He made no comment as I opened the door, though his body swayed and feet shuffled. I, on the other hand, started to feel hot as I took in the dark room.

Since neither Bryce nor I originally lived nearby, our room was nowhere near as cluttered as some of the others. We each had one suitcase pushed underneath our loft beds, and just enough clothes to fit in our dressers. Most of the things we'd brought from home were small, like plushies and special trinkets. Above my bed, I had a rainbow pride flag surrounded by glow-in-the-dark stars. The stars' low, blue light welcomed us.

While it was pretty, my armpits broke into a sweat as my gaze landed upon my bed, which looked like a tornado had ripped through it. The duvet was rumpled and had been kicked everywhere, a reminder of my struggle to wake up early that morning. My poor bear plushie barely clung onto the side of the mattress. Thankfully, Tyler didn't pay attention to any of that, focusing on the floor after his inspection.

"Feel free to shower and warm yourself up." I moved the bear onto my pillow before peeling my wet sweater off. Hopefully, the backup power would kick in and ensure I didn't die of hypothermia before Tyler was finished. "I'll grab you fresh clothes while you're at it. You can take the lantern, and I'll use my phone for light."

Tyler gave the lantern a distrustful look before setting it on the ground. He stood still for a moment, unsure, before pulling his drenched hoodie and T-shirt off. Handing them to me, he whispered, "I'll do the—do the rest in the bathroom," as if he had to justify why he still had pants on.

I opened my mouth to reply, but I froze as I took in the boy in front of me. His ribs stuck out of his sides. Littered along his chest and shoulders were scratches and bruises, warped by visible collarbones. He was a house of cards in a hurricane, ready to topple at any second.

I forced myself to face elsewhere, gripping his wet hoodie and shirt. "No worries."

He took the lantern and started for the bathroom. Right before he disappeared inside, though, I noticed the thin, long scars shining across his back.

When the door closed and locked behind him, I exhaled shakily and pulled out my phone, using the light to aid me as I laid Tyler's clothes on my desk.

The black hoodie was huge, frayed at the edges, and musty smelling, like it hadn't been washed in ages. It reminded me of a wet dog. His T-shirt was even worse: thin as a sheet, too small, and covered in little holes, which threatened to become a bigger problem.

Tyler's ungroomed, bruised appearance flashed in my mind. The image was followed by his quiet behavior, his jumpiness, and the almost lonely look in his glassy eyes.

Is he okay? It was a stupid question, but it tore at my heart. Something—or someone—had to have put him in that state.

I felt this sudden urge to call the police or child protective services. But that wasn't a part of Isabel's instructions, and what if it dug Tyler into a deeper hole? I didn't know the full story behind his visit to Indra Academy. I tucked the idea into the back of my mind, just in case.

Until I could inform Isabel of what I'd seen, the next best thing would be to help him relax here. I moved to my dresser and started to rummage through my things. I'd donated most of my old clothes, so finding something that fit him proved tricky. I opted for a long sleeve top and sweatpants.

After changing into dry clothes of my own, I leaned against the ladder to my bed, swiping my phone open to send a text to the chat I shared with Luke and Bryce. My fingers hovered over the keyboard for a minute, unsure of how to explain my absence. Before I could start, though, an email notification from Isabel appeared at the top of my screen. The message read:

Power won't be back for a few hours. Would you mind if Tyler crashes with you for the night?

It was an odd request, but given Tyler's state, I wasn't in a rush to send him back to wherever he came from.

"Not at all," I typed back.

That did, however, provide a new issue and prompt for the group chat. Returning to my original message, I sent: Sorry for disappearing. Isabel wanted my help with a visitor. Bryce, he's bunking with us tonight.

Bryce sent a string of texts exclaiming: *What the hell?*

I added hastily: *I'll explain when you get back. Just be nice to him, okay? Please.*

With that, I set my phone down and began searching for an air mattress.

Bryce swung the front door open just minutes later, slouching in relief to see our guest was still in the shower. He joined me on the floor, taking the air mattress package I was struggling to unfold. "Hey, what's going on?"

I watched him pick at the tape on the box. "It's a long story."

With a raised eyebrow, Bryce glanced at the bathroom door. "Then you better start talking."

My mouth opened, but no words came out. How could I even begin to describe this?

Slowly, I backtracked to earlier at dinner, starting from there. Bryce listened in silence. My pauses were filled with the sounds of him undoing the box and the shower running next door. I faced the ground the whole time, only looking up once I finished.

Bryce stared back at me with this wide-eyed, pale expression. "He got undressed in front of you to show you, Oliver."

"He's a little kid!" My voice cracked. The idea that someone had the nerve to hurt such a sweet boy made me sick to my stomach. "He's just a kid..."

"I know." Sounding just as pained, Bryce dug out his phone. "We need to tell someone."

But before he could do anything, the running water in the shower stopped.

"Shit, I don't want him to know we spoke behind his back!" I waved my hands at Bryce's phone, like a magician urging it to disappear. "Act natural!"

Bryce flung his phone away, ripped the air mattress out of its plastic confines, and blew into the little hole. After a long pause, he released it, and all the air flew out with a farting sound.

It caught me off guard, and I let out an unexpected, childish laugh. Perhaps the exhaustion had gotten to me. Bryce grinned before doing it again, and we were soon rolling on the floor acting like nothing happened.

That was perfect since Tyler emerged from the bathroom, wrapped in a towel, heartbeats later. Clearly thinking we were laughing at him, he grabbed the clothes I left out and disappeared into the bathroom again with record speed. The guilt quieted us down, and when he came back dressed, we apologized through our laughter and complimented the new outfit.

The clothes were too big for him, the sleeves of the shirt swallowing his hands while the ends of the sweatpants dragged on the floor. At least he looked comfortable. Tyler kept touching the material in awe, rubbing his hands along the fabric and smiling to himself.

When we explained to Tyler that he'd be staying the night, he didn't say anything. He simply allowed his head to droop, focusing on the ground, and nodding to show he understood. He kept rubbing his scarred knuckles with this distraught look.

For the rest of the night, Bryce and I drifted between doing homework and checking on our guest. With curfew about to start, the best meal we could offer was a pack of trail mix. Though he looked ravenous, Tyler hesitated, like he was unsure if he wanted to eat when we weren't. Slowly, he pecked at the trail mix when we promised it was okay.

While Bryce and I did our homework, Tyler occupied himself with watching downloaded movies on my phone. Every time a Disney song started, he turned the volume down.

Eventually, I gave up on homework, partially because I needed my phone for the last bit and didn't have the heart to take it away from Tyler. *Would he really care, though?*

He sat hunched over on the air mattress, hugging his knees as he watched *The Lion King*. From the blank look on his face, he was either fully invested in it or completely zoned out. His eyes sparkled every time the talking bird came on screen.

"Good movie, huh?" I piped up, sitting next to him.

He tore his gaze away from the screen, nodding stiffly at me. A moment later, he was back to watching the movie, trying to curl himself into an even tighter ball. It was probably a hint, and while I kept quiet, I didn't leave. Even Bryce joined in, flanking my side as we enjoyed the movie.

All was well until the scene where Mufasa died. Tyler turned the sound off completely, and he tilted his head away from the screen. I tried keeping my attention on the movie, but it was hard to ignore the stricken look on his face and the way he trembled beside me.

A minute later, he just returned the phone to me and crawled to the far end of the air mattress. Ignoring the questioning stares

Bryce and I shot his way, he flopped onto his side with his back facing us.

Neither Bryce nor I moved for a moment, just watching and waiting to see if Tyler would do anything else. Nothing.

"Maybe he's not a Disney fan," Bryce muttered into my ear.

"How could anyone not like Disney?" It was hard keeping my voice low as emotions surged through me. *We didn't even get to Hakuna Matata!* Disappointment and empathy wrestled in my heart. "Maybe he's just tired. It must've been a long day." I stood, grabbing the blanket I'd left nearby before carefully pulling it over Tyler's body. His eyes were closed, and only the twitch of his brow showed he was still awake. His mouth opened, maybe to say something. Again, nothing came out.

When Bryce and I got into our bunks for the night, though, I heard him crying under his blanket.

I found myself standing in a tunnel covered in glowing blue moss and mushrooms. All around me, water droplets splattered on the ground the way rain dripped from rooftops after the sky cleared. The sound was irregular, seemingly clinging to keep its pattern. A musty, earthy smell hung heavy in the air, like a damp blanket. A faint light pulsed from around the bend.

Even in the unconscious world, my heart skipped beats as I followed the glow like a moth to a flame. The walls around me widened, until they broke away and revealed a room brightened by luminous blue moss that draped the walls and hung from the ceiling. A large pool of crystal-clear water stood lonesome in the center.

When I craned my neck down for a better look, I swore I saw other faces looking back at me.

How unfortunate the serenity couldn't last forever. My toes brushed the cold surface, sending ripples across the pond.

"What are you doing?" a feminine voice rumbled behind me.

With a squeak, I spun around. Standing just paces away was a girl a little shorter than me. Her outline was white, and her body translucent. A trio of scars slashed across her face, which was framed by short, fluffy hair. It reminded me of a lion's mane.

Her wide eyes met mine. "What are you doing?" she repeated, this time louder and harsher. The pointy ears atop the sides of her head were pinned back like an aggressive animal.

I flinched, my mouth opening to explain myself, but nothing came out. Or came in, for that matter. The air in my system voided itself, leaving me to stare at the spirit, dumbfounded, as I wheezed for breath. She blurred before me as electricity jolted through my body.

There wasn't any relief when my eyes flew open, and my gaze landed on the familiar ceiling of my dorm. The glow-in-the-dark stars glued above me stared back quizzically. I was soaked in cold sweat, my mouth hanging open as I gulped for air. The dizziness I felt made me question if I'd even slept at all.

My gaze swept over the gloomy room before focusing on the dark shapes of Bryce and Tyler. Both were asleep and unharmed, which eased my racing mind ever so slightly. Outside, rain and hail slapped against the windows. Thunder rolled in the distance.

The calm was interrupted by a whisper breathing in my ear, *"You found him, now bring him to me."* I vaguely recognized it as the girl's voice from my dream.

I sat up, whipping my head around in search of the ghost. She was gone, and I was left with a ringing in my ear.

Sleep refused to return after that.

CHAPTER FOUR

DANCING WITH STRANGERS

TYLER

WHERE AM I?

Certainly not the apartment. It was too nice looking for that. I lifted my head with sluggish alarm, my sleepy eyes taking in the room. I was on an air mattress comfier than my own bed, wearing fresh clothes with a blanket pulled over me. Faint morning light poured through the windows, but instead of cars honking, there was the sound of voices floating in the air. The growing familiarity of them made me relax, and I dropped my head back onto the pillow with a sigh.

Oliver was nagging Bryce about the time, which was seven in the morning. Afraid I'd also be prodded, I quickly rubbed my eyes and looked over my shoulder to find the boys.

"See?" Oliver gently shook Bryce's loft bed. "Even Tyler is awake and ready for the day!"

Barely. Drowsiness crept behind my eyelids, and to make sure I didn't doze off, I forced myself to sit up properly.

"How's it that yesterday, you were the one refusing to get out of bed?" Bryce groaned, swatting his hand at Oliver's face. He sat up and leaned against his pillow, pushing his brown hair out of his eyes. "And you're ready before me, too?"

Bryce was right; there wasn't a trace of sleepiness left in Oliver. He was already dressed in uniform and had his bag slung over one shoulder. His hair was pulled back in a loose, fluffy ponytail, which rocked back and forth as he swayed in anticipation. He reminded me of an oriole bird with such vibrantly orange hair.

"Would you like a repeat of yesterday when you dragged me out of bed by the ankles? We can switch places this time," he offered when Bryce just flopped back down.

That was enough to get his roommate moving. Bryce tore his blanket off and stumbled out of bed. "I'll be ready in five!"

As he raced for the bathroom, I forced myself to take in the room once more. The fog lifted from my mind as I realized this was a stranger's home. There were no slamming doors or angry sisters muttering about school. I wasn't hiding under the covers until all was quiet.

It was already quiet. And it was a peaceful type of quiet.

But this isn't my dance! I shot to my feet, but with nowhere to run, I just spun in a dazed circle. *What am I meant to do? What do I say to them?* More importantly, what would my mom say if she knew I slept the night at a boarding school? My chest heaved up and down at the mere thought.

"Hey." Oliver's gentle voice pried me back into the moment. "It's okay. You're safe."

Safe? How could that be possible? "No..."

"Before classes start, we'll go to Isabel to check on the situation of...sending you home." His smile faltered.

Somehow, going home appealed to me more than his idea of safety. I nodded.

Oliver's pained expression cleared, and he nodded to his closet. "You can pick something out to wear, if you want."

I stepped around Oliver's offer, heading to his desk instead. Laid upon it were my clothes from yesterday. I was about to grab them when Oliver nudged my wrist away. I flinched.

He put his hands up like he had a gun held to him. "Sorry, I didn't mean to spook you." Clearing his throat, he nodded at my clothes. "The shirt and jeans are definitely too small, so let me give you an old pair or two I got. And the hoodie—"

"Not the hoodie!" I stiffened, surprised by the strength of my own voice. "I'm–I'm keeping that."

I braced myself, but Oliver smiled at my outburst like a proud parent. "Sounds good."

My muscles relaxed, and then, I grinned. I'd stood up for myself, and it worked!

My cheeks hurt from the strain. I couldn't remember the last time I smiled so hard.

∞

Indra Academy was more old-fashioned than I expected. The buildings loomed tall, made of brick and stone, with moss growing out of their crevices. Crows hopped around the dew-speckled courtyard, hunting for worms. Morning mist weaved through the dead trees, and for a moment, I felt like I was in a movie. It was magical.

The dining hall, however, was infested with rowdy teenagers. Their nationalities, sizes, and appearances varied, but they all wore the same outfit. Indra Academy's school uniform consisted of a black vest over a white button-down shirt, a tie, and in the winter, they got to wear a black trench coat. Other than the little, yellow lightning bolt embroidered on every vest, everyone wore muted colors. They made up for it with their attitudes.

That, plus the amount of chatter for seven thirty in the morning, was beyond nauseating. In my head, they were going *chirp, chirp, chirp,* in the worst way possible. As Bryce and Oliver started inside, I gravitated toward the wall as if it were a lifeline. Because my black hoodie was in the washing machine, blessed by the power returning and Bryce insisting I shouldn't walk around "smelling like a wet dog," Oliver let me borrow his beige coat. I was the only one in color.

"You don't think he'll get lost, do you?" Bryce murmured, pausing to shift his gaze from me to Oliver and back again.

"If he sticks close to us, I don't think so." Oliver flashed me a concerned look, his brows furrowed in a silent question.

I desperately shook my head, which only made me dizzy. *It's too busy here. I'll suffocate in front of everyone.* What if my legacy revolved around being the kid who couldn't handle cafeterias? *Who said you get a legacy in the first place?* I put my hands over my ears to muffle the chaotic noise, which made me feel like I'd plunged underwater. Was it too late to join the crows in the courtyard?

Bryce shifted his weight from one leg to the other, his expression softening. "Maybe we can find a quieter spot for today?"

Miraculously, I could make out the words with my ears still covered. "Please," I whispered, my shoulders relaxing when I saw they'd heard me. Hell, I could barely hear myself.

"Okay, but I'll grab us something to eat in the meantime. Wait here!" Oliver flashed us a smile before disappearing into the dining hall.

That left me with Bryce, who seemed okay. He was even taller than Oliver, with East Asian features and ears that were slightly pointy at the end. According to Mia, my ears were also a little pointed, but Bryce didn't hide it the way I did. Dominic's friend used to call me a mutt for them.

Bryce's outgoing streak faded without Oliver's presence. The chatter around us filled the silence. He frowned as he stared at me, glancing up and down my form. He didn't seem to care about my hands over my ears, instead surveying my body and face.

Before I could run for it, though, he nodded and asked, "Do you like Indra Academy?"

"It's..." The rest of my sentence fizzled out, and I frowned. *What if I offend him?* I dug my fingernails into the skin behind my ears. "It's cool." *It's big and scary.*

Suddenly, it didn't matter that everyone had funky, overly loud personalities. I was the loser without a uniform and the big letters "I don't go here!" hovering over me.

I wished Oliver would hurry up. My chest hurt without his soft presence nearby. A thread inside me pulled uncomfortably with the ginger-haired boy's absence.

Bryce nodded. "It's overwhelming at first, but it's a great place." It was a curt response.

An approaching flash of orange saved me from having to respond. Oliver returned, holding three bagels smeared with cream cheese in napkins. "Lads, I present your breakfast!"

Bryce took his, but I froze. On the days I was lucky enough to get breakfast, it was usually an expired granola bar. Guilt pressed down on me. Mom and Mia were probably going to work and school with little in their stomachs. Why did I get to eat when they didn't?

"If you'd prefer something else, I can go grab it," Oliver offered when I still hadn't moved.

That would make me more of a burden, so I shook my head and took the bagel. It was warm, making my stomach hurt in anticipation and mouth water. "Th-thank you." My whisper felt too loud to my unprotected ears. My chest no longer ached now that Oliver was back. The thread inside me fell silent.

We ate as we walked through the main hallway, which was lined with lockers and large windows, and dotted everywhere with students. Some hung out in front of classroom doors, while others were on the floor, quickly exchanging answers to their homework.

Voices echoed up and down the old corridors. Many students spoke about the storm from last night and how they hadn't seen something that severe before.

What if I get caught here? Just because the principal knew I was hanging around didn't mean everyone else did, too. *I'm contaminating their hallways, aren't I? They're giving me funny looks. I just know it.* It felt like the lockers were pushing against my rib cage. *I shouldn't be here.* Holding back the urge to run, I pulled the hood of my borrowed coat over my head. Seeing the woolly, white fabric in my peripheral vision didn't help. It was too bright. What if I went blind?

When I took my next bite of the bagel, I tasted more bile than cream cheese.

Before I could further panic, the sound of high heels clacking along the tiled floors caught my attention. It was Ms. Aysun, or as Oliver insisted, Isabel. She smiled once she spotted Bryce, Oliver, and me, which gave away her intentions.

"Hey!" Oliver wiped some stray cream cheese off his lips before grinning at Isabel. "Did I pass your babysitting test? I think Bryce and I did a great job!" He looked down at me for approval, and I nodded. Never had I been this pampered before.

Isabel chuckled. "A great job indeed." She fixed her stormy eyes on me, her smile turning a little forced. "I'd like to speak with you in my office. It's nothing bad—don't worry—and you can eat while we talk."

I glanced at Oliver and Bryce, expecting them to be upset, but they gave me encouraging smiles and nods. My brother used to do the same with me at playgrounds, coaxing me to play with the other kids. In the end, I always hid under the slide until it was time to go home.

There was no slide here, though. I gripped tighter at my bagel and nodded, pulling away from the older boys to follow the principal. Before I forgot, I turned around and offered Bryce and Oliver a half-hearted wave.

"I trust their judgment, but let me hear it from you." Isabel had a twinkle in her eyes as we walked. "How was last night? I hope those two didn't give you too much trouble."

"Th...they were nice." While I was being genuine, I struggled to make my voice sound lighthearted.

Isabel murmured, "I'm glad to hear it," and left it at that. However, she kept glancing at me.

I took another hesitant bite of my bagel, wondering if she was upset that I wasn't eating. It was fresh and didn't taste like plastic, so it'd obviously been made that morning.

Isabel's office was much more welcoming now that I could see the place. Bookshelves stood tall against the walls, with plants taking up empty spaces on the shelves and vines curling along the decor. The whole room smelled of baked goods and freshly brewed coffee. Gloomy light poured through the window, giving me a perfect view of the quiet street beyond the gate. Isabel had been right; you could see where I'd sat last night in the rain.

Balls of hail littered the lawn, mixed with debris that'd definitely come from a roof. *Nobody lied when they said it was a bad storm.*

Isabel took a seat in her swivel chair, gesturing for me to sit across from her. A steaming cup of coffee rested on her cluttered desk, which she rather absently swirled with a spoon. "Oliver emailed me last night with a concern," she began. As she faced me, her expression turned serious. "And it confirms something I found out while searching your public school records. You haven't been to school since fifth grade, correct?"

I nodded.

"Have you been homeschooled since then?"

The sound of the tardy bell overhead sounded. School hours had officially begun for Indra Academy.

"No." My voice was meek when I finally answered. I sank into my chair, wishing it could swallow me whole.

Isabel turned to her computer. "I also see that your older brother used to attend Indra Academy. Dominic Lynn?"

Hearing the name felt like a punch to the gut. My appetite gone, I rested the half-eaten bagel on my lap. "Yes."

"He was here on the scholarship program, which is for students from low-income families." Isabel fixed her gaze on me again with a frown. "What's life at home like?"

One of the first rules my mom taught my siblings and me was to never tell anyone about our situation: that every coin was for the apartment's rent. Mom said that if someone found out, we'd be separated. After all her hard work, that would be the end of the world.

I closed my eyes, trying to remember life when I *did* go to school, but that wasn't a relief. Instead, I recalled better times when Dominic was around. My insides warmed at how he always made sure I had enough to eat. How he checked on me whenever our mom got physical. How he made me laugh until my stomach hurt whenever we went to Central Park. Finally, I opened my eyes and whispered, "It's okay."

Isabel's eyebrows furrowed, and she looked doubtful. With a deep sigh, she lifted her cup of coffee and took a few sips, all while staring at me.

Maybe I truly was a ghost, and she was seeing right through me. I pressed a finger to my chest, feeling the aches as I pushed my bruises, just to make sure I was actually alive.

"And on the topic of home—" Isabel started.

I knew better than to interrupt someone, but now was my chance. Thinking of the apartment made my heart race, sweat beading under my arms despite wearing a coat. "When can I go? Go–go home?"

Isabel scrunched up her face. "I haven't contacted your mom yet."

"But–but the power is back!" I pointed to the window, where the patchy blue sky was beginning to poke through the clouds. My breathing hitched as I imagined what my mom would do when I returned. The longer I stayed here, the worse it would get. "It's not th-that hard!" *Is the air getting thinner?*

A better idea came to mind. I stuffed the bagel into my pocket, stood up, and spun around to leave. I could find my own way home.

Isabel was out of her chair in a heartbeat, her hand reaching for the sleeve of my coat. "Your safety is my priority."

A thread snapped in my mind. I yanked my arm away before she could touch it, shrieking, "This is kidnapping!"

We stood in stunned silence.

Oh no. My eyes filled with tears, regret welling up in my throat. Pressing myself against the wall, I cried, "Just let me go home! You don't have to protect me from her! I can protect myself!"

"From your mom?"

I lifted the collar of my coat to hide my mouth. I'd seen myself cry in the mirror before, and it was something I believed was too ugly for the world. So I just stood there, sobbing and whimpering apologies like an animal, because I missed the household that treated me like one.

Isabel tried resting her hand on my shoulder, but when I flinched, she backed up to give me space. "It's okay, don't worry. You haven't done anything wrong."

Breathlessly, I hiccupped, "I gotta go home. Please, please, please." Unconsciously, I chewed on the collar's fur lining.

Isabel still shook her head. All she said was, "I'm sorry. You *will* get to go home, I assure you. Last night's storm was only the beginning, though. Something is changing because of your appearance here."

I protested weakly. That was impossible. It just so happened that I stumbled upon Indra Academy. People liked to believe they're special, that they're more than a speck of cosmic dust, but I already knew about my insignificance.

"No...Please, no, I can't," I finally choked out.

"You must." Isabel cringed, her hands clenching and unclenching. Consoling a child on a Monday morning hadn't been in her plans—I could tell. "Okay, that does make this sound like a kidnapping. I assure you it isn't." Her eyes narrowed as she looked at me. "I believe some time away from home will do you well."

There it was again. She saw right through me. I swallowed my tears down, fighting to ask her to elaborate. But once more, I was drowning and unable to answer back.

To Isabel, that was my submission. "I just need some time to plan, okay?" she asked. "And until then, you will be cared for as if you're one of us." She backtracked to her desk, but instead of sitting, she simply gazed out the window. Right then, she looked old beyond her years.

"For how long?" Slowly, I removed the coat's collar from my mouth. It was damp with tears, snot, and saliva, and I froze once I remembered it was Oliver's coat, not mine.

"I'll have to talk to a friend about that. We've waited a long time for this." Isabel offered me a half-hearted smile. "Classes are in session, so you can hang out near the offices or find somewhere else to sit. Maybe there's a teacher that needs help running errands. Whatever you'd prefer."

I stood as stiff as a statue for several heartbeats before sniffling, "Okay." Rubbing my sleeve over my face, I wobbled to the door and inched it open. The world outside flooded back to me, the sounds of academic chatter echoing up and down the halls. Pausing, I looked at Isabel one last time. "S-sorry again."

Isabel shook her head. "The responsibility lies on my shoulders now. I promise I'll alert you when I'm ready with the next step."

Hopefully, the next step was going home. "Promise?"

"I promise."

Was it wrong of me to feel relieved, being at Indra Academy? My earlier comments about it being overwhelming and frightening still stood, but Oliver and Bryce were like my bodyguards against the fears pounding in my head. With them, I felt grounded. I followed them around the way I used to follow Dominic. When they talked to friends, I stood idly in the background. When they did homework, I peered over their shoulders but retreated when they jokingly asked if I wanted to do it for them.

No wonder I felt lighter being at the school Dominic used to attend. I felt closer to him. I felt...stronger. Every day, I sat in the library while waiting for Bryce and Oliver to finish their classes since I was too young to participate. I had never seen so many books before in my life, so I took the opportunity to read all the bird content I could find. The fifth grader inside me, the one who hid in the library every day at recess, was chirping with joy.

The days trickled by, and I started to recognize faces. There was one specific boy, Luke, who hung out with Bryce and Oliver a lot. He was also nice to be around. Other students would nod and smile at me in acknowledgment, like I was a puppy on a walk. A girl even said, "Aww, I never knew Bryce had a brother!"

To that, Bryce cried out, "I'm an only child!" while I muttered, "My family has blond hair." The assumption probably came from our pointed ears.

Nobody hit me for lurking. Nobody threatened me. Bryce and Oliver stopped reaching their hands toward me in innocent gestures, respecting that I didn't like physical contact. Unlike at my elementary school, I didn't have to hide from kids making unnecessary comments like "Woah, he *can* speak!" Instead, people nodded at me encouragingly, and nobody mimicked my stutter.

The crumbs from my hoodie's pocket were cleaned out, but that brought no relief. It felt wrong. So after every half-eaten meal, I put my crumb-infested hands into my pockets and let them spread again. I was always aware of Bryce watching, but he never said anything.

By Friday, I wasn't thinking of my next meal, and the bruises along my body were fading. I could sleep on my back and stomach again without pain. Everything felt so right around Oliver. It scared me to be out of his sight. Did it make me a traitor to my family by enjoying my time at Indra Academy? Bryce and Oliver let me watch movies with them before bed, and Oliver helped me brush all the mats and tangles from my hair.

I think the movies were my favorite part of every day. My family couldn't afford any technology, and we certainly didn't have the money to go to a theater. So every time Bryce opened his laptop to the homepage of a streaming site, and all those movie posters flooded in, I couldn't help but sway with delight. There were so many! And they were all at our fingertips! The possibilities were endless, but I always let Bryce and Oliver choose the movie in the end. They were the experts, after all.

It was a school night, so we said we'd quit at eleven. The time now read 11:26 p.m. and we were still leaning against the wall next to Oliver's bunk, watching some action movie in the dark. My eyes stung from the blue light, but my heart pounded with this rebellious adrenaline. Nobody said anything, maybe because the climax was upon us.

By nobody, I meant Bryce and me. From where Oliver sat between us, he'd dozed off against Bryce's shoulder, and it was around then my attention shifted away from the movie. I found myself looking to the side more often, stealing glances at the teenagers. Bryce was focused on the movie and Oliver was still out cold, so I didn't feel as guilty for staring.

I wondered if Isabel chose Oliver to look after me because of how motherly he acted. He always offered Bryce snacks while they studied together and encouraged us to take breaks from screens and go on walks around campus. He was the one reminding us to go to bed at reasonable hours, even if he disregarded his own advice and woke up just as groggy as he'd been the day before.

In the background, the hero cursed as the villain trapped him in a corner.

I carefully reached forward and lifted a strand of Oliver's ginger hair. It was feathery soft, recently washed and dried, falling in waves just past his shoulders. The faint smell of strawberry shampoo still clung to him.

There was an explosion on screen. I jumped and let go of Oliver's hair. The villain drew closer. Bryce remained unaware of what was going on beside him.

Suspenseful music started to play as I glanced downward to where all our hands sat. Another fictional explosion lit up our features. Oliver's fingers rested limp on his lap, and his nails were painted black. Something about that settled funny in my stomach.

Dominic had painted his nails once. Our mom made him scrub it all off an hour later. Her lecture echoed off the walls for hours, while I hid in the bedroom, crying because I was scared for him.

Oliver's nail polish, however, had stayed on for more than an hour.

The screen dimmed as the tense music continued. The room was just a little darker now. Shaking all over, I took Oliver's hand and lifted it closer to me, giving the nail polish a better look. His skin was soft. My stomach fluttered as if there were birds trapped inside it.

"If you're getting tired, we can—" Bryce cut himself off as he faced me, his eyes widening.

I dropped Oliver's hand so fast it was a miracle he didn't wake up. "Sorry—I just...I—" I stuffed my hands into my armpits, far out of reach. "I'm sorry."

Bryce smiled in the blue light. "No need to apologize. What's up?"

My eyes watered, and I didn't respond. What if I only started to cry? I glanced at the movie, where the hero was trying to come up with a last-minute plan. How could he sort through the mess in his mind so easily? I would need days in advance. The room spun as possible scenarios choked at me.

Finally, I croaked, "My mom wouldn't like him."

"Who?"

"Oliver."

Bryce's smile wavered, but it didn't disappear fully. "Why?"

I gave his sleeping roommate another teary look. "I can't—it's mean."

Bryce sighed when I looked away. My silence said enough. "Not everyone likes it—who he is and how he expresses himself and stuff, but that's just how the world works. Trust me, my dad wouldn't like Oliver either." Bitterness clouded his face, and he glared down at his stomach. "That's why I'm here at Indra Academy, where I'm...free from my father."

My lungs ached at the realization other people were here to hide from family, too. "I'm sorry," I said. Meanwhile, the movie played through the hero's tragic journey and how it was all about to end.

Bryce shook his head. From the way his eyebrows knitted together, I was glad to not be his enemy. His eyes were cold, amber steel. "It's okay. I'm doing a lot better now." He released the tension from his shoulders. "Being accepted here was the best thing that ever happened to me. Without it, I wouldn't have met Oliver and Luke, and learned great hair advice from—"

"What about hair?" Oliver echoed groggily. He pulled away from Bryce's shoulder, giving his roommate a bleary-but-intrigued look.

"Sorry, did we wake you?" Bryce asked. "Oh, and don't worry about it. I'm gonna take a bathroom break—you guys keep watching." Before Bryce stood, he leaned close to Oliver and whispered something in his ear.

Silence fell over Oliver and me as Bryce left, and nobody spoke even after the door locked behind him. The movie kept rolling.

"They say you should do what makes you happy in life," Oliver said quietly, breaking the tension. He paused to rub the sleep from his eyes, though it didn't seem to help much. "It's a basic saying, I know, but it's true. What good is living if we're hiding all the time? It doesn't cost anything to be kind."

On the screen, the hero's companion burst through the wall, kicking the villain. She had come to save the day.

Bryce told him what I'd said, didn't he? I focused on Oliver's hands, waiting for his fingers to seize up and clench with anger. That was how most lectures with my mom went: She'd start off sweet and let it escalate from there. But Oliver's hands, the same ones I'd held just a few minutes ago, stayed relaxed on his lap.

I took a slow breath. "I like that logic. I–I think it's cool that you're yourself. Because you're...cool." *Oh, Tyler, you idiot!*

Oliver paused as he registered my response before his face broke into a smile. It was as warm as the sun. "You're also quite cool."

I wasn't sure if I wanted to laugh or cry at that. I chose to laugh.

Despite starting to feel welcome at Indra, a little voice in my head kept following me around. It was panicking because I'd never been this far from home, and it was telling me to leave. Only now did I realize I abandoned my sister, who was all alone, having now lost both her brothers.

I had dreams of the apartment, of me trying to tell my mom what happened. She smiled this sickly-sweet smile every time, her eyes wide with fake concern as she asked, "Am I not good enough? After everything I've done for you?"

I woke up crying every time.

CHAPTER FIVE

OPERATION BABYSITTER!

OLIVER

WHEN TYLER WAS FIRST issued to me and Bryce, Bryce joked that Isabel should pay us babysitter money for keeping an eye on this kid. I'd laughed weakly in response, but the idea triggered a nagging question in my brain. How long was Isabel planning to keep this up for? It'd now been four days since Tyler arrived at Indra Academy, and there was no sign of anyone coming to pick him up.

I meant to ask Isabel about it. But every time I spotted her in the halls, she disappeared into the crowd before I could call out to her. She was constantly in meetings or on the phone, too. I could've emailed her, sure, but I felt this was something to discuss in person.

I made sure to keep my nerves tucked safely out of Tyler's sight. He might've been popular amongst my classmates and blending in nicely, but he still jumped at everything unknown, retreating into the safety of silence when he was stressed. The last thing he needed was to think his presence bothered me. Because honestly? It didn't. In a way, I enjoyed looking out for him and making sure he was alright. This strange discomfort filled me whenever we were separated for long.

Tyler was easy to care for. He didn't complain or demand anything from me and Bryce. He simply followed our lead and stayed quiet. Deep down, I wanted him to be difficult. I wanted him to act how most boys his age did, immaturely and loudly. It didn't feel right to have this shadow of a kid follow me everywhere.

The only time Tyler's obedience proved to be convenient was when Luke, Bryce, and I resumed our myth project. We decided to dig more into Indra Academy's past in order to better understand this wild claim that elemental magic existed. For that, we ventured to the school library after classes. We were still in our uniforms, making us feel like professional scholars as we scoured for information.

With the sunset's orange light bleeding through the bay windows, the library was ablaze with light compared to our break-in earlier that week. Students were scattered around, buzzing like bees as they went along with their afternoon.

While Tyler settled on a nearby cushion, reading, my friends and I spread all our sources out on the table in front of us. These leatherbound books were falling apart at the seams and coated with dust, similar to the nameless book we'd stolen. It was no wonder they didn't appeal to any other students with their weathered designs.

"We need evidence suggesting elemental magic is real," I reminded Bryce and Luke as we flipped through the endless pages. "Anything helps."

"Okay, Shakespeare." Bryce's snarky response was the last comment any of us made as we got to reading.

Ten minutes later, we'd all turned to different pages with a variety of images and maps. Luke's had a handful of necklaces printed in faded ink, mine documented strange plants and animals, and Bryce's showed networks upon networks of caves and tunnels. The dates scrawled on them ranged all throughout the late nineteenth and early twentieth centuries.

"So they're connected? I mean, just look at the plants in all those cave images. The white hue suggests they're glowing." Luke furrowed his brows as his gaze jumped from page to page.

Bryce scowled at me. "Go on."

I shot my roommate an equally exasperated look. "Well, don't expect me to know it all!"

Bryce opened his mouth to respond, but he fell quiet. His eyes filled to the brim with emotions you wouldn't expect a history project to summon. What stood out to me was the worry. It looked completely foreign on the guy who'd shoved the ancient book in his pocket a few days ago.

Luke must've noticed as well because he cleared his throat to get our attention. "I heard they made cake for high tea today." Grinning, he added, "Strawberry."

I scrambled to my feet. "You should've said so earlier! I'll get us a few slices. We need some sugar to perk us up." Glancing over my shoulder, I noticed Tyler, who was frozen in place after my jump. "Sorry, I didn't mean to scare you. You want some cake, too?"

"N-no, thank you." Tyler rubbed the corner of his book vigorously. But his eyes twinkled at the mention of food, and I caught him nibbling the inside of his cheek.

My heart sank. "Okay."

After instructing Luke and Bryce to continue researching, I left the library and started my quest to the dining hall. Since school was over for the day, most corridors were empty other than a few students lingering behind. All background noise came from the courtyards or clubs in session.

I passed the main office on my way to the dining hall, and logic told me to keep going. I'd been unable to speak with Isabel all week. How different would today be?

But my need to talk to Isabel about Tyler won over logic. I spun around to storm into the office. A navy-blue blur entered the corner of my vision, and I stumbled to a halt.

The principal herself stood several paces back, in front of one of the bay windows illuminating the hall. Isabel, clearly lost in thoughts of her own, turned my way.

"I've been wanting to talk to you," I breathlessly began. Even after a week of formulating my approach, I felt clumsy and unprepared. It was like dropping all my notecards on a stage before thousands of people.

"I figured." Isabel crossed her arms over her chest, returning her gaze to the frosty window. Every inch of her not exposed to the light was shrouded in shadow, including her beige trench coat. It twirled to the floor like a dusty waterfall.

I loosened my tie, which did little to combat my rising temperature. "It's about Tyler."

Isabel didn't respond.

"I think we need to call the cops or child protective services." It was weird to say such serious words. They didn't roll off the tongue naturally. I hated to admit this. "I–I enjoy his company and everything...but Tyler needs help from someplace other than a boarding school. Other than *me*."

Isabel shook her head, keeping her face to the light. Her eyes drooped, suggesting she agreed with me, even though all she said was, "The hailstorm started right as Tyler stepped foot on campus."

"So?" I asked. "That's just the weather."

"You'll understand in time." Isabel sighed. "But until then, Tyler must stay here."

A million different questions and accusations bubbled up in my throat. I choked on them all. "That's kidnapping," was all I managed to say in the end.

"And he's being abused at home." Isabel's words were steely. "Don't you dare suggest he isn't in a better place now."

"That's why I said to call for help!" I waved my hands in the air, unable to contain my frustration to only my voice. "It's up to us to make sure he's free from his mom once and for all."

Isabel didn't waver. "We are not getting the authorities involved."

"What? Why?" My breath hitched. "Why, Isabel? Why, to all of this? You don't realize how irresponsible this is of you!"

My last words echoed through the hall, coming back to taunt me for making such a poor move.

Isabel finally pivoted her body to face me. In the pale light, her blue hair seemed to dance and swim with dangerous strength, carried by this nonexistent wind. She bristled in a way that made me wonder if I was about to be struck by lightning. "Do not forget that I'm the head of Indra Academy. It would be wise for you to listen to me."

Frost spread along the windows at her bark. The faint patterns laced shadows across the floor and darkened the sky ever so slightly.

It shut me up. I shrank back but maintained eye contact with her.

"I assure you: I haven't forgotten about Tyler since he was put in your care." Isabel leaned back, and her hair relaxed. "This has just required some...intricate planning."

Well, your planning sucks. I couldn't afford to say it aloud, so I nodded mutely.

Isabel's shoulders slumped. "I promise, everything will fall into place soon. There's just some turbulence to deal with. Now, is there anything else you need?"

I glanced at the window, where the frost had stopped spreading. It didn't take a genius to realize that wasn't normal. My research with Bryce and Luke rushed back to me, and I snapped my head toward Isabel. I offered her a plasticky smile. "Nope, all good. Thank you!"

Before she could stop me, I ran to the dining hall with my mind full of strawberry cake and magic.

❧

Back in the library, we decided to eat first, knowing we'd never stop talking once we started. I split my slice with Tyler, who insisted he didn't want any but pecked at it anyway. He pulled up a chair next to mine and sat with us, hunched over with the book on his lap and crumbs speckling the corner of his lip.

"We came up with a system," Luke began when we'd finished eating. He smiled at the kid accompanying us. "If Tyler asks any question about the topic, we have to find an answer. Then, we write it down! He isn't biased since he doesn't know the school rumors, which helps."

"Oh." I eyed Tyler, hoping I was being subtle. How much of this secret could we even tell him? What would he think of this?

From the way he stared back at me, I guessed he was more afraid of disapproval than whatever crazy facts he learned.

"Alright, then!" With a forced smile, I allowed my hesitance to be washed away, as if at sea. The tide would return it eventually. "Let's hear it."

We all looked at Tyler. He shrank under our gazes, focusing on the books while twitching nervously. "Um...okay. If–if all this m...magic stuff was real, where did it go?"

Bryce, Luke, and I all opened our mouths, only to fall silent.

"We don't know." Bryce grabbed one of the old books, flipping through it. "All the books end after a mention of 'Dern,' and the pages beyond that are ripped out." He held the damaged binding toward us. "We couldn't find any mention of this magic on the internet, either. Not a single article, so it essentially disappeared. Consider it an extinct animal."

"Not necessarily," Luke piped up. "Extinct animals always leave their bones behind. We just gotta find the fossils of this magic."

Bryce grimaced. I wanted to assume the mention of bones made him queasy, but I knew his stomach was far stronger than my own. No, something about this project was definitely sitting wrong for him.

"A-and where would the, uh, bones be?" Tyler pressed.

I glanced over my shoulder, to the massive library surrounding us. "This is obviously unknown to most people. The answer will be here."

"Why don't we ask Isabel, then? As the principal, she must know a thing or two about the school's past," Luke quickly proposed. "Hopefully, that's not pushing it."

"Oh, that's definitely pushin—" Bryce started.

"That reminds me!" I cut Bryce off while bumping my shoulder against his. "I was talking to Isabel on my way to get the cake, and she was totally off."

Tyler snapped his head up at the mention of the principal.

"She wouldn't listen to me." I scanned my three-person audience. What if they didn't share my suspicion and simply thought I was crazy? "She's so set on this idea that..." My voice trailed off as my gaze fell to Tyler.

"S-sorry," was all he peeped.

"It isn't your fault." Luke offered him a gentle smile.

I nodded. "Isabel is the one keeping us in the dark. But, gosh, she was so weird about it! And you know what happened?" I leaned over the table, like a gossiping child in the middle of class. "The windows frosted over when she got angry. Does that sound normal to you?"

"Maybe we found our bones," Luke said, his face smug.

But Bryce's expression was tight and unmoving. "It doesn't prove anything. Oliver, you might just be seeing things. It's after a long day of school, and I know you get foggy when you're tired."

"Okay, now this is getting personal." I curled my hands into fists, fighting the urge to cuff him upside the head for that. Part of me wanted to mention our nights of debating and dissecting rumors before Tyler came along, when it was Luke and Bryce convincing *me* the Mageian stuff was real.

"What's your deal?" Luke twisted in his chair to face Bryce properly. "You agreed to take on this research with us. What, do you wanna back out?"

"No, that's not it." Bryce glared at the books around us. His eyes burned with so much emotion, I was surprised the pages didn't catch on fire. He kept rubbing his fingers over one of his ears—naturally pointed in a way that unnerved me. "I just think we should abandon the project altogether. What are we achieving through this? Clarity we don't even need?" Before we could respond, he rose out of his chair and shouldered his backpack. "I just need some time to think about this, okay? I'm sorry. I'll catch you guys later."

We watched him leave in stunned silence. His question lingered like a dark storm cloud.

"I think that's our sign to call it a day." The corners of Luke's lips twitched upward. "We can always come back to this."

"That might be best." I sighed, tried to expel the tension from my body. Still, my chest ached with the accusation of misinterpreting.

That's when I remembered Tyler was with us, staring intently at the table.

"Uh, what book were you reading earlier? The one in your hands." I nodded to Tyler's lap. I pushed Bryce's attitude to the back of my mind as I rerouted my attention.

Tyler's eyes widened, and his cheeks reddened. "Oh. It–It's nothing!" Still, he lifted the book and held the cover toward us. It was an encyclopedia with a cover that showed different birds scattered on a white background. You'd find something that simple in an elementary school library.

I smiled, remembering his previous fascination with the bird from *The Lion King* before he quit the movie. "You like reading about them, huh?"

Tyler's expression lit up. His lips curved into this giddy grin that he quickly slapped his sleeve over. "I suppose."

"What's your favorite bird?" Luke asked.

"Pigeons!" Tyler replied. His voice was quiet but excited. "They're un...underappreciated, y'know? They adapted to l-live in our cities." Tyler's voice strengthened, and he sat straighter. "They're smart, too! They served in–in war, and carried things, and..." He trailed off, turning even redder than when I asked him about his book. "Sorry."

"No, keep going!" Luke leaned forward in his chair. "What else?"

Tyler stared at him and shuddered. It was as if his body wasn't used to attention. He started to drone on about some sort of mirror recognition pigeons were capable of.

As I listened to him and Luke talk, I wondered if I should slip away and catch up with Bryce. It made sense to be uncomfortable with an idea as weird as magic, but I hadn't expected him to turn against it. Where had his sudden change of heart come from? Now, Isabel wasn't the only one acting shady.

It all started with that stupid, nameless book.

I glanced at Tyler again. What hidden power did this boy possess, and how did it connect to everything that'd happened these past few days? Why did he show up the day we discovered Indra Academy's true history? Why had his arrival marked the beginning of Isabel's sketchy attitude?

Oddly enough, these questions didn't worry me all that much. I was more mesmerized by the way Tyler spoke to Luke. He seemed to be coming out of his shell, his small voice stronger than before. He was a kid who appreciated the lesser-known critters, and from the looks of it, just needed a place to be himself.

Part of me wished to cling onto that rare smile of his. Who knew how long it would last for?

I wanted to protect it.

CHAPTER SIX

A NOBODY

TYLER

Isabel and I never spoke about what happened in her office that day again. Frustration for being kept in the dark continued to boil in my chest, especially when Oliver mentioned her refusal to act on anything.

Indra Academy proved itself to be a strange school once I learned of the rumors echoing up and down the halls. Isabel had mentioned something was set in motion by my appearance, too. A million different "what ifs" loomed over my head.

At least I knew Isabel was serious about confiding in a friend, because several times, I found her and another woman talking closely and looking my way.

According to Oliver, that was the nurse, Ms. Alvi, but just like Isabel, she insisted on going by her first name, Camila. She was shorter than the principal, always sporting long skirts like flower petals that matched her hijabs. Every day, it was a different color, and I enjoyed guessing what the next combination would be.

The two ladies seemed fascinated by my appearance. I felt like an animal on a wildlife documentary, except boring. Too bad I didn't know how to backflip or dance like the manakin birds. Those guys had serious skills. The best I could do was press close to Oliver for protection.

Somehow, it had been a week since Isabel brought me to Indra. It was a relaxing sort of day; Bryce, Oliver, and I sat in the courtyard while Bryce groaned over homework. Oliver was trying to help, and eventually, Luke came to join us.

Luke was just as tall as Bryce and displayed similar muscles whenever he rolled the sleeves of his shirt up. And like he did in the hallways, he smiled widely when he sat on the grass beside me A guitar case was slung over his shoulder, which he opened, and pulled the instrument onto his lap for tuning.

The way his long fingers effortlessly reached every chord fascinated me. They were full of calluses and the nails were painted with the same black polish Oliver wore.

Bryce and Oliver weren't necessarily fighting, but the tension of their previous dispute lingered in the air, leaving a metallic taste in my mouth. They didn't mention anything, I assumed, to preserve peace in the dorm, but I saw it in the way they spoke and acted delicately.

Other than Luke's gentle guitar playing and Oliver's hushed teaching, we remained quiet. If I were with anyone else, I would've been swimming in the guilt of not being interesting enough. But this sort of peace didn't leave me antsy or embarrassed.

I lay on my back, closed my eyes, smiled, and let the gentle music wash over me.

That night, I didn't dream of the apartment and my mother. Instead, I found myself in front of Indra Academy, but there wasn't a human in sight. Fog hung heavy in the air, the castle-like buildings standing tall in front of me. The silence was pierced by crows cawing, a swarm of the black birds flying toward me, away from the school. Their chatter was deafening, frantic, and panicky, as they soared overhead like they were escaping an enemy. I closed my eyes and ducked, waiting for them to pass before straightening up again.

The ground trembled below my feet. A crack sounded. With a gasp, I looked up to see the whole place falling apart. Bricks and stones came crashing down, dust and ash filling the air.

For once, I didn't see Dominic's face in my mind at the first sign of danger. Racing to the crumbling buildings, I screamed, "Oliver!"

The ground dipped below my feet before opening and swallowing me whole.

I jolted upright and saw the world had gone black. There were no glow-in-the-dark stars on the ceiling. Was I not in the dorm?

The ground below me turned to water, glowing blue and crystal clear. It came up to my ankles, sloshing as I moved forward hesitantly. *Gotta find Oliver. Gotta find him.*

Water splashed behind me, and I spun around with a smile. "Oliver!"

But it wasn't the ginger-haired teenager approaching me. It was a tall, unfamiliar figure, with slow yet strong and confident steps. Their amber eyes glowed in the dark, bright against the blue light coming off the water below us. His brown hair was short and slicked back. Gray streaks tainted the roots. He had long elf-like ears, with little notches cutting them up.

Upon meeting my gaze, he smiled.

I didn't smile back.

"Hello," he said, voice rumbling like thunder.

I'd heard that every face you see in a dream belongs to someone you know. I frowned at the man, pivoted my body to face him properly. *I don't think I know him.*

"Isn't this wonderful?" he purred. At first, I wondered if he was talking about the scenery, but he was staring my way, walking circles around me like I was a juicy piece of prey.

"What?" I finally whispered. "Who—who are you?"

"Child, the real question is, who are *you?*" He finally stopped walking, nodding to the water we stood in.

I followed his gaze to our reflections. The man beside me looked so strong and scarred, like someone right out of a fantasy book. I vaguely remembered elven creatures like him in the stories Dominic would read me. Next to this man, I was ordinary. "Tyler," I replied eventually.

"And who is Tyler?" The man faced me again. "Let me guess. He's a dropout. A runaway. An unwanted child." A smile painted his lips as he put a finger to my chest and said, "A frozen heart."

I backed away, rubbing my hand over my chest to wipe away the feeling of his finger there. My heart pounded. My stomach churned the way it did when dreams became nightmares.

Noticing my wounded expression, the man smiled. He cocked his head to one side and asked, "Am I right?"

My voice trembled as I asked, "Why does it matter?"

"Because that's all you are." The stranger shrugged. "A no-body."

∞

The next day, I focused on trying to rid myself of that dream's lasting impression. It'd seemed so real, almost too real. I didn't bring it up to Bryce or Oliver, just nodding when they asked if I was okay. When Luke saw me after class, he said I looked like I'd seen a ghost.

Had I seen a ghost? Was I being haunted? Indra Academy was ancient from what I learned through Oliver, Luke, and Bryce's myth mission. It wasn't totally impossible that I had angered a spirit lurking around. However, something inside me made sure I didn't tell them.

That night, I had another dream with the same man. I asked if he was dead, and he threw his head back and laughed. "Dead to your world, perhaps!"

"What does that mean?" I asked, my frustration rising. "Are you dead or not?"

His long ears flicked and swiveled, like an amused cat. "What a funny little human you are, Tyler."

I stiffened. "Are you not human?" It was a stupid question. The man had elf ears, and that said enough.

"Can humans do this?" He held out his hand. A flame as brightly orange as his eyes danced over his fingers. He chuckled at my amazed expression, bringing the fire closer for me to observe. While I watched, he asked, "Do you want to learn how to do this?"

"I'm dreaming," was all I said back. To make sure, I reached one finger into the fire. Pain pierced through my skin, and I recoiled.

I was, suddenly, back in the dorm. It was the middle of the night, the glow-in-the-dark stars shining. Oliver and Bryce were fast asleep, their soft breaths filling the air once captured by crackling fire. If all of that was a dream, though, why did my finger still burn?

That question stayed with me, and the next night, I awoke in the abyss, with water at my feet and surrounded by darkness. The man was waiting for me.

"I want to know." I pointed to his hand. "I want to know how."

"Oh?" He inspected his nails. "But first, you must answer another question. Are you willing to acknowledge what you really are? How much *more* you are?"

"That's the thing," I whispered in response. "How can I know how much more I am when I...don't know if there's anything to me to begin with?"

The man's ears tilted downward, mimicking those of an animal. He tutted and approached me. "Well, I certainly believe there's more to you." Leaning forward, he scanned me up and down. "Ah, yes. I see *potential*."

A shiver rolled down my spine. "What do you mean?"

"It means you have what it takes, but something is blocking you from achieving this greatness." His expression shifted into something resembling sympathy. "It's your environment. You can't learn in a place that doesn't accept you."

I winced. "But I–I haven't done anything!"

The man rolled his eyes. "This world doesn't revolve around you, little Tyler. Why don't you stop to consider what your presence has done to these new *friends* of yours?" He put air quotes around "friends," like it was so unrealistic for me to have any. "They had lives before you came along. They were able to have fun while being dedicated to their schoolwork and didn't have to constantly worry about an extra mouth to feed."

I opened my mouth to argue, but there was no point to be made.

The chill in his eyes melted. "That's why I'm offering you a great opportunity, Tyler. You'll have a purpose if you take this chance. I'll see to it that you're never hurt or betrayed again."

Was he implying that Oliver, Bryce, and Luke would do such things? I struggled to believe that. But this man's argument that I was dead weight hit close to home.

"And if you don't comply, then, well…" He smiled slowly as he summoned a flame.

"Okay." It spewed impulsively from my mouth. "I'll go. Just–just don't hurt them."

The man's smile turned into a wild grin, his ears perking up with delight. "Then follow the cat."

Before I could ask what he meant, I was back in the dark dorm room. I sat up and looked around with a frown. There weren't any felines on campus as far as I knew. At least, that's what I thought, until my eyes landed on something ice blue under the door to the hall.

Small, glowing paw prints disappeared into the corridor.

My whole body tingled with anticipation. The dance kept getting fresher, and the beat was changing.

Despite all that, I still hesitated, glancing at Bryce and Oliver. What was I walking into? How could I just go back to being alone after following them around so much?

I crawled off the air mattress, grabbed my new jeans and shirt, and left for the bathroom. But I didn't realize Oliver's backpack strewn by the base of his loft bed and tripped. Miraculously, I steadied myself before I could fall.

But my victory was cut short as Oliver shifted and lifted his head to face me. His eyes were barely open, half his hair sticking to the side. "Is everything okay?"

"Y-yes, sorry! I'm just going to the bathroom." I scrambled to get the sentence out in one go.

"No worries." Oliver smiled at me sleepily before rolling over and passing back out.

But that split-second grin imprinted in my vision, almost stealing my breath away. Oliver had a smile almost identical to Dominic's. It was subtle and warm, like the sun.

I couldn't burden him and destroy it the way I had with my brother's.

In the dark bathroom, I got dressed, and headed straight for Oliver's desk once out. I pulled out a blank sheet of paper from his drawer and wrote:

Going for a quick walk. Will be back.

But just in case, I added:

Thanks for everything.

I included a smiley face at the end and left the note on my pajamas.

With clothes on my mind, I remembered my black hoodie. It was lying against my pillow like a child's blankie. I pulled it on. If I had my shield, I'd be fine.

The paw prints were still glowing on the floor, and they continued in the hallway down to the staircase. They looked like the stars above Oliver's bed.

Wind from outside rattled the windows, reminding me of whispers, as I ventured through the sleeping school. It felt too familiar, as if I'd already walked these halls in another lifetime. Even without a flashlight, I knew where to go, trusting the paw prints to lead the way.

I found myself trudging to the Main Building, little flurries of snow spiraling to the ground before melting on impact. My skin was numb to the cold. All I could think about was this new mystery. Did Oliver, Bryce, and Luke feel this way about their own research? *Boy, do I have a story for them.*

Finding an open window, I had no trouble sneaking inside. I'd been to this place on campus countless times during my visit. It was a quiet section of the Main Building, mostly occupied by club rooms. The prints led to a dead-end, disappearing under the large doors of the library.

Some security guard must've forgotten to lock it, because when I grabbed the rusty knob, it twisted right open. I smiled to myself and slid inside.

The paw prints showed me exactly where to go, not a single claw deviated from the path. The marks led to the back aisles, and unable to contain myself, I jogged after them.

That surge of adrenaline crashed, though, as I turned the corner. The prints led to a bookshelf against the wall before stopping completely.

"Oh, come on!" I approached, breathing heavily as I willed the invisible cat to keep going. "Now what? What does this"—I raked my gaze over the dark bookshelf, touching my hands all over the surface to feel it—"mean?"

I pushed on the side of bookshelf, and the entire thing moved. It opened like a door, revealing darkness beyond the wall. A faint blue haze glowed in the abyss.

"Oh." I slid the shelf back and forth to make sure I hadn't imagined this secret passageway. Accepting it, I cautiously stepped into the hole. The ground sloped beneath me. *It leads underground!*

Clean air rushed into my lungs. I couldn't remember a time it was that easy to breathe. I stood, dumbfounded, trying to decide what next before a "plop" echoed around me. *Water?* And if the glow from everything around me was blue, it had to correspond to the paw prints I followed.

Forcing my legs to move, I pushed deeper down the trail, running my hand along the wall to stay balanced. Several times, smaller burrows leading elsewhere branched off of the main tunnel, but I didn't dare leave the original path.

I picked up my pace as the dripping sound grew louder and louder. Hungry to know what it was, I kept going until the tunnel widened and lit up around me.

I found myself stepping into a cave decorated with blue moss, crystals, and mushrooms sprouting from the walls and ground. In the center was a round pool, lazily rippling without a source.

"Is that it?" I asked no one in particular.

A gust of wind from behind pushed me a step forward. That was my answer.

Okay. Shoulders tensing up, I crouched down and peered into the water. My awed expression stared back at me. I couldn't see beyond my reflection to the bottom, though.

The wind pushed me again, coaxing me toward the water. I hesitantly stood up.

My skin tingled at the idea of diving into the water, but I'd never learned to swim. *You came all this way! Can't babies swim by instinct?*

If I turned back, the man would come and call me a nobody again. Was this what it took to prove otherwise?

I spent the next five minutes pacing around the pool, arguing with myself. Maybe the man would give up and leave me alone? *Okay, and if he doesn't? He could drive me to insanity. He might hurt or kill me with his fire. That is, if I don't drown. But what if he kills someone else?*

That realization chilled my whole body.

Was I putting Oliver and Bryce in danger by associating with this man? It was no secret I crashed their everyday lives. Maybe this was a sign to stop exploiting their resources and kindness.

Oliver had those motherly qualities, yes, but he was more like a brother. He was more like Dominic. And what had happened to the real Dominic? He was gone.

The man knew something was bound to go wrong. He was trying to save us all.

I backed up a few paces before hurling myself into the pool.

My body was tossed in different directions, like I was in the middle of an angry ocean. Water streamed around me, cold on my skin. The force of it almost knocked all my breath out, and panic clawed up my throat. There was nothing to grab onto as I thrashed.

My search for an exit was impossible with the blue abyss staining black, spreading like ink on paper. Bubbles streamed from my mouth as I opened it in a desperate plea for help. Nobody would hear me, though.

Just as I realized that, I went limp.

Chapter Seven

THE GHOSTS OF INDRA ACADEMY

Oliver

For once, the alarm wasn't what woke me up.

Bryce shook my bed violently, continuing even when I groaned and rolled to the other end of my bunk. He just climbed up the ladder and on top of me, yelling, "He's gone! Get up!" while shaking my shoulders.

I finally opened my bleary eyes with a frown. Unable to formulate an understanding or question, I just scowled at him.

"It's Tyler! He's not in the dorm!" Bryce's eyes were wide, his breathing heavy like he'd just run laps around the school to find the kid.

"What?" Sitting up, I pushed Bryce off me and scanned the room. He was right; Tyler's bed was empty and unmade, his pajamas on his pillow. "Oh no."

A new realization chilled me. "He was up and walking around in the middle of the night, but I thought I dreamed that! How lost did he get on his way to the bathroom?"

Bryce pulled a folded piece of paper from his pocket and handed it to me. "He left this behind."

"'Will be back. Thanks for everything,'" I read out loud. "Uh, there's a difference between saying you'll be back and thanking the people who looked after you!"

A lump formed in my throat. I kicked my blanket off and followed Bryce down my bunk. "Have you searched anywhere other than the dorm?" I wasn't sure if the world was spinning from the worry choking me or because I'd gotten up so fast.

Bryce shook his head. "No, I thought I'd wake you first."

I darted to my dresser, pulling my school trench coat over my pajamas. Checking my phone, relief overcame me to see it was only seven in the morning. "We have time until classes start, so let's look for him." I grabbed an elastic tie and fumbled my hair, trying to get it into a messy ponytail. "You call Luke for help, and we'll split up. I'll email Isabel, too."

Bryce stood frozen at the base of my ladder. "You don't think he ran back home, do you?"

"Let's check the campus first." It was hard to sound optimistic considering how queasy his words made me. I'd forgotten that Tyler had a home and a life outside of Indra. His presence here was so normal. It was the reality I once more began to dread.

I shoved my phone into my pocket, sliding my shoes on. "I really, really hope he didn't."

I knew better than to run through the hallways and shout, but some instinct in me said "Fuck that." This was one of those things I could throw all my energy into. So while Luke and Bryce were searching the English and Science buildings, I took it upon myself to check the Math and Main buildings, where I was right then.

Bitter regret and worry pulsed through my throat as I recalled my fight with Isabel the other day. Why didn't I try harder to convince her to help send Tyler elsewhere?

Look where that got us! I screamed in my head. *He's missing! Why didn't I follow my gut?*

"Tyler?" I yelled, my voice bouncing around the walls. In an office nearby, some teacher shouted "Hey!" I backtracked and poked my head into her classroom, giving her a guilty smile. "You haven't seen a boy here, have you? He's, like, eleven or twelve with brown hair and—"

"No." She scowled at me and went back to looking at her computer.

"Thanks."

I sprinted back into the hallway, trying to picture Tyler's ideal hiding spot. Before I could decide, I'd walked around the next bend. The entrance to the library was at the end of this hall, and to my surprise, the door was cracked open.

Worth a shot to check it out. I made sure nobody was around before peeling the door further open and sliding inside. Pale light flooded through the library's bay windows. The place seemed abandoned without any students hanging around.

"Tyler?" I called again. No response.

Oh, come on! I was about to leave, but something unusual caught the corner of my eye. At the far end of the library, where Luke, Bryce, and I had found the nameless book, was a crack in the wall. "That's definitely new," I muttered, jogging to the strange sight. There were no dents around it, so it couldn't have been from an impact of some sort. *An earthquake? No, I don't think those are common here.*

When I reached forward to touch the crack, my hand brushed the wall, and the nearby shelf shifted. *There's more?* Instinctively, I wanted to turn around and pretend I saw nothing. But what if this led me to Tyler? Besides, after how Isabel tied the earlier storm to Tyler's arrival, making his presence seem so important, I wasn't sure if I wanted this kid to stay missing for long.

I grabbed the shelf and pushed it to the side. With how easy it was to move, it must've been designed that way. I knew my own strength wasn't enough to commit property damage.

Once the gap was large enough, I shimmied inside and gasped. A whole tunnel was back there, the path evidently leading underground. Something about it was awfully familiar, clicking in my mind as I inched deeper into the passage. *I dreamed of this place a few days ago, didn't I?*

I broke into a run, letting the glowing moss around me lead the way. Déjà vu overtook my brain, reminding me where to go as I weaved through the tunnel. Water droplets echoed in the still air, ringing in my ears and getting louder with each step I took. *I swear if there's a—*

Sitting in the center of the approaching room was the round, aqua-blue pond.

"It's real?" My voice was nothing more than a whisper. I crouched over the edge, leaning forward and peering at my reflection below. My fingers tentatively hovered over the water, but I paused as I remembered my dream.

Everything had been real up until this moment. *If there's the slightest chance I could ask for help, let her reappear, too.* With that in mind, I plunged my hand into the water, gasping as an icy shock spiked through my whole system. It wrapped around my body like snakes, squeezing and stealing my breath. I tried to pull away, but the pool seemed to have its own gravity rooting me to the spot. There was lightning in my veins, bubbling up and trying to burst free.

A glow pierced the air in front of me, and I looked up. Six figures, all outlined in white and transparent, were staring back at me from across the pool. *Ghosts?*

I couldn't feel my fingers in the water anymore, nor could I feel the floor beneath me. Through the ringing in my ears, soft voices whispered, *"Bring him back."*

"You have to find him."

"Bring him back."

I yanked my hand free and stood up, only for the ground to rush forward and meet my body.

Water droplets from the damp ceiling plopped against my cheek. I forced my eyelids open, squeezing them shut again as blinding white pain pounded through my head. Maybe it was from the glow of the ghost hovering over me.

Wait, what?

I forced my eyes open again, scrunching them up as I faced the spirit. Alarm rushed through me as I recognized her. She had short hair, long ears, and a trio of scars slashing her nose. "What the—"

"You fainted, genius." Her foot kicked at my ankle, but it went right through and left a chill in that spot. That didn't faze her, though. "Come on, we don't have much time, and you've wasted enough of it."

"What's going on?" My voice rasped in my throat, and I coughed before continuing with more strength. "You were in my dream, so I must—"

"You aren't dreaming now," she interrupted again.

I sat up shakily, leaning on my elbows. "Would you stop interrupting me? Who are you? What do you want?"

The ghost huffed and straightened up, putting her hands on her hips. She looked like she was fresh out of another era, wearing a cloak over her puff-sleeved shirt, corset, and plaid skirt. "I'm Crystal Lacey. And you, Oliver Stylus, are quite the damn disappointment, I must say!" She threw her arms into the air, her gaze hardening. "You let him get away, just like that! We were so close!"

Her ominous words from my dream returned, and my stomach sank. "You're talking about Tyler, aren't you? Do you know him?"

Crystal's eyebrows knitted together. If she weren't a spirit, she'd probably be strangling me. "Not personally. But we needed him here! There are things coming—we almost had five of the six." She rubbed her temples like I was a headache she needed to ward off. "And you let him walk out! How stupid are you?"

Rather unceremoniously, I staggered to my feet, leaning against the earthy wall for support. "How about you make that clear next time? And what things are coming? Who's we? What six?" I wasn't sure if my head was reeling from hitting the floor or the fact every rumor about Indra Academy was probably true.

"For hell's sake, did Isabel never tell you?"

"You and Isabel know each other?" The floor swayed again, and I dug my fingernails into my palms to ground myself. When Crystal nodded, I groaned. "Okay, okay, let me get this straight. There were six of you when I touched the water, and now you're the only one here." Crystal wasn't objecting to any of it, a silent invitation for me to keep going. "And you need Tyler for something that involves five other people. Isabel knows about this, too."

Crystal made finger guns in my direction. "Bingo!"

"Fine." I straightened up, pulling out my phone to check the time. "There's still a while before classes start, so let's go. We need help." Brushing past Crystal, I started my way back to the entrance tunnel. But before I could lead her into the library, I paused. "Uh, will anyone see you?" Releasing a ghost onto campus sounded like a recipe for disaster.

"Nope, only you. Just keep quiet about me, alright? Let's not spread a mass panic."

There was a great deal of confidence in her words, and my gut couldn't tell if that was good or bad. I weighed my options before muttering, "Okay."

Once back in the library and after returning the bookshelf to where it covered the hole, I started for the hallway. As I passed the row of ancient yearbooks, my mind flashed back to the letter I found. It'd been dedicated to this very ghost, but given our circumstances, I didn't want us getting sidetracked.

With my attention on making sure Crystal didn't wander off, I hardly noticed the person I collided with a moment later.

"Oh!" I looked up. Luke stared down at me with an equally puzzled expression. "I'm so sorry—I didn't see you there."

Luke grabbed my wrist before I could dart away. "Still looking for Tyler? Bryce and I couldn't find him." Scanning me up and down, he frowned. "Are you okay? You look really pale."

Heat flushed through me, and I rubbed the back of my neck. "Would you mind coming with me to the main office?"

"Are you—" Luke started to repeat the first question, but it trailed off as he shook his head. "Fine, but why? Did something happen?"

Now it was my turn to grab him by the arm. "It's a long story," was all I murmured as I started to drag him down the hall. Crystal strutted ahead of us, her billowing cloak creating a draft. It took everything in me to hold my tongue and not snap at her to stop, especially when Luke shivered behind me.

He scoffed in amusement, shaking my hand away as he fell into step with me. "I'm assuming I'll find out in a moment, huh?" More quietly, he added, "Since when was this hallway so drafty?"

We walked the rest of the way in silence, which was filled by the sound of muffled chatter as we approached the main office. When we headed for the principal's door, the receptionist said, "She's busy!"

"We'll be quick. It's important." Luke gave her a wave, and before she could protest, he knocked on the door.

The talking inside stopped, and Isabel called, "Come in!"

I held my breath as I pushed the door open, pausing when I noticed a cop standing over Isabel's desk. Buff and tan, he had tattoos creeping up the back of his neck. Instinctively, I inched closer to Luke. "Should we come back later?"

"Stay a minute," the cop said before Isabel had a chance to speak. "I received a call from someone about a missing child." The cop adjusted his belt. "Sadie Lynn, I believe the name was. She's the boy's mother. Do you know anything?"

None of us spoke.

The cop took that as his chance to explain. "She had suspicions that he was hanging around this area, because her eldest son used to attend this school. Now then, we're gonna search the—"

"We don't know who you're talking about," I blurted out before I could hold myself back. "You have to describe him to us." It took everything in me to not waver under the stares of everyone else.

The cop didn't hesitate. "Tyler Lynn. A twelve-year-old boy with brown hair, one blue eye, and one brown eye. He's four feet and eleven inches tall."

Luke's confusion melted into understanding. He stepped forward with a relaxed expression. "We haven't seen anyone like that."

The cop scanned us up and down, and I braced myself. After a pause, he just glanced at Isabel to confirm our story.

The principal's face was as blank as stone.

"I'll talk to the guys I came here with. We're going to search the building, just in case," he decided.

We watched him leave in stunned silence. When the door clicked shut, I whirled around to glare at Isabel. "That's why we should've called for help sooner! Now, they're going to think *we're* the bad guys."

Isabel didn't flinch. "Everything is under control," she said. "Any news on finding Tyler?"

Crystal reappeared behind Isabel, reminding me that now wasn't the time to fight.

"Tyler's in the library. Well, more like in the walls. There's, uh..." I fumbled with my hands as I tried to explain using gestures, but Crystal pointed to herself vigorously and bounced on her feet. Finally, I groaned. "There's this secret tunnel leading to an underground pool."

"Seriously?" Luke's voice cracked with surprise. I nodded, and his eyes widened.

Isabel's shoulders trembled as she took a deep breath. "You found it, huh?" It came out as a fierce whisper, almost like it was meant to be heard by only herself. She cleared her throat and asked more professionally, "A pool?"

I started to pace, needing to get rid of this pent-up energy. "Yes! And it summoned this ghost! She told me you'd know about it. You should, because you're the principal and are bound to know every nook and cranny of this school." I pointed to Crystal, who was just empty air to Isabel and Luke. "Her name is Crystal Lacey, and she was all, 'Grr, what have you done, letting Tyler leave?'"

Crystal laughed. "Bravo—minus the impression. That sucked."

Isabel's eyebrows furrowed, and it took a moment for her neutral expression to return. "No wonder I felt a chill this morning." She glanced at her computer before standing up. "I'm going to grab the others. You two stay here."

"Others? What others?" Luke opened his mouth to ask more, but Isabel ignored him and power-walked out of the room. He then glanced at me with his face scrunched, questioning.

It was tempting to run after her. How dare Isabel continue to hide information from us, even if it might've cost Tyler his life?

"That son of a—" I whirled around and stormed to the trashcan beside Isabel's desk. With a yell, I kicked it as hard as I could. Crumpled papers and wrappers exploded into the air. "It's not fair! It's not fair! It's not fair!"

The lightheadedness rushed back. I stumbled to the side, and I would've fallen if Luke didn't rush over and steady me.

He gripped my shoulders with grounding strength. "Oliver, snap out of it! Please, at least sit down before you faceplant."

I wanted to fight out of his grip and scream for him to bring Tyler back. But I could feel everything draining out of me, my vision swimming in circles and the floor tilting beneath me. Shakily, I backed up, plopped into the chair across from Isabel's desk, and hung my head. "I'm sorry."

Luke stood in front of me, blocking my view of the trash I just kicked up. "No, don't worry about it."

"I dragged you into this mess."

"I'm glad you did." To my surprise, Luke's voice didn't waver with uncertainty. "Tyler's a good kid, and I want him to be safe."

At that last part, my gut twisted. "I don't like the sound of his mom calling the cops. Does that mean she's looking for him and wants him back?" I clenched my fists, another wave of anger washing over me. "You should've seen Tyler the night he came to Indra. He was bruised and hit all over. We can't let him go back."

"Think about it this way, Tyler's mom called the cops to find him. That means he's not with her, at least." Luke frowned. "Of course, that doesn't mean he's safe. Wait—are you seriously saying we gotta kidnap him?"

"I would consider this rescuing, not kidnapping," Crystal piped up even though only I could hear her.

I didn't respond to either of them right away. Luke's theory only eased the tension in my chest by a molecule. "Whatever it takes to make sure he doesn't get hurt again."

To that, neither Luke nor Crystal spoke. Luke grabbed one of the plastic chairs stacked in the corner and pulled it up next to me. We continued to ignore the trash on Isabel's floor.

Luke sat down. Eventually, he asked, "A real ghost?"

"It sounds crazy, I know." I lowered my head onto the desk, letting the cold surface of the wood spread along my forehead. "You don't have to believe me."

"Isabel believes you, and she's the principal!" Luke tipped his chair back, fixing his gaze on the ceiling. "Even if she didn't, I'd still trust you. This school is super old, and it backs our research up." He closed his eyes and let out a short laugh. "Tell this Crystal girl I say 'hi,' though!"

I turned to face Crystal, but she silenced me by raising her hand.

"I heard," was all she said with a smile.

CHAPTER EIGHT

THE FIRST DOMINO

OLIVER

ISABEL DIDN'T TAKE LONG to return, and this time, she had two students behind her. Both were familiar.

The first was Diana Divata, a fourteen-year-old freshman I'd met at the start of the school year. I'd helped her out at the orientation when some other kids gave her trouble for being a transgender girl trying to use one of the neutral restrooms. As soon as I'd walked my junior ass over there and asked what was going on, they ditched. I reported them to the counselors anyway.

Still, Diana always had a spring in her step, even on school mornings like today. She was from the Philippines, with black and gray ombré hair that bounced as she stepped inside and smiled at us. I was jealous of how silky it was. It complemented her tan skin and green eyes well.

Behind her was Vincent Ferris, who was distracted with wiping his foggy glasses. He was a sophomore, fifteen years old, with dark brown skin and black hair that swooshed to the sides. Dark circles sat under his eyes, giving away his lack of sleep, so no wonder he looked like he was supposed to be napping instead of standing here. He always wore this thin necklace with a small, circular gold pendant hanging from it. Most importantly, he was Luke's younger brother, so he made a face at us when he put his glasses back on. "What is this?"

"Please, close the door behind you and take a seat with Luke and Oliver." Isabel sat in her chair, and Crystal, who'd been sitting there in the meantime, disappeared. She reappeared on top of a nearby bookshelf, pouting.

The younger students exchanged an unamused look before Diana closed the door and Vincent grabbed two plastic chairs to place beside ours. They eyed the trash still sprawled on the floor but said nothing. Isabel was also ignoring the trash, though I noticed her eye twitching.

Once we were settled, she leaned forward with her elbows on the desk. "I don't want you guys to freak out, but I need you four for a special assignment."

Luke stiffened. "Is this about Tyler? Why do Vincey and whoever the other one is—sorry by the way—have to get involved?"

Diana raised an eyebrow.

"Because..." Isabel let out a frustrated sigh and opened her desk drawer. She pulled out a handful of dominoes and stacked them in a line on the table. "Do you know how these work?"

"Duh?" Vincent slumped in his chair like a toddler who'd been brought to their parents' meeting. He rubbed his necklace as he spoke. "I also know how wasting time works. For example? This."

Luke shot his brother a warning glance.

Isabel ignored his sour attitude. "We have a starting domino, and what happens when you tip it over?" She reached one finger out, tapping the domino. The rest of the line collapsed.

"They fall." Diana raised her eyebrows in confusion.

"Exactly. When one person sets something into motion, everyone else is affected as well." Isabel focused her gaze on the four of us again, her eyes stone cold. "I need you all to go after Tyler."

My heart jumped in my chest. "Isn't that what the cops are here for?"

Isabel shook her head. "The cops can't follow him where he's gone. Only you four can."

"Who's Tyler?" Vincent interrupted, sounding more disgusted than anything.

"Because like with the dominoes, one person has tipped the rest into motion." Isabel looked at me, then Luke, then Vincent, and finally Diana. "While you've never felt it, there's a thread that connects you all to each other. It's tied to Tyler as well, caused just by his presence here. You must bring him back before that red string of fate is severed."

I reached for my chest, tearing at the cloth shielding it. I thought the tightness inside was from worrying over Tyler or perhaps fainting earlier. But this ache was a vacant hole I'd never felt before.

Diana's eyes were round. "I don't get it. But who's Tyler? Is he a student?"

Isabel finally leaned back, like a large weight had been taken from her shoulders. "He's a very special asset. Would you believe me if I said our world was at stake?"

"No," Vincent said flat out.

My skin prickled. It might have been because of Vincent's disbelief or Isabel referring to Tyler as a "special asset," like he was some resource. "He's just a kid," I protested for maybe the hundredth time that week.

Isabel stared at me with the same storm in her eyes from the other day. "You must comply."

"Stop ignoring us!" Vincent jostled his brother's shoulder.

Luke held a finger toward Vincent, a sign for him to wait. He turned to Isabel. "Does the whole ghost-and-secret-tunnel story tell us where Tyler went?"

"Okay, the *what?*" Diana's eyes bulged wide.

Despite his bitterness, even Vincent perked up at the mention of ghosts and secret tunnels. He stopped rubbing his necklace.

"After the pool, it's a dead end." I ignored how the younger students gawked at me. "Where are we supposed to go?"

Isabel narrowed her eyes. "I'll show you, but once you know, there's no looking back. I'll have more answers when you return. Pack your bags as if you're camping for a few days, then meet in the library."

Knowing that was our dismissal, the four of us got up and filed out of the office. Students had flooded the hall outside, yet I still heard Vincent mutter "unbelievable" under his breath.

He spun around to face Luke properly. "What the hell is going on?"

Luke grinned at him. "Maybe next time, you'll pay attention when I tell you about the school rumors!"

"Does it relate to this?" Diana asked. Then, she offered Luke a weak smile. "Oh—and I'm Diana, by the way."

"You're the annoying girl in art class who talks too much. Fourth period. I sit behind you," Vincent grumbled before his brother could speak.

Diana sniffed. "Someone has to ask the questions, you know! And this is coming from the guy who always flips his pencil on the desk like it's a skateboard. It gets really annoying after five minutes."

I stepped between the two. "Shut up and listen. This is important."

Diana pouted. "Then who's Tyler? At least tell us that."

"He's a..." I struggled to finish the sentence. Was "friend" an appropriate title? I paused, imagining how Tyler would react if I called him that to his face. "He was visiting the school for a few days and Isabel wanted me to look after him."

Vincent's eyes twitched. "Isabel's sending us away to find someone we don't even know?"

"Let's just go with it, okay?" Luke said to Vincent, before turning to face me. "I think it ties into what we found—about the whole original concept of the school. Whatever books we found were telling the truth."

It killed me to agree. I nodded, but Vincent cut me off. "Why do Diana and I have to get involved if you two are so sure about this?"

I frowned at him. "If you're *that* unenthusiastic, why don't you tell Isabel you refuse?"

Vincent shuffled closer to Luke, rubbing his necklace again. "Because I'm not letting this idiot run into danger alone."

We gave Diana a questioning look.

"There's no harm in joining," she said tentatively. "It might be fun...and Vincent and I can find some inspiration for our final art project." She twirled her thumbs, not meeting our gazes.

"I guess that's reason enough." Strangely, I was relieved that all four of us were going. It felt right. Whatever thread was supposed to keep us together tugged at my insides. It yearned for Tyler's presence, too.

I smiled at the ragtag group and said, "Let's go pack."

CHAPTER NINE

I'M A CAT WHISPERER

TYLER

MY FIRST THOUGHT ONCE waking up was, *this is uncomfortable.*

I was lying in a dead bush, a million branches and thorns stabbing my back. A pale blue sky overhead stared down at me, framed by giant trees. Their bare branches rustled with a gentle breeze. Icicles hung from the trees, and powdery snow covered the entire forest floor.

New York City wasn't meant to have snow this heavy yet. That meant this was a new dance floor. Unfamiliar territory.

I tried to sit up, but I sank further into the bush with a gasp. Like a mermaid in a net, I thrashed my arms in a struggle to free myself. Branches scraped at my skin. I stopped struggling, defeated, and let my head loll back to face the sky. *That portal really worked, huh? No wonder it's hidden away.*

Something flickered in the corner of my eye, and a weight pressed down on my chest as a black blob appeared in front of me. I blinked, and the blob came into focus, exposing triangular ears on its head. It was a black cat, but unlike any cat I'd met, this one had glowing white eyes.

I screamed and threw the cat off me. The movement sent me falling further into the bush. Thorns stabbed my arms and face as I fought my way out of the makeshift prison. When I finally crawled out, I sat slumped on the snowy ground, breathing heavily, my legs numb.

The cat trotted after me, innocently peering up at me.

"H-h—" My throat burned, and I swallowed before trying again. "H-h-hello?"

The cat jumped onto my chest, its weight pushing me flat onto my back. "Hello!" she chirped.

It talked. The cat could *talk*.

"You don't have to look so afraid," she continued.

"What–what do you mean?" I grimaced. I was talking to a *cat*. "What are you? What is this?" Whipping my head around, I gawked at the massive trees surrounding us. "Where am I?"

"Derngate." The feline tilted her head to one side, her muzzle wrinkling in a smile. "The elemental realm."

I blinked a few times, trying to process the new information. "Okay," I exhaled. "As in...magic?"

The cat nodded.

If this was another realm, no wonder my stomach felt scrambled. I stayed still for a minute to ensure my queasiness didn't sky-rocket. The cat slid off me and I watched it trot circles around me. Only when I felt confident I wasn't going to hurl did I straighten up, plucking a twig from my hair. "So, this–this Derngate place...isn't part of our world?" I thought back to what that man told me, about how he was dead to "my world" but not his own. "A-and that explains why–why you can, uh, talk?"

"Yes!"

Her enthusiasm brought my nausea back. I muttered "okay" before pushing myself to my feet. After taking a few more breaths, I faced her again. "I'm fine now, so you can–you can scurry along."

The cat's eyes widened in dismay. "But I'm here to hang out with you!"

"I have...places to be." Ignoring her, I started to walk away, ice squelching under my sneakers. Dapples of winter sunlight spotted the ground. Birds chirped overhead, a strange peace in the air. I was so used to the hustle of New York City, it felt wrong to not see any buildings. Where were the people? The cars? My chest tightened.

Snowflakes fell daintily from the sky, carried by a weak breeze. Several fell onto my hoodie's black sleeves and didn't melt. Instead, they glowed. Upon closer inspection, I realized they were tiny, jellyfish-like creatures. They varied in size, their heads bobbing lazily up and down while their tentacles clung to the fabric.

Grimacing, I used my other sleeve to wipe them away. As they fell into the snow, their light faded. I shuddered and kept walking.

The crunching of my shoes against the snow was interrupted by a pattering sound. The cat was following me.

"What places do you need to be?" She jumped onto my back, climbing up to sit on my shoulder.

I opened my mouth to shoo her away, but that was a good question. Where *was* I supposed to go? Panic swept through me. I kept walking, afraid that she'd notice my anxious expression. "I'm figuring that out."

The cat pressed her side to my neck, causing me to teeter again. Her paws kneaded my shoulder through my hoodie. "Surely, you must know, because people don't go back and forth between worlds for nothing." She stopped kneading, and reached out and tapped my ear. "Especially half-Meraki."

"Half what?" I glared at her.

"Half-Meraki. You have the ears!"

I turned my head away, brushing my hair over my ears. "They're just naturally pointy." *In other words, leave me alone!*

The cat didn't take the hint, but she fell quiet as I traipsed around the forest. Her blessed silence made it easy to hear the faint trickling nearby. A stream?

Water always has a source. Maybe I could find someone and ask for directions. Hope stirring in my chest, I picked up my pace and followed the sound. Oh, how I hoped it would be freshwater. My mouth was dry and burned as bad as my body.

As predicted, there was a partially frozen river dividing the forest in half. The foam it carried bubbled upward before popping in the air. I couldn't think of a logical explanation for it. The river weaved downstream for as far as I could see, and upstream was just as bad. Which direction was I supposed to follow?

"You know, I'm familiar with a bunch of faces around here. Is there someone you came here for?" The cat hopped off my shoulders, neatly landing on all fours.

"I don't know his name." I approached the riverbank and sank to my knees. Cupping my hands into the freezing water, I brought it to my mouth and took a hesitant sip. It chilled my insides, but I'd never tasted anything so fresh. The bubbly foam popped in my mouth, a bit like an energy drink. I took another few sips before cupping more water and splashing it over my face.

The cat watched, her white eyes narrowing. "Then what does he look like?"

I stared at my reflection in the river. "He's a–a big guy. Uh, he's got long ears with a bunch of holes and scars in them."

"Are you sure?" The cat's head jerked back when I nodded. She looked around, a bit like a stray ready to bolt. "That would be Thierry Colliss."

Her reaction confused me. What about this man could've turned her off so easily? I hesitated, then repeated the name back to her. "Theory?"

The cat shook her head. "Thierry. Thee-air-ee."

Oh. I stood up, glancing up and down the river like it was a street. "How do I get to him?"

The cat opened her mouth, tasting the air. "Upstream."

The idea of going uphill made my lungs feel tight, but I sighed and started trudging that way. "Uphill it is. Thanks."

"Of course!" She raced after me, apparently not taking me turning my back on her for the hint it was.

We spent the rest of the morning walking and following the river. I occasionally took breaks to sit on a rock and question my life choices, but the cat didn't let me dwell on it for long. The more we walked, the denser the forest around us became. Long shadows covered the ground as a maze of branches shielded us from the sun, and I jumped at every hoot. I prayed it was just an owl.

Just an owl? I asked myself in a jeering tone. *The cat can talk, and the snow is alive. You think that's just an owl?* It both worried and intrigued me. I was almost tempted to go searching for the birds of this strange world. That would have to wait until later, though.

"Are you sure we're not lost?" I sat slumped against a boulder for the hundredth time. My legs ached and refused to keep moving.

"Yes." The cat jumped onto my lap, her animated expression rather serious. "I'm the local, after all."

She had a point. Back in Manhattan, I knew every twist and turn since my brother helped me memorize the subway routes when I was little. I could travel across the great city blindfolded, and the cat must have felt the same way about this place.

I curled up at the foot of the boulder, hugging my arms over my stomach, which groaned from hunger. While everything around me was different, I was the same as always: starving and hiding with animals. The chill of the icy floor soaked through my clothes, tickling my exposed skin and making my hair damp.

Aware of the cat still clinging onto my legs, I adjusted myself into a tighter ball. She was like a soft weighted blanket. My breathing slowed and my eyes closed.

Immediately, my hunger melted and the ache weighing down my legs lifted. Even without opening my eyes, I knew I was back in a dream.

I found myself in the familiar abyss of water and night sky. I'd done this so many times now, I didn't even waver with fear. "Thierry!" I called into the darkness. "That's your name, isn't it?"

"That took you a while to figure out," the man rumbled from behind me. I spun to face his calm smile. "And I see you've made a friend, too."

"She's not my friend."

"Oh?" Thierry made a flame with one finger, grinning to himself. "Then maybe we'll cook her."

I froze. "No!"

Thierry cackled. "I'm not that heartless!" His amusement over the sick joke faded into a serious frown. He closed his fist over the flame, snuffing it out. "You must leave her, though."

"She won't go away." I shrugged. There was a bigger problem at hand. "Are we going in the wrong direction? Is that why I need to leave her?"

Thierry nodded.

That damn cat! Biting back a yell of frustration, I muttered, "Great, thanks." I kicked at the water below, having to release the negativity somehow. "So, I'm supposed to go downstream? Is that where you are? Where do I go from there?"

"You'll give me a headache with all those questions," Thierry replied.

A lump formed in my throat. Guilt. Afraid to make it worse, I said, "Sorry."

"It's fine." He said it the way my mom always did when it actually wasn't fine. "Once you reach the end of the river, you'll find where the ground splits in half. That's where I am."

What is this, a riddle? I forced my breathing to stay even. "Okay. Thank you."

When I awoke, the cat was staring me down with wide eyes. The sky behind her was still light, and I was relieved to see I hadn't been asleep too long. The solace didn't last long, though, as my gaze returned to the feline. Without a word, I stood and started to walk downstream.

My legs trembled from the effort of walking on an empty stomach, my body slow and head reeling. After a week and a half at Indra Academy, I'd forgot what serious hunger felt like. I mentally punched myself. *Grow up! You've gone longer without properly eating before! This should be nothing.* Refusing to accept I'd grown soft, I forced myself to keep moving.

"Wait!" The cat was walking by my ankles in a heartbeat, trying to get in front of me. When I sidestepped all her attempts, she growled. "Wrong way, genius!"

"Says you!" I shot her a glare, not slowing my pace. "What did I say about managing on my own? Leave—leave me be!"

The cat raced a few feet ahead, and as I approached, she jumped at my chest. She ignored my surprised yelp and scrambled up to my collarbones so we were eye to eye.

Then she raked her claws across both sides of my face.

I jumped back, throwing the cat off and clutching my face. My cheeks stung like crazy, pain like none other flooding through me. Blood flowed down my chin steadily. I pulled my hand away from my face, bile making its way up my throat when I saw my fingers covered in red. My breathing became shallow and quick. "What's wrong with you?" I asked the cat.

She licked blood off her paws. "It's not my fault you don't listen."

The metallic taste in my mouth was so overpowering, I couldn't reply right away. For a cat with tiny paws, that was some unreal damage. I swallowed. "And you expect me to listen now?"

The cat nodded.

"Too bad." Wiping my sleeve over my bleeding cheeks, I began to stumble downstream once more. Crimson droplets left a trail behind me, and my vision shifted in and out of focus. Jelly-snowflakes drifted to the blood to feed on it, but I didn't focus on them. The ground was unstable beneath me, but I wasn't going to slow down and admit defeat to an animal.

So when the cat continued to follow, I continued to ignore her.

CHAPTER TEN

SWIM, VINCENT!

OLIVER

WHEN I GOT BACK to the dorm, I found Bryce rummaging through his desk. Alerted by my entrance, he spun around to face me. "I left something here, sorry. Did you find Tyler?"

I shook my head, grabbing my backpack from off the floor. "Kind of. Isabel is sending me, Luke, Vincent, and Diana to go fetch him."

"Why? Did something happen?"

I stared at the floor for a moment, unsure of how much I could explain. There was no way I'd leave him in the dark, but for his own sake, I wouldn't let him become one of the dominoes. Leaning against the ladder of my bed, I told the story as best as I could.

Bryce listened in silence, but the more I explained, the more nauseous he appeared. In the end, all he could whisper was, "Pointy ears?" It must've tied back to when I described Crystal to him.

"Yeah!" I looked around, trying to find Crystal, but the ghost had disappeared on me. Luckily, I'd talked enough at this point to know I hadn't dreamt it. "We've basically confirmed the school is haunted and that Mageia is real."

Bryce slumped in his desk's chair, burying his face in his hands. "You met my dad before, right? Remember how he always wore a hat and kept his hair over his ears?"

I hesitated, picturing Bryce's father in my mind. The one time I met him was at our freshman orientation years ago, when Bryce introduced me to him. I shook his big hand and remembered suppressing a shudder. His father had been wearing a hat, Bryce was right about that. Of course, I never questioned it, thinking it was just a fashion statement or something. But when I thought about it..."Oh my gosh, does he have those ears as well? How? The–the people with those ears in that book disappeared a long time ago!"

"It's something to do with the school." Bryce glared at the floor, absently rubbing one of his pointed ears. It was a nervous habit I'd been blind to in the past, but watching him do it now, I wanted to scream.

I already had an idea in my mind of how the school connected to why Tyler's tracks stopped at the underground pool. It made me feel ill.

"But when we found out about Indra Academy's origin, you seemed so cool and calm about it. And toward the end, you wanted us to stop researching." I narrowed my eyes as I recalled it. "That's because you knew about it already. Why didn't you confirm it?"

Bryce's eyes flashed with emotion. "Do you think it's easy being a mix of a human and something nobody believes exists? You would've called me a freak!"

I forced myself to remain neutral, despite wanting to strangle him for thinking I'd go against him like that. "You know I never would've, and the same goes for Luke. We've always supported each other."

Bryce looked me up and down, only relaxing when he seemed to believe me. "Whatever. I haven't properly seen him in three years, anyways. He made some sort of deal with Isabel, to keep me close but out of the way. I'm not complaining, of course. I'm glad to be here." Bryce swiveled in his chair, grabbing a sheet of paper. After a moment of scribbling, he handed it to me.

Bryce had drawn a portrait with his father's face on it. The hair was slicked back with stray stubble around his chin. His ears were pointy, just like Crystal's. But unlike the ghost girl's, his had scars on them and were full of little holes.

"Other than also having pointy ears, what does your dad have to do with this?" I folded the paper and slid it into my pocket for reference, just in case.

"If you're going to where I think you're going, you have to avoid him." Bryce stared up at me. "I've heard him talk to coworkers before. He—he tries to get people on his side, showing them magic and promising a world better than our own."

My eyes widened. "You don't think it was your dad that lured Tyler away, do you?"

Bryce shook his head. "We told him about the origin of Indra Academy. We roped him into this. My father must've seen it as an opportunity."

Seeing him look so defeated tore at my heart. I offered him a weak smile. "We'll be in and out, I promise. I'll make sure we don't even encounter your dad. We'll figure it out."

"No, you don't get it. My father—he's a two-faced snake. You have to be careful. Please, trust me." Bryce's words were strained and pleading. He stood up and grabbed at his sweater, lifting the cloth to reveal a shiny, pink scar that slashed over his stomach. "This is what happens if you're not careful."

I'd seen that scar a million times before. Bryce had a thing for sleeping shirtless in the spring and summertime, so it was hard to miss. Since freshman year, he'd told me it was a burn from hot water; that he was making tea and slipped. Although I knew a burn from hot water wouldn't normally look like a slash, I never said anything. I always figured Bryce had his reasons for not sharing the full story. But now..."Did *he* do that to you?"

A hollow smile appeared on Bryce's face. "You don't want to know how." When my expression shifted from surprised to horrified, he pulled his sweater back down. "But I trust you guys. If you keep your distance, you'll be fine. Now then, when do you have to leave?"

"We're supposed to meet in the library soon." I hesitated, tilting my head to one side. "Do you want to come with us? Since you seem to know more about this stuff, it might be helpful."

After several heartbeats of silence, Bryce scratched the back of his head. Red bloomed along his cheeks. "I don't think anyone would be happy to see me back there. Besides, I..." His smile vanished, and his arm fell back to his side. "Staying away from my father was also by choice. I'm not going back on my decision."

I couldn't blame Bryce for that. He bore a scar from his father on his stomach, and I'd listened to him whimper, sob, and talk in his sleep enough times to know what sort of impact had been left on him. "I understand," I finally said. "I won't pressure you."

Bryce pushed past me, opening a drawer in his closet and pulling out a pair of dark brown boots. They were the ones I always borrowed, the ones with white wool lining the insides. They were too small for him yet perfect for me. He held them toward me, and when I hesitated, he laughed. "I know you can't dress warm for shit."

That's fair. "Thanks," I mumbled, taking it from him with one hand. "I'll get dressed, pack, and be on my way, then."

"Sounds like a plan." Bryce's voice wavered, like there was more he wanted to say. Instead, he stepped forward and yanked me into a hug. "I just don't want my father to hurt you, too."

I relaxed in his arms, returning the hug. "We'll be okay." It was a promise I didn't know if I could keep, but for Bryce's and Tyler's sakes, I had to try.

"Yeah? Oh, and good luck, I forgot to mention."

Stifling a hollow laugh, I said, "Thank you." *We'll need it.*

Packing didn't take long, mainly because I didn't know *what* to pack. Where were we even going? Beyond the pool was unknown.

Being short on time didn't help. I must have looked through my closet a million times before stuffing some extra socks and shirts into my backpack. After tossing in a sweater, a flashlight, and some snacks, I was ready. I gave Bryce another hug goodbye, bid farewell to our dorm, and left for the library.

Luke, Vincent, Diana, and Isabel had arrived before me, standing in a small cluster at the library's entrance. When I got closer, I noticed that Camila was there, too. Like Isabel, she appeared fidgety. She wrung the straps of the tote bag slung over her shoulder, but she still smiled at me as I joined the party.

"Back in our day," Isabel started as we followed her inside the library, "we also had kids lured into the walls. Camila and I, plus a friend, were the first to see it again."

Vincent sighed. "This is bull—"

Luke knocked Vincent's shoulder with his, cutting him off.

"Is this something we haven't learned yet?" Diana shifted her gaze from Isabel and Camila to Luke and me. "Is it in the junior curriculum?"

Camila tilted her head to one side with a thoughtful hum. "It's not. There's a lot that's been hidden from society." More quietly, she added, "Knowing it all is a heavy burden to bear."

As we reached the back aisle that'd originally lured me in, Isabel stopped at the bookshelf. "Let me tell you four something." She leaned against the wall. I could see the faint outline of the crack beside her. "Camila and I visited this place a long time ago. We were seniors, with no clue of what we were walking into. We met some spirits and were warned of the fate resting on your shoulders." Isabel glanced at me. "One of those ghosts, you've already met."

"Crystal," I guessed.

Camila nodded. "After our first encounter with them, we went back several times that year to learn about the forgotten past of this school and what lies beyond it. Since then, we've been watching and waiting for the right ones that fit the calling. We found jobs here after graduation but never lost sight of that goal. After spending more time with these spirits, we learned how important the success of the mission is. That kept us going." Her eyes rested on Luke, Vincent, Diana, and me. "By being connected to each other, you have ties to the catalyst. We discovered that as you came to the school in your own time."

"Ties to this Tyrone kid?" Vincent asked. "Or was it Tyler? Why are you sending us away for someone we don't even know? I have no connection to him."

While Vincent's comment stung, he had a fair point.

"Not yet, but the people you *are* connected to have ties with him." Isabel nodded to Luke and me, the ones who'd already interacted with Tyler. "That's why this is a game of dominoes. When one tips, the rest follow." She scanned us up and down again with a sigh. "I know this is a lot, but I have faith in you all. You're more than what you think you are."

Diana scrunched up her eyebrows. "You still haven't explained why we're here or where we're going."

Camila gave her a kind look. "We'll explain once we're inside."

Inside? I frowned but didn't question it. "On that note, let's keep going," I said. I was itching to follow Tyler.

Camila rummaged through her tote bag, pulling out four, long pieces of cloth, and handing them to us. They were hooded cloaks.

We fumbled to put them on. I felt like I'd been swallowed by a shadow. The material was light and comfortable, and as I pulled the hood over my head, a sense of security washed over me.

Luke prodded me, and when I faced him, he struck a badass pose. We dissolved into giggles at how silly yet awesome we probably looked. Diana and Vincent watched, confused, which was very *in* character for Vincent and out of character for Diana.

"They're to hide your ears," Camila explained. "If the locals found out humans had slipped into their realm, they'd track you down in an instant."

"Realm?" Diana echoed in amazement. "Like, alternate realities?"

My stomach did a flip. We were confirming supernatural theories one after another. It wasn't that I didn't want to find Tyler—it was just daunting to be thrown into the unknown so quickly. *Do it for him,* I thought. *He's probably even more freaked out than you are.*

"Yes." Isabel put her index finger to her mouth, a shushing sign. Once we were quiet, she pushed the nearby bookshelf aside to reveal the hidden entrance. She and Camila slid inside.

We silently filed in after them, though Luke, Diana, and Vincent let out murmurs of awe when we entered the tunnel. This being my third time here, I wasn't as impressed as I followed Camila and Isabel deeper underground.

The adults were even more certain of where to go than I was. Illuminated by the moss around us, they looked like they were at home.

To my surprise, neither Camila nor Isabel paid attention to the glittering pool right away. Instead, they focused on the walls decorated with draping moss and ferns.

Camila brushed one of the fern curtains aside, revealing a portrait carved into the stone. It was of an elven girl with an afro and billowing cape, and she held the sun in her palms. Next to that portrait were five others, the subjects no older than me or Luke.

"This is the Assembly of Six," Isabel explained in a hushed voice. "They split the human realm, our realm, and created a portal to banish the Meraki, wielders of power, to a new world."

Luke stiffened. "Wait, Meraki as in Mageia stuff? That means everything Oliver and I researched was true! They disappeared because they were banished, then? Is that how Indra Academy became a regular high school?"

Isabel nodded, returning her attention to the carvings. "They were students, just like you. Since their passing, they've been looking for the right people to fix the balance between worlds. The requirements are very specific."

I followed her gaze and gasped. There was a carving of Crystal holding a cluster of ice shards, all poised and serious. "And one of those people is Tyler." The connection was made based off the ghost's request to bring Tyler to her. The rest of us were roped into it because of our relation to him.

"Yes. Tyler takes after her, the way the rest of you take after someone else." Camila gestured to the other portraits.

Each carving had a unique touch to it. The rest of them were each holding something different: a lightning bolt, a flame, an orb of water, or swirls of air. I felt especially drawn to the fire, held by a girl with braids and glasses. She had this imposing energy to her. The crystal pendant of her necklace floated in the air with embers surrounding it.

"There are going to be six of you, according to what Camila and I were told," Isabel continued. "The fact that we've found four is a miracle. Now that we've found the fifth, we need to bring him back."

Camila dug around her pocket and pulled out a folded piece of paper. Scrawled on it was a drawing of a necklace. Attached to the string was a gemstone of some sort, with a small flame engraved on it. It looked just like the one the fire Meraki wore. I glanced at the portrait once more to confirm it.

"The entrance to the place you're heading to is powered by six of these," Camila said. "According to our sources, you'll find Tyler with this necklace nearby." She handed the paper to me, and I tucked it away next to the drawing of Bryce's dad.

Isabel cleared her throat, and we faced her again. "There are six keys, and there will eventually be six of you. The necklaces were hidden after the Meraki were banished, so nobody would open the portals again. But somebody uncovered the fire necklace, and its energy grants the entrance enough power to let individuals through. Any person can slip between worlds at any time. I want you to retrieve it. Bring both Tyler and the necklace back."

Luke's eyebrows furrowed. "Where are we meant to find them?"

Camila and Isabel exchanged glances.

"You're looking for a man by the name of Thierry Colliss," Isabel said, her voice strangely bitter. "He'll have what we're looking for."

Vincent and Diana nodded, though they still looked confused. Meanwhile, Luke was trying to catch my eye. It was for good reason. The last name "Colliss" rang a bell I wished would've stayed silent forever.

The adults, however, didn't dwell on that. Camila released the tension from her shoulders with a sigh. "Okay, I believe that's all. Time moves faster where you're going, so don't panic over how quickly days pass. Just stay calm, and please, stick together." She looked to the pool, which pulsed with energy. "Do you four know how to swim? Or at least hold your breaths?"

"Yes," Diana and I spoke.

Luke muttered, "Kind of."

"No," Vincent said flat out.

"You must be the life of the party, huh?" Diana raised an eyebrow at Vincent.

"What does swimming have to do with parties?" Vincent glared at her before turning to face the strange pool. "The same question applies to this. What the hell? We'll be swimming in circles! Are you trying to kill us?"

Isabel rubbed her eyes with her fingers. "No, we aren't trying to kill you. Just jump in, and the portal will carry you. You might drown if you don't hold your breath, of course."

Vincent didn't have a comeback for that one, just looking away with a scowl. He brought his pendant to his mouth and bit down on it.

Camila kicked a pebble into the pond, which sank and disappeared. "You'll go in one at a time, as the portal doesn't have enough energy to take all of you at once."

"I say we let Vincent go first, so we don't have to hear his whining," Diana proposed.

Only silence followed, meaning nobody was objecting. I put my hand over my mouth to keep myself from smiling. *That's your payback for being rude,* I thought.

"I'll go," Vincent said, shoving past us. "Just so I don't have to deal with you." He lingered by the edge of the pool, focusing on his reflection before dipping the tip of his boot in.

The pool glowed brighter at his touch. Vincent yelped and tried backing up, but an invisible force dragged him into the water. He thrashed for only a second before disappearing under the surface.

"Vince!" Luke raced to the edge. "Holy shit, he's gone!"

"Once again," Isabel said with a sigh, "it's a portal. You'll see him on the other side."

Diana tossed her bag into the pool. "That's both ominous and cool. I'll see you guys there!"

She jumped in without a second thought. Luke grimaced before following more slowly.

I knew that was my sign to copy them, but I couldn't just run into the unknown without clearing something up. I pulled the drawing of Bryce's father from my pocket and lifted it for Camila and Isabel to see. "This is Thierry Colliss. This is the man we're looking for." It was more of a statement than a question.

The color drained from Isabel's face. "Yes."

"He's Bryce's father," I continued more harshly. "Who Bryce said we should avoid at all costs."

"This isn't a battle you get to choose." Camila's voice came out uncharacteristically serious. "We can't avoid this."

I clenched my fists, wrinkling the paper. "So you're blindly sending us into danger? What sort of man are we even talking about? Isabel, Bryce told me you made a *deal* with Thierry. You're hiding something from us!"

Isabel's stormy eyes glowed in the blue light around us. Her hair did that swimming thing again—taking on water-like movements. "It was to protect the school from the whole other realm lying beneath it. Thierry Colliss promised to leave us untouched if we boarded his son, who didn't have anywhere else to go."

I wanted to scream at how absurd that was, and the fact all this existed right under my nose. But I bit my tongue. I loved Bryce, I loved Isabel, and I loved Indra Academy. Now wasn't the time to start yelling over truths I wished to understand in the first place.

"Fine," I hissed. "But I want to talk about all this when we return."

"It's a promise." Isabel lowered my hand that gripped the paper, coaxing me to put it away. From next to her, Camila nodded with kinder eyes.

I shoved the portrait of Thierry away, almost able to feel his intense stare weighing my legs down. "Then I'll see you guys later."

I took a step forward before breaking into a run. The longer I took, the more scared I'd get. This was a Band-Aid I simply had to rip off.

I jumped into the water, and the gravity of the pool wasted no time pulling me down. It hit me with a blunt force, and I nearly gasped from the surprise. I was used to being thrown in the ocean from my days in California, but the intensity of the portal was on a whole new level. Time slowed and sped up simultaneously. Bubbles burst all around me, dimming as the water darkened and darkened, until I couldn't recall what came next.

Chapter Eleven

TITANIUM

Tyler

When I was younger, I always tried to pet every stray cat I found. Dominic used to smuggle me leftovers to feed them, both of us ignoring that we were just as starved. Mia thought we were crazy. Mom always yelled. Whenever I got scratched and cried, she turned her back and said, "You deserve it for touching the dirty thing. If it gets infected, you'll learn your lesson."

I eventually stopped petting the cats—once the shed on the roof got involved.

Now, as the sun disappeared below the horizon, I noticed the river giving way into a waterfall. But unable to take another step or tolerate the cat urging us to leave, I crawled into a bush and decided to save exploring until morning. Besides, it was getting harder to see the cat as she started to blend into the dimming forest. The jelly-snowflakes and icicles glowed as it got darker.

I didn't dream or even sleep this time. Exhaustion rooted itself deep in my bones, weighing me down, but I couldn't stop shivering. I really hadn't learned my lesson, had I? *You got involved with the cat and paid for it,* I scolded myself in my mother's voice. Salty tears rolled down my face and stung with the wounds on my cheeks, only making me sob harder. It was a pathetic cycle.

The cat just watched, and for a creature with only white circles for eyes, she looked rather guilty. She stayed by my side and silently kept watch.

All I focused on was the question Dominic always asked: "Where does it hurt?" I put a hand to my face, which stung in response.

I must've dozed off, because I opened my eyes to feel my lids heavier than before. The sky was light again, but that wasn't what caught my attention this time.

It was the hand hovering over me.

Even in my lethargy, my heart jumped, and I flinched at nothing. I shielded my face with my hands, watching the stranger through my fingers.

It was a young person crouching over me, maybe around Oliver's age. Their appearance was startling; long, elf-like ears stretched away from their face, framed by short, wavy blond hair. Their expression was a mixture of confusion and worry, their sage-green eyes narrowed.

"Hey, there." They spoke softly, like I was a stray dog. Their gaze focused on my head, all bloody and lacking magical ears. "You aren't from here, are you?"

I just stared at them through half-lidded eyes, mouth open but too dry for words.

"You're scaring the child," the cat piped up as if she'd known me my whole life.

They frowned, their breath clouding in front of them. Slowly, they started to unbutton the woolen coat they wore. "You must be freezing."

As they offered it to me, I shook my head and scooted further into the bush.

"Maybe you got lost," they murmured more to themself than me. "But that can't be it. What human accidentally takes a Shadow Guard for their own?"

Their words were turning to gibberish. What was a Shadow Guard? Why did it matter? Besides, it was the least of my worries. A hand was hovering over me, and that usually meant danger. Even if I had the strength to defend myself, what would I do afterwards?

Silently, I willed them to kill me already. Maybe I was insignificant enough that Thierry would forget I agreed to come here or that I'd ever existed.

The stranger started to offer help again, but their voice was replaced by boots crunching against snow. I curled myself into a tighter ball, expecting to be met by their backup.

It was indeed a long-eared person approaching us. But he was hauntingly familiar, a tall, broad-shouldered man with gray and brown hair and amber eyes like fire. In person, he looked even stronger, nothing like in my fuzzy dreams.

"Thierry!" The stranger immediately stood up and put their fist to their heart. "My apologies for the commotion. I found a trespasser and was about to—"

"Don't touch that boy," Thierry interrupted, pushing past them to crouch beside me. After a moment of staring, he slid his arms under my back and legs, lifting me up. "He's coming with me."

His words were met with silence.

The elf offered a weak smile. "Are you sure? I'd be more than happy to take him off your hands. It's a human, after all."

Thierry's grip tightened on me. "Don't question my judgment. This isn't the first human I've taken in, and you know that." His expression softened ever so slightly. "You're a knowledgeable soul, Reed. But surely you know better than to mess with me."

"Of course, sir." Reed suddenly seemed small next to this man.

Knowing that, amusement was the last thing I felt before the pain flared up again, this time dragging me into the depths of unconsciousness.

Wherever I was being taken, there were the rhythmic thumps of walking up stairs. Lots of stairs. Boots clomping on wood. Paws pattering.

There was a woman's voice, a deep one, exclaiming over my bloody face. The rough arms holding me were traded for softer ones.

The bed she put me on was so delicate, it felt like a cloud. She even pulled my shoes off. A wet cloth rubbed over my face, her voice soothing me. It was the first time someone mothered me in such a way.

From somewhere in my exhaustion, I heard a girl's voice ask, "Is that him?" She sounded amazed.

"Yes," the woman responded quietly. "Now come on, let him rest."

Maybe it was all a bad dream. Maybe I was still in my mom's apartment, and any minute now, I'd wake up to my sister nagging me about the time. Maybe Oliver and Thierry and Isabel didn't exist after all. My everyday routine would resume, and I'd wander the streets and dance the same old dance.

Or maybe the nightmare had started when Dominic disappeared. Maybe it'd be him waking me up, laughing about how he bought seeds for us to feed the birds with. Maybe Mom would be in the background, yelling that he shouldn't have spent money on something so stupid.

"Get up, I want to show you around!" a voice said.

Not now, Dominic, I thought.

"The sun is rising, and it looks really cool from the top of the gorge."

Five more minutes.

My body jolted and I hit the hard floor with a thud. My bleary eyes shot open, gaze landing on a pale girl crouched over me. The first thing I noticed about her was her hair: dyed an electric purple color that fell in thick waves down to her elbows. Peeking out of them were a pair of long, pointed ears. Large blue eyes complemented her body, which grew closer as she leaned in to poke me. She was a teenager, from the looks of it.

"You're a heavier sleeper than I imagined," she said in a fascinated tone. "Sorry 'bout that. I gave you a little shake and you rolled off! Are you okay?"

One strand of her hair was darker than the rest. On her cheeks were little scars shaped like lightning in the sky, which crinkled as she smiled. Her bubbly, purple vibe reminded me of the plumage on an overly friendly pigeon asking for more bread.

What? I thought, confused.I didn't move, only able to stare with my mouth open. Who was this? Where was I? With a gulp, I wrenched my gaze away from the girl and looked around the room.

It was a large, circular space surrounded by white walls and golden detailing. Massive windows, one of them leading to a balcony, let natural light flood the room. Similar to the walls, the closet and desk were pristine white. A spacious bed sat in the center, supported by a dark, wooden frame and white bedding with flowers embroidered on it. It was something you'd see in a Victorian child's bedroom. An open door led into a torch-lit, red-carpeted hallway.

"Where—where are we? What's going—what's going on? Who are you?" I faced the girl again. It was hard to sound threatening with a trembling voice.

She pulled away and sat cross-legged in front of me. Her old-fashioned outfit was as much of a shock as her hair. She wore a button-down shirt with black tie that sat under a long blazer falling to her knees, hugging her beige pants. Pinned to her chest was a small badge of a crescent moon with three dots curving around it. "You must've been beat up hard, then." Her smile was large, her voice carefree in a way that reminded me of Dominic and Oliver. "I'm Savana! And you are?"

"Awake and didn't tell me?" a new, lower voice cut in. I vaguely recognized it from earlier, and I glanced over my shoulder to see a young, tall, and fit woman leaning against the doorframe. The light around us warmed her russet-brown skin and the coily hair falling past her shoulders. What caught my attention was her lack of long ears.

"You're–you're–you're human!" I faced her with wide eyes. "Th-that—how?" Adrenaline encouraged me to stand up, but it shifted into dizziness when I did, and I sat heavily on the bed.

She came closer with a low chuckle. "Yes, I'm human. You're not the only one Thierry has taken in, you know. But tell us, kid, your name is...?"

"Tyler." It was hard to focus with both her and Savana gazing at me like I was an ancient artifact. There were a million questions on the tip of my tongue, but my brain was struggling to organize them.

"Well, it's nice to meet you, Tyler." The woman sat down on the side of the mattress, a little distance between us like she knew I wanted space. "I see Savana's already introduced herself. I'm McKenzie."

I looked from her to Savana and back again. "Um, is Thierry here? I'm...I'm here for–for him." Stiffening, I realized how rude that was. "Not that I'm not pleased to–to–to meet you! I'm sorry!"

Savana sat on my other side, pointing to my face. "Quite the serious one! You didn't even acknowledge our awesome bandaging!"

I slowly brought my hand to my face, fingers brushing against bandages plastered to my cheeks. I winced as I touched them, and pain stung me. "Sorry."

McKenzie stared at the dresser in the corner of the room. "I'm surprised you got it so bad. Shadow Guard bonds usually occur when a professional is present, as the process is indeed a little"—she gestured to my weary form—"painful."

"Bonds?" I echoed. I followed her gaze and saw the cat sitting on top of the dresser, staring back at me. "You! What did you do to me?"

The cat stood up and lazily arched her back in a stretch. "I bonded myself to you."

"What does that even mean?" I glared at her. "Just say 'attack' instead!"

McKenzie rested her hand on my shoulder, and while it made me jump, it also shut me up. She gave me an apologetic look for spooking me. "Sorry. Shadow Guards are companions in this world that come in all species and sizes. They're like pets but are immortal until their host dies." Nodding to my face, she added, "Pairs are bonded through a scarring."

"I only did it so you'd listen to me about going upstream," the cat said. "I sensed that Reed was downstream from the start and wasn't sure of how they'd react to a human." She hopped off the dresser, trotting toward us and jumping onto my lap. Staring up at me with those white eyes, she knew just how to make me squirm. "Yet you still didn't listen."

"You–you could've mentioned that!" Like a defiant toddler, I crossed my arms over my chest and tilted my head away. "I could've f...fought them–them off on m-my own."

The cat flicked her ear back. "This is coming from someone who hasn't eaten in how long? You're skin and bone, child."

I opened my mouth to protest, but I paused when McKenzie stood up.

"In that case, why don't I find you something to eat?" She smiled mischievously. "Savana, you can help me. Let's give Tyler a moment to settle things with his friend." Catching my dismayed expression, McKenzie sighed, "And I'll search for Thierry while I'm out there."

"Thanks." I leaned back, too offended by the feline's comments to muster a smile. I watched Savana and McKenzie exit the room in silence, leaving me with the cat.

Unlike how tense the feline had been at the mention of Thierry's name and in the presence of Reed, she seemed to observe Savana and McKenzie's departure without any emotion. Did she approve of them or something?

She sat down on my lap, quite heavily. "A Shadow Guard would be beneficial for you." Her voice had a matter-of-fact tone to it, like she was a genius or something. "I can feel the turmoil in your body."

"That's because you–you nearly killed me!" I picked her up and placed her on the mattress beside me before lying down. The bed hardly squeaked under my weight. It was soft and plush, not to mention the first bed I'd ever been in that had a frame and legs. "A name...do you have one?"

She blinked up at me, her earlier anger seeming to ebb away. "Usually the host picks it."

I hesitated. The only names I could think of right away were cliché and basic. She reminded me of a nagging crow, but it would be silly to name a cat after a bird.

"Think of your desires." The cat rested a paw on my heart. "Who are you? What do you stand for?" They were wise questions for an animal. "What drew you to this place?"

"I want to be protected. I want my existence to...have some sort of value." My voice came out quiet, the way it always did. *But how do I be more than this?* I asked myself.

I dug my fingers into the soft mattress below. "Something strong. Strong inside and out." Looking at the cat again, I surveyed her form. What did she look like to me? "Titanium. It's strong, isn't it?"

It was a little long, but it had a good ring to it. *Tyler and Titanium.*

The newly named Titanium smiled with her fangs showing. "Sounds perfect."

CHAPTER TWELVE

NO, YOU CAN'T EAT THE BUTTERFLY

OLIVER

A FIRM JOSTLE WOKE me with a start. My eyes shot open, my gaze landing on the fuzzy form of Luke sitting over me. "What—"

"Rise and shine." He gave my face a few light slaps for extra measures.

"I'm here, I'm here," I said, my voice grating in my throat. I pushed Luke away and sat up. The world swayed, and I doubled over to make sure I didn't lose my breakfast. "Did it work?" We were all dry, despite the chill nestled deep in my bones.

Luke glanced over his shoulder. "It must have. Look around."

I did as I was told, squinting as sunlight blinded me. We were no longer underground, now surrounded by massive trees that touched the sky with their bare branches. Icicles had formed where the leaves would be. The ground was covered by thick snow, the cold air biting my lungs with every inhale. "Are...are you sure we didn't just time travel? It wasn't as snowy this morning."

"Nah, this is definitely not our usual world. Look." Luke tilted my head to the side, where a butterfly the size of two basketballs was sitting on a rock. Its vibrant colors made it look like it belonged in the rainforest. "I don't think that type, uh, normally exists for us. It's larger than the Queen Alexandra's Birdwing."

I opened my mouth to call him a nerd, but the sound of wheezing behind us cut me off. Turning around, I saw Diana and gave her a questioning look. She was sitting up, clearly fine, with an expression that was just as confused. We all looked a little past her, in time to see Vincent retch into the nearest bush.

Luke raced to his side in an instant. He shifted into big brother mode as he murmured soothing words and rubbed Vincent's back while he threw up and fought for air.

"He really isn't the life of the party," Diana muttered to me. More loudly, she called, "Vince, you okay?"

Vincent wiped the dribble off his chin before shooting her a death glare. "That's Vincent to you. Only Luke"—he coughed—"can call me Vince." He took in a deep breath, scooching away from the contents he just heaved up. "And I'm *fine.*" When we gave him skeptical looks, he stood up to prove it. "We just went through some sort of magic portal. What else were you expecting?"

"So long as you're fine." I also stood and looked around once more. Everything spun, and I took a moment to collect myself before speaking again. "Okay, maybe we should've asked this earlier, but where are we even supposed to find Thierry?" I pulled out

Bryce's drawing of his dad and held it for the others to see. "That's his face."

Vincent put his hands up in surrender, starting to pace around. "Nope. Nope. Not doing this, not when we're so unorganized. Where's the damn portal? Let's go back and ask."

He stormed away, and after exchanging weary glances, Diana, Luke, and I trailed after him. I shoved the drawing back into my pocket, hovering my hand over it to make sure it was safe.

"There's a den of some sort over there." Luke pointed to a thick cluster of trees past a line of silver, leafless bushes. He was right. A gap in the snow revealed a dark hole, surrounded by a handful of crumbling ruins.

We approached the den and cautiously peered inside. Past thick roots sticking out of the soil was a pool of crystal blue water, framed by shining gems. Without looking closely, one could assume the pool was just another one of the shimmering jewels.

"But if the portal is here, how did we land up above ground?" Diana asked what we were all thinking.

Vincent tensed. "Doesn't matter. I'm not questioning the logic of this place. Okay, on the count of three?"

Luke nudged his brother. "I think your stomach would implode if you hopped back in."

Diana put her hands on her hips. "Yeah! Not to mention we're supposed to be doing this as a group, all four of us. I'm just as scared as you are, but you don't see me wanting to run home with my tail between my legs."

"I'm not scared!" Vincent stepped away, pouting. "Nope, not at all!" He lifted his necklace and bit it again, but when we noticed, he pulled it down and resorted to twisting it.

"It looks like we won't need to go back, then." With that settled, I wandered a few paces away, surveying the white forest for any signs or directions. "Maybe we can ask someone for help."

Diana lifted the edge of her cloak with a frown. "Are we sure this'll be enough to hide our ears?"

Luke pulled his hood over his head, letting a shadow cast over his face. "It's all we got."

The strange butterfly from earlier finally lifted off the rock, weaving past us before landing on the ground a few feet away. It slowly opened and closed its marvelous wings, almost like it was inviting us to follow it. I gasped when I saw footsteps on the trail it sat upon.

"I assume we're supposed to follow it?" Diana glanced my way, the question clearly aimed at me.

Everyone else faced me, too, and I stepped back. "Why are you guys looking at me? Aren't we deciding together?"

"I mean...you're the one who seems to understand what's going on." Diana flashed me an embarrassed smile.

I shook my head. "We'll decide together, as a group. There's no leader."

Luke straightened up. "Okay. Then, is everyone in favor of following the butterfly?"

Nobody objected. Vincent raised his hand like we were in a classroom before asking, "Can we eat it afterwards? We'll have to think about food and water while we're here, too."

"This is coming from the one who threw up five minutes ago." Diana shot him a mischievous look before strutting past him, following the butterfly's trail.

We watched her leave, Vincent's face scrunched up with embarrassment. Slowly, we followed her.

"I don't know how it works here, but colorful things back home are usually dangerous," Luke said finally, a delayed answer to Vincent's question. "We'll find something, though."

We kept walking through the forest until dusk rapidly approached. Darkness swallowed the sky as the trees thinned behind us, elongating every shadow. Strange, glowing snowflakes bounced and mingled in the air. Below the hill we stood upon were a bunch of yellow dots, which we soon realized belonged to glowing candles. It was a whole town!

When we came to that discovery, the butterfly that'd been leading us lifted off and flew away. Its job was done.

We had a bit of an argument over whether we should visit now or wait until morning. Shockingly, Diana and Vincent were in agreement on exploring the town now, using hunger as their motivation. Luke and I reasoned that the stores were bound to be closed, and we didn't know if bars or restaurants would let broke teenagers in. That is, if they existed in the first place.

Instead, Luke and I picked some harmless-looking berries and insisted on sharing the batch with them. Vincent and Diana didn't look thrilled with the idea, but knowing it was pointless to fight, they begrudgingly split the berries between the four of us. The berries were surprisingly hot, like I was chewing a piece of lava. Whenever we swallowed, a tiny puff of smoke would slip from our lips. We got a good laugh out of pretending to be fire-breathing dragons.

Gathering some sticks and using the lighter Vincent had packed, we started a pathetic fire and huddled around it. Overhead, wind rustled the dead branches and stirred the bare trees. We jumped and covered our ears at every snapping twig, worried we'd be exposed as humans. Wings flapped and critters growled, but nothing dared to show its face.

"All we need now are some marshmallows and spooky stories." Diana hovered her hands over the flames.

Luke scrunched up his face. "We don't have marshmallows, unfortunately. I could totally settle for a spooky story, though."

"Right before bed?" I frowned. "This whole place is spooky!"

Vincent huffed. "Don't be such a wuss, Oliver," he said before digging into his backpack again. He pulled out a pocket-sized notebook and flipped through it. Looking me dead in the eyes, he recited, "The crystals are not lost, but waiting. They bare their teeth. So sleep well—they'll whisper your fate. They are calling."

Was I feeling sick because of exhaustion or his use of the word "crystal?" I grimaced, swallowing my discomfort. "That's not even a scary story."

"It made you squirm, so it is." Vincent grinned smugly, probably his first smile all day.

Diana peered at the black leather cover of his notebook. "Did you just have that ready?"

"What can I say? I get bored." Vincent nonchalantly waved the notebook in the air. "Most of it's just bits of dreams I remember."

Dreams? I surveyed the air around Vincent, searching for signs of a ghost hovering near him. What if his unconsciousness had been tied with the Assembly of Six this whole time, despite his complaints? I wanted to ask, but I was certain I'd sound crazy. Besides, what if I was wrong?

Diana, however, had been ensnared by the poem. "Read another one!"

"Nope." I shuffled back, kicking dirt over our makeshift campfire. "I think that's enough for one night."

Luckily, Luke jumped to my defense, reminding us that we needed to save our strength. He offered to take the first shift, moving to sit a little up ahead after we'd put the fire out.

Diana and Vincent were both out like a light, huddling with their backs to each other for warmth. I laid a short distance away, staring at a clump of snow for a rather long time. These strange, tiny jellyfish melted into the frost. Watching the intriguing sight made my eyelids heavy. Still, sleep wasn't coming for me. Vincent's cryptic letter played on a loop in my mind.

Rolling onto my side, I glanced at Luke, who was hugging his knees and staring up at the sky. Guilt formed a lump in my throat at the sight of his tired eyes, even if he was guarding voluntarily. I unfurled myself and crawled closer to sit beside him. "Hey, we can switch if you want. You look ready to crash."

Luke gave me a weak smile. "I'm okay. Check out all the stars, though!"

From where we sat, we had a better view of the sky beyond the canopy of branches. My eyes drifted upward, landing on the black night splashed with vibrant purples, blues, and greens. They swirled together to create galaxies adorned by massive stars. There were two moons, one to the west and the other to the east.

I could've sworn the stars and constellations were dancing up there. After a minute, I just breathed out, "Wow." I couldn't bring myself to blink in fear the sight would disappear. *Stars never disappear, though,* I reminded myself. *They're always there.*

A tiny voice in my head asked, *Are there stars where Tyler is now?* We'd find out soon, but this time, the reminder made my stomach cramp. Or maybe that was just the berries from earlier.

I laid down on my back, letting the night sky flood my vision. "Say, Luke, how long do you think it'll take us to go there and back? To–to fetch Tyler, you know?"

Luke lowered himself next to me with a small hum. "Isabel and Camila said it shouldn't take too long. I hope not, because we have winter exams next month. I also told my dad that Vincey and I would visit for Thanksgiving break." He frowned up at the stars. "It depends on how long we take finding the place, getting there, fetching him, and coming back. We also need that necklace Isabel wants."

Hearing it like that, it sounded like rocket science. My mind flickered back to this morning, to the cop in Isabel's office looking for Tyler. Would he be back when we returned, regardless of how long it took? "What if they take him away?"

"Who?"

"The police." My voice came out as a pained whisper. "Will they give him back to his mom? We–we don't even have proof that he's been abused."

Luke shook his head. "That doesn't mean we can't try. First, we gotta find him and bring him back." He grabbed a clump of snow, holding it up in front of him. "It sucks that the teenagers have to do all this."

A chilling realization took hold of me. "We're responsible if something happens to Tyler from this point on." I looked over to where Vincent and Diana remained fast asleep. "We're responsible for them, too."

Luke's eyes darkened with worry. "I think you're setting yourself some crazy expectations."

"But Isabel wanted me to keep Tyler safe!" My voice was strained with a pain I hadn't expected. "She put him in my care and..." Crystal's earlier words rushed back to me, and I gripped my chest. "I let everyone down. That's why I have to make it right. And that's why I can't afford to let Diana and Vincent get hurt, either."

"Hey." Luke rested his hand on my shoulder. "I'm right here alongside you. It's unfair for you to think you have to do this by yourself. You aren't alone."

Groaning, I rubbed my hands over my eyes. "There's just so much to worry about. I know we were chosen for a reason, but I just hope we're the right ones."

"What, you think we aren't worthy of this?" There was more tired amusement than offense in Luke's tone.

I squirmed. "Not exactly! It's just like what you said. We're only kids."

Luke's hand trailed down my shoulder. "Maybe it's because kids are freer than adults. We aren't as restricted as they are." When I didn't reply, he sat up and offered me a smile. "You can take the next shift if you still want it."

"Sounds good. Sleep well." I leaned up on my elbows, watching him stand and move to where Vincent lay before he plopped down next to him. More to myself, I whispered, "I hope you're right."

There was great vulnerability in being the only one awake in a forest. Most of the town's lights had gone out, leaving only the stars and moons to keep me company. All I could hear was my breathing.

The silence was interrupted as a gust of wind brushed my side, lifting my hair and buffeting my coat.

"Hope what?" a voice piped up as soon as the gale calmed down.

I whipped my head around to see Crystal sitting inches away from me. Only after my heart rate calmed did I respond. "Hope you're not luring us into a trap. Nice of you to show up again, by the way."

Crystal grinned and rose to her feet, shifting to stand right in front of me. Her white outline glowed in the dark, her translucent body turning the space behind her purple. It was hard to believe there was a carving of this girl under our school. "Oh, Oliver Stylus, with time you'll learn that I'm a friend." She brought one hand to her heart, preening under her self-praise. "Especially because if it weren't for me, you never would've known where Tyler went! You're welcome!"

She had a point, as much as I hated to admit it. I basically let Tyler sneak away right before my eyes, a fact that made me squirm. "What do you want?"

Crystal nodded to the town just down the hill. "I want you to keep going, duh. There's a life at stake! Come on!"

She thought I didn't know that? I crossed my arms over my chest and looked away. "The others are sleeping, and we promised to move as a team."

"Huh. Then I guess Tyler will die." Crystal's response was a blow to the chest.

"Shut it, will you? And besides, the guy Tyler is here for is the dad of my friend. I–I don't think he'll kill him—I hope not." I muttered the last bit under my breath as I refused to show Crystal how her words were getting to me. Vincent's eerie poem from earlier trickled back into my mind.

Crystal nibbled the inside of her cheek. "Whatever the case is, you must get Tyler back before Thierry Colliss changes his mind.

The rest of you can be replaced if the worst happens, but Tyler? He's the reactant, as Isabel put it. If he dies, who knows how long we'll have to wait before another opportunity strikes? I literally told you to bring him to me in a dream, didn't I? We could've secured him, and this never would've happened."

There she went, talking about this chosen group again. "Don't describe Tyler like he's an object. He's a person, not to mention just a kid!" I dug my hand into my pocket, pulling out the crinkled paper Camila gave me. The illustrated necklace was barely visible in the darkness. "Besides, Isabel needs this, too. We wouldn't be able to get it if it weren't for Tyler's disappearance. That's one kind of a plus to this, right?"

No response. When I looked up, Crystal was gone. My last words hung heavy in the night air, and not even I could summon an answer.

My dream that night was in a cave of some sort. Right away, I started searching for Crystal, but there weren't any lights to guide me. It was only me and the bare, dusty, earth walls.

Besides, Crystal had a white, blurry glow to her. The figure at the back of the cave was a shadowy mass.

Wait, what? My heart jumped in my throat. "Hello? Who's there?"

"How disappointing." The cave shook as the voice reverberated around it. A flame appeared between us, held by the person with the deep, rumbling tone that spoke up. Dust fell from the ceiling at his powerful words. But that didn't alarm me as much as his face.

"You're Bryce's father," I said. It came out meek, like I wished I didn't have to say it.

He grinned. "That's more like it. At least I'm kind enough to remember names." He paused, giving me five seconds to say it out loud. But when I stayed silent, he purred, "Thierry Colliss. Don't forget it." The flame he held flickered under my chin as he drew closer, looming over me. With his free hand, he lifted a strand of my orange hair. "It's the color of fire. It's a window to your soul, all alight with ambition. We're awfully alike, don't you think?"

His words sent chills down my spine. I worked saliva into my dry mouth. "Are we?"

"We have common goals." Thierry's fire transformed into the shape of a boy. To my horror, it was Tyler.

It raised the hair on the back of my neck. I stepped away from Thierry, with my eyes locked onto the fire. "What are you doing with Tyler?"

Thierry tossed his head back with a laugh. "You talk as if I'm a monster! I'm not doing anything bad to him!" Relaxing, his smile turned sly. "Tyler *chose* to come here."

"Unless he was manipulated." I looked Thierry up and down with a scowl. "That's what you do to people. Bryce told me!" As Thierry's face darkened, my heart clenched. "Yeah, your precious son let me know all about you."

"Bryce's judgment has been clouded for years now. He's a coward and a disappointment." Thierry wrinkled his nose. "This is why Tyler is so great! He needs a purpose, and I'm the only one who can give him that. He's like a little puppet." He closed his fist, and the flame vanished. He loomed over me in the darkness. "You could join us and reunite with Tyler. Isn't that what you want? You don't have to be crushed, Oliver Stylus."

My heart thundered in my chest as I pulled away. Bryce's warnings about his father blared through my mind. "I'll never join you."

Thierry bared his teeth, revealing sharp canines. "You're making a grave mistake." The fire rekindled above his palm, stronger than before.

He slashed it at me.

I jolted awake, my muscles screaming from adrenaline.

It was morning, and the others were already stretching and groaning over their sore backs. I'm pretty sure Diana asked me something, but I couldn't hear it over my panicked breathing. I sat up and patted myself down, searching for injuries. Everything felt fine, but in a missing sort of way.

Bryce had been right. I didn't want to know how he got burned.

Chapter Thirteen

A Taste of Home

Tyler

THE APARTMENT WAS SMALLER than I remembered. It was never cluttered, because we barely had any belongings, but the walls were closer. Standing in the bare room Mia and I shared, I stared at our empty mattress. Mia's old doll sat on her pillow, and I frowned. She got rid of that thing ages ago.

"Tyler?"

My mom stood in the doorway, her eyes wide and jaw taut.

I tensed up. It was wrong of me to be in my own room.

Thump.

She came forward and wrapped her arms around me. Her hug was warm, making me feel gooey and melty. "I was so worried," she whispered.

Thump.

As I raised my hands to hug her back, I paused. My knuckles weren't scarred or bloody. "I'm sorry," I croaked finally. The walls were closing in and pressing against my skull.

"It's okay, darling." She pulled away to search me up and down. "You aren't hurt, are you? Oh, you poor thing…" She put her hands to my wounded cheeks.

Thump.

I relaxed. When was the last time she'd spoken to me in a motherly, or even caring way? "I'm alright."

"I missed you."

Thump.

"I'm sorry." Shakily, I began to explain the past few days to her, pausing every few minutes to apologize. I kept looking down to her fist, watching it clench and unclench. "I'm fine now, though."

Thump.

Mom frowned, a bit more like her usual self. "Are you?"

Before I could answer, I blinked awake.

Am I? I wondered.

I sat up in my bed, freezing once remembering where I was. There was no Mom accepting my apologies.

Pale light shone through the large windows. Was it morning? Had I slept through the rest of the previous day? Embarrassment crawled up my throat. Maybe I hadn't fully recovered from the fatigue, and the bed had been so soft that I couldn't get enough.

A shadow fell over the crack under the door, and instinctively, I flopped onto my side and buried myself under the blankets. It took everything in me to not whimper as the door slammed open. What did I do wrong this time?

Heavy footsteps approached my bed. "Alright, peasant, Thierry wants you."

It was a hauntingly familiar voice. Snappy and deep, I could recognize it in any crowd. I sat up and twisted my body to face the newcomer.

Standing over my bed was a tall, tan boy in a tank top that revealed the muscles of his upper body. Pinned against his chest were two small badges: one of a crescent moon with three circles, just like Savana's, and one with two lines of red fire. His pants had scorch marks where they met his scuffed boots. Without taking his eyes off me, he absently ran a finger through his light brown hair. It was the same as it used to be, fluffy and falling over the side of his forehead. All he said in the end was "oh."

Every muscle in my body was screaming to make a run for it, but my feet refused to move. Pleas to be left alone pooled in my tight throat, but nothing spilled out.

"Strange to see you of all people around here. Has Dominic come back?"

My stomach dropped as he dared say his name.

"What, don't remember me or something? Come on, how could anyone forget Noah O'Quinn just like that?" His confidence returned, a cocky smile taking over his face. When I didn't answer, his amber eyes darkened. "What about you? Cat still got your tongue?"

I clamped my teeth together, hunching up my shoulders as I shrank back. There were so many things I wanted to scream at him, but he had a point. Something *did* have my tongue, that's for sure. All my words were frozen in my throat.

Noah rolled his eyes, but instead of turning away, he stepped even closer to me. He seemed to loom higher than all of New York City's skyline. "The last time I checked, ignoring someone when they're talking to you is awfully *rude*." He rested one hand on my small shoulder. Digging his fingernails into the fabric and skin, he asked, "Don't you think so?"

My lips trembled as I fought for the right words. Finally, I croaked out, "Sorry."

His hand on my shoulder seemed to set my skin ablaze. Slowly, I pulled away.

Noah just glared down at me, his lips in a thin line as he debated what to say next. He'd always been a tough guy, towering over me and even making Dominic look small. Now, he looked like he could end me in a split second.

I shifted back to put more distance between us. "You–you-y—Is...Th-Th...Th-Thierry here?"

"I can't tell what's more annoying, your silence or your damn voice." Noah pulled away and started to pace around the room. "And yes, Thierry is here. That's why I came. Weren't you listening? I was told to bring you to him."

"Right." I stumbled out of bed, running my fingers through my hair the way Noah always did. It wasn't to make myself look cool; I just wanted to look presentable. If anything, I felt stupid doing the gesture.

Noah rolled his eyes again, finally turning around and starting toward the door to the hall. I followed, but the view beyond the balcony caught my eye, and my pace faltered.

Ignoring Noah's questioning stare, I wandered to the window, opening it and stepping onto the balcony. A cold gust of air welcomed me, but it was the sight below that summoned my gasp.

Right away, the architecture reminded me of Indra Academy. We were in a castle-like building crafted of cobblestone, several stories up. Dark red wooden details lined the edges and tips of the roofs. Resting just feet away from the back of the structure was a deep ravine that stretched on until the fog swallowed it. On the closer end of it was a waterfall, which must've come from the same river Titanium and I fought over a few days ago.

The wintery forest stretched along the other side of the split land. Rooftops from what must've been a town filled the gaps between the trees. The dense overgrowth shielded the gorge from the naked eye. A field-length of empty land surrounding the ravine made a clearing in the woods.

"No way," was all I could whisper.

"What, you never bothered looking outside?" Noah's gaze was scathing as he looked me up and down.

I shrugged, but under his burning stare, it turned into a guilty nod. Perhaps it'd been fueled by my exhaustion or the uncertainty of what to do without instructions. If nobody said I wasn't allowed out of the room, I couldn't simply assume it was fine to go outside!

After flashing me another disgusted look, Noah yanked the door handle to the hall and pulled it open. The violence of the action brought me to his side almost immediately, but before we could leave, a gentle thud from behind made us pause. We turned around to face Titanium, who'd jumped down from the dresser.

"Where are you going?" she asked.

I shooed her away with my hand. "To see—to see Thierry. You stay here."

Titanium didn't look convinced, her glowing white eyes narrowed. Her paws flexed, revealing her claws, but she sighed and said, "Fine."

"Thierry doesn't like it when people waste his time. Hurry up, mutt." Noah tried grabbing my wrist and glared at me when I pulled back.

He ignored my apology and left the room, with me hot on his trail. We entered a long hallway lit by flaming torches along the dark walls. Our footsteps were muffled by the maroon-red carpet below us, lined with intricate black details. Portraits in gold frames loomed above us, their eyes seeming to watch my every move. Low voices echoed and murmured around us, but as the sounds were blocked by the walls, I couldn't make any of it out.

After turning the corner, Noah opened a door leading to a cobblestone staircase spiraling downward. He didn't hesitate, walking down with speed and precision. His long legs only made him quicker, and I had to move twice as fast to keep up.

Normally, a trek like this would've been a breeze, considering how often I walked long distances in Manhattan on an empty stomach. But my body truly had grown accustomed to the soft treatment of Indra Academy, so two days with limited food and water made my pace falter. Going in circles was dizzying, and I had to focus all my strength on not tripping and pitching forward like a sack of potatoes. It must've been obvious, because Noah gave me this amused look when I finally reached the bottom. His stance was poised and steady, unlike mine with my wobbling knees and fluttering chest.

"Quit the dramatics. We don't want to keep Thierry waiting." Noah gestured for me to keep moving. He shoved open the next door and stepped outside.

I glared at Noah's back but followed him. We found ourselves in a courtyard of silver-leaved trees and dead grass sprinkled with snow. A large, wooden gate stood tall, proud, and open at one of the stone walls. Armored, elf-eared people stood guard around the courtyard and entrance. They didn't give Noah a second glance yet did a double take as I passed them. My skin crawled, and I threw my hood over my head.

After passing the gate and walking along the path, I turned around to take in the building as a whole. My breath caught in my throat. Jutting into the sky, hugged by fog, was a castle.

"There's just no way," I said, echoing my words from the balcony. Thierry never mentioned a castle! I was so mesmerized, I almost tripped as I stumbled back and faced the right direction. I wanted to ask Noah about the castle, but I couldn't formulate the question.

With him facing forward, I could finally stare at Noah without him seeing. Noah had been Dominic's best friend since elementary school, and while Dominic had tons of buddies, Noah had been with him no matter what. He was like a leech.

Having grown up without any friends, I'd spent my free time following Dominic and Noah around. Noah had always tossed me dirty looks, loudly whining to my brother, "Why does he have to hang out with us?" As if silence equaled stupidity. Dominic used to say, "I'm here to be both of your friends!"

Noah would reply, "He's your brother, not your friend. You spend all day with him."

Noah was the kid who threw rocks at birds. I was the one who cried because of that.

Knowing I was a hassle, I never said much to Noah other than the occasional apology. I knew I was always getting under his skin. I knew I was a burden to babysit. But I didn't have anyone else to hang out with.

Of course, when Dominic applied to Indra Academy in eighth grade, Noah did the same. They both got accepted. It was during the winter break of their freshman year they came back to Manhattan to visit, and that was the last I ever saw of Dominic. Noah went back to Indra Academy and never returned. I never thought much of it.

Was he here the whole time, though? I wondered. My stomach hurt. Noah seemed at home in this hostile world.

The point was further proven as I let my gaze stray away from the path. It settled on a feathery blur of colors pecking around some tree roots, and my heart soared. Finally, a bird in this place! I stopped to admire the creature, with its long legs and crest of stray feathers sticking out of its head.

Noah paused and tossed me a scowl. "We don't have all day."

"But look!" I shuffled closer, excitedly scanning the bird over. It had the characteristics of a secretary bird, though the feathers on its head were made of kelp fronds, and it was living nowhere near a savanna or grassland.

"You'll have time to look at your stupid bird later." Noah stormed away, toward the river and waterfall.

"Secretary bird," I corrected him under my breath. The clenching of his fists had me darting away from the avian creature. My heart was as heavy as a water balloon, but I held my breath and tucked the memory of the bird into the back of my mind.

The hum of voices, growing louder, overlapped my thoughts. I dragged my gaze up to see two elves nearby, standing side by side, their expressions filled with anticipation. One of them was twisting the reins of a furry, almost bear-like horse. Both people had scratches and bruises on their faces.

Thierry Colliss loomed over them, like a shadow that consumed all the nearby light. He was a terrifyingly thrilling sight in real life and when I wasn't foggy with fever. His shoulders were broad, and his form was muscular. His hands were large and calloused. Perched on his head was a thin band of gold, and two pillars of red fire flickered from them in a shape reminding me of devil horns. It looked just like the badge on Noah's chest.

But it wasn't the crown that brought the familiar sense of dread tugging in my stomach. It was the sight of his hands. They were weapons. I shuffled behind Noah, watching Thierry's fists clench and unclench while he spoke to the elves. None of them seemed to notice Noah and me lingering about.

"All I asked was one simple task from you two," Thierry was saying to his companions, voice thunderous. His fangs, an eerie feature I hadn't noticed before, glinted in the dull light. "This forest spirit is endangering lives and my research!" He paid no attention to the elves' wounds. Leaning forward, he asked, "Are you really going to drag Derngate down with your fear?"

The first elf's ears pulled back. His fingers tightened around the reins he still clutched. "That *thing* was impossible to beat with just the two of us."

Thierry's lips drew back in a snarl. "I'll give you an impossible fight if you're looking for it. Now, get out of my sight, or I'll make a fine meal out of your transport."

The bear-horse—whatever it was—made a strangled sound as if it could tell its life was in peril. Newly motivated, the elves hopped onto the tandem saddle and galloped off.

After several moments of silence, Thierry turned around and gave Noah a bored look. His eyes shifted, and he focused on me with his ears perking up. "Ah, glad to see you're feeling better."

Smiling felt impossible knowing he just threatened to roast an animal.

Noah cleared his throat and asked, "Is there anything else I can do, sir?"

Thierry waved his hand nonchalantly. "Thank you, Noah. You may leave now."

Noah frowned at the quick dismissal, mouth opening like he wanted to pry for more. He must have remembered how that went for the other elves and kept quiet. He shoved past me with a glare, storming back to the castle gates.

Neither Thierry nor I spoke, each challenging the other to start.

I forced myself to look at him, focusing on his ears instead of his eyes. Mesmerized by the way they twitched, I mumbled, "You never...never mentioned a c-ca-castle." I then focused on the flickering of twin flames on his crown. "Or a crown."

"I was afraid of the impression I might leave if I revealed everything about myself." Thierry gave a lighthearted shrug. "And you listened to me without knowing the entire truth. What admirable yet foolish faith you have."

"I'm sorry," I quickly piped up. "Um...King...?"

"Emperor, actually. But just Thierry is fine."

"Okay." I fought the urge to shrink back. This was a ruler in front of me. A man with status and power. A man with a castle and free rooms for troublesome children. "S-sorry if...Sorry if my–my timing w-was bad."

"No, my apologies for not giving you proper instructions." Thierry scanned me. He sighed and shook his head, like he'd failed to find something he was looking for. "Allow me to give you a proper introduction." His arm swept to one side, gesturing to the gorge below us instead of the castle. "This is the Cataclysm."

"I thought Ti-Titanium call-called this place, uh, Derngate?"

"That's the name of the realm." Thierry nodded to the system of stairs and slopes entangling the eerie ravine. "This organization I have going on is the Cataclysm. We have several other locations around the continent. My most important work is done here, assisted by the brightest minds I know. I'm sure you've already met McKenzie Evans, who's in charge of this location."

"Oh." I buried my hands in my pockets to hide the way they fidgeted. "It's–it's cool. McKenzie's cool, too." I risked a glance up at Thierry, my skin burning when I realized he was already staring at me. "But look, I..." My voice trailed off, and I fought to speak up. "I th...thought about it, a–and I don't think this place is for me." *Especially after seeing Noah here.*

Thierry tilted his head to the side. "Oh?"

That was my sign to keep going. "I just...I'm not big enough to be here." I was half convinced my mom's shadow was looming over me, nodding for me to continue. She was telling me to come home.

"There are no size restrictions."

I shook my head. "N-no, not like that. I mean I don't...I don't have the guts." Absently, I squeezed my arm. I was almost able to loop my fingers around it.

Thierry sighed. "You came here to learn your Mageia, correct? You haven't gotten there yet. Of course you don't feel ready. You're the same boy from the human realm, after all. Everything will get better when you learn to love this place. You just have to be open." He smiled, almost uncharacteristically. "You have a great purpose here, you know?"

"I do?" I almost laughed.

"Yes, you do." Thierry raised his palm, tracing the lines like they were a maze. "The goal of my project, and the goal of the Cataclysm, is to return the Meraki to where they rightfully belong.

In your world. We were chased out a long time ago. And you"—he pointed at me—"are the missing piece I've been waiting for. Don't you want to save the world?"

Don't we all? I shrugged, but it turned into a guilty nod. It was an average person's foolish dream to think they were needed.

But this was no dream.

Thierry must've read my mind. He scoffed. "That's what I thought. I'm offering you something great, Tyler. I've seen your dreams. They're filled with jeering laughs and cramped spaces. You don't have to face that ever again if you stay here."

"But my mom—"

"Will be incredibly proud of you!" Thierry cut me off enthusiastically. He patted my shoulders like I was a dog, ignoring how I flinched. "Just think about this. You can show her everything you've accomplished when we're finished. We'll have nudged this world into a new era of prosperity and hope. Unfortunate souls such as yourself will have new opportunities. Nobody wants to be forgotten, after all." His expression darkened as he glanced at the snowy forest. "You don't have anywhere else to go, I hope you know that. But I can give you everything you need. Resources. A warm place to stay. A purpose."

My heart twisted as his words sunk in. "Right," I said. But Thierry had a point. No one else wanted me, and the offer of a lifetime was dangling right in front of me. "Right," I repeated with more strength.

"And if that's not enough of a push..." Thierry began to laugh to himself. "I have information on your precious older brother. If you care about him, you'll listen to what I say."

Time stopped.

Thierry had...*what?*

I took a step back. "Dominic Lynn? You–you have information on Dominic? Is he alive? Oh my gosh—please, tell me!"

When Dominic first went missing, Noah and I searched like crazy for him. It was the only time we ever united under a similar cause. However, neither we nor the police could find any leads. The search quickly faded away, especially when Noah moved. Dominic's case was shoved under the rug, left to burn a hole in my heart for three years.

Thierry's eyes twinkled. He knew he'd found my weakness. "Yes. But remember what I said! First, you must do as I say."

Thierry meant serious business. My heart lurched. It gravitated toward his authority and promises. He had the one thing I'd never get at Indra Academy. Information about Dominic.

This was perfect. Mom would see me change the world, and maybe I could reunite her with Dominic. Her beloved son would be back. My beloved brother would be back. A smile pulled at my lips, making my cheeks hurt. "Yes, sir!"

Chapter Fourteen

DINE AND DASH

Oliver

I'D NEVER SEEN SO many—what were they—elves? *They're Meraki, remember?* I reminded myself. *That's what our research said.*

Everywhere I looked in the town, which was called Audun, people had pointy ears. It was fascinating how they swiveled, perked up, and pinned back. Everyone looked like they were fresh out of a historical film with their suits, puffy dresses, and fancy hats.

Even with our ears hidden, us humans must've stuck out like a sore thumb. Security was easy to slip past in the crowds. We got a few weird looks, but thankfully, nobody struck up a conversation with us. Everyone was going about their morning, hustling to work or meeting with friends.

Audun was a well-sized town, with a high cobblestone wall hugging its perimeter and a wooden gate letting people in and out. Citizens didn't have to worry about outside threats from the looks of it. Looming in the near distance was a castle, which explained the guards posted every few blocks. The sight of the stony palace made my stomach hurt, but I still felt drawn to it. But messing with those in charge could get us in big trouble, so any curiosities I had stayed untouched.

Amongst the loud chatter and bells echoing in the distance, I also picked up on hushed whispers. I overheard murmurs along the lines of "Do you think he's serious about restoring peace?" and "It's a stupid necklace. What good can it be? What we really need fixed are the attacks from the forest spirit."

A shudder rolled down my spine, and I quickened my pace. Either the others didn't share my nerves, or they were simply better at hiding them. Diana excitedly pointed out every little detail, and while most of her thoughts seemed directed at Vincent, it was Luke who responded and joked with her. Vincent listened but his face said he'd rather be caught dead than participate.

We were walking along what appeared to be a shopping street of some sort. Several spots seemed to be under construction. Brick buildings lined the cobblestone streets, most colored white with wooden details and slanted roofs. Near each door were tiny ball-shaped flames wedged into the ground, keeping the snow from piling up. The Meraki certainly didn't have to worry about shoveling.

When I mentioned my observations to Luke, he whispered back, "These guys disappeared from our world around the early twentieth century, so it makes sense that they dress and act like it. They must've evolved in different ways."

I was about to ask what he meant, but the nearby sound of applause cut me off.

A buff, shirtless guy stood in front of a clothesline that had fish hanging from it. He put his hand under one of them, and a blaze of fire erupted from his palm. In just half a minute, the fish was well-cooked. The crowd applauded him again with enthusiasm.

"I don't like the look of that." Diana pulled her hood even further down her face to consume her ears. Her black-and-gray hair fell over her eyes. "Let's get out of here. Just one gust of wind or a knock sideways and we're done for!"

Vincent nodded eagerly. "On that note, where can we get breakfast?"

Luke patted his pockets, then froze. "More importantly, what do we pay with? Using dollars is just screaming 'We aren't from here!'"

Vincent strolled away, and to stick close, we raced after him. Once we were back in earshot, he said nonchalantly, "We'll dine and dash."

"That's illegal!" Diana hissed.

"So?" Vincent rolled his eyes. "Do you want us to go hungry?"

I was about to call the idea absurd, but my growling stomach had other ideas. "How about we find a place to eat and ask what their payment method is, okay? We can say we're travelers and don't know the currency here. Technically, that's the truth."

Luke gave me a thumbs up. "Sounds like a plan."

∞

We found ourselves at a coffee shop called The Audun Peaberry that was brimming with life. It reminded me of the café Bryce worked at back in Manhattan, and homesickness tugged at my heart.

Flowery wallpaper surrounded the place in a blur of nauseating color. Everything was crafted from dark wood, which contrasted nicely with the pink petals and the white-and-green stripes of the upholstery. The pale light from the windows clashed with the golden glow of the dimmer corners lit with lanterns. Business was booming as people laughed at the bar and occupied the tables either with a date or a larger group.

The lady working at the front told us to sit wherever, without even glancing at how busy the place was behind her. Scared shitless of getting our ears noticed, we mumbled "thank you" and went inside without asking about the currency.

Miraculously, we found an empty round table on the second floor, which was just as packed as the first. The window next to us displayed a perfect view of the bustling street below and graced us with natural light. I squeezed in between Luke and Diana.

"Let's be quick, okay?" I said. "We still gotta search for Tyler." The nervous lump in my throat wrestled with my hunger.

Vincent rolled his eyes. "At least let us eat in peace. Gosh." From the way he impatiently played with his necklace, I feared he'd start gnawing it down.

No waiter approached us. Instead, a gust of wind brought four menus fluttering our way. We hadn't heard of most of the items, but it wasn't like we could ask anyone for clarification. We resorted to peeking at what was on everyone else's plates. In the end, we ordered what looked like pancakes.

Just like with the buff fish guy, our food took an impressively short amount of time to arrive. After surviving off berries for dinner, we were practically salivating to see this meal.

The syrup was crystalized on top and inside of the pancakes. I took a bite. It was...savory? Yet still fluffy and delicate on the outer part. After hearing my review, the others dug in.

"We should get the recipe," Luke mumbled around a mouthful of pancake. "These are awesome!"

"What, trying to outdo Dad's pancakes?" Vincent wasn't eating as quickly, but I saw his eyes sparkle behind his glasses.

Luke grinned at his little brother. "Never!"

Diana faced the brothers. "Your dad cooks?"

"Yeah! He even owns a small restaurant in Manhattan." Luke waved his fork as he spoke. "He teaches me new recipes every time we come home."

Vincent gave us a sideways grin. "You'd be surprised to hear Luke's not entirely shit at cooking."

While the others chatted, I kept glancing around the shop, unable to shake off this nagging feeling. We should've been searching for Tyler. Crystal's urgent words from last night came back to taunt me, leaving the pancakes to form a lump in my throat as my mind wandered. How could we be sure we were on the right track? Tyler could be somewhere completely different in this strange world.

The cops were already searching for the missing kid.

Bryce sounded so stressed over his father's involvement.

Luke and Vincent wanted to be home by Thanksgiving break.

What if we had to keep moving away from the portal?

"I think I'm done," I mumbled, pushing my half-eaten pancake away. Instead, I reached into my pocket, pulling out the drawing of Isabel's necklace. The ink seemed to blur as I stared at it.

Diana peered over my shoulder with a little hum. "That's a pretty crystal."

"I think it's fire quartz. Look at the shape." I ran my finger along the rough outline. "It stands for stability and balance."

"You know about crystals?" Diana stared at the drawing in awe.

I nodded. "My moms had a ton when we lived in California."

Vincent raised an eyebrow at me. "Moms?"

"Two," I confirmed.

Vincent fell silent, his mouth parted. All he said after a moment was "cool."

Before I could reply, a shadow fell over our table, and we looked up to see two middle-aged women standing over us. Neither looked pleased, and I tensed up. Not once had I thought about how a place like this might accept someone having two moms. The hairs along my neck rose as I prepared to defend myself.

Yet all they did was scowl at the table. The shorter and plumper of the two pointed an old-lady finger at our mostly empty plates. "Are you done yet?"

"What?" Luke blinked at them before looking at our table. "Um, I don't think so."

"This is our reserved table," said the other woman. "If you're so cocky, you must know that."

Vincent straightened up, glaring daggers their way. "Excuse me? You don't get to kick us out! There's no sign saying it's reserved."

"Yes, it is! My husband owns the place and keeps this table just for us! He'll ban you forever," the first one shrilled.

Vincent slammed his hands down on the table and shot to his feet. His fingers curled into fists, his body tense like a snake waiting to strike. "We're not leaving!"

One of the ladies shoved him back. Vincent tripped over the leg of his chair, and he crashed right into Diana. Her chair broke under their combined weight, and they toppled to the floor, knocking into the table and bringing it down with them. Luke and I scrambled to our feet, narrowly missing the collision. The sounds of plates and glasses shattering stilled the happy atmosphere. Suddenly, we had every eye in the shop looking our way.

More worryingly, Vincent's and Diana's hoods had fallen off.

"You–you–you!" The ladies cried in unison. They pointed their fingers at Diana and Vincent, shaking and holding each other. "You're from the other world! You're from the other world!"

The plump one whipped her head over her shoulder and screamed, "We need backup! We need backup!"

"We've dined, and now we dash!" Luke grabbed Diana and Vincent with one hand each, easily hauling them to their feet. Once they were up, he grabbed my wrist and bolted for the stairs, dragging me behind him with the younger students following.

Just like that, the place was ablaze with roars. Food was thrown our way. Customers got out of their seats and charged toward us. Someone even threw a fork.

We burst out of the coffee shop with at least five angry dudes coming after us. One threw a cup of water our way, and while it missed horribly, the water inside shot at us like a water gun. It hit me right in the neck, and I nearly lost my footing on the frosty, cobblestone ground.

And speaking of the ground, why was it rumbling? It was cracking right below our feet, and looking to the side, I noticed someone with their palm to the ground. The cracks were coming from his direction, spreading along the street in front of us before splitting wide open.

"We can't jump that!" I grabbed Luke's arm, tugging hard to disable him from jumping over the hole. In the corner of my eye was an alley, and seeing an opportunity, I led the way straight for it. "We just gotta lose them, okay?"

"I owe you!" Luke's voice was garbled from the adrenaline roaring in my ears.

"You don't owe me anything!" I replied, but I couldn't even hear myself.

We erupted onto the other side of the alley, only to see another mob forming at the end. "You've got to be kidding me!" Vincent groaned as we backtracked into the alley. On both sides, angry Meraki waited to tear at us. We were stuck.

"Maybe next time, don't piss off the locals!" Diana hissed. "Or at least watch your footing when you do so."

Vincent feigned remorse. "Oh, I'm so sorry, Princess!"

"We have bigger problems, so shut it!" I watched as the Meraki started to aim their hands at us. Some had smoke rising from their fingers and nostrils, and others crouched next to puddles of water with flexed hands. Several were collecting nearby bricks.

A new, deep voice cut in, "Yoo-hoo, have you tried going up?"

We looked up to see a black bunny sitting on a ladder leading to the rooftops. Once we acknowledged him, he started to hop up before disappearing to safety. It was either follow the bunny or be killed, so one by one, we scrambled up the ladder after him. The mob charged, little balls of fire and pointy rocks flying past our ears.

The ladder retracted by itself, flinging us onto the roof.

"Duck back here," the voice said again. The bunny darted to a chimney, his back foot drumming against the roof, almost like he was pointing.

We followed him, listening to the whirring of supernatural weapons calm down. Shouts ebbed, and I heard someone grumble, "They can't stay up there forever. Spread out and keep close watch. They'll be dead in no time." Their footsteps disappeared down the road, silence taking hold.

For a good moment, we were unable to do anything but gulp for air. My muscles felt like they were on fire, all heavy and ready to give up. I refused to keel over despite how tempting it was.

Only then did we realize the absurdity of what had just happened. We faced the bunny with mouths dropped open.

"Did you just talk?" Vincent demanded.

"I think you mean 'thanks for saving us,' but that works, too." The bunny scratched his ear.

Diana squealed and scooped him into her arms. "You're so cute!" She drew out the word "cute" and held him in the air, only for her smile to dim. "Oh, your eyes are so shiny!"

Now that I looked at him, I understood where Diana was coming from. The little guy had pure white eyes, the pupils lacking.

"It's not anything fancy. Shadow Guards are just like this." The bunny wiggled out of Diana's grip.

"Shadow Guard?" Luke echoed dazedly.

The bunny sighed and started to hop away, to the edge of the roof. "You humans have daisies for brains. Come on. Let's get out of here before those mobs find us."

We watched him jump to the next rooftop, stunned with the new vocabulary. I offered the others a weary smile. "It might be the safest option. We can ask if he knows anything about where Tyler is."

"Me?" The bunny raised his ears before shaking his head. "No, no, I wouldn't. My host would, though. Reed should be in their library by now. You can talk to them instead."

Our options were to either test our luck with the mobs or trust the bunny. So, one by one, we hopped to the next rooftop, following our new companion.

The rooftop trek to Reed's library brought us to the center of Audun, giving us an aerial tour of the town. Every time a crowd came within sight, we hid until the bunny said it was safe. Extra time was dedicated to making sure we weren't spotted by any Meraki. I still felt my heart jump into my throat every time I imagined being caught and our journey ending before it truly began. Luckily, the street the library was on was empty.

If Indra Academy's library was impressive, there were simply no words to describe the one our new friend led us into. Shelves stretched all the way up to the high, domed ceiling, stacked with more books than I'd ever seen in my life. Tiny balls of fire, like the ones on the street, floated around to make the air nice and toasty. The roof was made of glass, letting winter sunlight flood the spacious, tiled floor. Benches lined the open space, complemented by a grand piano in the center. Ladders of all sizes were pushed against the shelves, and at the top of the highest one was someone rearranging books.

"Reed, you got company!" the bunny bellowed. He had quite a voice for a little fellow.

"Huh?" Reed glanced over their shoulder, the ladder rocking as they stiffened in surprise. They grabbed the nearest shelf, steadying themself before calling, "I'll be there in one second!"

Almost as if it was second nature, Reed easily slid down the ladder, their boots hardly making a sound as they landed. They jogged over to us, smiling. In the roof's sunlight, their blond hair shimmered, curling just above their chin. They couldn't have been any older than Luke and me.

"I see Dewey went exploring," Reed said. "Did he get into your garden patch or something? I'm so sorry." Before any of us could answer, they bent down and picked up the bunny. Unlike with Diana, Dewey melted into their arms with a purr.

"Anyways, welcome to Hamilton Library. My parents own the place, but I do most of the work while they oversee bigger changes." Reed stroked their bunny's ears as they spoke. "I don't think I've seen you guys around before, and trust me, almost everyone in Audun has visited this place at least once."

Diana gave the vast library a dreamy look. "I can see why."

"Are you by any chance related to—" Vincent started.

I elbowed him in the ribs, cutting him off before he could mention one of America's founding fathers. "You have a beautiful library," I said, redirecting Reed's attention. "My name is Oliver, and these are Luke, Diana, and Vincent. We're new in town." *If that was the truth, why did it feel so bad to say?* I wondered.

"We're looking for someone." Luke leaned toward me, fishing out the drawings of Isabel's necklace and Bryce's father from my pocket. "We believe he's with this guy. Dewey, uh, said you'd know."

Reed took the papers, scanning them as they walked over to a bench table. We followed, watching as they sat down and continued to look them over. "That's Emperor Thierry. What business do you have with him?"

Hearing the word "emperor" was like a punch to the gut. The other students stiffened, and though I had the urge to hurl, I repeated, "Emperor Thierry?"

"Yes. Why?" Reed tilted their head to the side.

Nobody mentioned Thierry is an emperor! I wanted to scream. The castle's looming presence over Audun suddenly felt ten times more significant. This new information meant so many things. We had to save Tyler from the monarchy. Isabel was making deals with a ruler. Bryce was a *prince.*

The others were staring at me, clearly waiting. The longer we stayed silent, the more suspicious we'd seem. *We'll need to talk about it later,* I decided. *Now isn't the time.*

"We're looking for a kid who went searching for Thierry," I finally responded. I pointed to my face. "He has shaggy brown hair and different colored eyes—his right is blue, and his left is brown."

Reed's fingers twitched, gripping the drawing's edge tighter. "I saw him the other day. The poor kid was bloody all over, and Thierry took him away." When they noticed Diana's nauseated expression, they quickly added, "He should be fine, though! From the looks of it, it was an unsupervised Shadow Guard bonding."

Vincent grimaced as he watched Reed stroke Dewey's ears. "Something like *that* did the damage? Ew."

"You don't know about Shadow Guard bondings? They're quite special!" Reed stood up and faced Luke, who'd been watching the Meraki in awe. "This friend of yours—that kid—wasn't from here, either. He was half Meraki." Slowly, Reed stepped forward, and as quick as a striking snake, they grabbed Luke's hood and tossed it down.

"Hey!" Luke finally snapped out of his trance, putting his hands over his ears.

Reed's lips formed a thin line. "Just as I thought. You're human." They glanced at the rest of us. "You *all* are."

Vincent looked ready to knock them out cold and run for it. I rested a hand on his shoulder, giving Reed a nervous smile. "We don't want any trouble! We just need to find our friend and leave." I wanted to ask what they meant when they said Tyler was half Meraki. How could that be possible?

"Trouble? Oh no, I'm not looking for that, either." Reed gestured to the library around us. "Unlike the majority of this town, I did my reading."

Luke took in the ocean of books with sparkling eyes. "Quite a lot of it, I'm guessing."

Reed nodded enthusiastically, but a thought must have struck them, because their expression dimmed. "Both sides are so ignorant of what happened. There was no clear villain." They glanced at the drawing of Thierry again. "Okay, let me piece this together. Thierry took in some kid, yes? He's taken in humans before, but it's uncommon. This is something special, and now you guys are here." Taking the other paper I'd given them, the one with the necklace, their eyes widened. "This confirms it. You're Indra Academy students, aren't you? So you must be—you must be—" They looked up at Luke. When they made eye contact, both took a flustered step back.

"The ones?" Vincent guessed with a raised eyebrow. There wasn't a trace of delight in his tone. "We know."

Reed waved the drawing of the necklace. "No wonder you have a sketch of this. As far as I'm aware, Thierry has it with him, too."

Diana bounced on her toes. "Then getting both the necklace and Tyler will be a breeze!"

"First, we have to find them." I gave Reed a questioning look.

Their ears drooped downward. "Messing with Thierry is a deadly game. Do you know what his name means? It means the ruler of the people.It's not too late to turn back, you know."

It pained me with how eager the idea made the others look. Everyone was doing this for someone else. Bryce had told me a similar story, too.

"I'm not leaving Tyler out here by himself." I was surprised by the steadiness of my voice.

"Oliver's right," Luke said. "I don't like the idea of Tyler hanging out with someone dangerous." He shot Reed a pleading look. "Please, help or at least guide us."

Reed fell silent for a minute, their expression torn. Finally, they sighed, "Fine. Let me grab you a map, first."

CHAPTER FIFTEEN

HIS SCREAMING REFLECTION

TYLER

FOR THE REST OF the morning, I followed Thierry as he spoke with different patrols delivering reports. I shadowed him, mimicking his strong posture to see how it felt. He introduced me as if I were someone important.

The patrols brought news of how the surrounding territory was doing, mentioning fallen, charred trees and abnormal paw prints. Thierry approached them more calmly than the pair from earlier, offering solutions and alternatives. Most of the discussions revolved around the mysterious beast I'd overheard about before.

Picking up on my tense posture and how my gaze darted between the trees, Thierry smiled and said I should talk to McKenzie about unlocking my Mageia.

Before directing me to the gorge, he pulled out a small badge, just like Noah's, with twin red flames that symbolized Thierry's crown. "It's a message to the Meraki that says your presence is approved by me," he explained.

Thierry...approved my presence? That meant he wanted me here! He wanted others to know that!

I wore a stupid grin on my face as I trekked behind the castle, through the dead flowers and weeds, to find the entrance to the gorge. Running my eyes along the ravine, I came to realize that there wasn't a set entry point. A network of staircases ran up and down the steep walls, stopping at various ledges. I picked the one that led to the very bottom and slowly started my way down. As wildly as my heart was thumping, I made sure to take my time. I didn't come this far only to slip down a flight of stairs and die.

Reaching the bottom of the ravine was like stepping onto a new planet. Rocks towered far above me, stretching toward the sky, and disappearing into the midst of fog. Beneath my feet was an uneven cobblestone path, and the walls structuring the gorge looked just as unbalanced. How much pressure could they withstand?

Dead, silver shrubbery sprouted from the cracks in the walls, littering the sidelines and drooping in the gloomy light. Through the fog, I could make out ancient architecture between the crags of the ravine. Bridges ran across the perilous gap, their frames keeping the walls upright. Carvings of skulls peered over the ledges.

For a good minute, I just stood still and took in the sight, with my mouth open in awe. The caw of a bird overhead finally dragged me from my admiration-filled thoughts, and I scanned the base of the gorge. McKenzie's name kept getting stuck in my throat when

I tried calling for her, so I resorted to wandering around in hopes I'd find her.

Swift pattering came from behind. I sighed, seeing my stumbling had only attracted Titanium. Facing her, I demanded, "Where's McKenzie? And...how did you get down here?"

"She's in her room." Titanium angled her ears upward. The gesture drew my attention to a small staircase leading to a door etched into the wall. "And I'm not a prisoner here, either! I can roam where I want!"

"Thanks." I spun around and raced for the door, only to stop when the pattering continued. Glaring at the cat who weaved around my ankles, I stepped to the side. "Don't follow me."

Titanium's eyes rounded. "Why not?"

I pushed past her, jogging up the stairs. When she trailed after me, I groaned. "Why should you?"

Titanium hopped onto my shoulder like a parrot. "As your Shadow Guard, I'm supposed to protect you and make sure you don't do anything stupid. I can feel something brewing in your chest."

What a genius you are, I thought. Rolling my eyes, I didn't comment, instead preparing myself to speak with McKenzie. Would this "unlocking" hurt? I reached out, hesitating before grabbing the doorknob. Maybe I could lie and tell Thierry I did it. Would he know the difference?

And then what? What comes next? Where do you go if it doesn't work? This was my only resort. On that note, I knocked and slowly pried the door open. "McKenzie?"

"I'm here."

I welcomed myself inside, pausing as I took in the room. The walls were made of shelves, covered in books and glass bottles containing hell-knows-what. With no windows other than the one in the door, it was a cozy candle-lit space.

While I gawked over her room, McKenzie chuckled from where she sat at her desk. "It's nice, isn't it? Is there something I can help you with?"

"Y-yes!" I straightened up, struggling to keep myself from swaying under Titanium's weight. "Th-Thierry mentioned a Ma...Mageia thing? He said that–that you'd h...help me."

"Ah, right. I've been expecting you." McKenzie stood, tucking her chair under her desk before approaching one of her bookshelves. She grabbed the wooden edge and pulled the shelf forward and to the side, revealing a dark path carved into the wall. McKenzie stepped inside, beckoning me forward with a tilt of her head. "Come on."

The sight was all too familiar. It was only days ago I went through a similar secret door at Indra Academy. At least this time, I wasn't alone. That made up for the lack of glowing moss here and there. Unlike at Indra Academy, this place was devoid of life.

McKenzie, Titanium, and I only followed the trail to the next bend, where McKenzie stopped and turned to face us. "You must walk the next part alone," she said. I was about to ward off Titanium when she raised her hand and added, "Shadow Guards don't count."

Of course. I gave the rest of the tunnel a wary look, unable to tell where it ended. "Will–will this, uh, hurt? Wh...what am I supposed to do?"

"Once you reach the end, find the large stalagmite." McKenzie curled her fingers in a similar way to Thierry, and an orange flame flickered over her hand. It lit up her face, illuminating the seriousness etched into her features. "The whole process is to see if one truly has the heart for an unlocked Mageia. It digs into the deepest, darkest parts of your brain. You can't run if you want it to work."

I lived with the deepest, darkest parts of my brain every day, something that seemed rather amusing now that it was mentioned. This would be easy. "Okay, th–thanks." Giving her a small wave, I pushed past the bend and continued down the trail.

The light from McKenzie's fire dimmed the more I walked, and suddenly, I was grateful for Titanium's company. *What if I get ambushed? This could totally be Thierry's way of getting rid of me. Oh no, but it won't work if I turn back now.* Was I really going to rely on trust for this?

My pace slowed before stopping, and Titanium rubbed her cheek against mine. "You're almost there," she murmured, her voice softly echoing around us. "Just a little further. Don't give into your fear."

"I know," I whispered back. My legs felt like they were encased in ice, but I forced myself to keep walking.

Titanium hopped off my shoulder, neatly landing in front of me, and took the lead. She disappeared into the darkness right away. Before I could panic, she called, "In here!"

The tunnel gave way into a large cave. Tips of stalagmites and stalactites glistened in the gloom, water droplets echoing around the walls. I stood frozen in place, afraid of bumping into something hidden by the dark.

"This is it." Titanium trotted to the largest stalagmite, which jutted out of the center of the room. "Give it a tap."

It was taller than I was, and I had to crane my neck to see the top. I inched forward, tentatively poking the jagged stalagmite with my finger. When nothing happened, I put the palms of my hands on both sides of it.

A bright blue glow erupted from the top of the stalagmite, illuminating the room in brilliant color. Blue orbs began to glow at the tips of all the other stalagmites and stalactites, too. My hands were glued to the large rock, wrists aching from the way I tried to flinch away. I was forced to stare upward, watching as images took shape in all the orbs surrounding me.

Scenes started to play in the orbs as the images became clearer. Voices blended together, swirling all around me. They were familiar, but I couldn't put my finger on why until a laugh pierced the air.

It was me from years ago.

One of the visions playing was of me and Dominic running in the street, chasing pigeons. I must've been seven, meaning he was twelve. We didn't look out of breath in the slightest, and I was the one taking the lead with a giant smile on my face.

The scene blended with a million more. Some were of Dominic, some were of Mia, some were of my family all together, some were of my elementary school. As they grew clearer, though, the laughs turned to whimpers. The praise turned to lectures.

Teachers were yelling at me to speak.

Classmates were giggling behind my back.

Mia was ignoring my cries.

Dominic was saying over and over, "It's okay. It won't happen again."

It wouldn't happen again.

There was screaming.

It wouldn't happen again.

He promised me.

Fists breaking skin.

The Tyler of the past was screaming.

"Where does it hurt, Tyler?" Dominic asked.

And Mom yelled over the noise, "Why are you making me do this?"

What had I done?

I forced myself to face the large stalagmite again, jaw dropping when I saw what was playing in front of me. My mom was dragging me to the roof by the wrist, muttering to herself. I was drenched in sweat, crying, skin red from being beaten.

She grabbed a key and opened the door to the shed.

"You're staying here while I clean the mess."

She shoved me inside.

It was the first of many occasions. That time, I accidentally broke a plate.

I pleaded for forgiveness, saying that I was sorry. I was seven. Only seven.

She didn't let me out of that shed until a day later. There I was, punching my fists on the door, shrieking and screaming for someone to hear me while my knuckles bled. It was deafening.

It went on like that forever. Those five years were playing all at once, full of crying and wailing like I was a tormented animal.

Then, the noise grew even louder. I didn't realize I was screaming, too, until I nearly passed out.

My legs buckled, and I knelt, gasping for air. Tears flooded my eyes, heart pounding. I jumped at every shriek from my past self.

"Make it stop!" I howled over the noise. "McKenzie! Titanium! Stop it! Help!"

As I was shouting for them, the younger me was shouting for Mia and Dominic, with each cry more desperate than the last. It felt like the cave was going into implode from all this chaos.

That's when this growing ache in my muscles spasmed into pure agony. I doubled over with another guttural scream. All the blows I'd received in the past rained down at once, the pain tearing through my veins and lodging in my bones. Hot and cold flashes washed over me until I was shivering and covered with sweat.

The blue in my vision was overpowered by red. I frantically yanked at the stalagmite, trying to free my hands from the source. They didn't budge.

On the final tug, though, the sound of shattering glass exploded through the room. My hands were free, but it brought no comfort. The air was sucked from my lungs as I looked up.

Surrounding me were massive ice crystals sprouting from the ground. They were shielding me, their sharp edges dug deep into the vision orbs. The scenes flickered before fading. The icicles glowed dully. I stared at them.

Someone started crying. I realized, vaguely, it was me. I brought my hands to my mouth to hide it as I sobbed for nothing in particular. My vision blurred and sparkled from the tears, like I was seeing the world through the loneliest disco ball.

Titanium reappeared from who knows where, jumping onto my lap and licking the salty tears under my eyes. "You did it. Hey, look, you did it!" She brushed her cheek against mine, a purr vibrating in her throat. "Breathe from your stomach. Not so shallow."

I sniffed and hiccupped, fighting to control myself before I could puke. Holding Titanium close to my chest, I straightened up with my head turned away from her. Little whimpers shook my body. Only when my lips stopped trembling did I look her way again.

Titanium frowned up at me. "Are you okay?"

A flurry of footsteps near the entrance answered before I did. I glanced over my shoulder. Past the ice crystals was McKenzie's blurry form running closer.

"Kid, you alright? I heard screaming and..." Her voice trailed off, eyes widening as she noticed the mess. "So, Thierry was correct. You're an ice mutation."

"Mutation?" I echoed weakly. *Have I done something wrong? Did I fail?*

McKenzie smiled as she said quickly, "It's not a bad thing, don't worry! Mageias can sometimes branch off with mutations such as ice, lightning, solar power, and light, otherwise known as illusion." She nodded to my trembling hands. "Ice mutations are incredibly hard to find nowadays. You're special, kid."

Me, special? I would have laughed if I hadn't felt so lightheaded.

"Let's go tell Thierry. He'll be thrilled to hear the news." McKenzie approached and offered her hand, but I dodged and hid my face. She didn't move, only sighing a moment later. "It's a difficult process, I know. I'll let you gather yourself in peace, then." As she left, she offered, "You'll feel at home here in no time. Savana is also a mutation, a lightning one, so she'd be more than willing to help you out."

I let her final thought fade into silence. Sighing, I dropped my head until my chin touched my chest. "I–I knew all of that stuff," I finally whispered to Titanium. "It just...I just didn't–didn't expect it to–to play all a...at once." In the dark corner, I swore I saw the Tyler of the past, all weepy and withered. Had I always looked that hideous when I cried?

I was so appalled by the sight, I barely heard Titanium say, "You're strong, Tyler. With or without an unlocked Mageia."

I lifted my hand, staring at the pale skin in the dark. The scars from punching the shed so many times shone along my knuckles. My fingers twitched and trembled.

Titanium didn't blink, staring up at me like she was searching for something. Rather quietly, she asked, "Did all of that really happen to you?"

I pulled her off my lap and staggered to my feet. Somehow, I managed to smile at her, my face wet from tears. "Yes." My voice, while scratchy from screaming, was oddly calm. There was certainty in my answer. "But don't worry. Like you said, I'm strong. I'm used to it."

"Just because you're used to it doesn't mean you should have to endure it."

Titanium's words were met with silence. I shook my head, slowly navigating my way to the entrance tunnel.

The cat sighed from behind me, but she didn't pry as she followed.

Chapter Sixteen

Love Is Like a Book

Oliver

"It's just like a hotel!" Diana laughed as she threw herself onto the bed. She landed softly on the mattress.

Dewey, who'd unlocked the door for us, hopped off the knob. "Reed says to make yourselves at home. They'll still be in the library for a while, cleaning up."

When we admitted to Reed earlier that we didn't have a place to stay, they'd willingly let us take their spare bedroom for the night. Apparently, they lived in the library with their parents, who'd gone on vacation.

"It must be fun having a big place to yourself, huh?" I'd asked.

Reed had shaken their head. "It's lonely during the quiet hours."

That must've been why as soon as we had dumped our bags on the floor, Luke was already heading to the door again. "I'm gonna go hang out with them!"

"Not so fast, lover boy." Vincent grabbed him by the arm and yanked him back. "We need sleeping arrangements."

I was about to ask what he meant, but a single glance at the room answered the question for me. The room was average size, with a closet right next to the door leading into the bathroom. Oil lanterns lit up the space. Two queen-sized beds were pushed against the wall, with sage-green pillows that matched the long curtains. There was a thin, beige carpet below us.

Looking from the two beds to our group, I frowned. There were four of us.

"I'll pair up with Oliver," Luke said. "Vince, Diana, you two figure something out." He nonchalantly waved his hand before spinning toward the door. "If that's settled, I'm off to find Reed. Have fun!"

Dewey silently hopped after Luke, leaving us to stare into the hall, dumbfounded. I hoped my face didn't look as red as it felt.

Diana scooted off the bed to face Vincent properly. "We can share on the condition we're flipped, so you're by my feet and I'm by yours."

"Seriously? I—" Vincent squinted at her. "Whatever. Fine."

When Vincent went to stroll around and inspected the room, Diana prodded me. "Do you have anything to eat?"

"I think I packed a snack or two back at Indra." I threw off my cloak to make it easier to slide my backpack onto the bed. Diana hovered over me as I unzipped it and rummaged through my spare clothes. Back in the library, I'd grabbed a few map scrolls to check out later. Now, it felt like they were staring at me, silently asking, *Well? Aren't you gonna read us?*

My original plan had been to crash for the night, but what would the others think if I turned in so early? *Fine.* I took out what Reed had explained to be a map of the continent and three granola bars. Once I handed one to Diana, I called to Vincent, "Do you want one as well?"

"Huh? Where were those when we foraged for berries last night?" Vincent looked at me from where he was busy pulling the curtains aside. "But yeah, sure. Check this out!"

The curtains had parted to reveal a large window overlooking the town of Audun. It being dark already, the lights outside glowed.

Vincent fumbled with the latch and swung the window open. A gust of wind whistled through the room, which he ignored as he climbed over the sill to sit on the roof.

"Are you sure that's safe?" Diana called.

"Probably not," he said. "Whatever."

I approached carefully, with Diana on my heels. Just below the window was a tiled roof, slanting downward at an angle that wasn't too dangerous. I'd sat on roofs before with my middle school friends in futile attempts to find stars. Now, though, as I crawled onto the tiles, I was welcomed by a sky full of them. Tonight, the galaxy consisted of green, pink, and dark purple splashes, lit up by the two visible moons.

Diana gasped in awe as she joined us. "I've always wanted to do this!" Her breath clouded in front of her.

Vincent lay down, taking the extra granola bar from me without even looking. He seemed at home up here. "It's nice to bend the rules, isn't it, Princess?"

"Hey!" Diana scowled at him, but with me between the two of them, there wasn't much room for fighting.

We ate in silence, staring up at the sky and listening to the lazy chatter of night-dwelling folks on the street. I felt awfully naked without a hood over my ears, but I knew we were far away enough to not be caught. Just to be safe, though, I pulled my hair out of my ponytail and brushed it over my ears. It warmed my neck from the nippy air.

When I finished the granola bar, I unraveled the scroll, letting the map fall over my thighs. Jellyfish-snowflakes perched on the edges, giving off light.

The printed letters "DERNGATE" were chipped and faded, like the rest of the ink outline. The map showed a continent of jagged mountains bordering the north and southeast coasts. In the center was a massive cluster of trees, which I assumed represented the forest we started in. Little towns were scattered across the great plain, with what looked like cities at our current location, in the mountains, and on beaches scattered along the coast.

"How are we supposed to find Tyler in such a huge place?" Diana scanned the map with wide eyes.

Vincent scowled at the rooftops below. "As long as we don't have to follow him to the edge of the world or anything."

I would, I silently pledged. The bold statement remained hidden under my tongue. Just thinking about Tyler all alone in this strange, new world made my heart skip a beat.

Hugging my knees, I fixed my gaze on the roads below us. Two young women were on the corner of a street, waving goodbye to each other before one crossed the road. But a moment later, she ran back to the other and jumped into her arms, planting a kiss on her cheek. Both looked giddy with delight.

I hadn't realized Vincent was following my gaze until he sighed from next to me. His glasses fogged up as he exhaled. I half expected a scathing retort about my silence, but his next words went in a different direction. "Oliver, you don't like girls—as in you're gay—right?"

I faced him, surprised. "Yeah. What about it?"

Vincent propped himself on his elbows, looking me up and down. There was no challenge in his eyes, only curiosity. "Don't you think it's strange this old-fashioned place is more open about such a topic?"

"Reed uses they and them pronouns, too," Diana piped up. "Nobody seems to have a problem with that."

"It's clear this place evolved differently from Earth," I quietly theorized out loud. "The Meraki must have accepted and normalized it quicker than us." I watched the ladies part ways again after blowing each other a kiss. Nobody started anything with them. Nobody even batted an eye.

I, too, had grown up in a welcoming environment. But the world was a scary place, and not everyone was so fortunate.

"Why?" I finally faced Vincent again. "Were you worried or something?" He'd mentioned possibly being both asexual and bisexual a year ago, closeted to everyone but Luke and me. To be put in an uncertain location must've been nerve-racking.

Vincent looked down at his fingers. The black nail polish he wore was chipping, the reason revealed as he absently scratched at it. "I just thought it was scary to be outed as a human here. To think that back in our realm, it's who you love that people will try to kill you for." For someone who always paraded around and spewed blunt comments, Vincent sounded awfully small.

"We're lucky enough to live in New York City, which is really accepting," Diana offered with a nervous smile. "You got allies back home."

"Oh?"

"Yeah!" Diana pointed to herself, looking rather proud. "Bisexual and trans, right here."

Vincent looked her up and down, his mouth agape. The smile he flashed her was genuine. "That–that's really cool."

I nodded. "And Luke is pansexual, but I remember him telling you that."

Vincent glanced over his shoulder to the open window. "Speaking of Luke, where the hell is he?"

"Still hanging out with Reed, I think." I crumpled the wrapper of my granola bar into a ball, stuffing it into my pocket. The map was rolled up and safely tucked away as well. But before offering to find the missing duo, I paused. "Is...that all you wanted to talk about?"

Vincent nodded, but his body remained tense.

"What about you? Is something on your mind?" Diana frowned at me.

"I mean…" I gave Vincent a shy look. "I was wondering about those dreams you mentioned having—but since you're stressed enough, you don't have to—"

"They started about a year ago," Vincent cut me off, "when I was a freshman. Nothing from those dreams really made sense. Voices were begging me to listen and search for something…" He turned to me, his eyes dark. "But I'm realizing they must've meant some*one*."

Diana leaned forward with interest. "Tyler?"

Vincent sat up and hugged his stomach. "It only makes sense."

"I hate to say I told you so, but I totally did." I smiled weakly at Vincent. "Don't you see? You say you aren't connected to the Assembly of Six, but you've been getting mystical messages you haven't been able to piece together until Tyler showed up."

Vincent rolled his eyes. "Whatever. I never signed up for the cryptic messages. The only reason I came to Indra was so then I'd stay with Luke. I assume you guys have similar stories?"

Diana tilted her head to one side. "I applied to Indra Academy so I wouldn't have to go to school with anyone I used to know. Didn't want to introduce myself only for everyone to know me by a different name." Her lips twisted with a wry smile. "I still got picked on at the orientation anyways. But then Oliver came to chase those girls away, and…it was like something clicked. It felt like Indra Academy was the place to be."

My insides warmed at hearing my gesture had such an impact. "I first heard of Indra Academy from my moms. They were eager to send me here. I—I thought it was about the circumstances and stuff going on for me, but there must've been more to it." I made a mental note to phone them about it when we returned home. "And when I met Luke, everything seemed to fall into place. My presence at Indra Academy suddenly felt right."

Vincent grinned at me. "Are you hitting on my brother?"

"No!" I shrank away from him. "Absolutely not. I'm just stating a fact."

"Sure."

I huffed and slowly rose to my feet. "I better go see what he and Reed are up to, anyways."

Vincent and Diana were just murmuring their goodbyes when a sound like thunder roared through the town. All three of us stiffened, glancing outward in time to see a blast of white fire rage through the streets. Shouts rang and heads peered out windows to observe. They looked small from the roof we sat on.

"What in the world?" Vincent tensed, looking ready to bolt.

Diana pointed to where a wooden roof caught fire. "There!"

From a distance, the attacker was nothing more than a glowing blur of flames. Meraki raced to the scene, lashing water whips to put out the fire and drive the mysterious beast away.

"Come on!" I shakily started to inch down the sloped roof. "We have to help."

Vincent also stood. He grabbed my wrist, yanking me back. "Are you out of your mind? There's nothing we can do to help!"

"But—"

"No buts!" Vincent blocked my view of the fire. "We're not throwing ourselves into danger for the people who tried to kill us this morning!"

I struggled to free myself from his grip. "It doesn't matter! Innocent people might get hurt." I gave Diana a pleading look, hoping she'd back me up. She just stared at Vincent and me with this frozen expression.

"The only one who'll get hurt is you, and that makes you more idiotic than innocent." Vincent shoved me back, ignoring how I slipped and fell on my rear. He planted his boot on my chest, pinning me down. "You can't save everyone. Don't you know that yet?"

I stared up at him. Sharp wood from the roof poked against my shoulder blades. In a heartbeat, our delicate truce broke. "That doesn't mean I'm not gonna try," I said. I pushed Vincent's foot away, scrambling toward the window. Before he or Diana could argue, I hopped back into the room.

They watched in stunned silence for a moment, but as I opened the door to leave, they began to talk. I could tell Diana was trying to soothe Vincent, though I was out of earshot and didn't bother to spy.

That surge of adrenaline was quick to fade. I didn't want Vincent to see that he was correct, that I had no idea of how to help put that fire out. That this wasn't my battle.

The candles in the hallway were blown out, so I trailed my hand along the wall to find my way. In the distance, the gentle melody of a piano hummed in the air before fading, as if it were hesitant to let the world hear. Then it picked up again, and the familiarity of the tune made my ears ring. I followed the song to the library's main room. Like water extinguishing a fire, the music soothed my tense muscles.

Blue moonlight poured through the glass dome ceiling, making it look like we were in the ocean. The stars shone even brighter up there.

Luke sat at the grand piano I'd noticed earlier, demonstrating that song to Reed, who sat on the bench beside him. The Meraki cautiously pressed a key, and Luke put his hand over theirs, guiding them through it. Reed smiled at the piano, delightedly swaying to the melody. Meanwhile, as Luke's fingers worked effortlessly, he watched Reed with this dazed, awed expression.

Oh, Luke, you can't afford to get attached now, I thought help-lessly.I curled my fingers around the corner of the wall, my heart aching as I watched the two. Perhaps it was jealousy. Not that I was jealous of those two, but jealous of the concept—of thinking a person is the coolest in the world.

After a moment of just standing there, I turned around and left.

Vincent and Diana were getting ready for bed when I returned, grumbling over having to share the bathroom between four peo-ple. I dismissed their whining, taking a lightning-fast shower be-fore putting fresh clothes on and flopping into bed. The tangles in my hair were obvious, but I couldn't be bothered to brush them.

I was aware of Vincent shooting subtle glares my way, but right then, he was just another burr in my hair. Something to deal with later.

He must've been thinking the same thing, because only Diana mumbled "goodnight" when the lights switched off.

At some point, though, I awoke to the feel of the mattress shifting. Glancing over my shoulder, I caught the blurry shape of Luke finally getting into bed beside me.

"Sorry, did I wake you?" he whispered once he caught me staring.

"No." The grogginess of my tone gave away the truth.

Luke mumbled another apology, laying on his side so our backs touched. I was just about to nod off again when he murmured, "I'm guessing we leave in the morning, right?" He sounded wide awake.

"Hm?" I watched the curtains in the dark, how they flowed with the window's breeze. The song from earlier was playing in my head. It fought against the echoing screams from the fire in the distance. "I assume so. Why? Did you want more time here?" When silence was my only answer, I sighed, "Since this town is on our way back to the portal, we can visit Reed when we go home. I promise." I couldn't tell if my words slurred out of exhaustion or annoyance.

Luke shifted, taking a while before replying. "I owe you."

I nestled deeper into my pillow. My eyes drifted shut. Familiar words from earlier came back to me. "We don't owe each other anything. I already said so."

"Fine." Luke didn't sound convinced, but he didn't press the issue. "Goodnight, Oliver."

I was asleep before I could reply.

My dream was of an empty black sky. I stood atop a glowing blue lake that stretched forever. There were no stars to greet me, nor was there Crystal's presence. Remembering how my last dream was interrupted by Thierry Colliss, I didn't dare call out in case it triggered his appearance.

The lake stirred beneath me, but when I looked down, it wasn't my reflection staring back at me.

It was Tyler's.

I stepped back with a yelp. The watery kid copied me.

"It's just a dream," I reminded myself aloud. "I'll wake up any second now."

That's when my back bumped into someone else's.

I spun around to face the culprit. Again, it was Tyler, but his actual flesh-and-blood self. Nobody else had such unruly hair and those dual-colored eyes. When he faced me, his jaw dropped, and he jumped back. The color drained from his skin as he whispered, "You aren't real."

I scanned him over, my veins constricting at the sight of the bandages over his cheeks. He seemed fine otherwise, carrying himself with the same tense posture that always made it look like he was ready to bolt.

I looked down again. His reflection, like mine, wasn't of himself. His reflection was mine. It was weird to see myself so...stressed.

"No," I replied finally. "I'm pretty sure I'm real."

Tyler crept closer, leaning in until his nose was an inch from my chest. Upon noticing how it rose and fell with each breath, he scrambled back with a gasp. "You are!"

"What is this, a lucid dream? A supernatural summoning?" I glanced around, but once I'd confirmed we were alone, I sighed with relief. "Well, that's convenient. I'll make this quick. Hang on tight—the others and I are coming to find you."

"What do you mean?" Tyler stiffened. He glanced around, his shoulders hunching up. "I...I don't need to be found."

I was about to pry for more when the sound of slow applause cut me off.

Thierry entered the clearing, stopping by Tyler's side. "Well said." He gave the kid a firm pat on the shoulder.

Tyler scrunched up his face but didn't move.

"We're not falling for your little party tricks." I straightened up, though it had no effect on Thierry's stance.

"What 'we?' What party tricks? Can't you see that Tyler is doing well?" Thierry gave me an innocent look. "He's unharmed and is being looked after by adults. Who knows what the influence of teenagers might have done to him if he stayed at your school. We're going to raise a real hero here." He glanced down at Tyler. "Would you like to tell Oliver how you feel for yourself?"

Tyler grimaced as Thierry tightened his grip on his shoulder. He nodded at the ground. "I chose to come here." His voice was stiff and hollow.

I wanted to scream about how absurd this was. But Tyler would never listen with Thierry peering over his shoulder. I clenched my fists as I faced the watery floor. In the reflection, Tyler and I were still swapping places; it was my shoulder Thierry held while Tyler watched helplessly.

"You see?" Thierry purred. "You don't have anything to worry about. You and your friends can go home. I know how eager they are to leave."

"No!" I shouted, stirring ripples from below. The blue light wavered across my features. Desperately, I searched Tyler for some sort of weakness. "What made you choose *him* over Indra Academy? Over us?"

Tyler stared straight ahead, past my soul. Only the twitching of his brows showed he could hear me. "Thierry is an adult." His voice was rough, like stone scraping together.

"That's right!" Thierry said it with so much enthusiasm, you'd think Tyler was a dog being called a good boy. He smiled at me, his eyes narrowing to cold chips of amber. "You're the only one twisting words here. If it comforts you, though, I might let you visit each other in dreams. I might."

I exchanged a glance with Tyler. Very subtly, he was shaking his head. Was it a warning? Whatever it was, I wouldn't let that stop me. I forced myself to smile at Thierry. "Thanks."

Just a little longer. I promise.

I had to prove Vincent wrong. I had to save at least *one* person.

Chapter Seventeen

Why I'm Not a Doctor

Tyler

THERE WAS EVEN A training area in this place.

Thierry had thought of everything. Through the barren land separating the castle and gorge from the forest was a well-trodden path through the snow, leading to an arena. Little balls of fire spread along the outskirts kept the soil from disappearing under the snowflakes. A wooden fence that came up to my stomach bordered the arena. It looked like a horse paddock that lacked the hooved animals.

Savana was busy vaporizing little puddles of ice when McKenzie and I approached. Somehow, she could put her hand over the target and then *zap!*

That only made my morning weirder. Just half an hour ago, McKenzie woke me up to say my training was starting. I was still processing the dream I'd seemed to share with Oliver. How was Thierry able to unite both of our unconscious minds like that?

More importantly, what did Oliver mean when he said he was coming to find me? *That's impossible. He doesn't know where I am, nor where the portal is.*

I hated to admit that Indra Academy was *his* school, so there was a chance he already knew about such a thing.

That notion had my heart racing before the training even began.

It took me a few tries to swing my legs over the arena fence, which, luckily, neither McKenzie nor Savana commented on. Cushions of snow by each wooden post muffled my landing. The arena stretched about half a field in length, making me feel small as I tentatively ventured closer to the middle.

Of course, Savana didn't acknowledge my dazed state when she noticed McKenzie and me. She faced me with a grin, straightening up with a wave. "Hey! You're just in time—check this out."

She raced over to me, cupping her palms in front of her so I could see. Strands of her purple hair stood on end as her hands glowed. Little snakes of lightning began to weave around her fingers.

That can't be real! I carefully reached one finger forward, only to be zapped with electricity. With a yelp, I jumped back, clutching my finger as it tingled.

"That's the first rule of the Cataclysm. Don't poke another's power when activated unless you have a death wish." McKenzie gave me a wry smile as she entered the ring.

I gave the ladies an apologetic look. It basically confirmed that my power was also able to kill. The way my ice stabbed the visions during the unlocking ceremony proved it could impale someone.

But how much control do I have of it?

I held one palm toward the ground, trying to replicate how Savana, McKenzie, and Thierry all did it. They all took in this deep breath, and...

The tension building in my wrist snapped, and a massive shard of ice erupted from the dirt. It towered feet above Savana, McKenzie, and me.

I stumbled back, lightheaded, as I stared at the crystal. Was that seriously my doing?

Savana looked at me with amazement. "You're an ice mutation? No way, that's incredible! McKenzie, I was right!" She pointed to me while grinning widely at McKenzie. "He's the one!"

McKenzie blinked up at the pillar of ice. "You were right, indeed."

"What?" I frowned at the two of them.

"Remember when I said that ice mutations are rare?" McKenzie was looking at me as if I were an ancient artwork. "You're literally the only one."

I glanced at the ice again, focusing on the pointy tips stretching toward the sky. What if I accidentally aimed that the wrong way? Crossing my arms over my chest, I stuffed my hands into my armpits to dull the power. When I backed up, however, more tiny shards appeared by my ankles.

McKenzie stepped toward me, only to pause when I flinched away. "It's okay. Just stay still. Let's learn how to use that power before you unleash it all over the place." She nodded to Savana, who'd been watching. "Go grab the blanket from the fence."

"How are we supposed to guide a mutation that hasn't been around in, like, forever?" Savana grappled with the blanket draped over the nearby wooden post.

My eyes stretched wide. "How long?"

My comment flew right over McKenzie's head. "All Mageias comes from the same source." She brought her hand to her heart, squeezing it over her chest. "All living things have a Mageia, regardless of who or what they are. Meraki are naturally born with them unlocked. While physically different, Mageias are managed and controlled in similar ways."

Savana dropped the blanket by my feet and dusted her hands off before crouching down. McKenzie and I followed her lead.

"I figured we should start with the basics. *Mageia* is Greek for magic. There are four main groups, based on elements, and while they're kind of obvious, you should know anyways. They're fire, water, earth, and air. Those, plus their mutated versions, all come with special bits granted by the Mageia." McKenzie pointed to herself as she added, "Those with a fire Mageia, such as me and Thierry, focus on combat, destruction, and navigating." To demonstrate, she lifted her palm. A small flame flickered over her fingertips.

Like with Savana's lightning, I wanted to touch it to make sure it was real. But I controlled myself this time, slowly nodding.

The flame disappeared and McKenzie smiled at me. "Ice mutations spring from water Mageias. They're most known for defending, building, and," she tapped the blanket, "healing." Before I could question it, she grabbed the fabric and ripped it with surprising strength. When she let go, it flopped uselessly back to the ground.

Noticing my nervous expression, Savana cleared her throat to make me look up. "I know how McKenzie babies beginners, so you'll practice on the tear first. Right?"

"Right." McKenzie rolled her eyes in a teasing way. "Don't teach the lesson so well that you put me into retirement."

"H-how do I...?" My voice trailed off, and I pointed to the blanket in hopes they would guess the end of my sentence.

"It's your frost that has healing properties. You can use it to mend and ease swelling, as well as close open wounds. The blanket replicates that since the ability transfers to inanimate objects. Unfortunately, the frost doesn't work for severe injuries." McKenzie held her palm down, and it started to glow orange. "It works the same way you release power from your body. But you must imagine a barrier, letting it build under your skin without seeping through. Like an ice or heat pack. That's how you keep the power from slipping out at random times, too. It takes great mental strength to keep it from going haywire."

I carefully held my palms out, hesitantly holding them over the tattered blanket.I closed my eyes, trying to picture a wall in the darkness. There it was, though it was cracked and ruined. Anger surged through me. Who the hell had broken my wall?

My eyes shot open as something pierced the air. My palms were glowing blue, and an icicle had impaled the blanket into the ground. My anger immediately shifted into horror. "I–I killed it!"

Savana was laughing her butt off, but I was bracing myself for a hit or yell. This was a dance everyone knew but me. It was like they were expecting me to bust out a whole routine without any experience.

McKenzie only chuckled. "Don't worry—it's hard to get on the first try. It's an old blanket, anyways. Would you like to try again?"

The risk of further humiliating myself was high. *But to turn her down, after everything?* My chest still ached from crying my heart out yesterday, and I could feel McKenzie's and Savana's gazes digging into my skin. It felt like the castle was watching me, too.

After a moment of hesitation, I nodded.

I must have been at it for an hour, sitting on the floor while trying to mend the damn fabric. But the ice shards kept slipping through, and it started to look more like a frozen porcupine than a blanket. Savana eventually got bored and went to shoot lightning around the other end of the arena.

Every time I heard thunder rumbling, I paused to watch her. *Why can't I do something cool like that, instead? Ice is so...stagnant.*

McKenzie was still next to me, and every time I looked away, she cleared her throat to redirect my attention. The longing on my face must've been obvious. She just encouraged me to try again, saying that if I got it down, she'd teach me what Savana was doing. I nodded, but deep down, I feared I was wasting her time.

I was on my last attempt before giving up when I felt something other than the ground being stabbed. Opening my eyes, I gasped. A thick layer of frost covered the mangled rip I was trying to fix. Slowly, the strands of threads were inching together to mend themselves. I glanced up at McKenzie.

McKenzie's expression warmed and she nodded. "There's still room for improvement, but that was better."

It was the type of praise I'd been craving but never received after Dominic's disappearance. The smile that spread across my face felt so unnatural, the movement foreign after all these years.

McKenzie went to help Savana, leaving me to continue with the blanket. Now without supervision, I leaned back and grabbed a stray icicle by my ankle. Surprisingly, it didn't hurt to hold the way most cold things did. I tossed it from hand to hand, waiting for a sting that never came. Instead, it felt right to hold such a object.

I put the shard down, holding my hand in front of me. Imagining the wall in my mind to soften, another crystal of ice shot from my palm, which I caught in the air. It was an infinite supply!

"It looks like someone's having fun," a voice rumbled behind me.

I turned around to see Thierry standing behind the fence, watching me with this mesmerized expression. It grew as I held up the shard for him to see. The twin flames of his crown expanded, almost as if excited, before mellowing down again.

Thierry nodded in approval before fixing his gaze on the young ladies. "McKenzie, mind if I steal him for a short while?"

Savana pouted, but McKenzie gave him a thumbs up.

I stood, focusing on the ground as I stepped forward. When no ice crystals appeared by my feet, I broke into a jog and climbed over the fence, so I stood beside Thierry.

He walked away, leaving me to trail after him once more. Without looking back, he asked, "How are you doing with your training so far?"

"I-It's cool." I held my hands up, staring at my palms that had been glowing blue a few minutes ago. They were back to normal now. Only the shaking of my limbs told me I hadn't imagined it.

Thierry didn't reply to me, and I couldn't blame him.

He veered toward the forest. The winter sun cast willowy shadows across the snow-covered landscape. I hadn't been there since Titanium mauled my face, but that wasn't the source of my hesitation. My memory closed in on those wounded elves, or Meraki, as McKenzie called them, Thierry had snapped at when Noah brought me to him. They'd been talking about a...a *thing*.

I wasn't truly terrified, though, until I saw a paw print larger than Thierry in the snow. With bated breath, I hurried to catch up.

Questions about Dominic I'd been unable to ask previously were on the tip of my tongue: How did Thierry know him? Was Dominic healthy and thriving? But I couldn't find it in me to ask, so I focused on keeping pace as Thierry led me deeper into the trees.

Finally, he stopped next to a fallen log. "Sit."

His command reminded me of my mother, and I sat down immediately. The log was adorned with silver, frosty moss that had white mushrooms growing on top. I kept my distance, just in case.

"Have you wondered if it was a coincidence that we needed an ice mutation for this project, and voilà, here you are?" Thierry glanced up at the sky while he spoke. He didn't give me a chance to respond, looking down at me with a grin. "No, it's not a coincidence. You see, while the Mageia comes from the heart and soul, genetics also play a part in it."

"Do I—do I g...get it from my mom, then?" I brought my hand to the right side of my face, where my blue eye was.

"Partially. Your mother has a water Mageia. How do I know?" Thierry sat down next to me, pulling something out from the inside of his shirt. It was a golden chain with a locket attached to it, and when he clicked it open, there was a photo of him and my mom inside.

Thierry was wearing a hat to hide his ears, but his face was exactly the same, if not a little younger. My mom stood right next to him, smiling with all the light of the sun in her eyes. Never before had I seen her so happy. Both looked young and at ease, in fancy attire, like they were at a special occasion of some sort.

I leaned closer to the image, blinking to make sure it was real. "How?"

Thierry tilted the locket, so a dapple of sunlight caught the image. "I find that humans are fascinating creatures. Both worlds are flawed, and both inhabitants tend to seek escapes. I met Sadie on an expedition to Manhattan, what, twelve or thirteen years ago?"

"I'm twelve." The observation slipped out before I could stop myself.

Thierry gave me this knowing smile.

My heart dropped, and I scooted back to face him properly. "No."

"You are half Meraki, after all." Thierry reached his hand toward my ear.

I flinched away, eyes widening. "No...no, that can't be." Hot and cold flashes racked through me as I stood up, facing Thierry with my hands in fists. "But you're an emperor! You're an—you're an emperor, and I've never seen you before."

Thierry's unwavering gaze didn't betray any hint of a joke. A lifetime of silence passed before I whispered, "Does that make me a prince?"

"Yes." Finally, Thierry smiled. "The prince of Derngate."

There were so many things I wanted to shout and ask. It couldn't be true. I had no dad. And there was no way the prince of a magical realm had been living in the slums of Manhattan this whole time. But suddenly, my spacious room in Thierry's castle made sense. He could've dumped me in the gorge with Savana and Noah, but he hadn't.

And Thierry had a point. How could he have known I was the one to summon otherwise? I wanted to feel awed and powerful with these new discoveries, but I felt awfully small. I crossed my arms over my chest, further shrinking away from the man who just called himself my father. All I could think to ask was "Where were you all this time?" My voice was hollow.

Thierry glanced in the direction of his castle and the gorge. "Building a better world, son."

"Mom struggles, you know?" For once, sadness wasn't what overcame me. It was something sharper. I started to pace around. "She does everything by herself! My older brother is gone. He–he–he isn't there to help her anymore!" My breathing grew shallow and quick, muscles taut and head racing. "You're–you're an emperor w...with all the power in the—in the world...You could've done something. Yet you left us all alone!" Those last words came out as a scream that rattled the spindly branches above us.

Thierry wasn't facing me, and instead, he was focusing on my feet. A cluster of ice crystals had shot out of the ground, reaching up to my hips. He leaned forward, breaking a piece and inspecting the pointy edge. "My goal wasn't to raise a family. I needed an heir and an ice mutation, and with a water Mageia, Sadie was the one who could give both to me." A shadow fell over his fiery eyes. "Complications arose and I had to return to Japan, where most of my work took place at the time. Because of your mother's financial situation, I was never able to keep contact with her, and therefore, I couldn't keep in contact with you, either. That's why I'm grateful my connection in dreams runs as far as Indra Academy."

My mouth opened, but I couldn't find the words. Instead, I crossed my arms over my chest and turned my head away. Scowling at the ground, I whispered fiercely, "You just wanted an ice mutation—a precious gem."

"And would you look at that?" Thierry stood up, opening his arms in an invitation. When I didn't move, he closed the gap himself, carefully pulling me into a hug. "I got my precious prize, indeed. You know what they say, kid. Better late than never."

I didn't return the hug, leaving me to stand awkwardly against him. With a soul full of fire, his body was warm, but none of his energy reached me.

Thierry pulled away, giving me this uncharacteristic smile. It was soft and slow, nothing like his hardened appearance. "I see you've grown into a fine young man without me, though. Sadie did a good job. We're going to do something amazing. You're going to help both humans and Meraki with what we're creating." He hugged me again. He stroked the top of my head gently. Why did that make my eyes burn?

Did I do a good job? I wondered. *Did Mom?* Thierry knew nothing of our struggle for money. Nothing of Dominic or Mia. Nothing of my failed grades, or how I dropped out of school. Nothing of Mom's disapproval or the shed.

Considering how awful that reality was, maybe it was a good thing Thierry had shielded himself from us. I forced myself to smile, though I felt numb. "Yeah."

"I would be careful with how you talk to me, though." Thierry's expression darkened. His embrace tightened. "Don't disrespect your father if you ever want to see your precious Dominic again." Finally, he released me and turned around. He started to walk back towards the castle. The moment was over.

I watched him leave, my mouth parted open.

Of course.

How could have I gotten angry at him like that? Everything in me screamed to catch up to him and apologize for getting snappy. Such behavior around my mom would've landed me in the shed. I half expected Thierry to come back and start yelling, but his silence was just as terrifying.

With shaking legs, I slowly followed him back home.

Chapter Eighteen

A Build-in Flamethrower

Tyler

I spent the rest of the day in the training arena with Savana. If Thierry changed his mind about being angry, I didn't want to be alone. Thankfully, Savana didn't mind me watching from where I sat on the fence.

As the sun dipped below the horizon, her lightning glowed. The little purple scars on her cheeks did the same. My ice shards had a similar effect. In the dark, they were bright blue. It gave the arena this ethereal vibe, even more so when reflected on the pearly snow.

The vibrant colors blurred in my vision as I kept thinking back to my talk with Thierry. I repeated the phrase *Prince Tyler* in my head, but it didn't ring right. It was like wearing clothes that were too big and too small at the same time. I felt constricted, trapped by my own presence. I was so insignificant, disappearing under the velvet cloaks of every emperor before me.

How would my former classmates and bullies react? How would my mom react? That was if she didn't know already. And if Oliver knew, would his warmth for me fade? Or would it burn into an artificial flame in reaction to my new status?

Watching Savana move in the arena, I asked myself, *What would* she *think?*

From the looks of it, she didn't have a clue of my relation to Thierry.

"You can make ice crystals with your feet, right?" Savana asked, joining me on the fence. The nippy, winter air didn't seem to bother her. Her smile was so bright it could be a substitute for the sun. "I can teach you how to use that to your advantage!"

I looked at my battered shoes with a doubtful frown. To be polite, though, I nodded.

Savana led me to the center of the arena. "Similar to how we balance our abilities with our minds, we release them through our minds, too. You have to imagine what you want to create, and..." Extending her arm, lightning blazed from her palm and into the dark sky. A clap of thunder rang out with it. It didn't faze her, whereas I jumped with my hands over my ears. The lightning sizzled out in time for me to hear Savana add, "It's a game of trust with yourself. If you don't know what you want and aren't willing to take control, it'll be half-assed."

"Right." I sounded like a strangled bird.

"No, no, no. That's your first mistake." Savana made a fist and gently knocked on my head like it was a door. When I jumped back, she sighed heavily. "You have no trust. You're a shriveled ball of self-consciousness!"

I opened my mouth to apologize, but Savana kept going.

"Alright. New plan. I want you to stretch your arms out wide." To demonstrate, Savana threw her arms out, her palms reaching for the sky.

Slowly, I copied her. But my elbows refused to straighten, making me look more like a soccer goalie or frightened crab.

Savana shook her head and straightened her arms out even more. "It doesn't matter if you look stupid! Pretend you're doing yoga!"

I'd never done yoga before in my life. Cringing, I extended my arms until they were straight.

"Now, I want you to scream."

"What?"

Savana looked dead serious. "You have to let your tension out somehow! I think we can all use a good scream sometimes."

She's absurd. I squirmed, unsure if it was because of the prompt or my arms growing sore. Half-heartedly, I went "ah..."

"No, silly! Like this!" Savana lifted her head to the sky and let out a piercing scream. Lightning sizzled around her. Her sound was like a war cry, coming from the depths of her chest. As it echoed, she turned to me and said, "Your turn!"

I put my arms down to shake the tension out. As I put them back up, I went "ah!" again. It was louder, but it didn't have the length Savana wanted.

Savana started to yell again. Her carefreeness amazed me. How could she just...do things? It reminded me of Dominic. He was always able to express himself loudly without the words ever catching in his throat. I'd wanted to be like him for years.

Maybe that's what pushed me into joining Savana's scream-fest. It was easier when I couldn't hear myself. My spurts got longer and stronger, and every time I paused for air, I giggled to myself. We sounded ridiculous, shouting into the sky. By the time we finished, I was doubled over and laughing to myself.

"So? How do you feel now?" Savana wiggled her eyebrows.

I smiled up at her. "Better."

She beamed in the darkness. "Then let's get some ice going. Imagine a line in the dirt and stomp your foot on it. Remember that the intensity will impact the size."

I faced the ground, narrowing my eyes as I envisioned a path. My foot hesitated in the air before slamming down. A row of ice crystals shot through the ground, glowing in the night.

Savana had just started to squeal in amazement when a voice snapped, "Who the hell is screaming bloody murder?"

It was Noah stomping toward us, with his classic deep scowl. He'd been gone most of the past day to investigate the mystery of the forest. Clearly, he was still sour, so he mustn't have found anything. "I bet they heard you all the way in the next town over."

A lump formed in my throat. I mumbled, "Sorry."

At the same time, Savana said, "We were just warming up for practice!" To prove it, she pointed to the line of ice I'd created.

Noah looked us up and down, his frown deepening. When he noticed the ice, though, it softened ever so slightly. Like he couldn't decide whether to be mad or intrigued. "Just warming up, huh? Alright. Sav, go sit by the fence. Things might get heated."

Savana pouted, but she must've known better than to argue with him. After whispering "good luck" to me, she trudged to the fence.

Good luck? I shuddered. I never considered Noah's purpose in the Cataclysm, and something in me didn't want to know. To be safe, I summoned an icicle in my hand, gripping it tightly. Pointing to his hands with the sharp tip, I asked, "Do you—do you also have one?"

Noah paused, probably wondering what I meant, before it clicked in his mind that I was talking about an unlocked Mageia. He grinned at me, backing away to put distance between us. "Of course. I'm a solar mutation! Check it out."

When Noah kicked his foot forward, a blast of white fire came out. It lit up the whole arena.

"Fire?" I knew so much better than to argue with him, but at least I had a weapon.

Noah glared at me. "Shut it, mutt. The difference is that solar fire is more powerful. You know about how Mageias come from the heart—all that lovey-dovey stuff?" When I nodded, his anger seemed to ebb, and he puffed out his chest like he'd won an award. "The human body has limits. Solar mutations, however, get their power from the sun. And the sun has infinite power!"

"Oh." I extended the ice shard in my grip, just to be safe. "S-sorry."

"So, Savana has shown you how to visualize targets, yes? Why don't you channel all that energy into one big crystal?" Noah nodded down at my trembling feet.

"Okay," I said, my voice barely a peep.

Noah moved to the center of the arena, beckoning for me to follow. "As McKenzie, hopefully, told you, ice mutations do a lot of building and defending. You can make good shields with those." He put his hands on his hips, giving me his classic, cocky smile. "I'm gonna shoot fire at you, and you'll make a wall to defend yourself. Keep it going until I stop."

My eyes bulged wide. "Really?"

"Yeah! Experience is the best teacher, after all."

I looked at my hands, which were visibly shaking. "How–how do I...?" I glanced at Savana, hoping she'd back me up, but she said nothing.

Noah tapped the ground with the tip of his boot. "Your ice crystals appear from your feet, so to make a big one, you just need extra force. Give the ground a big kick for me." Before I could react, he'd backed up and held his palm toward me like he was aiming a flamethrower.

There was a flash of white light and roaring in my ears as heat crashed over me. I brought my hands to my face, slamming my foot on the ground. A wall of ice erupted from the ground, and I crouched behind it as white fire pounded the shield.

Only then did it occur to me that heat melted ice.

"Stop!" I yelled, but I could barely hear myself over the blazing attack. "Noah? Noah! Stop!" Water was starting to drip down the wall, the heat seeping through the melting surface. Earlier, he'd said to keep it going, but my mind was already five steps ahead. I rolled away from the shield just as it collapsed from the fire. My hand slapped the frosty ground, and a line of ice crystals shot straight for Noah. The last one was the largest, the blunt tip hitting him right in the face, sending him toppling.

The fire died out, and Noah sat up to glare at me. "What the hell? I said to stay where you were!"

I shook my head, too busy trying to calm my breathing. "You–you–you–" Groaning in frustration, I stumbled to my feet, my hoodie damp from the mud and dirty snow. "You almost—you almost killed me!"

Noah also stood up, and I couldn't tell if he was more disgusted over getting dirty or my whining. When he faced me, his eyebrows furrowed. "And?"

I threw my hands into the air, like my body language could answer for me.

"I'd never kill you, little mutt. Thierry would maul me if he found out." Noah wiped his hands on his pants before running his fingers through his hair, like a cat trying to smooth its fur.

"Speaking of Thierry," Savana cut in, "do you guys hear that?" She hopped off the fence and walked over to us. Her long ears were perked up like a tensed animal's.

We fell silent, and I caught Noah's unamused expression. But before he could call her stupid, a faint voice shouted, "Get back here!" It was Thierry.

"You'll have to catch me!" A new, feminine voice cackled.

There was more, indistinct yelling, before a gust of wind blew through the arena. I glanced up, gasping, to see a giant pair of wings flashing in the darkness. It was a girl, and she was holding something that shimmered orange in the night.

"No way!" I huffed right as Noah shouted "Thief!" He shot a blast of white fire at her.

She dodged with ease, laughing to herself as she flew over the forest. In a matter of seconds, she was out of sight. Noah's fire sizzled out like a firework.

It was a real bird lady! My heart soared, but when I glanced at the others and only saw anxious expressions, it plummeted.

"Mystral," Savana groaned. "The collector of shiny things. I should've known."

A flurry of footsteps approached. Thierry skidded to a halt just outside the arena. His palms were fiery and glowing orange, smoke billowing from his nostrils. Thin cuts laced his hands, like he'd lost an arm-wrestling match with some nasty talons. "Did she escape?"

"She headed west," Noah offered. In Thierry's presence, he straightened up like we were in the military.

Titanium, who must have followed Thierry, jumped onto my shoulder. She opened her maw, tasting the air. "To the ocean, specifically. I can smell the salt. And considering she went west, it must be the Timber Coast."

Thierry rolled his eyes. "That was a sacred necklace she took."

Out of the corner of my eye, I noticed guards slipping out of the castle gates, lining up several feet behind Thierry.

"Should we go after her, Your Majesty?" one of them asked.

Thierry paused, his gaze shifting from his guards, to us, and back again. "No. Stand down." When he faced Savana, Noah, and I again, his eyes were bright. "Why don't you three retrieve it for me? You want to be of help, correct?" He stared at us each individually. We seemed to stand taller under his gaze.

The guards exchanged unamused looks. But none of them dared to argue with the emperor.

Noah pushed Savana and me aside, his eyes alight with childish eagerness. "Sir! I can do it myself. I assure you, these two will only get in the way."

"Not fair!" Savana pouted.

Thierry scowled at Noah. "You will not disrespect your comrades. Especially my son."

His words were met with silence. Noah and Savana turned to face me, stunned.

After several agonizing heartbeats, Noah roared, "You're Thierry's son?"

I shrank under the weight of his anger, only able to nod.

Noah whipped his head from me to Thierry and back again, like he didn't know who to be angry at. "That can't be true," he hissed.

"I can see the resemblance between them!" Savana offered. "If Tyler closes his right eye, he's almost a perfect, small copy."

Was that supposed to be a good thing?

Thierry cleared his throat. "You're all going on this mission. That's final."

Such an opportunity made my heart pound. This was a chance to make it up to Thierry. He was showing me hospitality, so I had to pay him back, right?

You can't disrespect him, a part of me thought. *Do as he says.*

But, another part of me reasoned, *if Oliver is truly looking for me, am I only making things worse for him? Maybe I should stay put...*

No! the sharper corner of my brain snapped. *Oliver is a thing of the past! He doesn't exist anymore!*

This was my life. I had to show Thierry I was a good son, that I hadn't been an experiment or an heir born for nothing. I finally had another parent. Another chance. A *future.*

When Thierry turned to me, waiting for an answer, I nodded and gave him a wobbly smile. "Y...yes, sir. We—we won't let you down!"

More importantly, I won't let you down.

CHAPTER NINETEEN

WHO NEEDS A GPS WHEN YOU HAVE A GHOST?

OLIVER

WE WALKED ALL DAY, taking detours around town when necessary to avoid anyone who'd recognize us humans. Civilians went about their business as usual. A cluster of earth Meraki stood around a blueprint next to a house half burned to the ground.

The fire had been put out hours ago, but the damage remained very real. I made that observation while glaring at Vincent. As we traversed the streets, he grew real interested in watching the ground roll by.

Reed had organized a change of fresh clothes that were in fashion for us, so we could blend in better. We looked great no matter how much we denied it, even if our cloaks swallowed the outfits. Vincent seemed relieved to hide himself, muttering about how stupid we looked. Diana, Luke, and I couldn't understand how.

Diana had this billowy, sage-colored skirt that matched her green eyes, and frankly, I was a little jealous. Her shirt was white, tightened around the waist, and had puffy sleeves. She kept doing little twirls for us, quietly squealing to herself and demanding compliments from Vincent, who kept looking away in embarrassment.

The rest of us received a selection of old-fashioned coats. I took a bloodred one, Vincent took a black one, and Luke took a navy-blue one. Our trousers were dark gray, and despite the light material, I felt warm as we walked through the snowy streets.

"The fabric is made with fire Mageia," Reed explained. "The wielders use a special thread to keep the material nice and toasty in the winter."

Even with night rapidly approaching, I was bundled up and comfortable. The human realm could learn a thing or two about making winter clothes.

We ended up at the edge of the forest we'd started from yesterday. Vincent's first comment was "Are you seriously kicking us out of the realm?"

Reed rolled their eyes. "No. The Cataclysm's base is right under our noses. Literally!" They smiled as if there was some inside joke to it all.

Because of the terrain, they suggested we make camp for the night and keep going when we could see the ground beneath our feet. With our legs weary from so much walking, we didn't argue the slightest bit. All we had to do was find a safe place to stop. In the morning, we would look for a Cataclysm member by the name of McKenzie, who often visited the library. Apparently, she could help us.

Only Vincent seemed skeptical. At one point, he muttered, "Are we sure this isn't a trap?" He fixed his gaze on me. "What's so bad about this Thierry guy other than kidnapping? That can happen anywhere, you know."

Reed returned the glare. "You don't know what he's planning, do you? You special ones are involved, so I hope you pay attention." While they spoke, a twig snapped under their boot. "Emperor Thierry wants to reunite Derngate and the human realm. Those necklaces you're looking for are the keys. And you still don't know the history, do you? Why do you think you're wearing hoods? Why do you think those Meraki attacked you on the street?"

Luke grimaced. "The two don't mix well, huh?"

Reed's expression was one of regret. "Unfortunately. There are centuries of history behind it, but basically, the humans drove the Meraki out. That's why we have two different realms. The Assembly of Six created Derngate, separating humans and Meraki to stop the fighting. Thierry agrees with the leaders of the past, that Meraki shouldn't have to hide themselves away."

Diana's expression hardened, which was strange to see on her face. "That Meraki need to hide? Uh, what did you literally just tell us? *We* are the ones who have to hide!" For emphasis, she tugged her cloak.

"That's what I meant by saying history is tainted." Reed stopped walking, looking up at the spindly canopy above. Glowing snow fluttered to the ground like glitter. "It's a touchy subject for both sides."

"We believe you, though." Luke rested a hand on Reed's shoulder.

Reed's green eyes shimmered with warmth. "That means a lot." Luke seemed to glow at that.

My insides twisted. It felt strange to see a human and Meraki stare at each other with such admiration. They were supposed to be enemies. Instead, they looked longingly at each other.

Only two factors separated us from Reed and the other Meraki. Humans couldn't use magic and didn't have pointy ears. That was it. And to think those two, simple things made such a difference? I eventually grumbled, "Let's just keep moving."

Diana halted and glanced over her shoulder, completely disregarding my statement. Her hands hovered over her hood, almost defensively. "Did you guys hear that?"

We fell silent. Reed's long ears twitched and swiveled, then stopped. "Why now?" they groaned.

"What now?" The hairs on the back of my neck rose.

A bright yellow glow flickered around the corner. I tensed, worried that it was a Meraki, but the light was too strong. That, and whatever it was, it was growling.

A massive glowing lion lumbered toward us, pale yellow with a white outline making it ghostly. It towered over us, the tips of its flaming mane reaching just below the treetops. Its glowing white eyes were narrowed and its muzzle wrinkled in a scowl.

"What the hell is that?" Diana screamed.

At the same time, Reed bellowed, "Scatter!"

We dove in different directions. I felt like a mouse, hiding in a bush, but I wasn't about to become a chew toy. Besides, from where I was on the ground, I got a perfect view of the beast.

Unlike the rest of us, Reed stood their ground. They crouched down, placing their palms to the earth, unnaturally calm as the lion charged forward. The snow under their fingers glowed green as roots erupted from the snowy ground, lashing at the beast. It roared and reared onto its hind legs, swatting away the vegetation. Its flaming mane expanded, threatening to set the branches above ablaze.

My blood turned to ice. "Is that what attacked the town last night?"

"Yes!" Reed manipulated a root to wrap around the lion's forepaw. Sweat beaded on their forehead as they fought against the writhing beast. "He's the solar mutation guardian named Ruslan! Something's been upsetting him. My bet is that it's the Cataclysm keeping him here. He's—" They grunted and summoned another root to keep the lion in place. "He's been taking his anger out on the town!"

"How do we get rid of him?" Diana, who was hiding behind a nearby tree, made a fat snowball and chucked it at Ruslan.

The big cat growled, shaking his head. White fire trickled from his eyes. His mouth opened, revealing teeth that glowed like the rest of his body. Fire shot from his maw, lasering the ground just inches away from Reed.

"That's it!" Reed's face scrunched up, maybe at the thought they nearly got flamed alive. They glanced around, calling, "Who's the solar mutation in your group?"

"The *what?* Are you out of your mind?" Vincent shrieked, already halfway up the nearest tree.

"No, trust me! I—" Reed was cut off by Ruslan spinning around, his massive tail smacking them right in the stomach. They went flying until their back hit a tree. The lion advanced toward them.

I struggled out of my hiding place. "Distract that thing!" I ordered Diana and Luke before racing to Reed. Helping them to their feet, I sighed in relief when I saw they were just winded and scratched.

"Thank you." They flashed me a grateful smile, blissfully unaware of the jealousy I'd held toward them last night.

That must've been Luke's signal to have a go with the lion. He took his job of distracting a little too seriously, standing right behind the creature, yelling and waving his arms to get Ruslan's attention. The beast finally turned around to face him.

"Luke, don't—" I started to call.

Reed put their hand over my mouth, muffling my sound. "Shh."

I wanted to tell them they were foolish, but we had bigger problems. Ruslan was taking Luke's bait, and from the panic spreading across his face, I could tell he didn't have a plan beyond this. The snowballs Diana threw at the beast weren't working anymore.

Ruslan jumped forward at an amazing speed, but I didn't see him land. There was a white flash and a bellowing roar. Heat flashed through the clearing, so hot you'd have expected the snow to melt. Jelly-snowflakes flurried like crazy as they fled the scene. The flash died, and then there was silence.

The lion had disappeared, and Luke was left lying motionless in the snow.

"Luke? Luke, hey!" Vincent jumped down the tree, racing to his brother's side. "Hey, idiot! Get up!"

Reed, Diana, and I quickly followed. As we neared, Vincent shielded us from Luke and snarled, "Go away!"

"Let me just see—" Reed offered a hand forward.

"It's your fault!" Vincent cut them off. "You put us in danger! You put *him* in danger!"

"Luke *chose* to put himself in front of the lion," Diana said. "Nobody forced him to do it."

Vincent's glare was as ferocious as the beast itself. "Oh yeah? What do you know about any of this, Princess?"

A cloud of breath trickled past Luke's lips, and he winced from where he lay in Vincent's arms. "Don't–don't fight. I'm okay." He opened one eye only, as if the moonlight was too much for him.

I would've cried with relief if it weren't for the shock overtaking me. Just as Luke finished speaking, the freckles under his eyes started to glow yellow. It reminded me of the lion we just faced against. "Say, are you feeling alright?"

"What?" Luke sat up with Vincent's help, touching his cheek with his hand. "Oh, that tickles."

Reed rubbed their temples. "You absorbed the lion."

Diana, Vincent, Luke, and I echoed in unison: "What?"

"Yeah." They sat down on a nearby log, giving Luke a weary smile. "That's why I asked who the solar mutation in this group is. Ruslan was born from the early solar mutations, and the guardians of each element are fiercely dedicated to their creators."

"We...didn't know humans could have, um, Mageias," I admitted.

Reed tilted their head to the side. "All living things have a Mageia, but Meraki unlock them naturally. They don't teach you that at Indra Academy?"

Us students shook our heads. Reed looked confused, but they didn't pry.

"So now you're Ruslan's...what? His friend? His protector?" Diana managed an intrigued expression, though her voice trembled.

Vincent continued glowering at Reed. "Give us a proper answer, will ya?"

Reed bowed their head, accepting the anger thrown their way. "It's rare for a guardian to take someone as their vessel. I've only ever read about it. They usually do so with a goal in mind."

I flitted my gaze from Luke to Reed and back again. "Does that mean you got, I don't know, sun powers?"

Luke raised his palms up and made a constipated face. After a moment of straining, he released his breath. "No."

"You unlock your Mageia through a different ceremony," Reed said. "Ruslan's strength might bleed into your own, but that's it until you summon your own power."

Luke clutched his chest. "I can feel him inside me. Not physically, but his presence is there." As he relaxed, the yellow glow around his freckles faded into nothing. "He's not gonna eat me from the inside, is he?"

"Hopefully not." Reed scanned him up and down. "I just pray he won't use your body for anything bad."

"You did mention a goal," Diana murmured.

"Again, I only read this, but..." Reed gazed into the dark forest around us, their expression unreadable. "The spirit guardian for each Mageia and mutation group resides in a designated area. When I was little, Thierry tricked Ruslan into leaving his home, confining him to this forest in order to scare citizens away from the Cataclysm's base. If my theory is correct, Ruslan wants Luke to bring him home."

We all looked at Luke.

"That depends on where his home is." Luke didn't sound opposed or thrilled. He frowned at the slushy ground. "But I'll try my best."

We fell into tense silence. I could tell Vincent was itching to call the idea absurd from the way his mouth opened and closed, but he didn't say anything. Deep down, I hoped we were able to help Ruslan. Homesickness was a pain I knew all too well, and returning Ruslan would also help the town of Audun.

We were all shaken from the experience and Luke was clearly exhausted, so we made camp in that clearing, deciding to take shifts in case any other fantastical beasts decided to check us out.

Lying on my back, I thought selfishly of how when we returned, Luke and I could boast to Bryce that we'd fought and harnessed a spirit of the sun. But thinking of our absent friend snuffed my amusement out, and the snow beneath me chilled my spine. We were deliberately going against Bryce's advice by searching for his father. What would he think? How upset would he be?

I sighed. This whole mission was held together by a thread. If our fight against Ruslan failed horribly, or if our impending encounter with Thierry went south, it would all be over. Tyler would succumb to the danger surrounding him and all hope would be lost.

And I'd thought our battle against the lion spiked my nerves to their limit.

Around halfway through my shift, I could no longer ignore my drooping eyelids or the ache in my muscles. But I didn't want to bother anyone because I was just tired, so I curled up on the ground in hopes of getting more comfortable. I should've known I'd be out like a light.

I'd wondered if I'd escaped the strange pool underneath Indra Academy. It turns out it had grown unbelievably large in the time I was away. So large, it covered the floor for as far as I could see, crystal-blue water reaching up to my ankles. The sky had gone black, leaving only the water's glow to illuminate the area.

Ripples hit me from behind, making me turn around, only to stop in my tracks. There was Tyler, looking up at me with those round, different-colored eyes. As always, he didn't say anything. He just stared at me with a puzzled, worried expression.

I took a step closer, giving our surroundings a wary look. "Are we alone?"

Tyler didn't budge. He made no gesture to show he heard me. Not even a blink.

"Tyler?" My heart fluttered in my chest, desperation seeping into my tone as I moved forward. I reached my hand out, but when I tried resting it on his shoulder, my fingers went right through his body. He crumbled before my eyes, turning to ash and flying into the darkness.

My stomach lurched and I scrambled backward in surprise. "What in the—"

Something disturbed the water behind me, and I spun around to see at least a hundred Tylers staring back at me. They multiplied like bunnies. They all wore the same confused face.

I raced toward them, but as I drew near, they, too, started turning to ash. "Wait!" I cried out. They weren't stopping for me, though. Rapidly, they disintegrated until I was only surrounded by dust.

That, and a voice whispering in my ear, *"Why haven't you found him?"*

"You have to find him."

"You have to find him."

"You have to find him."

I jolted awake in a cold sweat, lying on my side. A trail of drool had frozen on my cheek. Not much time had passed since everyone was still fast asleep. *At least nobody saw how you bailed out of your shift.* Ignoring the racing of my heart, I lifted my head and tried to slow my breathing. My eyes were heavy, and I felt just as tired as I was before the dream, if not even more.

A gust of wind whooshed through the trees, a familiar gale that no longer surprised me. My stomach didn't even drop when I looked up to see Crystal crouching in front of me.

As soon as our eyes locked, she scrambled closer and whispered with a grin, "I found a shortcut."

"What?" I kept my voice low, making sure the others were still asleep before sitting up. "How? Were you just wandering around?"

Crystal rolled her eyes. "No. I felt Tyler's energy nearby and followed it. Come on, I'll show you."

The dream still fresh in my mind, I quickly caved. It didn't matter how tired I was. We had to pick up the pace. I twisted around to grab my backpack, standing up once I made sure I had my flashlight inside. Before leaving, though, I crouched down next to Vincent and shook him awake. Now *this* was worth disrupting someone for. "You're taking the next shift."

Vincent rubbed his eyes, groaning in protest. Still, he sat up and put his glasses on. He frowned when I started to walk away. "Where are you going, then?"

I paused, remembering he couldn't see Crystal. "Bathroom. I'll be back in a minute."

There weren't even any crickets or owls, leaving Crystal and me—the only idiots in all of Derngate—to wander around at such an hour. Just a minute or two into our walk, a fat jelly-snowflake hit the bridge of my nose and plopped to the ground, followed by another and another. Snow spiraled from the sky, nipping my skin and leaving me hunched over as I followed the ghost. Crystal seemed to glow in the night, the snow passing right through her like she didn't exist.

I lost track of how long we walked for. Several times, I asked how much further, but Crystal always responded with "You'll turn into a child by asking so many childish questions." It left me glaring at her billowing cloak from behind and wondering if this was really worth it.

Every time the thought of giving up occurred, though, Tyler's face flashed into my mind. We came all this way for him. A little bit of snow and walking should've been nothing. Even if it was hard to keep a brave face when the wind roared between the trees.

I picked up my pace and hurried to where Crystal had stopped. In front of us stood a massive wall of thick trees. Not a light or sign of life at all. The glowing jelly-flakes no longer reflected on the snow. "Are you sure?"

"When have I ever been wrong?" Crystal grinned and breezed inside. The darkness of the dense forest didn't seem to bother her.

I looked like a pathetic mouse creeping after her, wincing at the muddy snow squelching under my boots. Dead bushes and tree trunks brushed against my coat, each tug threatening to pull me farther from Crystal. But if I told her to slow down, she'd think

I was weak or a coward. I was *not* about to be ridiculed by a dead person.

Crystal weaved through the trees effortlessly, and I had to jog every few minutes to keep her in sight. She disappeared at one point, her voice ringing over the wind, "Down here. Be careful, it's kinda steep."

Before I could ask what she meant, I stepped forward, only for my foot to slip. I lost my balance, gravity yanking me down a slope. My scream was muffled by the wet snow that had me sliding me around like a clumsy penguin. Finally, I landed in a puddle of slush right by Crystal's feet.

"*Kinda* steep?" I grumbled.

"You humans amaze me," Crystal said with an amused grin. "Come on, we're almost there."

"I'm okay. Thanks for asking," I called as she kept walking. When she didn't stop, I groaned and pushed myself to my feet. My damp cloak was quickly growing a layer of frost.

Crystal was right; the trees were starting to thin out, and I heard the rush of water nearby. Thierry's castle loomed in the sky.

"Okay," she said, "now you *really* need to watch your footing. If you fall, I can't catch you."

I stepped forward, and the pebble I kicked went flying ahead. However, I couldn't hear it land. Squinting in the darkness, I sucked in a sharp breath. The ground was ripped open, a mass of darkness in its place. A ravine lay right below us.

Facing Crystal again, I couldn't help but feel impressed. I was about to praise her, but the ghost appeared solemn for once. "Hey, it's a good find! Come on, let's get closer and bust Tyler out while it's dark."

Crystal stepped in front of me, shaking her head. "You were assigned this task with the others for a reason. Wait until morning and bring them here. Besides, you think you're good enough to scale down a cliff in the dark? That's plain suicide."

My mouth opened to protest, but she had a point. If something happened to me with no living witnesses, the others would never know, or they'd be too late. Besides, the thought of something going wrong with the cliff made my chest tighten. Hoping she wouldn't notice, I adjusted my damp cloak and sighed, "Very well, Crystal Lacey."

When I looked up again, she was gone.

∾

"Are you sure you didn't hit your head or something?" was the first thing Diana asked when I told her and the others about the gorge in the morning.

Even Luke was looking skeptical. "Or maybe you dreamt it."

"Seriously?" I paused my pacing to glare at them. "Come on—Vincent, you believe me, right?"

Vincent looked up from where he was busy drawing in the slush. "You must've taken a hell of a long piss last night if you stumbled upon a *ravine*."

Reed, who'd been listening in silence, finally cleared their throat. "The gorge is the right place to go, actually. I'm more surprised you found it by yourself, in the middle of the night, while it was snowing. The odds were in your favor, huh?"

I didn't know how to explain it was Crystal who did the work. "I got lucky." *Sorry, Crystal.*

"It's not completely impossible," Reed continued. "The easiest way to get to the Cataclysm is to follow the river. This shortcut will probably lead to the side." They smiled reassuringly. "It's worth checking out."

Since they were our escort, their word was pretty much law. I pumped my fist in the air. "Thank you!"

After organizing ourselves, we set forward on the trail Crystal had led me down last night. Only my footsteps were visible in the snow. The spirit's footprints had washed away with the storm, if she left any prints in the first place. Mine, too, would've been difficult to spot if it weren't for Reed's tracking skills.

I thought it would've taken less time to find the gorge in broad daylight, but having to do so with a bigger party slowed us down. At least I didn't have to worry about slipping in the dark every two seconds.

However, a new concern arose. Because I'd visited at night, I didn't know anything about the gorge other than where it was. How deep was it? How were we supposed to get down?

Luke must've read my mind, because as the trees started thinning out, he jogged to the front and asked.

Reed laughed. "There are stairs, of course."

An answer to the question regarding how deep it was appeared in front of us. A familiar rush of water met my ears, and the forest broke away to reveal a jagged rip in the ground. It was as deep as your average Manhattan building—maybe a building and a half. Ledges and stairways jutted out of the walls, none seeming to be in use.

"Right, well…" Vincent paused, then asked, "How are we supposed to get into the enemy's base without being seen?"

Reed held their palm up to silence us. Once we were quiet, they walked over to a nearby tree, where a black, four-eyed bird was pecking at the bark. They pulled some dark red berries from their pocket, holding them up for the creature. Reed pursed their lips and emitted a series of whistle sounds.

The strange bird hopped closer, bending down to examine the berries. After several moments of listening to the whistles, it took the berries and flew right into the gorge.

"What was that for?" Diana craned her neck toward the cliff, trying to spot the bird.

"I don't think I *want* to know," Vincent grumbled.

Reed scoffed. "They're messenger birds! They're wild and take jobs from travelers, for a small price, of course."

A cawing sound echoed through the gorge, and the bird swooped back into the air. When Reed held their arm out, it perched right onto it and let out a series of chirps and squawks.

Reed's eyes widened. "The base is empty?" They turned to us humans, their expression hard to read. "Then be quick. I assume the others are out elsewhere. No sign of any guards, either. McKenzie's room is on the last level, about three doors left of the waterfall. She'll help you from here on out."

I faced the Meraki with a dip of my head. "Thank you for all your help. It means a lot."

The bird let out one last caw before retreating to the branch it started on. As if that was their cue to get moving, Reed shook their head and returned the smile. "The pleasure was all mine. Good luck!"

We didn't dwell on the goodbyes, wishing Reed well and telling them to give Dewey a carrot for us. I did, however, notice Luke rubbing his eyes a little. When Reed left, Vincent put his hand on his brother's shoulder and whispered, "You okay?"

Luke nodded and turned his head away from us. Even when we started our descent down the gorge, he took the lead so we wouldn't see.

Little pebbles tumbled down the cliffside. The silence before they hit the ground was agonizing. I kept watching and waiting for a rockslide. My heart rate shot through the roof.

Distracting myself from the perilous drop was a futile effort. Repeatedly, I asked myself, *But what if the wall does cave in?* My legs grew shakier and shakier, and my vision kept going in and out of focus. I was sweating despite the cold. Afraid of losing my balance, I came to a stop, leaning against the wall with hands tightly gripping the crevices. I squeezed my eyes shut, trying to pretend I was elsewhere.

"Is something wrong?" Diana stopped to glance over her shoulder.

I started breathing out of my mouth, shallow and quick. No words left me. Why was the air getting thinner? I couldn't feel the ground, even when I lowered myself down to huddle on the stairs. All hot and shaky, my priority became making sure I didn't pass out on the spot.

Boots shuffled, and a pair of footsteps drew near. A warm hand grasped mine, followed by Luke's voice saying, "I got you." It was closer than it'd been a second ago.

I opened my eyes a crack, squinting, to see that he'd climbed back up to join me. He crouched in front of me, somehow able to remain calm and collected. Vincent and Diana watched from several steps below in interest. "No," I croaked finally, but I was unable to risk pulling my hand away. "If I slip, we'll both slip." Every syllable shook in my throat.

Luke squeezed my hand. "I'm stronger than you. If you fall, I'll pull you back up." When I didn't reply, he stood up, gently tugging my arm. "You know I'd never let go."

That forced me into motion. With bated breath, I crept after him. I feared my legs would buckle with each excruciating step. My vision filled with spots. Every other moment, I had to stop and re-collect myself. Luke didn't seem to mind waiting, even if he cringed every time I squeezed his hand for dear life. I probably broke a finger or two of his.

Diana and Vincent had been on the ground level for a while by the time Luke and I joined them. They observed curiously but didn't say anything. Vincent had gone back to biting his pendant.

I sat heavily on the final step, burying my face in my knees, and fought to slow my racing heart. Luke put his hands on my shoulders, rubbing them gently. Nobody spoke, but the wordless question in the air was obvious.

"Sorry about that." I offered the three of them a weak smile. "I must've looked down and gotten dizzy."

"You're fine. I nearly pissed myself, too." Vincent didn't sound convincing in the slightest bit, but luckily, he didn't linger on it. Instead, he turned around to face the gorge we were in. "We better start looking for McKenzie, I suppose."

CHAPTER TWENTY
SUPERHEROES
OLIVER

WE HADN'T EXPLORED FOR long when a nearby door flew open, nearly scaring the living daylights out of me for the second time in ten minutes. In this narrow part of the gorge lined with carved skulls, intricate designs, and stairs, a stranger could've meant good news or guaranteed death.

The person who came out was a young woman with russet-brown skin, who ran one hand through her coily hair upon meeting our spooked gazes. Stopping in her tracks, she smiled, betraying no sign of shock. "You must be the ones Reed whistled about."

"Are you McKenzie?" Luke approached slowly, his hands balling into fists.

"I am." She paused, studying us for a moment. "Why don't we go inside where it's warmer? Let's talk." Without waiting for an answer, she turned around and disappeared past a door set into the cliff face.

The rest of us exchanged glances before following.

As we stepped into the candle-lit room, I understood what Reed meant when they said McKenzie visited the library often. The shelves lining the walls were piled with books. Papers and scrolls were scattered around the floor and the desk McKenzie made her way to.

"Make yourselves at home." McKenzie waved to the bed pushed against the wall. The blanket covering it looked like it'd been passed down through generations. She pulled her chair out, swiveling it to face us before sitting. "I saw that messenger bird swoop around and knew you were on your way." Her gaze flickered to my head, which was partially swallowed by my cloak's hood. "Please, you don't need to hide it. We're all on the same side here." She tucked a strand of hair away from her face, revealing round ears just like ours.

"You're human!" Diana gasped.

"So we aren't the only ones!" Luke tilted his head to one side. "Um...is it okay if I ask why you stay here? Since you're the only other human we've seen here. This place is kind of intimidating, you know?"

McKenzie hesitated, clearly considering something, before rummaging around her desk and grabbing a picture frame. She handed it to me, and us kids swarmed it.

In the frame was a bunch of polaroid photos glued together, of three figures. McKenzie stood taller than the duo, her hair in an afro and posture hunched over, like she was trying to appear more feminine. Indra Academy was in the background of most of the images. What caught my attention were her friends.

I was about to comment on their familiarity when Diana blurted out, "Hang on, is that Isabel and Camila? How do you know them?"

McKenzie played with her hands. "We were classmates. These photographs were taken during our senior year. We were all going through a lot of changes, and honestly, I wouldn't be who I am today without them. We helped each other for the better." Her expression was one of nostalgia and maybe pain. "We did everything together. So, when Isabel found Derngate, of course Camila and I were right behind her."

"That didn't end well, I assume?" Vincent finally spoke up.

McKenzie looked somber in the dim light. "This world was too good to be true. Thierry's promises got to my head, unlike Isabel and Camila. I thought that if there was anywhere I could make a difference, it would be here."

Diana's shoulders slumped. "So, you guys aren't friends anymore?"

"Well…" McKenzie tilted her head thoughtfully. "We were out of touch for quite a while. It was around two or three years ago Isabel snuck into Derngate, found me, and said she was starting to find members of the new Assembly of Six." Her gaze fell upon Luke and me before continuing. "We've been writing letters to each other since then. She and Camila continued searching for other members of the party while I worked to slow Thierry's progress down."

Vincent cocked his head to one side. "Why should we trust you if you're on Thierry's side, then? Reed might've led us into a trap for all we know."

"I never claimed to be on Thierry's side." McKenzie's voice remained even. "I simply stayed where I was needed."

"You helped the enemy," Vincent pressed.

"Try leaving a situation you've spent twelve years in." McKenzie bristled. "It's not as easy as it sounds. Does it look like my morals are out of line to you? I'm not the clueless eighteen-year-old I once was. Get this in your thick skull, boy. I do not stand with the Cataclysm."

Only silence answered. We all glared at Vincent, who just lowered his head in submission.

"I was wondering about that for a while. The whole acceptance thing," Luke mused, probably to cool the situation. "Considering this place has so many, uh, old-fashion vibes to it. I haven't seen any hostility over our differences."

"What deems a person lower on the social pyramid here works differently." McKenzie gave him an understanding smile. "It's the Mageia you're judged on. Nowadays, it's a lot better, but back when ice mutations were around, they were the ones cast away and stripped of rights." She paused before rubbing one of her ears. "Of course, humans are easy targets, too."

"Wait, back up a little. What do you mean by the ice mutations? Uh, are any of us that?" I looked around our ragtag team. Our powers were unknown. The exception was Luke, who Reed had called a solar mutation.

McKenzie grabbed a blank scroll, scribbling on it with her pen. "I hope at least one of you met the original Assembly of Six?" When I nodded, the tension seemed to leave her body. "Thank goodness. I assume Isabel has mentioned there are meant to be six of you to follow their footsteps. Your Mageia matches the one of that who came before you. Let's see…We got fire, water, air, and three mutations: ice, solar, and lightning."

Diana counted those on her fingers, frowning. "What about earth?"

"Earth Meraki stayed out of the fighting all those centuries ago. They weren't involved. The same goes for light mutations." McKenzie finished drawing on the paper, holding it up for us to see. There were six necklaces; one had the fire quartz crystal Isabel had sent us here for.

"That doesn't answer Oliver's question," Vincent said. It was probably the first and last time he would stand up for me. "Who's the ice mutation? What happened to the rest of them?"

McKenzie looked reluctant, but under Vincent's stare, her shoulders drooped. She began talking, defeated. "Ice mutations lived within water Meraki communities, as that's where their mutation sprung from. But water Meraki deemed them lower class citizens, as I mentioned. They helped to build, construct, and heal. That was it. Pay was very little for them, too."

My stomach clenched. I already knew this wasn't going to end well.

"The ice mutations broke into riots and tried to start a revolution. Water Meraki teamed up with fire Meraki to put them in their place." McKenzie squirmed and hesitated, looking like she wanted to leave the next bit out. "And by that, I mean the ice mutations were all killed. The world was industrializing, and nobody needed their skills anymore, especially with new, reliable modern medicine and building techniques. Survivors died out because their bodies were unable to handle global warming on the rise." She ducked her head, focusing on the palm of her hand. "The ice mutation in your group is Tyler. Thierry knew all along."

Luke grimaced. "He's timid, from what I remember. Was he okay to hear all that?"

McKenzie shook her head. "Nobody has told him. He's so fragile and riddled with anxiety, I fear such news would break him."

"I don't blame him. That's kinda scary, knowing your lifespan is cut because of how much warmer it is now." Diana hugged her knees, eyes full of sympathy. "But speaking of Tyler, where is he? And this necklace, too."

"You just missed them, actually." McKenzie smiled nervously as we stared at her. "The necklace you're looking for was stolen. Tyler and two other Cataclysm members, Noah and Savana, left to retrieve it. Thierry sent them off."

Vincent buried his face in his hands with a groan. "You've got to be kidding me! I didn't sign up for a wild goose chase! Besides—"

"None of us did!" McKenzie interrupted him with scary strength in her voice. "This isn't a wild goose chase. The futures of both Earth and Derngate rest on finding Tyler and these necklaces. Now quit your whining or leave."

Vincent blinked in surprise. He glanced at Luke, mouth open for another retort, but clearly, he thought better of it and bit his tongue.

I shared Vincent's dismay, but I forced optimism into my tone. "Where are Tyler and the others headed? Maybe we can catch them before they're too far off."

McKenzie narrowed her eyes, gaze trained on the floor, humming in thought. "According to what Savana told me, they're going west to the Timber Coast."

"More swimming?" Diana and Vincent asked in unison. One looked excited and the other horrified.

"No. The thief, an air Meraki named Mystral, lives in a cave by the cliff. You don't have to go near the water."

Hearing that, Vincent relaxed, but the earlier tightness in my chest threatened to return.

Luke nudged me with his shoulder at the mention of the cliff. "You'll be okay?"

I blinked at him, taking a deep breath. "Yeah. Can't be picky with where we go, after all."

McKenzie leaned forward, resting her chin on her hands. "I must ask, though, what will happen once you've collected Tyler and the necklace? You're going home, I assume?"

"Yeah!" Diana straightened up. "Do you want to come with us? If you haven't been back since your senior year, you probably miss it."

"I never returned because I was busy looking for you guys." McKenzie took the picture frame from us, tracing her finger over the outlines of her old friends. "But since it's all coming together now, perhaps." Despite her light words, her expression was hardening once more. "I asked on Tyler's behalf. Even if it hadn't taken so long to find him, it's obvious he's too young to be an Indra Academy student. What will happen to you as a team?"

We fell silent.

McKenzie pulled open her desk drawer, pulling out a stack of worn papers. "I found these in Thierry's room. They flooded in at the time I arrived here, about twelve years ago. They're from who I believe is Tyler's mother."

I snatched the papers, reading them over as Luke, Diana, and Vincent crowded around me to see. Most of them were short, the words drawn together with messy handwriting. Many had crinkled edges and little stains, like ghostly tears.

They told Thierry she was pregnant.

That she and her two kids were being kicked out.

That she was all alone now.

She begged Thierry to come back.

She had to juggle taking care of a newborn and two toddlers by herself.

She told Thierry that she had his kid and she wanted him to take him away.

These letters must have never gotten a response, because each one sounded more desperate than the last. She even threatened the child, but no reply.

"You're helping the world," she'd written in the final letter, "but at what cost?"

"Piece of shit," Vincent muttered under his breath. "Why's she getting mad over a kid she agreed to conceive?"

I stared at the letters, which blurred before my eyes. Somehow, I couldn't tell what was more appalling: the fact Thierry was the father, or the fact he abandoned the woman he impregnated. "It makes sense that Thierry tried for another kid, despite raising Bryce in Japan. Bryce wasn't the ice mutation he wanted." Putting race aside, I could see it now; Tyler and Bryce's similar hair and pointed ears, and how Bryce kept looking at Tyler like something was off, but he couldn't explain it. "They're half-brothers, aren't they?"

That's when a newer, more shocking realization hit. "Hang on, that makes Tyler a prince, doesn't it?"

Diana let out a low whistle. "Well, that makes this ten times more interesting. We're rescuing a prince!"

"It's more like kidnapping, since this is technically his turf." Vincent scowled as he thought about it.

Luke glared at the papers, his fists clenching the bed's blanket. "Have you *seen* how negligent his parents are? We're not the villains here. None of these letters excuse the actions of Sadie and Thierry."

Diana looked Luke, Vincent, McKenzie, and me up and down rather than focusing on the ugly letters. "Who said that taking Tyler home means taking him back to his mom? People are looking for him. So what? We'll hide him until they go away. It's simple." She focused on McKenzie. "Right?" When nobody responded, she laughed at herself. "I know that's basically kidnapping, but wouldn't that work best? At least for now? We just won't rat him out."

"Yeah. Who knows how far Tyler would be taken away if authorities got their hands on him?" Relief bubbled in my stomach knowing I wasn't the only one with that anxiety.

McKenzie chuckled. "I'm glad you guys have it sorted on your own. I'm sure Isabel and Camila would be more than willing to assist. Now come on, I want to show you guys something. To have a chance at making it out of here, you'll need your own Mageias to be free."

"As in powers?" Vincent asked in a hoarse voice.

When McKenzie nodded, we exchanged uneasy looks. None of us ventured into this thinking we'd emerge with elemental abilities.

"It's a big change, I know. For now, one volunteer would suffice," McKenzie added in an attempt to ease the tension.

Nobody budged. I was mainly eyeing Luke, since he got a good taste of Mageia-like power last night, but he didn't seem to be feeling the same way. His attention was actually on me, as were the others'.

"Fine." My stomach knotted at the mere thought of gaining inhuman powers. But maybe going first would encourage the others.

"You'll be okay." McKenzie nodded to me. "I see the eyes of someone familiar within you." She stood and headed to the nearest bookshelf. She pulled it aside—just like the bookshelf in the library at Indra Academy—to reveal a dark tunnel. "Follow me."

Shooting the others a look that meant *thanks a lot*, I trailed after McKenzie.

My first concern came from the lack of light, other than the fire McKenzie summoned above her hand. Something in me wanted to ask if this was a trap, but I bit my tongue. If McKenzie knew Camila and Isabel, this had to be fine. As she said, she was on our side.

McKenzie must've noticed my anxious expression because she offered a gentle smile. She came to a stop, right where the tunnel turned a corner. "This next part is for you to walk alone."

"Okay." I pushed past her, letting the darkness of the tunnel consume me.

The temperature dropped right away, and a cloud of breath puffed around my face. I wrapped my cloak around my body, awkwardly navigating along the tunnel. The lack of noise made everything ten times eerier. It would've been a great time for Crystal to appear and guide me, but the spirit was nowhere to be found.

Matters were only made worse when I noticed a skull wedged between two rocks. I stopped dead in my tracks. My gaze slid past it, landing on yet another skull, and then another, and another...I couldn't count how many there were, trailing through the tunnel. Other bones were scattered around them.

That's just what I need to see right now: dead people! The thought tightened around my throat like a noose, trying to tug me backwards.

I forced a deep breath, wrenching my eyes away from the graveyard. *Remember why you're doing this. Everyone is counting on you.* Still, my legs felt like lead as I carried on.

The tunnel opened into a dark cave adorned with jagged stalactites and stalagmites. Whisps of wind swirled around the largest stalagmite in the center. It was almost as if they were pointing at the stalagmite.

I cautiously approached, tentatively touching my palm to the rough surface.

Glowing, orange spheres appeared above every jagged tip in the cave, warming my body. Blurry images flickered in every direction. Muffled voices and laughter danced around me.

Why's it all so familiar?

I glanced around, gasping as I saw snippets of the Malibu Lagoon State Beach in the visions. The voices belonged to my birth parents, coaxing me into the water while I stubbornly sat on the sand.

How long has it been since I heard their voices?

The sound mingled with many others, belonging to classmates and friends and crashing ocean waves. And somehow, something wasn't sitting right in my stomach.

Did my classmates always sound so taunting?

It was my fifth-grade classroom. October. I remembered.

We'd had to draw people in our lives who inspired us and present them to the class. We'd had to make them superheroes. I drew my neighbors. They were two kind young men my parents often invited for dinner. When my mom started her own garden in the front yard, they were the first to help. I loved taking their poodle for walks. They ended up moving because our other neighbors made them feel so unwelcome. I knew they'd never see my drawings and I'd never see them again. Still, I'd thought they were cool people.

When I presented it to the class, my peers laughed. The teacher was on her phone. My friend at the time shouted, "Superheroes can't be gay!"

Superheroes couldn't be gay? I stood in front of the class, shrinking into myself and trembling with this emotion I couldn't understand. Watching the scene play out before me, the sixteen-year-old version of me teared up. *No, don't listen to him,* I told the younger image of myself.

"Why not?" the younger me asked his friend.

"They just can't!" My friend was cackling at that point. He gave me this crazed smile. "Oh my gosh, are you one of them? Are you a—"

He said a slur.

I punched him right in the face.

The sound of a nose breaking.

"Shut up!" I was screaming while he repeated the ugly word. "Shut up! Shut up!" I was on top of him, grappling with and punching him while he laughed, drunk on adrenaline. He wasn't fighting back, so I knew I'd take the blame, but I couldn't stop myself.

They suspended me. We had to pay the medical bills for the broken nose.

My parents and I moved to Santa Monica. They said it was for better job opportunities.

Different faces appeared in the orange spheres. They were the new friends I'd made.

One particular boy had long, curly black hair. *Boys can have long hair?* Fifth-grade Oliver looked amazed. I could feel the longing in my chest now. Anything to be friends with that boy.

And we did become friends. He and his group took me in.

It all flashed by in the spheres. Skateboarding, surfing, eating popsicles, hiking, sitting on rooftops, searching for stars and sunflower fields.

Our first slumber party. It was just the two of us, me at his house. My parents were going into the mountains for the weekend, and they let me stay behind. They knew steep roads made me sick.

There was that last night, the one before the morning my parents were supposed to come back.

I didn't want to keep watching, but my hand was stuck. I couldn't pull my body nor my gaze away.

The cops showing up in the middle of the night. Red and blue lights flashing.

"There was an accident."

No.

"A mudslide on the Pacific Coast Highway."

No.

"I'm sorry."

"You're a liar!" my younger self screamed. "My dad is the best driver in the world!"

And that poor friend listened with wide eyes. Even his older sister came to see what was happening. Their parents were hurriedly talking to the rest of the cop's squad.

When the Oliver of the past started to cry, I felt tears slide down my own cheeks.

What was fate gaining by taunting me?

It didn't scare that friend away. He held me close and comforted me in silence. There wasn't much he could say. He had both his parents. He had his older sister and pet bird. He had all his belongings.

They couldn't even break the news to me in my own house.

The next three years blurred before my eyes. My parents' best friends took me in, two women who'd recently gotten married. Who'd have thought their extra wedding gift would be an orphaned kid?

Self-exploration.

Longer hair.

Things settled. I was so tired. I couldn't shake it off. I started to quit the things that put strain on me. Biking. Skateboarding. Surfing.

Eighth grade.

"Oliver, sweetie, we have to talk to you."

No.

"We're thinking about moving to France. The countryside, in the southeast."

No.

Hours of research.

I wasn't ready.

Hadn't I moved enough? Cities. Houses. Schools. Even parents.

I begged to stay with my aunt and cousin in New York. It wasn't California, but it was closer than France.

I didn't want my soul torn away from the beach, regardless of how it was both saving and killing me.

Past Oliver's fear coursed through my veins.

My moms handed me a pamphlet for Indra Academy on Long Island.

It wouldn't be a goodbye.

"You really wanna live in a shithole like New York City?" my friend cried when I told him.

"It's New York or France!"

"What about everyone else? What about *me?*"

I'd smiled at him, despite feeling like I was crumbling behind that mask. "It's not a goodbye!"

"It might as well be." His voice rang furiously. Desperately.

A shithole like New York City.

"Fuck you, Oliver."

Fuck you. Fuck you. Fuck you. It echoed around the cavern.

"Oliver?" This voice came from inside my head.

"Wait, no, come back!" As the images began to fade, I teared up again. "Wait!" I pressed my palm harder against the stalagmite to keep my friend's face from disappearing.

All that did was bring searing pain to my chest. My heart twisted with strength that brought me to my knees. I let out a guttural cry as heat blazed through my muscles, seizing my limbs and spreading all over my body.

The orange silhouette of my friend appeared before me, his expression blank. He crouched down to meet me at my level.

Delirious with pain, I barely registered I was reaching forward, trying to touch his cheek.

Then he was gone, and I was sitting in darkness again. I wanted to scream but was too stunned to let it loose. The ache in my chest returned. Cold settled in my bones, coaxing me to lay down and never get back up. But there it was again, a warm voice asking "Oliver?" from behind me.

Luke stood at the entrance to the cave, his freckles glowing yellow. He frowned once he caught my expression. "Hey..."

The stalagmite released my other hand, allowing me to run and fall into Luke. He hugged me back, and for a minute, all I could hear was our breathing and my sniffles. His sunshine enveloped me. Eventually, he asked in a whisper, "Who hurt you?"

"Nobody. I just needed a hug." I pulled away, rubbing my face clean and offering a shaky smile to show I was trying to be okay. "Thank you, though. I owe you." Was the wobbling of my knees obvious at all?

Luke's expression was one of doubt, but as he looked me over, his eyes widened. "Uh, your freckles..."

"My what?" I raised the palm of my hand to my face, gasping when an orange glow reflected onto it from my cheeks. When I pulled the sleeves of my coat up, the spots along my arms were also lit up. "Oh!"

"That's your Mageia, isn't it?" Luke's lips formed a small smile. "It worked!"

"Yeah." I exhaled shakily, rolling back my shoulders to appear more composed. My legs still trembled from the weight of my memories, but for everyone's sake, I had to keep it together. "Come on, why don't we find the others?"

I started to leave, but Luke grabbed my wrist. "Are you sure you're okay, though?"

I hesitated. We stood alone in the dark, him glowing yellow and me glowing orange. We were warm compared to everything around us. There was no way to explain why my muscles relaxed. Then, the weight on my heart lifted. The blazing fire no longer hurt.

I finally smiled and sighed. "I'm okay."

INTERLUDE

OLIVER

I KNEW WHAT IT was like to drown. To have your eyes roll to the sky before everything goes blue. To ask yourself why you aren't fighting the ocean.

The most vivid memory was foam and bubbles blooming all around me like falling stars. And I was a meteor, the heaviest anchor sinking to the ancient sediment below. I remembered the agony pierce my lungs, craving air, but doing nothing to satisfy the desire.

I wanted to sleep.

I think I did. I remember my bare back touching the jagged seafloor. I remember the hazy image of white foam exploding at the surface as a new comet entered the atmosphere.

I think it was my friend.

I...

The rest of the memory tape burned, just like the seawater in my throat.

Then it all came crashing back. The ocean. The sun. The sand. Time.

For once, the shift in my dream brought me to an actual location, not a warp in space. I stood in a dark shed, surrounded by boxes and steel shelves. Old toys decorated the empty spaces. Unidentified stains covered the walls and floor. Everything was blue and blurry from the sea. When I exhaled, bubbles floated from my mouth.

And as if this place couldn't get creepier, then came the sound of crying.

My legs moved on their own, toward the despairing wails.

Huddled by the entrance was a little kid no older than ten. He wore nothing but his boxers, his bones jutting out of his gangly body. His head drooped until his chin touched his chest, eyes hidden by shaggy hair, and mouth covered by shaking hands.

My gut dropped. "Tyler?" It couldn't be! This kid was clearly younger, but nobody shared Tyler's unique appearance enough to take his place.

"Dominic?" His words were muffled by the fingers over his mouth. His eyes were wide and watery, tossing and turning like the ocean. Once he'd taken in my presence, he started to cry again. "Dominic, I can't do this! I keep missing school! She—she punched my last baby tooth out." He removed his hands from his mouth, revealing swollen lips coated in blood.

Nausea and horror surged through me. I crouched next to him, taking in the broken sight. "Who's she? Your mom?"

Tyler ignored me, hiccuping and sobbing. "I was playing with it, and she got mad. She told me to stop and then changed her mind and offered to help." He punched the air weakly to replicate it. Losing his balance, he fell onto my lap. "Then she yelled because I swallowed it."

I froze in place, hands hovering over him but refusing to make contact. Part of me wanted to tell him to snap out of it—because he was scaring me, and I knew he didn't like touch. But this kid, Little Tyler, curled against me as if I were someone else. I mentally apologized and carefully patted his bony shoulder. He nestled into my lap and wept.

My unconscious mind was racing five steps ahead. Was this another one of Thierry's games? A glance around provided no clues. This was a simple shed, and this was a younger version of Tyler. I had to be in the moment to make up for all the times I hadn't been there for him. So, I offered mindless comfort to combat the agonizing sound with gentle murmurs, only able to ask myself, *What have I gotten into?*

TYLER

What have I gotten into?

I had dreamed my way into an empty room with bare, beige walls and a single bed pushed into one corner. A desk, some cabinets, and a wardrobe stood empty. Trash bags were stacked up next to the door, where some kid was busy rummaging through them. His hair was fiery ginger, just reaching his freckle-splattered neck. Every few seconds, he sniffled or paused to rub the back of his hand over his face.

Such a suppressed, upsetting sound didn't sit right in my stomach. But it wasn't like I could exit unnoticed. He was blocking the entrance.

Slowly, I backed up, only to hear something crunch under my sneaker. I lifted my foot and noticed a picture frame below. Thankfully, it hadn't cracked or dented. I craned my neck for a better look, only for shock to sweep over me. It was of a small family—a mom, a dad, and their kid in the middle. He was no older than nine or ten in that photo.

"Oliver?" I gasped.

The kid busy with the bags looked up with a frown. His eyes were a startling, familiar green, and they widened upon meeting mine. Without a doubt, that was Oliver Stylus.

But he's so small! His height barely matched mine, and his hair was shorter than I remembered. He had no ponytail, and the freckles on his cheeks were faded against a pale, teary face.

"They said I could decorate the place however I wanted to." He gestured to the room, enthusiasm lacking. "But it's not my house. What if they won't let me paint the walls?"

I pointed to myself, a weak way of confirming he was speaking to me. "Um..." I followed his gaze to the empty walls. Little Oliver was definitely asking the wrong person about this. My bedroom walls had only ever been colored in the form of pencil scribbles.

I could still feel my mom's reaction between my shoulders. The pencil had been rubbed off as best as it could, but the stain still jeered at me for years after.

Little Oliver's puppy eyes brought me back to the moment. I swayed on my feet, nodding to the wall. "What, uh, what color?"

"Dark blue. They're good for stars." Oliver grabbed something from a nearby bag and approached me. He opened his fist to reveal a handful of plastic glow-in-the-dark stars. His weak, hopeful expression quickly dissolved, and his lip quivered. "You said these would help, but it's not the same. It'll never be the same. I...I don't feel them in the stars."

I said that? Confused, I lifted the picture frame with care, holding it at an angle we could both see from. "Your parents," I guessed numbly. Vaguely, I remembered Oliver talking about having two moms. That must've been a lifetime ago we spoke about it, but the silent realization of mine had never left.

That Oliver had reached that point through loss. He'd been removed from the nest prematurely.

He rubbed his eyes again, only for the tears to come rushing back. "It's my fault. If only I held my temper. If only we didn't move to Santa Monica. They'd be here. I...I killed them!"

I shook my head, leaning down to meet his eyes. His words had a frightening familiarity to them. "You didn't kill them. It wasn't your fault."

OLIVER

"It wasn't your fault," I whispered into the silence. "Your mom shouldn't have hurt you over a tooth."

Little Tyler faced the ceiling, eyes wide and unseeing. "I keep messing up. That's why she punishes me. If only I were better…"

I focused on his bloody mouth, parted to reveal the gap where his baby tooth used to be. The words weren't coming to me.

"You can't blame her." Little Tyler rubbed his knuckles, which were scabbed and infected. "She–she said that if I don't start talking at school, she'll pull me out. I keep missing school for the punishments, and she keeps having to pick me up early because everything hurts. I'm making it worse for her. You aren't there to help anymore, and Mia doesn't care." He glanced up at me. "Dominic?"

I choked back a sob. I didn't have the heart to tell him I wasn't whoever this Dominic was. "Yes?"

"How do you do it? How do you have friends and your words don't get stuck? I–I can't even ask to use the bathroom at school. All my boxers are ruined, and Mom won't buy new ones."

That explained the stale, rank smell of the shed. "What comes easy to one person might not for the next. That doesn't mean something is wrong with you, though." In all honesty, I didn't know how to continue. I wasn't popular in the way this Dominic person seemed to be. My circle of friends was tight. "And I'm sorry. I'd buy you new boxers if I could."

Little Tyler's head drooped, almost sliding off my lap. His nose rested inches from the cold floor. I would've thought he'd passed out if not for his hoarse question a moment later; "Is it going to get better?"

TYLER

"Is it going to get better?" Little Oliver asked. He held one of his plastic stars to the ceiling as if deciding where to place it.

I sat on the edge of his clean, new bed. "People say it does, but..." *I don't believe them.* Those bitter words lodged in my throat. Even if this was a dream, even if this wasn't real, I wouldn't crush Oliver's hopes. "It takes time. It–it doesn't heal overnight."

"How many nights, then?"

"As many as it takes."

Oliver lowered his arm back to his side, expressionless. At first, he seemed to relax at my words. But then he seized up, like a cold tsunami was crashing through his insides. He faced me, eyes wide and face pale. "Did I tell my parents I love them?"

"What?"

"Before they left. Did I?" Little Oliver's breathing hitched. "I–I can't remember! What if they died never knowing? Oh no, oh no..." He started to pace around the room, tearing his hands through his hair. Under his breath, he kept repeating it until his voice cracked.

This tiny part of me wanted him to shut up—because of how terrifying his words were. Imagine feeling so strong for a person, and never being able to express how much they meant to you before they left.

I had only seen death occur once: a pigeon getting hit in mid-air by a speeding car. It happened in the blink of an eye. One moment, I was admiring the pretty feathers, and the next moment, I was crouched on the sidewalk, vomiting, as those same feathers rained down from the sky like snow.

If that was the pain I felt about a bird, I didn't want to know what it might feel like if it were a human. Or was it the same?

My mind kept flashing to Dominic. The edges of my vision blurred. Little Oliver's hysterical voice rang in my ears. I was fighting to stay asleep and in the dream. Without even realizing it, I stood up and pulled Oliver into a hug. My whole body felt like it was on fire, every muscle screaming to pull away.

OLIVER

That's when Little Tyler hugged me with all his strength.

"Someday, you will grow up," I whispered. "You will leave your home. Nothing is permanent. Not the good. Not the bad. No night lasts forever."

TYLER

"So tell the stars you love them." I brought all my power into my words. "Tell the stars every night. It will be worth it."

Little Oliver's face melted into my shoulder. His tears were acid against my skin. "How do you know?"

OLIVER

"How do you know?" Little Tyler asked into the darkness.

And both boys answered, "Because someone out there will hear you."

PART 2

Chapter Twenty-One
SIGNATURE SCARS
Tyler

There's this moment when your sleepy consciousness recalls the dream you awaken from. Then you reach forward, trying to grasp the pieces before they disappear. That's when your fingers close around empty, cold air. The dream is gone.

Still, I felt some sort of void building in my gut. It chipped away at my insides. Every time I tried remembering my dream, the despair came rushing back.

Some dreams are meant to stay fuzzy.

I hadn't spent this much time around Noah since before he and Dominic left for Indra Academy. Every day, he used to accompany Dominic when he fetched me from school, whisking us away to Central Park until the sun went down. My mom was never the biggest fan of Noah, but when it involved taking me out of the house, she seemed fine with him. That was one of the few ways I could please my mom, despite how scary Noah was.

To stand by his side without Dominic between us felt unreal. Would my brother have wanted this outcome? Would he have wanted us to become friends? Wherever he was, was he smiling? Asking myself that, I watched the fog-shrouded sky as Noah, Savana, Titanium, and I trudged along. We'd been lost in our own worlds ever since Thierry sent us off.

We were going in the opposite direction of the river and neighboring town, now in unfamiliar territory. At least, it was unfamiliar to me. Savana and Noah seemed to know where they were going. They didn't even need a map.

The trees thinned before giving way to a large, frozen lake. It stretched on for as far as I could see. Large, scattered patches of frosty grass created a path across the lake. Similarly grassy islands floated in the air, defying gravity. Thick mist made it impossible to see where the lake ended.

Deciding this was a good resting point, we stopped at the edge for lunch. It was only bread rolls and jam, but it fit the fantasy world nicely. Savana and Noah quietly chatted about the mission while I sat on a rock several feet away, coaxing myself to eat. They weren't paying attention to me, but I still asked myself, *Is my chewing too loud? What if I didn't put enough jam and appear ungrateful?* Back under my mom's roof, jam was a delicacy. Or maybe I feared gorging myself too quickly and getting sick. It'd happened to me enough times in the past when my mom would free me from the shed and toss a pathetic sandwich by my feet. I always wolfed it down, only for my stomach to seize and reject it.

The only reason I forced the food down my throat was because Titanium couldn't eat it herself. She said that Shadow Guards share energy with their host, so it was crucial that I ate for both of our sakes.

Normally, I would've rolled my eyes at such words. Now, I gave her a small nod of acknowledgment and kept pecking away. It would be wrong of me to be mean, especially after how she helped me unlock my Mageia. That dreaded sensation of guilt returned.

"I never got to apologize," I mumbled to the cat.

Titanium looked over from where she surveyed the floating islands. "For what?"

"For not—not being kinder." I cringed at how childish it sounded. My fingers dug into the soft bread. "I thought—I thought I could do everything without your help. You...you just wanted to be nice. I didn't listen." Absently, I brought my hand to my cheek, where the bandages from her claws still sat.

"Don't be silly," Titanium purred. "It's okay. We're friends!"

Are we? It was a term I didn't toss around lightly, not even risking to use it with Oliver. Titanium was no human, though. Only humans were capable of destruction. With that in mind, I sighed, "I guess we are."

I managed to choke down about half the roll before I began to fear it'd resurface. Making sure Noah wasn't looking, as he'd teased me for this numerous times, I stuffed the roll into my hoodie's pocket. That little spot was a nesting ground for crumbs. It no longer bothered me, and I didn't think twice about it as I stood and approached the frozen lake. With only Titanium's attention on me, I crouched by the edge and grabbed the bandages over my cheeks. I ripped them clean off, wincing as they peeled away from my skin.

"At least I gave you a cool design!" Titanium chirped, moving to stand beside me.

I looked at my reflection in the ice, a warped version of Tyler staring back at me. Two triangle-shaped scars traveled from my jawline to my nose. They almost looked like whiskers. I glanced down at Titanium, pointing to my face. "These aren't, uh, these aren't going to fade?"

"Nope. We're bonded for life." She looked proud of herself, like a kid on their first day of art class.

Before I could reply, a shadow fell over us. I peeked over my shoulder only to find Noah standing right there. To be out of any sort of kicking range, I scrambled away before standing.

"We're gonna keep going. Are you coming, or are you going to keep admiring your reflection?" Noah studied the scars on my face before rolling his eyes.

I wasn't! My mouth opened to say it out loud, but all I managed was, "Sorry."

"I think the scars looks cool!" Savana looped her arm behind my neck, ignoring how I jumped. "Let's go. You're both dawdling now."

I ducked away from her touch, scratching the spot her arm had rested on to ward off the tingling feeling left behind. To make sure no one touched me again, I picked up Titanium and followed Noah, who was storming away. Savana bounced after us.

Noah hopped onto the first mini-island jutting out of the frozen lake. Savana joined him, and once I'd seen the platform was stable, I followed. In a single-file line, we jumped from island to island. With every move forward, the mist followed and created a bubble around us.

At one point, the ground trembled and an agonized groan echoed through the air. I yelped, dropping Titanium and covering my ears with my hands. "What was that?" I couldn't hear myself over my pounding heart.

As the tremors faded, Savana glanced at the frozen lake. "Oh, those are just the whagers. Whale-tigers. See?" She pointed to a blur of navy-blue stripes under the ice.

It took a moment of squinting before I saw how the stripes outlined the shape of a massive whale frozen in the lake. "What the—is it okay?"

"It's just hibernating, so don't worry. When the ice thaws, it'll take the underwater path back to the Timber Coast." Savana shrugged the question off, hopping to the next island. "Sometimes, it cries out like that. I wonder if it misses the ocean."

"Probably." There came the secondhand grief again. With a tight chest, I picked up my pace.

Reaching the other side of the lake brought sighs of relief from everyone. My legs were weary from leaping and my eyes were heavy from straining against the fog. Seeing how the sun was already dipping below the horizon, I expected another break of some sort, but Noah didn't even bat an eye. He simply carried on walking. Unfortunately for both of us, Savana didn't argue.

We found ourselves in a valley with tons of rocks and shrubs. Patches of snow and ice were sprinkled along the ground. The wind carried the scent of salt as it whistled through the open land and nipped at our bare skin.

"Is—" I started to pipe up, but the words got stuck in my mouth. *It's a stupid question, though. You're supposed to know this already!* But everyone was looking at me as we walked, meaning I couldn't stay silent and pretend I didn't blurt that out. "Is–is all this—is all this, uh, important? The–the whole...thing." *Because you're all acting so determined like this is your life's mission.* While the rest of the sentence flowed in my mind, I knew I couldn't manage to say it out loud.

Noah grunted as he kicked a stray twig. "What, getting the necklace back? Of course it is. That gem is one of the six that powers the portal. The further it gets, the weaker the portal."

"Mystral isn't evil like that," Savana added. "She's neutral. Like I said, she just wants shiny things." A smile twitched along her lips.

I frowned at her, confused.

Savana shrugged. "We met when the Cataclysm was recruiting when we were little. She didn't like it, though, and dropped out. We went our separate ways, but we still write letters to each other." Her blue gaze warmed as she spoke about her old friend. "Working for Thierry gives you a bunch of connections."

"Or maybe you just have a big mouth," Noah retorted from up ahead.

Titanium crawled into my hoodie from the bottom and poked her head up through the neck hole. Her forehead bumped against my chin. "You're human, Noah. Don't shame Savana for knowing her own species."

Savana and I nodded to back her up. Titanium had a point. I studied Noah's ears, the way they didn't twitch like Savana's or even have a point like mine. He was simply human. Still, he didn't hide it in a world of strange Meraki. He'd gone through the same process McKenzie and I endured to unlock his ability.

What do I have to do to be strong like that? I wondered. I watched the way strands of Noah's fluffy hair bounced over his forehead. His eyes were set and locked on an invisible target. I'd asked myself that question for years.

Without the luxurious protection of undergrowth and trees that we'd had in the forest, we made camp by a cluster of ruins jutting out of the valley ground. Having on solid concrete before, I didn't even think to complain.

There was no late-night chatting, unlike at Indra Academy, where Bryce and Oliver always whispered across the room to each other. It was usually about homework or scheduling, or something funny that happened in class. I was unable to relate to any of it, but I still enjoyed falling asleep to their hushed voices and tired giggles.

Noah had rolled onto his side almost immediately without a "goodnight," simply turning his back to us and leaving it at that.

Savana watched the stars for a while, holding her hand up toward them like she wanted to high-five the sky. I curled into the tightest ball possible, holding Titanium close like a stuffed animal until her snores and the wind faded away.

My first thought upon entering my dream was, *Thierry needs to get more creative with these landscapes.* It was the same black sky and blue lake as always. At first, I didn't think much of it, having gotten used to these dreams. That's when a large hand rested on my shoulder. Without a doubt, it was Thierry's.

I didn't dare move. But the feeling of it made me want to pull my hair out and scream or kick him. Whatever fragile peace was in the air threatened to collapse.

"You're acting like I'm going to do something evil," Thierry laughed around my tense posture. "Do you really think that badly of me?"

I let out a guilty "no."

Thierry finally removed his hand from my shoulder, observing the black landscape around us. "I can help you on the road, you know. McKenzie has always had a weak spot. She fluctuates between assisting me and rebelling against my ideas. Why learn from someone unreliable?"

Does that make me unreliable, too? "I'm sorry—and okay."

Thierry looked down at me, raising one eyebrow.

"I'm sorry," I repeated. Had I done something wrong?

"Is apologizing all you're good for?" he asked.

"I'm sorr—"

This time, Thierry cut me off with a slap across the face. I stumbled back, staring at him in shock.

He smiled, and it was so warm yet so cold. "We'll break that habit."

I wanted to apologize again, so I bit my tongue.

"But yes, allow me to teach you something new."

I nodded vigorously.

Thierry's smile became one of satisfaction. He walked until there were a few feet of distance between us. "Noah told me about your earlier training session regarding defense. Why don't we make this a lesson in both that and offense?" He paused, nostrils smoking, before he nodded to himself. "Yes, let's do that. But why don't we turn it into a partner session?"

He snapped his fingers, and the water around me rippled. I spun around to see Oliver standing a few feet away, patting himself down, seeming confused. He must've been teleported from another dream.

Once he spotted me, his eyes brightened, only to narrow once he saw Thierry. "What's going on?" The rigidness of his tone made my stomach churn.

Thierry grinned at him. "I'm giving you and Tyler some training. I can feel your unlocked Mageia. You'd appreciate the help, right?" In the dream, he created a pair of floating hands that hovered over Oliver, stroking his hair and touching his cheeks. "I'm so curious to see the bond I sense between you and Tyler," Thierry continued. "I want to see the Assembly of Six reborn for myself, before it's torn apart."

Oliver balled his hands into fists, swinging them to shoo the extra hands away. "I would never—"

He was out of his mind for fighting back! I stormed over, grabbing his collar and yanking him down so I could meet his eyes. Only the urgency of the situation allowed me to use such force. "You be quiet!" I hissed.

"What? Why?"

I could see my angered reflection in his eyes. "You can't argue with him. He's the emperor! The authority! You're supposed to do what he says."

Oliver gawked at me.

"It's for both our safety," I added in a whisper. "Please."

"Is he hurting you?" Oliver's voice was dangerously low. He was focusing on my newly uncovered scars.

"No." The cheek Thierry had slapped throbbed as I lied. "But he could if we make him angry. That's why you have to listen."

Oliver opened his mouth to protest, but he hesitantly said, "Alright." He pulled away from me and faced Thierry with suspicion glinting in his emerald eyes. "I'll accept your help."

"Excellent." Thierry's ears relaxed. "Now, then, as I was telling Tyler, I will fire a series of attacks at you both. Unlike Noah, I'm not a solar mutation, so don't fear anything too serious. Of course, that doesn't mean you should let your guard down."

"H-how is—how is that offense, though?" I dug my fingernails into my palms, shoulders tensing up.

"Because your job is to come closer and tap my shoulder." Thierry grinned wider, like he'd been waiting his whole life for this. "In a real scenario, you'd be able to stab or freeze me."

I shuddered. "I won't."

Thierry raised his palm toward me. "I know you won't." With that, fire blasted straight at Oliver and me.

I dropped to the ground, hitting the shallow water to let an ice crystal erupt before us. It shielded Oliver and me, but the orange glow on the other side reminded us that time wasn't our ally.

"This seems like a bad time to admit I don't know how this works," Oliver said with an embarrassed smile.

"You'll bore me to death like this," Thierry called.

I gritted my teeth, trying to decide if I should leave Oliver or not. This wasn't a scenario I wanted to become a sitting duck in. *So why should Oliver?* I scolded myself. I pulled Oliver into the open, creating a wall of ice for us to run behind. An inferno blasted the other side. Heat tickled my scarred cheeks.

"Pretend there's a barrier in your mind!" I barked as we ran. "And then let it loosen up. Go crazy!" *Just not in my direction.*

Oliver shook my hand away, holding his palm in Thierry's direction. His freckles glowed, and moments later, fire blasted from his fingers. "That's unreal!"

It was exhilarating to be the expert for once, not overshadowed by Noah and Savana. Thierry's attack let up just long enough for me to whisper, "Get him from the other side."

"Predictable!" Thierry shot ribbons of fire into the sky, letting embers fall toward us like little comets.

Oh yeah? Before I moved, the sloshing at my ankles made me pause. Looking down, I caught the crystal blue water and my reflection. *Water and ice are the same, aren't they?*

Praying that Oliver would cover me, I raced for the open, jumped, and landed on a sheet of ice. In a matter of seconds, the ground froze over into an ice rink. With Thierry's feet stuck in place, I skidded closer, swerving and ducking around the fire lashing from his arms.

Maybe I was a little too cocky, because while avoiding another attack, I swerved too far and fell right onto the ice. At the speed I was going at, I crashed right into Thierry's legs.

His fiery palm hovered right over me, and suddenly, I was reminded of my mother's lashing fists. The next thing I knew, I was cowering against the ice.

But before Thierry could do anything, Oliver leapt forward from behind my father, punching his shoulder. Thierry and I stared at him in silence for a moment before his proud expression faltered. "Oops."

"We're sorry." I scrambled to my feet, taking a few steps back.

Thierry just stared at his feet, still trapped in the ice, watching as smoke rose from the spot. The ice melted enough for him to step out of the hole and onto solid ground. "You're both inexperienced, but that wasn't half bad. You have a decent sense of agility."

"Right!" I stood taller, trying to control my smile. "Th-thank you!"

We continued to practice that tactic for the rest of my dream, pausing after every round for criticism. It made me guiltily happy when Oliver earned more lecturing than me. Where had this praise been all my life? There was something special about hearing it from an adult. It felt *real*. It was different from the type Dominic used to give me.

I can see your practice is paying off.

Our mission is safe in your hands.

I'm proud of you.

Oliver listened to every comment with narrowed eyes, frowning at me like he couldn't believe it. For some reason, it upset me that he didn't share my enthusiasm. What had happened to the kind, accepting teenager from Indra Academy?

I awoke sore and exhausted, like I hadn't gotten a wink of sleep, and yet, I was smiling. While the dream felt like it had lasted for-ever, the sky was still dark. The two moons stretched high into the sky, meaning daylight wouldn't break for a long while. Everyone else was asleep, or at least I thought so.

Glancing over my shoulder, I noticed Noah sitting atop one of the rocks we made camp beside, looking in the direction we'd come from.

Catching my stare, Noah faced me with a blank expression. "What?"

"Nothing," I whispered. *Sorry.*

Noah huffed and turned back to where he'd been facing before.

I followed his gaze, trying to see what was so interesting. It was nothing, but maybe that's what made it special. It was random. From where I lay stiff on the ground, I adjusted myself into a sitting position.

"Hey, do you ever, uh…" Once I realized I said it out loud, my voice died.

"What?"

It's too stupid. I hugged myself, wincing at the soreness in my shoulders. "Do you miss him?"

The following silence was filled by Titanium's snoring.

Noah didn't need to ask who "him" was. He narrowed his eyes at the dark horizon, lips pursing. "Of course I do. What kind of shitty friend do you think I am?" He finally pulled his gaze away from his target, focusing on me. His glare could kill if it wanted to.

I squirmed under the intensity of his attention. "Thi-Thierry said that he knows information on Dominic. I think he's, uh, I think he's alive."

"Yeah." Noah grimaced. His next words came out softer than his glare. It was almost uncharacteristic. "I think so, too. Remember the water trick he pulled that day?" He surveyed his hand, his fingers twitching from the white fire they held within. "That was Mageia. I just know it."

The day Dominic left us was blurry in my memory. It was overshadowed by my mom's reaction. A record-breaking three days in the shed dulled all the details. But when I thought back hard enough, I could see Dominic crouching by the lake at Central Park, weaving a stream of water around his fingertips as if he was a mermaid. Noah and I were at his side, gasping in awe. The whimsical moment didn't last long, of course.

However, I'd never forget Noah screaming for his friend and Mia's shattered expression when she heard her role model was gone. I'd never forget how my mom audibly wished they'd kidnapped me and not Dominic.

"Which means he's somewhere here," Noah continued. "It's been three years, but I'm positive. Hell, I'll search for three hundred years. I've been trying to get help from Thierry, since he's so well known around Derngate, but he won't listen to me. If he keeps it up, I'll take matters into my own hands, I swear."

Something about his speech tugged at my heart. How was it that big, scary Noah actively cared so much about a childhood friend? Did that make me feel jealous or stupid? Maybe a little bit of both. All this time, I'd been accepting defeat; that Dominic wasn't coming back. Even now, with Thierry's promise to tell me more, I'd left it at that. Looking Noah up and down again, guilt pulsed in my throat. Was that the reason he'd run away to Derngate, too?

I carefully pulled away from Titanium and stood up. Instinctively, I slid my hands into my hoodie pocket, only to pull away when I remembered the half-eaten roll stuffed in there. Crumbs stuck between my fingers. Aware of Noah's curious gaze on me, I muttered, "Going for a walk."

As I left, like it was a sign, tiny snowflakes began to spiral to the earth.

CHAPTER TWENTY-TWO

THE ICE MUTATIONS

OLIVER

MCKENZIE HAD SHOWED US a shortcut to the Timber Coast so we could easily catch up with the Cataclysm group. Still, night had fallen before we found any traces of Tyler or the other teenagers with him. We made camp where the forest broke away into empty land, deciding to stick to the sheltered area. Tension remained thick in the air. I could tell I wasn't the only one thinking about our farewell to McKenzie.

"Since Thierry is staying behind, it's best if I do, too. I don't want him to grow suspicious if I disappear as well," she'd explained. "But don't worry. I won't be staying here for much longer. I was his right-hand woman for almost twelve years. It'll sting to leave him, but I know it's the right thing to do."

She'd given us some gold coins and told us to buy supplies and food with them if we stumbled upon another town.

I'd flashed McKenzie a reassuring look. "Isabel and Camila will be happy to know you helped us, even in the shadows."

Something had flickered in McKenzie's eyes, but it was gone when she blinked. She smiled, but she looked tired. "I hope so." Her final piece of advice was that we should keep something shiny on hand to distract Mystral, at which Diana nodded solemnly.

Even in the dark, part of me wanted to keep searching. The irritation I felt when the others refused to push on almost surprised me. Vincent kept snapping back, insisting I shouldn't nag them because "we're only human." Diana didn't stop him and simply looked the other way.

Luke tried to find a middle ground for us. As we huddled together for the night, he rested one hand on my shoulder and murmured, "Pushing yourself will only save the consequences for later."

I tried to go to bed early while the others got a campfire started. Not only did it take a while to doze off, but my unconsciousness was plagued by Thierry summoning me and Tyler for a training session. When I groggily rejoined the others at the campfire, Luke asked, "Are you alright?"

"I'm fine," I whispered, lowering my head. The younger students were watching, and I didn't want them to see how the distance between us and Tyler was getting to me. Tyler was skating on thin ice around Thierry to keep himself safe. He believed that if he did as his father said, he wouldn't get hurt.

We had to save him before that ice cracked.

Vincent examined us from across our mini-circle, crossing his arms over his chest. But before he could say anything, Diana intervened with a nervous laugh. "Say, Luke and Oliver, what are your plans when we get home? Since you guys are juniors and all. Do you know what you want to pursue after high school?"

"Well…" Luke fiddled with his hands. He mimicked holding a guitar before his hands fell back into his lap. "I've always been passionate about music and stuff. If that doesn't work out, I can build on my cooking skills. Maybe I'll help my dad with his restaurant."

When everyone turned to me, I frowned and focused on the fire. "For a while, I considered something like being a marine biologist." I pulled my hair out of my ponytail, twirling one of the ginger strands around my finger. "But I've been away from the ocean for quite a while."

"What does that have to do with it?" Vincent finally looked up from where he started rummaging in his bag.

"I mean…I moved away from the Pacific Ocean to attend school in New York. Besides, I don't really have the stamina for swimming." Saying it out loud had heat crawling up my throat. Who was I to complain about work when I'd never had a job before? Bryce had a part time job in the city, but he always came home feeling fine—maybe just a little hungry. Meanwhile, I'd been joining him and Luke on journeys downtown less and less over the years. It required energy I just didn't have.

Vincent looked me up and down but didn't comment. Instead, he turned to Diana. "Why did you ask? As a freshman, you still have a lot of time before you need to think about the future." As he spoke, he slowly pulled his black notebook from his bag.

Diana let out a short laugh and glanced at the dark scenery around us. "Why not? It's never too early to start planning." She nodded in my direction. "Weren't you already making big decisions at fourteen? You came to New York all on your own!"

"Yeah. It wasn't an easy choice to make, of course." The lie left a sour taste in my mouth. At the time, I'd been so sure my best friend would support the move. I chose New York to be that much closer to him. Even when that backfired, I held no regret in my decision. My moms had tried teaching me a little French, and it didn't take long for me to realize the trouble I'd have in a different country.

"Traveling solo must be fun," Luke mused. "I'd love to try it someday."

Vincent stiffened, frowning at his brother. "Where would you go?"

Even I could tell that translated to "please don't abandon me." I remembered Vincent being inseparable from Luke as a freshman, so I could only imagine how stressful it was to think of his big brother leaving home someday for good.

Luke didn't hesitate. "I'd visit Mom."

"But that's so far away!" Vincent groaned.

I dug through my memory for the times Luke had talked about his mom in the past. "She's in...South Africa, right? That's, like, two long flights away."

Luke wasn't fazed by our lack of enthusiasm. "Yep! The traveling part is easier now that I'm older. Besides, we visit every winter break,"—He grinned at Vincent mischievously—"so get ready for next month!"

Vincent laid down on his back, rubbing his eyes. "That's only if all this blows over by then." His notebook slid off his lap, pages fluttering and folding as it landed awkwardly.

No one responded right away. Vincent had a point whether we liked it or not.

"Do we have any guesses on how long this'll last?" Diana asked in a rather small voice. "We don't even know what our ultimate goal is. What happens after we find Tyler and the fire necklace?"

"From the looks of it, we gotta stop Thierry from using the portal separating our worlds." I narrowed my eyes as I recalled my shared dream with Tyler from just now. Thierry knew about the Assembly of Six and said he wanted to see the connection for himself. Did that mean he was onto us and already recognized us as obstacles?

Luke frowned. "We don't have much information other than that. I want to assume Isabel and Camila will tell us more when all of us are united."

"It's a gamble to assume they'll tell us," Vincent huffed.

Seeing his notebook again reminded me of the dreams he mentioned a few nights ago. I cleared my throat and gestured to it with the tilt of my head. "Got any more ominous dream-messages for us?"

"Why do you care?" Vincent wrinkled his nose but sat up and flipped through the pages anyway. "Nothing precise as of recently. It's a whole bunch of whispering nonsense about shit like clocks freezing over and eyes watching from all angles."

I'm certain the air around us chilled at such images. A sharp wind blew through the clearing, snuffing the fire out.

"I definitely feel the pressure of a million eyes watching us." Diana swept her gaze around our little circle. "You guys realize we might have to do this whole search again for whoever the sixth person is, right?"

We all groaned.

"That's why it's so important we—" I started to say.

Luke clamped his hand over my mouth. "So important we get some rest." When I glared at him, he shook his head and murmured, "I know you want to find Tyler, but it won't help if you burn yourself out."

I shoved his hand away from my mouth. "I know, but—"

"I'll take the first shift," Diana cut me off.

She sounded a little too eager, but I muttered my acceptance anyway.

I was roused from my dreamless sleep by a strong wind blowing on my face. My eyes opened slowly to see the bright appearance of Crystal Lacey crouching over me.

"What do you want?" I whispered furiously. Just like after every other sleep I'd had recently, there was nothing refreshing about waking up. No new alertness.

"Your friend got up and left." Crystal pointed to the vacant spot where Diana had been sitting earlier.

That caught my attention. I sat up and glanced around. Diana was nowhere to be seen, and Luke and Vincent were fast asleep. *Didn't bother to wake one of us up to take her shift, huh?* My annoyance didn't hinder my concern, though. "Did you see what direction she went in?"

Crystal nodded to the empty valley beyond our resting point. "Somewhere around there. I can see her tracks in the dark, so let's go."

"Thanks." I stood up, only to hesitate. My hand was already reaching for my flashlight, but didn't I have my own light...in my body?

Tyler's advice from our dream came rushing back to me, and I relaxed my hand. A small flame flickered into existence.

"Just don't burn the forest down," Crystal said. With that, she spun around and walked away. I followed, carefully balancing the fire.

The spirit moved as swift as always, but she offered no other words. She just stared straight ahead as we walked. She didn't even make a snarky comment or bad joke.

As annoying as her presence usually was, I could tell something was different. I jogged until I fell in step with her, taking time to soak in her appearance. She wasn't as regal as she was in the carving by Indra Academy's magic pool, looking more like a regular teenager than a powerful being. Recalling the carving now, I jolted upon remembering something.

"Are you helping us because Tyler is your successor?" I asked into the silence. "That means you match Mageian powers."

"Yes." Crystal's voice was small.

"So, you were an ice mutation."

"Yes."

I studied her again, focusing on the three scars across her face. "Were you...killed for being one? Like the rest?"

Crystal stopped walking. She looked up at the sky, where tiny snowflakes flurried around. "When the news came out, that everyone was going after the ice mutations, I went into hiding at Indra Academy. My friends—the original Assembly of Six—they did their best to protect me. But my–my, uh—" Her voice faltered, and she gave me a nervous look. "My lover...She was a fire Meraki, on the side assisting the murders. She tried to ignore the pressure, but we kept arguing and arguing until we both finally snapped." She let out a shaky laugh. "We were fighting it out with our powers, but fire always wins against ice. That didn't really matter in the end, though. We killed each other."

I was left in stunned silence. For a moment, I wondered what I would've done if I found myself in that situation with Luke or Bryce. I wasn't afraid to admit I didn't have the brawn to kill either of them, but they could wipe me out in a heartbeat. Would they ever go to such measures if it was needed?

"Oh." I finally forced the word out, realizing I was just staring at her silently. "Oh, man. That must've been intense. I'm sorry."

I was suddenly reminded of the abandoned letter to Crystal in Indra Academy's library. Was that her lover who wrote it? Had they died before she got to read it?

Crystal smiled brightly, as if she hadn't just described her death. "It's alright. We're on complicated terms, both being part of the old Assembly, you know, but we manage. She had the fire Mageia in the group, just like you do!"

"Good to know." Weirdly enough, I felt guilty hearing that I had a fire Mageia. I was in the same group that helped to wipe out ice mutations. *But that was ages ago. You aren't directly at fault.*

I was about to speak again when a low growl cut me off. "What was that?"

Crystal's long ears perked up. "Trouble, from the sound of it."

We broke into a run toward the sound. Looming in the near distance was a yellow orb of light, and as we drew near, it turned out to be the same lion from the other night.

Diana was pinned under Ruslan's bright paw, writhing and grunting but, luckily, unharmed. She was snapping "Let me go, you dumb cat!" when we got within earshot. As she glanced to the side, Diana gasped. "Oliver, great timing!"

"What happened?" I shifted my gaze from her to the lion and back again. I extinguished my flame to put my hair into a ponytail before relighting it back. Adrenaline combated my sleepiness.

"He decided to go for a walk, and I tried to bring him back! And he got mad at me!" Diana squirmed some more, punching the lion's ankle. "Let me go!"

I stared at Diana and the lion, not quite sure what to make of it. All I knew was that Luke was still safe and asleep at our camp, meaning Ruslan must've acted on his own consciousness.

I looked to Crystal, who didn't seem fazed in the slightest, for help. "I'm a ghost, so I can't interact physically, but I'll give you assistance. First, ramp up that blaze! Make gestures that the fire can copy."

I willed the flame to grow until it covered my whole hand. It turned into a toasty glove. *Don't fail me now,* I begged myself silently.

"Hey, Ruslan!" I yelled at the top of my lungs. When the beast noticed me, I jumped and waved my hand. "Get off her! Hey, over here!"

Ruslan bared his fangs. He made a sound like groaning metal before launching himself at me. Unsheathed claws stretched in my direction, making a swipe for my body.

I raised my hand in front of my face with a yell. As it made contact with the massive paw, a slamming wave of heat knocked me backwards. Miraculously, I was unscathed. The freckles along my arm glowed orange. Flaming threads and embers weaved around my body.

"Well, don't just stand there!" Crystal teleported to my side with her hands on her hips. "Keep moving! Use your fire to deflect his and push forward."

"We really should've gone over this earlier!" I snapped in response.

Diana glared at me from where she struggled to sit up. "This is no time to be talking to yourself, Oliver!"

Ruslan advanced again, but this time, I dodged and raced over to Diana. Helping her to her feet, I hissed, "Go back to the others! Or at least fetch Luke to control his lion!"

"But I want to help!" Diana snapped, pulling away from me. In the firelight, I caught the endless superficial cuts and scratches spotting her skin.

I slashed at the lion as it tried again. Sparks and flames erupted as we clashed. It turned the snow below us orange. "You can help by bringing back up! I don't know if I can control him by myself."

Diana ducked behind me to protect herself from the embers. "What do you think he was trying to do by himself?"

Sweat beaded my forehead as I parried Ruslan back. "I don't know! Just find Luke and get out of here. You aren't exactly in fighting condition."

"Are you for—ugh, fine!" Diana grabbed a nearby stone and chucked it at Ruslan's forehead. He reared back in confusion. While he was distracted, she made a run for it as best as she could in flats.

That left me to face the beast by myself. What was I supposed to do? Kill him? Make friends with him? The lion was using Luke's body as a vessel, and I didn't want to accidentally hurt him by hurting the creature.

I wasn't sure if Ruslan was aware of that. He kept swatting at me like I was a mouse, his agitation only growing when I fought back. Eventually, he must've realized this wouldn't work. He stood straight, like a hunting dog, and opened his mouth wide, teeth angled at me, and started to glow.

White fire exploded from his mouth, right in my direction. I barely managed to scramble out of the way, but not without singeing the sleeve of my coat. The ground caught fire, pale flames licking hungrily into the night sky. Dead grass spared from the slushy snow crackled as it spread the fire around.

"How hot is that stuff?" I wheezed.

Crystal blew gales of wind around the fire, trying to contain it. "It's strong enough to cook you alive, so I wouldn't recommend finding out the hard way."

Just as I caught my footing, Ruslan tried again. This time, he turned his head, creating a whole zigzag of fire. As the blast approached me, I took Crystal's advice, raised my fire, and ran right at the beast. My flames acted as a shield, parting the inferno all around me. Still, that wasn't enough, as the force of Ruslan's power swept me off my feet and sent me flying backwards.

I must've hit my head because Crystal's nagging turned into a hazy, underwater-like annoyance. Somewhere nearby, a new voice shouted, "Hey!"

A hooded figure had caught Ruslan's attention, leading him away from the blazing grass. They dodged every attack with ease, a small and nimble body allowing them to navigate quickly. Their facial features glowed bright blue in the dark, as did their palms. They shot ice at the ground, freezing the spreading flames in place.

The hood covered their eyes, but I felt them glancing my way. Just like that, the figure paused their attack, mouth slightly open.

Ruslan took that as a chance to bat at the new enemy, swatting them feet away.

I stood and raced back to the fight. My arm swung in the empty air, like I was playing tennis, sending a wave of orange fire right at the lion.

As he twirled around to face me, the newcomer continued to freeze Ruslan's fire. Every so often, they chucked an icicle at the lion. We went back and forth until the creature was chasing its poor tail.

Once the fire was extinguished, the mysterious figure slammed their foot in front of them. Massive ice crystals erupted from the ground, trapping Ruslan in place. The beast tossed his head and roared, sending a stream of white fire into the sky. Little embers fluttered like snowflakes.

"I owe you," I sighed. I turned to face the newcomer with a smile, but it dropped almost right away.

An ice mutation. I hadn't been able to connect the dots earlier due to the fight.

The hood fell off the figure to reveal none other than Tyler.

He was staring back at me with an expression just as dumbfounded. The blue markings along his face flickered before fading. Before I could speak, he turned and fled into the darkness.

"Wait!" I took a step after him, but it was too late. He was gone. The toll of the fight and my panic from earlier caught up to me, and I sank to my knees. Hot and cold flashes coursed through me.

Crystal stared into the darkness Tyler vanished into. After a moment, she sighed and evaporated into nothingness. Her job here was done for now.

The trapped lion made a low sound, to which I responded with "Don't patronize me."

A flurry of footsteps from behind made me turn. Luke, Diana, and Vincent were heading my way, their faces lined with surprise as they took in the frozen scene. They were carrying our belongings, as if they'd expected needing to make a narrow escape. But once they saw the fight had already ended, they dropped our things with sighs of relief.

"Diana said the lion got loose?" Luke looked around, his shoulders drooping once he spotted Ruslan partially encased in the giant icicles. "Great." He approached the lion, murmuring soothing words to relax him.

Vincent wandered around the clusters of ice, running his hand along their jagged surfaces. "I thought you had a fire Mageia, Oliver." He paused to register me on the ground. "You good?"

"I *do* have a fire Mageia." I extinguished my flames and dusted my hands off. "Someone else came along to help me. And yes, I'm fine."

Diana clutched her skirt, tightening her fists around the soft fabric. In the dark, her eyes shone with tears. "I just wanted to help. I'm so sorry—I thought I could do something like navigate up ahead but then the lion followed me and...I lied when he said he got loose. He came to stop me from running off. I'm sorry."

Ruslan let out another low groan, and Luke pat the ice separating them. "That's right. I think Ruslan only attacked Oliver thinking he would let Diana leave again."

"That...makes sense." I gave Diana a reassuring smile. "Hey, don't worry about it. You actually did help a lot. Were you the one who sent that other guy to help?"

She straightened up. "Yeah! I saw him lurking around and asked. He was closer, so I figured he could help while I fetched Vincent and Luke."

"That was exactly who we're looking for." I wanted to laugh, but she still looked shaken, and I didn't want to risk further bruising her pride. "That was Tyler! It means we're on the right track!"

"Seriously?" Diana grinned. "That's great!"

I rose to my feet unsteadily, trying to ignore how the floor swayed. I was seeing double the amount of ice crystals I thought there were. "If we get moving, we could easily catch up with him."

"Have you not learned anything from this?" Luke sighed. "Oliver, I think you've had enough action for one night. You look ready to crash."

I started to protest, but the sounds died in my throat. Even in the dark and with all my efforts to conceal my growing fatigue, Luke could see right through the act. As I settled back down on the ground, I had to accept that I probably would've passed out long before I found Tyler in this state. When Luke continued to watch me, perhaps to see if I was alright, I rolled onto my side and faced away from the group.

How are you meant to keep everyone together if you can hardly do the same for yourself? The question burned into my mind.

In the corner of my vision, I saw Vincent sitting against an ice crystal. "We'll catch up with him tomorrow," he said, closing his eyes. "I was having a great dream before we were rudely interrupted." He reopened one eye, gaze landing on Diana. "Nice work, though, Princess."

At that, Diana beamed with enough light to outshine Ruslan.

CHAPTER TWENTY-THREE

DAMP FEATHERS AND DAMPER HEARTS

TYLER

I DON'T REMEMBER FALLING asleep. One minute I was running, and the next, I was jolting into Thierry's dream world again.

The racing thoughts hadn't left, though. Heaving for breath, I paced around, pulling my hair. *Oliver seriously followed me here. He meant it.*

"But why?" I shakily asked the empty, black sky. "Why is he putting himself in danger like this?"

"Because he's a fool," Thierry answered from behind me.

"You!" I spun around with my fists clenched. "Why am I back here? Leave–leave Oliver out of this!"

Thierry's expression was flat, almost bored. "You don't want him here?"

I shook my head. He was the last person I needed to see. I had to sort my thoughts before then.

"Very well." Thierry came closer, only to scowl when I backed up. "What? Do you not trust me? I don't recall doing anything bad."

I mentally punched myself. "I trust you."

"Good." Thierry snapped his finger, and the water between us gurgled and bubbled. The ground caved in, creating a bottomless sinkhole full of water.

"One key trait of those with a water Mageia is how they function in water," Thierry began. "They can hold their breath for long periods of time. A fraction of ice mutations should be able to do the same." His dark gaze swept over me, his lips twitching in a smile. He pulled an old-fashioned stopwatch from his pocket. "It's research I was never able to conduct due to the rarity of ice mutations."

Cold dread tugged in my stomach. *Is he going to make me swim in November? When it's the middle of the night and snowing in the real world?*

"You're going to get in and stay underwater for as long as you can. I'll time you."

I froze in place as I stared into the hole. He wanted me in there? What if I drowned? *No, no, remember what he said. Ice mutations should be able to hold their breaths. He needs you, Tyler.*

I couldn't disappoint him.

Aware of his burning gaze, I shimmied closer to the edge. My faint reflection stared back at me, subtly shaking his head as if telling me to back down. It disappeared as I sucked in a breath and jumped.

Icy shock rippled through my body when I hit the water. My limbs seized up. My mouth itched to open for air. Every rational fiber in my body screamed at me to get out, but it was overridden by the need for praise. My eyes opened, blinking rapidly as they struggled to see in the dim water. I was expecting to feel pins and needles piercing my skin, but I felt oddly comfortable.

Fish swim in water the way birds fly through the air. This is fine. Do birds see the wind? Do fish see the water? I can see it…

I felt no tightness in my chest. No aching. It was just me, the darkness, and the bubbles slipping past my cheeks.

I'm not sure how long I floated in the quiet for. An eternity must have passed before a sharp ache pierced my lungs. It felt like my rib cage was starting to cave in on itself.

Immediately, I thrashed around, kicking out instinctively. My hand scraped the edge of the hole, and I used it to pull myself up. Like a clumsy mermaid, I shot out of the water, gasping and spluttering for air. I tried hauling the rest of my body out, but I was shaking too much. My gaze darted to Thierry, hoping he'd notice my struggle.

He just stared down at me with a scowl. "Who said we were done? You were only down there for a minute."

Only? I let out a heavy exhale that formed a cloud in front of me. *I've never held my breath for that long before!* With a little whimper, I shook my head and tried freeing myself from the hole again.

"I'm not asking much of you, Tyler." Thierry's voice was as frigid as the night. He placed one hand on top of my head and lowered me back into the water. "You're looking at me as if I'm doing something wrong again. What did I tell you just now? You're the only one who thinks that way."

Am I? I was so busy trying to catch my breath, I didn't have the time to think about it. "But—"

"Let's not forget our promise. Will information on Dominic get you to cooperate?"

My silence said enough. Thierry reset the time on his stopwatch. His frown softened into something less frightening. "Now start again."

I cycled through floating underwater and coming back up for critique more times than I could count. Some of the icy water I swallowed, and the rest went up my nose as my energy faded.

"You can do better than this." Thierry shook his head. "Did you know the ice mutations were ended because they were so powerful? Don't taint their legacy."

In my head, I apologized a million times.

But it was all worth it to hear Thierry say "Dominic is somewhere in Derngate" at the end.

I awoke lying on my back, to the sight of three faces shoved in front of me, belonging to none other than Savana, Noah, and Titanium. Behind them, the blazing, winter sun told me it was almost midday. Titanium and Savana looked beyond relieved, while Noah kept an unwavering, unamused expression. We were still surrounded by the valley.

"Um..." I wasn't sure of where to begin. My mouth tasted like salt. At first, I thought the thundering in my ears was leftover water from Thierry's experiment. A distant crash corrected me; it was an ocean wave. Was this the Timber Coast?

"Titanium said she found you unconscious in the middle of the valley." Savana scanned me for injuries with round eyes. She probably would've poked me if she didn't know I'd jump five feet out of my skin.

Noah glared down at me. "What the hell were you thinking? This isn't the time for fooling around."

I sat up and patted myself. My shoulder ached. I must have landed on it when I collapsed. *But how did that even happen?* I had no recollection of feeling faint after fighting the strange lion with Oliver. I had just abruptly stopped running, my mind sent straight back to Thierry's little world. *He made me pass out, didn't he?* Unease churned in my stomach.

Only when Titanium had climbed into my lap did I snap back to the present. I stiffened and glanced up at Noah. "Thierry said—Thierry confirmed Dominic is here. In–in Derngate."

"What?" As predicted, that didn't ease his moodiness. "Did he tell you that in a dream?"

I nodded.

Noah groaned and started to pace. He kicked at the dead high grass. "That's so unfair! Thierry *knows* I've been looking for Dominic. Why didn't he come to me? Why is he going to you, of all people?"

"Maybe because Tyler is Dominic's actual brother?" Titanium balanced herself on my shoulder. She dug her claws into my hoodie as I stood up.

"Whatever the case is, we need to get moving," Savana said before Noah could start yelling. She stood, dusting off her pants as if that concluded the squabble. "We should've reached Mystral's cavern by now. It's not that far."

I glanced behind us, sighing when I didn't see Oliver or the strange, giant, glittery lion. Maybe I imagined it. *No, no, you were clearly running from something.* It was probably best if we didn't stick around. "Okay."

"Actually," a new voice said out of nowhere, "you're closer than you think."

Yelping, we whirled around. Standing a few feet away was an insanely tall girl, her head cocked to one side like an intrigued puppy. She couldn't have been any older than seventeen or eighteen. Her hair was a tangled, dark brown mess that fell over her shoulders. Her bangs covered her eyes, leaving us to guess her expression from only her mouth and elf ears. She wore a tattered black dress with matching pants, as if her outfit had been mauled by crows on Halloween. Where her feet were supposed to be were a pair of talons.

What really caught my attention were the magnificent, black wings folded behind her.

No way! I was itching to run forward and touch them, but shock left me rooted in place. *They're real! She has real wings!* Could she talk to birds? Could she turn *into* a bird? My throat swelled with the questions, but I was left to choke on them while Savana squealed.

"Mystral! It's been so long!" She raced forward, pulling the bird lady into a tight hug. "How have you been?"

"It's about time you visited again!" Mystral hugged Savana back with enough strength to lift our purple-haired companion off her feet. Once Mystral had set Savana back on the ground, she turned her head in our direction. Under her thick bangs, I felt her staring at Noah, Titanium, and me. "Oh!"

"You know how Thierry is about taking days off." Savana waved her hand nonchalantly despite the sad words. She gestured to us with a nod. "You remember Noah O'Quinn, right? And over there is Tyler, who's—"

"A child!" Mystral cut her off with a squeal. A few, long strides later, she was looming over me. She was even taller than Noah, casting a shadow on everything below her. Leaning down to reach my pathetic height, she smiled at me, revealing her fangs. "He's so cute! Aw, he even has a kitty. Hi, kitty!"

I gave her a speechless, half-hearted wave. Her salty breath tickled my nose, giving me the urge to sneeze. Luckily, I managed to suppress it. Sneezing into the face of a talon-footed lady didn't sound like the best idea.

Noah cleared his throat. "We aren't here to play games. You have something of ours."

Mystral glanced around the dead valley. Her feathers fluttered in shiny, black waves. "I don't see anything of yours here."

"That's because—"

"Ooh!" Mystral let out an ear-piercing squeal. "You want a tour of my place, don't you? I've rearranged some of the rooms." She gave us all what appeared to be a hopeful look.

There wasn't a building in sight, but I didn't want to upset her. Carefully, I nodded.

"But can we please talk to you about something afterwards?" Savana asked. Now that she'd been reminded of our mission, Savana no longer matched the winged Meraki's bounciness. I never knew she could sound so calm.

"Yeah, of course!" Mystral ignored Savana's serious expression. She sauntered over to a patch of dead grass. With a simple flick of her finger, a trapdoor was flung open. A narrow, stone staircase spiraled downward.

Mystral had no trouble fitting her giant wings into the tight space, leading us down with great confidence. Her talons scraped the stone with every movement. Titanium went next, her glowing eyes acting like a flashlight. Savana and Noah followed, while I took the rear. I didn't trust Noah behind me on such a perilous staircase.

The more we descended, the more the walls widened. Cobwebs weaved through the air, spiders coming out to watch us visitors. They were glowing little critters, their backs adorned with neon patterns. It reminded me of Oliver's glowing freckles.

No, no, no! You're not supposed to think about Oliver. My inner voice spoke so ferociously I nearly slipped. I tried to ease my pounding heart with the thought *Thierry is just testing my loyalty. It's okay.* Could Thierry hear my thoughts? Was I soothing him as well as myself?

It wasn't totally impossible. He'd pulled on my consciousness the way a puppeteer pulls on a string. I couldn't tell if my light-headedness came from the stairs or the fear of Thierry doing it again.

The walls eventually broke away to reveal a massive cavern littered with stalagmites, stalactites, and glowing white mush-rooms. Ghostly, six-legged bunnies hopped from burrow to bur-row, scampering into hiding as we reached the ground.

The stalagmites reminded me of unlocking my Mageia, and I hugged myself tightly. There wasn't a chance I'd touch one and risk viewing another piece of my past.

Savana squealed in delight. Now that I thought about it, maybe it was a trait she'd picked up from Mystral. She pointed to one of the burrows. "You got seabunnies! How've they been?"

"Oh, they're great! They do a fantastic job with cleaning." Mystral waved her hand dismissively, like it wasn't totally weird to have a collection of six-legged bunnies. "My crystal collection has never been shinier."

I prayed her wings weren't those of a predatory bird that feasted on rodents.

She led Savana down a nearby corridor, their voices echoing through the cavern. It left Noah and me in silence. The ocean rattled in the background, which could only mean the Timber Coast was nearby.

"We'll find our necklace and get out of here," Noah said, even-tually breaking the silence. He scowled down at the seabunnies, who'd finally emerged from their burrows to scamper around again. "The sooner we get it back to Thierry, the better." His voice was thick with urgency. I recognized that tone.

It was familiar because the urgency came from the fear of disappointing someone.

CHAPTER TWENTY-FOUR

THE DAGGER AND THE HORSE

OLIVER

EVER SINCE MOVING TO New York, my head always shot up at the sound of an ocean wave. I never imagined myself missing the sea that much. This was the first time it didn't bring me comfort.

It was what woke me in the morning, and my heart clenched immediately. We were nearing the coast, which also meant we were closing the distance between us and Tyler. The anxiety I had about finding him was evolving. Was it fear that bringing him home wouldn't be as easy as we imagined? When we saw each other the previous night, he'd bolted like a stray cat.

I expressed my concern that it might happen again as we trudged our way through the lifeless valley. Each step brought us closer to the ocean. I could hear it.

Luke smiled at me tiredly. He seemed to be fine after last night's ordeal, after reabsorbing Ruslan. "I want to hurry as much as you do, but we, uh, got another issue." He nodded to Diana. "Wanna tell Oliver and Vince what you told me?"

Red bloomed on Diana's cheeks. She slowed to a halt and tugged at the top of her shirt, exposing a thin slash across her collarbones. The skin around it was inflamed. "It's nothing awful, don't worry. Ruslan just scratched me too hard when he pinned me down."

"Girl, what do you mean?" Vincent cried. "That's straight up infected!" After looking for a split second, he turned his head in the other direction, very interested in the ground below.

Diana scoffed and released her grip on the shirt's collar. "Don't be so dramatic. I'm fine."

"But..." I imagined Thierry's shadow perched behind Tyler. It made my blood boil. "What about Tyler? Um, can we split up for a little bit? Someone takes Diana to find help while the other two continue searching?"

Luke blinked in surprise. "We're not separating. Besides, saving time won't mean anything if you collapse from exhaustion or hunger."

I would've argued if he hadn't hit the bullseye with that comment.

"Yeah. We need food." Vincent cut to the point his brother was tiptoeing around. "We can multitask while we find Diana help." When she gawked at him, he shrugged. "What? You don't know how things in this weird place work. For all we know, an infection from a magical beast might mean serious trouble."

Diana shuddered. "Whatever. Only if we don't dine and dash again! Dewey and Reed aren't here to save us."

"She and Vince got a point." Luke seemed apologetic even though he'd shot down my idea. "I saw some smoke in the near distance, probably from a chimney. It's worth checking out. Maybe we can stock up on other supplies while we're at it."

"Do you think they've got batteries for our flashlights? We shouldn't risk them dying out here in the wilderness." Diana tugged the straps of her backpack.

Vincent raised an eyebrow. "I think batteries are the last thing this place will be selling."

The village of Ikrel proved him wrong. Half an hour later, we found ourselves in a cute town square, traipsing around and collecting free food samples from outdoor vendors. Nobody started with us. Maybe they didn't want to get involved with the hooded, cloaked teenagers, which I couldn't blame them for.

While Audun had been full of all sorts of Meraki, Ikrel seemed to mainly harbor those in the air category. Almost every Meraki we passed had wings, each uniquely colored like a different bird's. I kept thinking of Tyler, and how he always read those non-fiction bird books from Indra Academy's library. Would he have liked this place?

We found a small clinic that wasn't horribly overrun with patients. Only when we were waiting for a doctor did Vincent ask, "What if the doc wants to see Diana's ears?"

"That's what you're worried about?" she groaned.

Luke frowned at her. "Why wouldn't we be? You remember how being caught as human ended in Audun."

Diana paused before crossing her arms over her chest and looking the other way. "Yeah, yeah," she said through a grimace. Several heartbeats passed before she continued in a softer voice. "I just don't want to get undressed."

"That's okay. Why don't you talk to whoever looks you over?" I smiled. "I'm sure they'll understand."

"I'll beat them up if they don't," Vincent offered weakly.

Diana couldn't suppress a short laugh at that. "Sounds good."

I never caught the doctor's name, but she was a kind Meraki with silky, silver and yellow hair, a bit like a tropical fish. She didn't ask any of us about the hoods covering our ears and managed to inspect Diana's wound by only tugging the collar of her shirt down. Still, to ensure we didn't cross a boundary, us guys paid close attention to the flowery wallpaper.

"Has it been hurting you?" the doctor asked while washing her hands.

"It stings," Diana admitted. "In a way, it feels like a burn. But it's such a shallow cut!"

The doctor nodded. "Our bodies react to the magic of organisms in strange ways, huh? And you said you got this from a spirit lion?"

"Yep." Diana weaved fake fear into her expression. "It's been terrorizing Audun."

She, Vincent, and I glanced at Luke, who whistled a casual tune in response.

Instead of using antiseptics or tools like what we'd see back home, the doctor summoned an orb of clear, fresh water. She directed it over the slash. Diana tensed, then relaxed into the healing.

"Is that how you clean it?" I asked like a true foreigner or perhaps idiot.

"Well, yes, but I'm also healing it. Do you see the wound closing?" The doctor nodded to her hands controlling the water, which formed smaller threads that weaved along the crevice in Diana's skin. "Of course, water healing is nowhere near as powerful as ancient ice mutation methods."

We all hummed in acknowledgment.

Diana was given some ointment in a small vial to take with her, but when she asked how much it costed, the doctor laughed. "Young lady, why should you pay? It's free of charge."

There wasn't a way to explain the American healthcare system to her. Diana just fished one of McKenzie's gold coins out from her pocket and handed it to the doctor. "Take it anyways. Thanks for everything."

"Of course."

As soon as we'd waved goodbye, Diana strutted away and called, "Time to shop, boys!"

"Is she allowed to boss us around like that?" Luke looked more conflicted than angry.

After a moment of silence, we shrugged and followed her.

Ikrel's town square was lined with pop-up shops of all sorts. Luke, being the chef among us, took charge in buying some fruits to eat on the road while the rest of us explored.

What caught my eye were the stands labeled "CLEARANCE!" scattered around the town square. They were stocked with items from the human realm. I recognized books, an iPod, hair dye of all colors, plushies, and other little trinkets. My assumption would've been they were relics of the past if not for how modern they were. Most of the authors in the featured cookbooks were still alive!

"Why would anyone try selling an iPod when much better phones exist?" Diana eyed the table suspiciously.

"Well, they don't have iPhones here." I tapped the screen, and a message that the iPod was dead popped up. *Good luck to whoever buys this without a charger.*

"Screw the iPod. I heard there's a stable just outside the square." Vincent grinned, an expression that looked so foreign. "I wanna steal some horses."

"Huh?" Luke gawked at his brother. "Dad refused to let us get a dog—he won't even let us get a goldfish! What are you gonna do with a *horse*, let alone multiple?"

Vincent shrugged.

I had to stifle a laugh because it was so absurd. But at the same time...it made me think. "It might help us with transport and reaching Tyler quicker."

Diana blinked in surprise. "You too, Oliver?"

"But what happens when it's time to go home?" Luke's voice cracked.

Their comments flew right over my head, something I could blame Luke's tall height for. I nodded to Vincent. "Show me the stables." As we left, I waved to Luke and Diana, saying, "Just wait around here!"

I heard Diana call me an idiot under her breath, but I let it slide as I followed my unlikely ally.

The stables were built as a rectangle around the town square, and luckily, the place was empty other than the horses. They were startling creatures, with shaggy fur adorned with patterns of all sorts. Their red eyes reminded me of a rat's, with fangs protruding from their top lips. Low growls and snorts filled the air, which reeked of manure and hay.

While Vincent wandered around the stalls, I gravitated toward the nearby workbench. Different tools were scattered over the wooden surface. Again, I recognized modern, human inventions. How was that even possible?

Something glinted under a messy stack of papers, and I carefully moved them aside. Laying underneath was a twelve-inch dagger with a beautiful, wood-carved handle.

I sucked in a sharp breath. "Vincent, check this out!"

"Huh?" Vincent looked over his shoulder from where he was stroking one of the mutated horses. The creature bit his hand, and he jumped back with a yelp. "Damn thing! Ugh. What the hell is a knife doing in a stable?"

"It's a channeling dagger," a new voice spoke from the stable entrance. He had a surprisingly French accent. "You drive all your Mageian power into it, and boom! It gives you magic and a blade all at once."

Vincent and I stiffened. We spun around to see a tall air Meraki leaning against the wooden frame, twirling one of the feathers he'd lost. His wings resembled a peacock's, a gorgeous mixture of greens, blues, browns, and yellows. He wore a casual suit and a top hat that plastered his sea-green hair to his neck.

"*Bonjour!* Hello!" His lips twitched into a smile. "I saw you peeking around and thought I'd introduce myself. I'm Ludic, founder of the Tunnel Runners. We're the ones who bring human items to Derngate."

"But the portal is—" I cut myself off. Any ordinary Meraki probably didn't know about the portal. Tugging my hood further over my ears, I mumbled, "How interesting. Er, how, exactly?"

Ludic's feathers ruffled with pride. "The humans' side of the portal leads to a whole network of tunnels. They run all over New York! My team and I forage for items in need of a new purpose." His eyes narrowed on Vincent and me. "We're always searching for new recruits, if you're interested."

Vincent rubbed his bitten hand. "We're good. Can you tell me about the horses, though?" As he led Ludic over to the stalls, Vincent made eye contact with me before gesturing to the dagger with his head.

His message was clear, so once Ludic and Vincent had their attention directed elsewhere, I crept to the table and lifted the dagger. It was light and easy to grasp, my fingers fitting perfectly into the grooves of the wood.

It was a dumb idea, one I never imagined myself actually doing. But such a tool would be perfect for our mission, and should we come face-to-face with Thierry, at least I'd stand some chance.

"Well, your creatures are beautiful," Vincent declared as I inched my way to the exit. He reached for the stall lock.

Before Vincent could release the horse, Ludic snatched his wrist. In a flash, he'd leaned forward and grabbed mine, too. He had an iron grip. "Not so fast!" Ludic's voice was still cheerful, but in a scary sort of way. "You're not leaving with my things."

"Oh, come on! You have a whole bunch of other horses—what difference does one make?" Vincent writhed, unable to shake himself free.

The blood had stopped flowing to my fingers, making them tingle. Diana's comment about me being an idiot was only now sinking in. "Okay, okay, I'll leave the dagger! And we won't take the horse! We're sorry."

"No!" Vincent pleaded. "Come on, don't back down now."

Ludic's feathers puffed up. "Oh? Are you looking for a challenge? How about we have a chariot race to settle this rather than jail time?"

Vincent paused, absorbing the new information, before breaking into a large smile. "Now you're talkin'! Can we keep the stuff if we win?"

"You can keep your lives!" Ludic said with matching enthusiasm.

I glared at Vincent. "This clearly isn't worth it. We're not gambling our lives away on a chariot race, especially when neither of us knows how to ride!"

"If you insist." Ludic snapped his fingers. "To prison, then!"

A whooshing sound came from outside, followed by Diana's and Luke's yells of surprise.

"Wait, don't bring them into this! Leave them alone, you ass!" Vincent tried breaking Ludic's grip again.

"What?" Ludic's said with feigned innocence. "Your options were to be arrested or race for your freedom. Now, come along!"

Since he spoke primarily to Vincent, him being the louder of the two of us, I found a split second to shove the dagger into my boot. I forced myself not to wince as the side of the cold blade rested along my lower leg. When Ludic glanced my way again, I straightened up and tried to look neutral, remaining silent as he whisked us away.

Being thrown into a prison cell with Luke, Diana, and Vincent was one hell of an "I told you so!" moment, which was exactly what Luke and Diana shouted once we were alone. Their voices echoed off the stone walls surrounding our pathetic room.

The gloom of the prison didn't help. We were underground, with a tiny window providing a sliver of light from above the dirt. A single cot and toilet stood in the corner. Beyond the hall, a handful of other Meraki, arrested for whatever reason, leaned against their cell bars to eavesdrop on us. With their curious eyes on us, we couldn't remove our hoods.

"A horse?" Luke seethed as he paced around our confinement. "Seriously, Vincent?"

"What? If it were Oliver's idea, you totally would've gone along with it." Vincent sat heavily on the cot, which was so stiff, it didn't budge under his weight.

Luke halted to face him. "What does Oliver have to do with this?"

Vincent scowled, looking the other way. "And nobody gave Diana shit for sneaking out and getting herself hurt!"

"Are you trying to make a point here?" Diana raised an eyebrow at him.

"Yes! Why is it okay if you guys mess up but not me? What's wrong with me being in charge for once?"

Luke's eye twitched. "Because you got us arrested for hell knows how long."

"So?" Vincent faced his brother with a foreign bitterness on his face. "Isn't that better than carrying out Isabel's dirty work?"

I clenched my fists at hearing him call our mission a cheap job. "Don't you dare suggest we shouldn't be rescuing Tyler and getting that necklace. Can't you guys feel it? The urge to keep going? The...the *pull*? Isabel mentioned ties being severed if we're separated for too long."

Vincent shot to his feet so we were eye to eye. "I was right to call this a wild goose chase. This matters too much to you, Oliver, especially for one kid. How far are you willing to go for Tyler?

Would you kill for him?" His eyes blazed when I didn't respond. "Even better, would you *die* for him?"

"I..." My voice failed, leaving me in stunned silence.

Would I?

"That's unfair of you to ask!" Diana said fiercely. "Vincent, you're only here because of Luke. What do you know about independent choices?"

Vincent whirled around to glare at her. "This is coming from the one who's here for fun! For fucking fun! You think this is exciting? You're unbelievable!"

Diana grabbed him by the collar, pushing him into the cell bars. "Yes, I like it here! Why don't you take a moment to stop and think?" While she lowered her voice, it carried the same intensity. "So many people back home don't see me. They...they see someone else. At least here, I am Diana Divata. When Reed took us shopping, they didn't care or ask about my body. Nobody questions me here. It's like I got to start over."

"Diana..." I reached my hand forward to rest on her shoulder.

"But it's not like an entitled brat like you would see that!" Diana's screech echoed through the prison, making prisoners jump and me immediately lower my arm back to my side. The window's sliver of light illuminated her teary eyes. "Maybe all I wanted here was a chance to pretend all the bullying and issues in the human realm didn't exist for a while."

Vincent opened his mouth, maybe to snap back, but instead, he relented and bowed his head. His chin dipped until it rested inches from where Diana held his collar. "I envy your sense of individuality."

Diana released her grip on Vincent, took a large step back, and tilted her head away. "You should, unless you want to die a lemming."

"Nobody is going to die." Luke's voice was firm. "I appreciate the communication going on here, but can it wait until after we're free from jail? We're too young to be criminals."

Diana patted herself down. "They took all our stuff, remember? We don't have anyone nearby to bail us out, either."

Vincent finally moved away from the cell bars, rolling his shoulders back. "Ludic challenged me to a chariot race happening today."

"What happened to none of us knowing how to ride horses?" I chided. Again, I was reminded of the cold dagger tucked in my boot, pressing against my skin. For half a second, I thought about suggesting we fight our way out of the prison. But with only my Mageia unlocked and one dagger for defense, we'd be overwhelmed immediately.

Luke scrunched up his face. "Judging by the name of the sport, people don't actually ride on the horses' backs."

He, Vincent, and Diana turned to me with expectant faces.

We certainly couldn't save Tyler if we were in jail or dead. "Fine." I hid my pounding heart with a forced smile to the team. "I guess I'll participate too, since I'm the one who encouraged Vincent to steal a horse."

"Great." Diana approached the bars and screamed into the corridor, "We need the peacock man!"

A minute passed before Ludic flew into the corridor, tucking his wings in to glide forward. He tipped his hat to us. "Have you reconsidered my offer?"

"Yes." Vincent gave him a shit-eating grin. "We accept your challenge. But regardless of what happens to me and Oliver, you must release Diana and Luke. They're innocent."

"*Magnifique*! Your wish is my command! They'll get to watch the race, too. We shall begin at noon." Ludic pivoted and called down the hall, "Guards, prepare these two juveniles for the chariot event!"

When Ludic walked away to address his comrades, Vincent grabbed Luke and me by the arms, yanking us closer to Diana, so we formed a group huddle.

"There's no guarantee Ludic will be true to his word—that his goons will free you two," I murmured to Luke and Diana.

Vincent nibbled the inside of his cheek. "If you two are allowed to watch us, then..." He leaned forward and whispered into our circle.

Diana cringed at the idea, but clearly thinking better of it, she sighed in defeat. "Sounds good."

"You got your wish of being leader for a minute," Luke scoffed. "How does it feel?"

"Shut up," his little brother muttered.

I joined the others in a half-hearted laugh, but Luke had a good point. Now, we would put trusting Vincent to the test.

∞

Vincent and I got out of being arrested, but I couldn't say the same for Diana and Luke. The Tunnel Runners' idea of "watching them" was putting them in a prison transport wagon, which was just a wagon with bars that ensured nobody could escape. The horses attached to it lazily grazed on bits of grass poking through the ground, ignoring how the humans in the cart rattled their cage and shouted for attention.

I itched to reassure them that this would work, but I didn't want to fill them with empty hope. Besides, Vincent and I were whisked to the racetrack before I could get any words out. Meraki poured through the streets after us, all whispering about seeing the show. The jail horses slowly followed, so Luke and Diana could witness our humiliation.

From what I could see from our backstage stall, the racetrack was massive, at least the size of a football field. In the center were large objects on a raised surface, which created an oval sand ring around them; that's where we would race. Seats were already filling up, and I was pretty sure I heard people making bets.

"Circus Maximus," Vincent muttered as we inspected the chariots given to us. They were small, rickety, and on their last legs. The blue banners—blue was our team color—attached to the rotting wood didn't make it any prettier. "That's where the ancient Romans held chariot racing. I wonder if Ludic knows how many people it killed."

"That might be his intention." I shuddered at the thought of the chariot breaking mid-race. Or of the dagger in my boot slicing my foot off. Or my horses losing control. One was a nippy black and white stallion, while the other was a chestnut mare with a mean glare. I'd rather not test their stomping hooves and sharp fangs.

The shake of Vincent's head brought me back. "Whatever. We'll just prove him wrong."

I looked outside again, where the jail cart had been placed in the corner of the arena. It was within reach of the track. While it was a safety hazard, it played right into our favor. "We have only one chance to fix this. Please don't half-ass it because you aren't a fan of our Assembly of Six destiny. Right now, this is about saving a kid." When Vincent remained quiet, I whispered, "He's just a kid. He needs our help."

Vincent's expression softened slowly. "Fine. And if it means anything to you...my chest does ache a little with this...*pull*...you mentioned."

I managed a weak smile. "That means a lot."

A horn blew in the stadium, and the crowd cheered. It was showtime.

A couple Meraki came over to help bring the horses and gear to the starting line.

Chariot racing must've been a common pastime for the town of Ikrel. There were three other teams of two that Vincent and I were racing against. As we fell in line, they glared at us. They probably wondered why they were competing against a couple battered teenagers.

That's when I realized Ludic wasn't in the lineup. He was sitting leisurely in the announcement booth perched above the grandstand, lazily twirling a microphone with his feet on the dashboard. The device was connected to a ball of wires surrounded by snakes of electricity.

"Seriously? Are you too chicken to race against us?" Vincent shouted at the booth. "Or should I say you're too peacock?"

Ludic put the microphone to his lips and said, "I'm the commentator, duh! Now, then, why don't we get started?" He stood and stretched his free arm out wide. "Everyone! Welcome back to another chariot race, but this time, we have more than prize money on the line. Two new faces from...somewhere...are here to fight for the freedom of themselves and their friends! Can they survive all seven laps? Place your bets!"

The horn blew again, echoing through the stadium. Instinctively, the horses leapt into action, galloping down the track at top speed.

I'll admit it. I screamed, gripping the reins for dear life. The small platform trembled beneath me, threatening to give way. Dust billowed all around me, making it hard to see past my horses' ears. I was aware of the others passing me, and at first, I thought, *Thank gosh! Vincent can take the lead on this.* But what if something happened to Vincent? Could I really trust he'd manage by himself?

"Come on!" I said to my four-legged companions. "Let's catch up to th—"

The horses didn't need to be told twice. They shot forward, scorching the sand with their speed. My hood flew off, and someone yelled about my ears, summoning shouts and screams from the crowd.

Someone from the red team glanced over his shoulder, raising his palm toward me. As we turned the corner, a gust of wind lifted one of my chariot's wheels into the air, threatening to topple my whole platform.

A slam of my foot brought the chariot back onto both wheels, giving me an idea at the same time. Gripping the reins in one hand, I bent down and grabbed the dagger from my boot. It would channel my Mageia, huh? I focused on the Meraki who tried bringing me down, closing the gap before swinging the blade forward. A wave of fire erupted from the dagger, slicing the wheels clean off my opponent's chariot. He went tumbling to the ground, his horses stopping skittishly.

"Sorry!" I called as I passed him.

"What's this?" Ludic howled into the microphone. "The human has an unlocked Mageia? What a twist! But don't kill him just yet, folks. Look, he's speeding up!"

I passed by the jail cart at the next bend. Luke and Diana were screaming, "Go, go, go! Go blue!" Their cheers flooded me with new strength.

From second place, Vincent looked over and grinned. His gold necklace bounced and flapped with matching enthusiasm. Without a doubt, this was what he'd been searching for in me. He soaked up the audience's attention like he was made for the competition.

We kept this up for another two laps. Vincent stayed at the front while I lagged. Every so often, I fired at our rivals, picking them off one by one. It wasn't long before the crowd was cheering for us. What they didn't notice was how every time I passed Luke and Diana, I slashed at the wooden bars of their cage.

On around the fifth lap, Luke managed to break the bars and get out right as Vincent turned the corner. He grabbed his brother's arm and jumped into the chariot.

The amazed energy in the crowd thrummed into shock. They would be on our tails any second now. I picked up my pace, reaching my hand out to Diana. "Let's go!"

Diana took my hand, letting herself get swooped into the cart as I passed by. She gripped the wooden edge tightly, cackling with delight. "That was so cool! You're amazing, Oliver."

"Yeah?" I looked over my shoulder to see the remaining competitors redirect their horses to start chasing us. "Well, don't relax just yet. Hang tight!"

Vincent and Luke veered into the stables, which must've been a narrow fit with how the horses shrieked in response. I pushed my guilt aside and followed.

"Well, would you look at that?" Ludic's voice still rang overhead. "They're escaping! Wait...they're escaping? Oh no! Get them!" His final words screeched through the microphone, loud enough to make my ears bleed.

Our opponents chased us into the town square, summoning gales of wind to throw us off balance. I ordered Diana to take the reins as I swung my blade, letting every barrier down to summon all my fire. The buffeting draft only sent the flames whirling back in our direction.

I ducked, and as the others yelped in alarm and did the same, I shrieked, "Sorry!"

From up ahead, Luke shouted something, but the wind carried it away. Vincent looked shocked, only focusing on the road in time for us to break free from Ikrel's main gate.

The ground trembled behind my chariot. Ruslan had emerged to create a wall between us and the Meraki, who gasped and yelled at the beast's sudden appearance. Our fantastical feline wasted no time in batting the chariots aside, roaring and preparing to stomp the Meraki out.

That bought us enough time to escape. The last I saw of Ikrel was Ludic trying to fly after us, only for Ruslan to swat him into a wall like a mosquito. I cringed, somehow hoping he wasn't dead. He'd been a charming enough guy with a hot accent.

Only once Ikrel was out of sight did the horses slow down. When we finally stopped, nobody said anything. Everyone just stood and gulped in deep breaths, trying to process what happened.

I slid the dagger into my boot and hopped out of the chariot. "Thanks for your help," I murmured to the horses, leading them to a nearby large puddle that hadn't frozen from the cold yet.

All four horses crowded by the water with delight, and once they'd drunk their fill, they lumbered over to the dead grass and started munching. Their fangs stabbed at nearby bugs to eat as well, a reminder that they could've pierced my arms but hadn't. Hopefully, that trust meant we could take their gear off with our limbs intact.

The others joined me on the ground, but as Luke landed, his legs buckled, and he fell on his knees. As we hurried over, he panted, "I'm okay!"

"Are you sure?" Diana looked him up and down.

"Yeah." He paused to take in a shaky breath before laughing. His forehead was beaded with sweat. "It was my first time summoning Ruslan on my own will. I'll get used to it."

Vincent muttered affectionately, "You're an idiot. That saved us, though."

Diana watched the horses for a minute, then turned to us. "They still stole our bags, but at least this detour wasn't a total bust. We got my scratch taken care of, had a small bite to eat, Vincent stole his horses, and Oliver now has a knife."

"Channeling dagger," I absently corrected her. "Now then, can we please—"

"Yep, we can keep going." Luke pushed himself to his feet, wiping the dust off his pants. He smiled at me. "I owe you and Vince for getting us out of jail. Anyways, I think that was a nice breather from traveling."

Diana eagerly nodded as we went to free the horses from their chariots. "It was! Oliver and Vincent looked so awesome out there.

You had the perfect plan and were all like *whoosh* on the track! You should've seen the other guys' faces. They had no idea what hit them."

We all laughed at that. For just a moment, the tightness in my chest eased. Vincent and I had synced up as a team. Luke and Diana had understood our intention with no words needed. I was reminded of how good it felt to share joy with a group of friends.

All I hoped was that it would last.

CHAPTER TWENTY-FIVE

KELP ENTHUSIAST

OLIVER

FREEING THE HORSES FROM the chariots was a success, and soon, we were traversing the valley on our new four-legged friends. I'd never ridden a horse before, let alone bareback, so I couldn't help holding onto a tight fistful of the stallion's shaggy mane. He didn't seem to care, luckily.

"So, when we get to Tyler..." I started, but once I realized I'd said it out loud and not in my head, I stiffened. The others didn't say anything, an invitation to continue. "Will you guys not jump down his throat right away? We—we don't know what'll happen when we find him, nor do we know about his companions."

Vincent raised an eyebrow. "You assume we'll jump down his throat?"

Diana grinned at him. "That's ironic, coming from you. Oliver has a point, though. Remember what McKenzie said? Ice mutations were wiped out a long time ago. For Tyler to be distrusting might be in his blood."

"Then we'll be patient." Luke gave me a reassuring nod. "It's just like at Indra Academy. Everything will be okay."

Vincent stuck out his tongue at such sweet words, only for his face to scrunch up. "I can literally taste fish in the air!"

We pulled our horses to a stop and opened our mouths to taste the air. Vincent was right. The salty, fishy smell was overpowering. The silence was filled by a crash, and where the ground met the horizon, sea spray erupted into the air.

"Great. So where's the cavern?" Vincent turned his head, surveying the empty land. "There's nothing here other than the cliff!"

"Exactly!" A feminine voice spoke from overhead. "Meaning you have exactly two seconds to leave. One, two...Oops! Looks like time's up."

I glanced up, jaw dropping, to see a young woman with giant, black wings hovering above us. Her hair was as shaggy as our horses', brown bangs covering her eyes and blowing in the wind.

"Damn, girl!" Vincent called. "Those wings are *fine*."

She frowned down at him. Ignoring his flirtation, she asked, "What business do you have here?"

Luke cleared his throat. "Are you Mystral?"

"I don't see how that's relevant."

In other words, this was definitely Mystral. McKenzie had mentioned the thief was an air Meraki, and those wings said enough.

"We're here to meet with some...comrades," I piped up.

"Well, you can't! You're trespassing and I already told you to leave!" Mystral stomped her foot in the air like a toddler.

I clutched my horse's mane with one hand, wondering if I could grab my dagger without falling off.

That's when my stomach dropped, and my body went weightless. A strong wind engulphed me, lifting me off my horse's back. Similar funnels of air carried Luke, Vincent, and Diana off their horses, too.

Mystral flicked her finger, flinging us to hover past the cliff and above the ocean. With her other hand, she summoned another *zap* of wind to whip the horses. In a panic, they galloped away.

"Yes! Run free!" Luke called to our fleeing companions. From beside him, Vincent groaned, and I wasn't sure if it was from motion sickness or the fact his horses were gone.

"Wait, what are you doing?" Diana writhed as Mystral combined our funnels, tossing us all into one small tornado. "You aren't even giving us a chance to leave!"

Mystral shrugged. "I already did. Now you threaten my friends?"

"Woah, woah, woah!" I struggled to stay upright. Falling would result in plummeting into the unforgiving sea below. I was extra careful to not glance downward. "We never threatened anyone! We just want to talk! I'm sort of friends with one of them. The short one—a half-Meraki kid."

"You'll just take them away from me!"

Vincent glared at Mystral. "You're not making any sense. We haven't done anyth—"

The pocket of air beneath him disappeared, and Vincent dropped. Screaming, he grabbed onto my ankle.

His weight was enough to drag me down, too. Everything in me wanted to kick him off, especially with his ear-piercing shrieks. That's when I remembered something Vincent mentioned back at Indra Academy. He couldn't swim. And now, he was dangling over a wild, rocky sea.

"Hang on!" Luke grabbed my wrist before I could fall out of the spiral, too.

Diana grabbed Luke's collar to make a four-person rope. She faced Mystral, her ombré hair whipping all around her face. "So your solution is to kill us?"

Mystral clapped her hands. "Finally, someone understands!"

Vincent tried to claw up my leg, but he couldn't do much besides dig his nails into my ankles. "Is it because I flirted? I'm sorry! I'm sorry!"

"Well, that's just part of it. My friends are visiting and you're going to chase them away." Mystral flexed her talon-like nails, like she knew she could throw us off balance but hadn't made up her mind.

"That's not why we're here!" Diana's voice raised above the roaring ocean.

My sweaty hands nearly lost their grip on Luke's arms. "What are you doing? That's not—"

Diana grinned at Mystral, which felt like a dismissal of my protests and our perilous situation. "We came because we've heard so much about you! Mystral the air Meraki, supreme collector of shiny things."

Mystral had a dreamy, absent look in her eyes. "I do like my shiny things."

"Exactly, and that makes you so awesome!" Diana sounded sure enough to convince *me* that was our mission. Genuine excitement filled her voice. "We're your biggest fans!"

"Really?" Mystral gasped.

Diana nodded, ignoring how Vincent, Luke, and I groaned our denial. "Really! If you let us down, I'll even give you a shiny thing."

That was enough to convince Mystral. With a snap of her fingers, we were flung back onto the cliff's edge.

Only after I frantically crawled away from the edge could I relax. Luke gave my shoulder a brief squeeze to remind me we were free from any land or mudslide. Then, he went to check on Vincent, who was crouching down and kissing the dirt, muttering, "Sweet, sweet earth!" under his breath.

Diana grabbed one of the pearls decorating the collar of her dress and ripped it off. She whispered an apology for ruining Reed's generous gift before holding it up for Mystral. "Isn't it nice?"

Mystral took the pearl, hovering over Diana as she inspected it under the wintery light. "Very shiny! Would you like to see the rest of my collection?"

"Of course!"

"Um, hello?" I stood up, wincing at the feel of scrapes along my ankle from Vincent's nails. You'd think I was a scratching post for a cat. "Are we invited, too?"

Mystral didn't even bat an eye. "Sure!"

It turned out Mystral's cavern was sitting under our noses. She led us to an underground staircase that spiraled into the earth. Only after some reassurance the structure was stable did I follow the others.

Her system of caverns was adorned by glowing jewels, mushrooms, and stalactites. The roar of the ocean returned, making the walls tremble. Its echo surrounded us, like we were in the jaws of the beast itself.

Mystral and Diana led the way through the tunnels, geeking out about the crystals. Vincent, Luke, and I trailed behind. I couldn't really blame Diana for leaving us in the dust. She'd been with us the entire trip, and spending time with another girl probably appealed to her.

At last, Mystral brought us to what she considered her den, or the living quarters. We arrived at a giant cave, one of the walls missing to reveal a perfect view of the gray sea below.

"We're literally *in* the cliff?" Diana stared at the ocean with a wide smile. "That's awesome!"

I was just starting to agree when the quiet patter of shoes in the tunnel cut me off.

"Um...Mystral? Do you know where—" The thin kid fell dead silent as he took in the scene and made eye contact with me. It was just who we were looking for, strolling in. Several agonizing heartbeats passed before Tyler whispered, "What are you doing here?"

He looked the same. His dual-colored eyes were still wide, and his small frame was still protected by his black hoodie. As always, it was dusty and in desperate need of a wash. If everything was the same, though, why was his expression so unfamiliar?

Just like when we'd first met, I was rendered speechless. Only once I'd pinched myself to confirm I wasn't seeing things did the words come to me. "Please don't run—we don't mean any harm."

"You're Tyler, right?" Diana faced him with an awed expression. "Hi! Thanks for your help last night."

Tyler shuddered, tightly crossing his arms over his chest. Silence. Taking a step back, he looked over his shoulder and whimpered before facing us again. "Why are—why are you here?"

"Hello to you, too," Vincent hissed under his breath.

Tyler flinched, but his distraught eyes met mine instead. "Why?"

"We're here to bring you home, actually." I offered him a nervous smile, hoping it would soothe his jumpiness. Just seeing him in the flesh had lifted a massive weight off my chest. The tense threads around my throat loosened.

"No, you're not."

Luke frowned. "What do you mean we're not?"

Tyler tugged at a strand of his hair. "Just...no."

He was as great at conversing as Mystral was.

Speaking of Mystral, she was milling around the edge of our group, watching with perked-up ears. As she leaned down, though, two necklaces slid out from under her shirt.

Everyone tensed up upon spotting the jewelry. They each had a crystal attached to them; one was purple and the other was orange. The latter was what we were looking for.

Tyler pointed to the necklaces. "Mystral," he breathed out, "I'm here for that."

"No way," Luke whispered to me. "Did he know we needed it?"

I watched Tyler approach the strange Meraki, only able to murmur, "I don't know."

Mystral stepped toward Tyler, bending down to reach his pathetic height. "What do you mean?"

Tyler shivered, his muscles twitching. "Necklace, please. E-Emperor Thierry needs it."

"Seriously?" Vincent shouted. "You're siding with the enemy now?"

Mystral loomed even closer to Tyler, a shadow falling over both their faces. "Are you really?"

Tyler lashed his hand out toward the fire necklace.

Mystral didn't even hesitate. She grabbed Tyler by the back of his hoodie, slamming him onto his stomach. Her foot knocked his face into the ground.

"Stop!" I yelled, but Luke grabbed me before I could race over. "He's with us!"

"I'm not!" Tyler shrieked.

Mystral's wings expanded to their full length, her feathers ruffled and spiky. "Nobody takes my shiny things!"

Diana grabbed a small rock and chucked it right at Mystral's forehead. It didn't even leave a scratch. "He won't take it if you get off him!"

"Will you?" Mystral glared down at the kid.

Tyler writhed, too busy trying to free himself. When Mystral relaxed her grip, he frantically crawled away with a scratched face and haunted eyes. His chest was heaving a lot for simply being pinned down.

Luke finally let go of my arm. He approached Tyler cautiously with a hand held forward. Quietly, he asked, "You okay?"

"What did...what did I tell you?" Tyler swerved away from the gesture, standing on his own. "I said leave!"

Mystral clapped her hands together. In a heartbeat, all of her aggression seemed to fade. "No need. You're all welcome to stay! It's been so long since anyone's visited." She grinned, revealing her fangs. "Ooh! Who wants kelp cakes? I'm gonna go make kelp cakes!" As she jumped around and strutted into a different tunnel, her crystal necklaces bounced. They were taunting us.

Tyler pulled at his hair again as he started to pace, eyes darting around before settling on us. "You ruined it!"

Diana's jaw dropped. "We just saved you!"

"You li-li...You lied." Tyler lowered one hand to touch his chest, where the necklace would have been had he retrieved it. "I had it!"

I cleared my throat. "Let's all take a deep breath. Can we have a civil discussion about this, please?"

Tyler just walked past me, back into the tunnel we arrived from. Not a sound left him.

Luke nudged me. "We better clear the air with him."

"You're right." With slumped shoulders, I slowly started after Tyler again. The others trailed after me.

To think there was a time it'd been Tyler following me.

Chapter Twenty-Six

I Need Soap to My Mouth

Tyler

I so desperately wanted to look at Oliver and Luke and feel the same warmth and protection that'd blanketed me back at Indra Academy. I wanted to be relieved they made it here in one piece, all by themselves without experts joining them every step of the way. I wanted to lean into their gentle smiles and questions if I was okay.

Do I look okay? I screamed it silently, letting it bounce and rattle around my head like the ocean's echo in the tunnel. It was suffocating. What if I drowned? Or was I already halfway there?

It isn't real. It can't be real. That's what I repeated to myself as I stormed through the tunnels. I needed a plan as soon as possible. Mystral didn't seem to mind the Indra Academy students around, and I knew Savana and Titanium would be excited to meet them. The real issue was Noah. Noah would flame them and tell Thierry all about their presence.

Oh no. What would Thierry say? Didn't he know Oliver was in Derngate? *What if he does something bad? Thierry might hurt them!* It was up to me to make them leave before things went wrong.

Boots thumped against the ground. I glanced over my shoulder, stiffening when I saw the Indra Academy students catching up to me. My brain told me to run for it, but my heart begged me to do otherwise. I stopped and faced them.

"I just want to talk." Oliver's voice was hushed, like he was afraid to wake the tunnel around us.

I pressed my back to the damp wall, crossing my arms over my chest. My mouth was dry, so I only shrugged. If I listened, he'd leave me alone, and then I could find the others.

Oliver also leaned against the wall a short distance away, giving me space like I was a hostile animal. His friends surrounded us like bodyguards. "Look, I'm sorry if we spooked you by appearing so randomly. We're probably not who you expected to find here."

I jerked my chin down a tiny bit.

"You aren't hurt anywhere, are you? Like—has anyone hurt you?"

It was a rhetorical question. Oliver was staring at my cheeks, where the scars from Titanium's claws were embedded in my skin. Still, in a weak attempt to distract him, I shook my head. I was like a robot programmed to do that and nothing else.

Oliver's eyes fell downcast. "Isabel sent us here to bring you home." When I opened my mouth to argue, he shook his head and kept going. "Did anyone ever tell you how Derngate came to be? How the humans and Meraki split up?"

"No." *I assumed it just happened.* It was impossible to say the rest in front of an audience.

"It was through war. Meraki started tormenting ice mutations and humans," the boy next to Luke muttered. I vaguely remembered his presence at Indra Academy—I believed the two were brothers. *Vincent, right?*

The girl nodded and said, "Six kids separated the worlds, and Thierry's goal is to undo their work. Their successors must stop him."

A lump formed in my throat. "But Thierry is doing a–a good thing! He's going to help people!"

"Diana's right. He's going to take over the human realm." Oliver's voice was strained. "Derngate was cut off for a reason. It's up to us to keep Thierry from causing chaos and destruction. The only reason nobody has done so is because there hasn't been an ice mutation in centuries. That is, until you came along. You've started a domino effect."

"It's all lies," I hissed. "Thierry has been nothing but...nothing but nice to me! He gave me my power! He's helping me find my brother! He cares about me." *Which is why you need to leave.* "He's picky with those—with those he likes."

Was I trying to convince Oliver or myself? Either way, I forced certainty to weave around my fingers, just so mine wouldn't tremble like Oliver's. It felt like all these threads within me were pulling and twisting, yearning for his affection but restraining themselves.

"He cares?" Oliver echoed in disbelief. "Thierry doesn't come across as a caring guy."

I glared at him. "You don't get to say that. You–you barely know him!" I pushed off the wall, spinning to look at the group properly. They didn't know that my mom would be proud of my work once she saw it. They didn't know I was doing this for the greater good. "Thierry's the emperor, you know? You can't...you can't disrespect him!" More sharply, I added, "He's also my father."

I expected their faces to stretch in shock, for them to back up and apologize for insulting Thierry. But their expressions stayed grim and unmoved.

My stomach flipped. Why didn't they look surprised? *They know Thierry is my dad. Who told them? Who else knows?*

Diana shook her head, eyebrows furrowing. "Thierry needs you for the wrong reason. None of us ever heard of these Meraki before arriving here. It's been erased from history for a reason. What good will reintroducing it do?"

"Are–are you scared?" I found myself smiling as I asked that. It felt wry and reminded me of Noah. *What am I turning into? Why am I trying so hard to keep them away?* "As the—as the prince of Derngate, I can order you to leave."

Vincent sized me up, gritting his teeth. "You're not the prince of me!" He clenched his fists and started toward me, but Luke pulled him back.

That allowed me to focus on Oliver again. Why was I shaking? "You didn't have to come here. If...if you wanted me to stay so bad, you–you would've stopped me. It's your fault."

Luke frowned. "You left in the middle of the night. Don't blame Oliver or the rest of us for your own actions." For a moment, I feared he'd unleash his feisty brother on me.

"It's okay." Oliver moved away from the wall to put his hand on Luke's shoulder. His next words were directed at me, though. "I promise, I'm so sorry all this happened." He mustered a weak smile, but as quickly as it appeared, it vanished. "I won't give up on you, Tyler."

My last thread of patience snapped. I balled my fists and screamed, "You're just jealous! You're jealous because Thierry needs me! You're jealous because I have a dad and you don't!"

My childish shriek echoed all around us, making my head pound and my chest throb.

Time slowed as I watched Oliver's eyes widen and his mouth part with absolute shock. In the distance, the ocean roared and crashed without a certain melody.

Nobody spoke.

"I..." Had I really just said that? Usually, someone raises their voice to feel powerful or in control, but I felt the complete opposite. The floor was going to give way beneath me. Someone was going to hurt me. Someone was going to shout back.

I put my hands over my ears, barely able to hear myself whisper "I need to go," before pushing past the Indra Academy students. I expected pain between my shoulders. Fingernails raking over my spine. Whips at my neck.

What truly hurt was the fact nobody touched me.

I hadn't realized the weight of that confrontation until I finally found Savana, Titanium, and Noah. They were back in the cave overlooking the sea, eating the kelp cakes Mystral had mentioned earlier. With a quavering voice, I relayed what I said to Oliver. Savana and Titanium's expressions were a mixture of dumbstruck and disappointment, but Noah started laughing.

He clapped me on the back and cackled, "Finally, you did something useful!"

I winced at the contact. "I didn't mean to. I...I just got so mad."

"Why?" Savana sounded oddly upset that I insulted someone she hadn't even met.

"Th-they were talking bad about Thierry." I cringed as I said it.

Noah grunted. "Then it's a good thing you put them in their place. If they start with you again, I'll burn them alive."

Titanium sat next to me, rubbing her cheek against my arm in a soothing gesture. "Let's not resort to violence."

Noah let out a scoff but didn't push it.

"Anyways!" Titanium shook out her void-like pelt, as if ridding herself of the tension surrounding us. "Mystral said I can show you where we'll sleep."

I glanced at the open wall. "But it's still light out."

"She said she understands that kids get cranky without their naps." Titanium grinned at my horrified expression. "Those are Mystral's words, not mine!"

"I'm not a kid!" I hissed under my breath. The last thing I needed was to cause another scene, so I clamped my jaw shut. Through clenched teeth, I seethed. "Show me the way."

Titanium breezed to the far end of the cavern, where a small stone archway led into a smaller—yet still spacious—room. Portholes along the wall let gloomy light shine through.

Instead of beds, a bunch of giant nests made of grass, straw, and dry kelp were spaced throughout the room. Kelp again, huh? As I stepped into one of the makeshift beds, it crunched under my feet. I grimaced as I cautiously lay myself on my back, facing the shiny jewels embedded in the ceiling. None were as alluring as Mystral's necklaces, though.

Titanium must've read my thoughts because she sat on my chest and peered down at me. "I assume you didn't get the necklace?"

"She was too quick for me." I brought my hands to my face, rubbing my sore eyes. "We need a distraction so someone can swoop in and grab it."

"Well, you have a whole bunch of people to ask for help." Titanium smiled at me like an encouraging parent. As she purred, her vibrations traveled from her body to mine.

I cringed, unsure if it was from her words or the bumpy massage. "You can help me, instead."

Titanium tilted her head in thought. "You're here with the others for a reason. It's not a solo mission."

Surely, there was no harm in trying by myself. Traveling here with other people was difficult enough. I didn't want them holding me or my victory back, because if I pleased Thierry, maybe he'd let Oliver go unnoticed. Then, he would tell me where Dominic was.

I only shrugged in response and rolled onto my side, using the hood of my jacket as a pillow. Titanium slid off my chest in the process, sitting next to my stomach instead. I brought my hands to my ears, and the roaring of the ocean subsided. It sounded like I was underwater, inside whatever shell sat at the bottom of the vast blue.

Finding myself in Thierry's dreamscape again, I couldn't bring myself to say anything or even smile. How was I supposed to explain our situation?

It wasn't needed, because the first thing Thierry said was, "I see you've made some friends."

He means the Indra Academy students. I stiffened, my hands curling into fists. "They aren't my friends."

"Do you know them?"

"We've met before."

Thierry cocked his head to one side, looking doubtful. "And yet, they followed you all the way here?"

His skeptical tone reminded me of my mom. I stood straighter, even though I was no match for his large size. "They aren't my friends," I repeated.

"You'll make them leave, then." Thierry moved closer. "They're against you. They'll only get in your way."

Instinctively, I stepped back. "I know. I'm trying."

A blunt force hit my collarbones, and I stumbled with a gasp. Thierry hadn't moved a muscle. It happened again, but this time it came from behind me, with more strength. I fell to my knees with a grunt. "Please—don't!"

Thierry grinned down at me. "I like that expression. You look like you're about to cry, but have no tears left to spare. Poor child."

I jolted when I saw my reflection in the water beneath me. I used to make that face when I was younger, but as I grew used to my mother's punishments, I learned her patterns and when there was something worth being afraid of.

This was new, though. This was unpredictable.

An invisible punch to the spine brought me closer to the ground, and I curled up with my hands over my head. A million apologies sat on the tip of my tongue, but it would only worsen if I dared say sorry. "Please!"

Thierry crouched down in front of me, his eyes wild. "This is called shaping, young man. I'm teaching you something valuable." His hand lashed forward and he gripped my chin so tight, I feared my jaw would break. He forced me to meet his gaze. "Go on. Disobey me. Run off with your red-head friend. You clearly love him more than your own family."

Get off, get off, get off!

I grabbed his wrist, summoning all my fear into freezing his hand in a block of ice.

While he was distracted, I scrambled away, my arms crossed tight over my body.

"I am not his friend." My voice was steady yet so hollow.

"Good. Then you know how imperative it is to get that necklace back. Actually, bring me both." Thierry put his hand over the block of ice, using his fire to melt it. He approached me, patting my head like I was a dog. "If you're a good son, you'll do it."

When I awoke, the world was dark, and everyone was sleeping around me. For the first time in weeks, my body flamed at the formation of bruises. *It's okay,* I tried reassuring myself. *Thierry still loves you. It's just shaping.*

Curling into a tighter ball, I brought my sleeves to my mouth to prevent myself from screaming. I sucked in a deep breath. *It's tough love. Why are you overreacting?*

I lowered my sleeve and forced a smile at the ceiling, but I couldn't feel my muscles. I couldn't feel anything. All that mattered was keeping Thierry from hurting anyone.

To the sleeping universe, I whispered, "I'll do it."

CHAPTER TWENTY-SEVEN

SHINY THINGS

OLIVER

Tyler had every right to be upset or stressed or whatever it was he felt.

I had every right to tell my side of the story.

Unfortunately, it wasn't a combination that went well together.

So now what? Pale light filtered through the porthole windows, shining into my eyes. My back ached from sleeping in an oversized bird's nest, little bits of dry kelp and straw digging into my scalp. The strain of getting here was finally sneaking up on me. My fatigue was like a hunting fox, and while shrouded in shadows, its blinding pelt made it hard to miss. I imagined myself staring it down, asking, *Dude, really? You could try being more discreet.*

Luke, Vincent, and the other boy—who we'd earlier learned was Noah—were all still asleep. My classmates and I had slept a little further away from the Cataclysm students, having gotten used to being physically vulnerable around each other. Honestly, I didn't think twice about it. I'd fallen asleep against Bryce or Luke on the subway in the past more times than I could count.

Just from a glance, I could tell Noah was the kind of guy who'd do more than draw on my face with a sharpie if I was close enough.

Tyler was still in his nest, too, staring at nothing as he absently stroked his cat's fur. Despite having been the first to go to bed the previous evening, he looked exhausted. Maybe that was what stopped me from approaching him.

Or perhaps, more realistically, it was because his words from yesterday were still lodged between my shoulders, like a stab in the back. Tyler hadn't been completely wrong; I'd been devoid of fatherly love since I was ten. As the years passed, though, the fury, grief, and jealousy of seeing other kids with their dads had turned into a simple pang in my chest. Tyler had been without a father for all twelve years of his life. His need to bring it up wasn't invalid.

The point I refused to say out loud was at least I could talk about my moms without wincing at the title. Back at Indra Academy, Bryce and I stopped mentioning Tyler's family when we realized the abuse he faced at home. Only when I was instructing Tyler how to brush his matted hair did I once ask if Sadie ever helped him. He'd shut down immediately.

Maybe Tyler knew I was strong enough to face retorts about my dad. I knew he couldn't handle such taunts about his mom, but what about Thierry? Tyler *had* to see that Thierry wasn't a good guy. Just knowing what he'd done to Bryce and what he planned to do to Derngate and Earth...

Great. I'd just woken up and I was already dealing with a headache. Instead of lingering on the pain behind my eyes, I focused on the fact Diana and Savana weren't in the room. They'd hit it off well yesterday and must've woken up already. Considering how Savana was a ray of sunshine compared to Noah, I figured I might as well take this opportunity to get to know her.

I carefully rose from the nest, making sure I didn't wake the others before creeping out of the room. The main cavern was empty, not even Mystral in sight. Before I called out, though, the hushed sound of giggling provided me what I needed.

When I looked over, I caught sight of Savana and Diana sitting on the open wall's ledge, talking amongst themselves. *Of all places!* Gripping the end of my cloak like it was my favorite blanket, I slowly approached.

"Good morning, Oliver!" Diana glanced over her shoulder to smile at me. "Want to join us?" When she noticed how I hesitated, she crawled away from the edge. "We can sit over here if you'd prefer." Her hood was off, exposing her human ears.

I sat down next to her, murmuring, "Thanks," under my breath.

Savana scooted back to join us. She stared at me with round eyes that revealed the blue depths to them. "Tyler never mentioned having human friends!" she snickered. Her purple hair had initially startled me, but after meeting the Tunnel Runners, it made more sense. She must have bought dye from them.

"Ah." I faced the view in front of us. The sky was a patchy mess of blue and white, while the ocean was a miserable gray. Savana's purple hair was freakishly bright in the corner of my eye. "I don't think he considers us friends right now. I knew him for around a week. The principal of our school asked me to look after him, and then, poof, he ran off."

It was bittersweet thinking that maybe, just maybe, we could've become actual friends if he'd never run away.

Savana's pointy ears drooped. "McKenzie always described the way she arrived here in a similar manner. While everything seemed to be going okay, she still disappeared at the first given opportunity. Some worlds aren't meant for their occupants."

Diana frowned. "So, is Tyler really with the enemy now? Shit—sorry, I didn't mean to call you an enemy! You, uh, aren't an enemy though, right?"

Savana grinned, bringing her index finger to her mouth in a shushing motion. "Noah would kill me on the spot if he knew. But yes, I'm on your side, and yes, Tyler is kinda with the enemy."

"Kinda?" I echoed.

"The way his posture changes around Thierry shows he wants to make him proud, but his eyes tell another story." Savana glanced behind us, like she was worried the kid would sneak up on us. "It's a tricky situation, with the whole Assembly of Six business."

Diana leaned forward. "You know about that?"

Savana winked at us. "Of course I do!"

"How much?" I struggled to keep my voice upbeat. "We've been hearing bits and pieces of it, but it feels like some of the story is missing." My mind kept flickering back to the tunnel at the gorge. "I saw a bunch of skulls back at the Cataclysm's base...Do those have anything to do with this? My friend back home mentioned Thierry has a thing for luring people in."

"Basically, the portal must be unlocked through a massive amount of Mageia. Mageia lies in your heart, too. It's your life source." Savana lowered her voice as she continued. "For years, Thierry has been extracting Mageia from people and collecting it to unlock the portal. That's been his way of substituting the missing necklaces."

Diana wrinkled her nose. "And by extract, you mean kill."

"Yes." Savana's gaze darkened. "The Assembly of Six holds an even stronger amount of Mageian energy. To kill them would give Thierry the push he needs to merge the worlds." She looked at Diana and me again, her expression stone cold.

Her words sent a chill down my spine. "So why doesn't Thierry kill Tyler if he's already in his clutches? My school principal called him the starting domino." Calling him such a thing felt weird in my mouth and didn't roll off the tongue. "If he dies, this whole thing gets messed up. Thierry could end it right away."

Diana shook her head. "Tyler's an ice mutation. McKenzie told us about how rare they are. Thierry might not want to kill the last one."

Savana nodded. "Exactly. Why kill the precious ice mutation when you can use him and kill the rest? Not to mention he's the heir to the throne. Thierry intends to keep him on the Cataclysm's side."

I stiffened. "Go back to that part about using him. What do you mean?"

Savana didn't respond right away. "Killing to extract Mageia isn't the only way to unlock the portal. This is where those necklaces come in. Like us, they carry vast amounts of Mageian life. Right now, the portal is powered by the fire necklace alone. It's only strong enough to let individuals through—not whole groups of people. When all six necklaces are united and activated by people with matching Mageias, the portal will fully open."

"So that's why Isabel wants the keys at Indra Academy. To prevent the gates from opening." Diana cringed, like she'd never imagined herself having this kind of conversation. "Great. Does Tyler not know this? He got all defensive yesterday."

"He's just unaware. We'll tell him this stuff." I paused, replaying everything in my head before frowning. As I said the next part, I counted on my fingers. "Wait. Vincent, Luke, Diana, Tyler, and I only equal five. We still need the sixth."

Savana grinned. "Who do you think it is?"

Diana and I fell silent as we thought about it. Finally, I faced Savana with wide eyes. "No way—is it *you?*"

"Did nobody mention it?" She threw her head back with a laugh that echoed around the cavern. "Yep! I'm the lightning mutation. Cool, huh?"

"Wait, so if we're bringing Tyler home—as in reuniting all six—does that mean you're coming with us, too?" Diana looked thrilled at the idea, maybe because she wouldn't be the only girl in the group anymore.

"Yeah!" But Savana's smile dimmed, and she averted her eyes. Her shoulders tensed up. "I've known for a while. A ghost from the original Assembly informed McKenzie a few years back, who then told me. I got comfortable with being the only member she had her sights on. So, when Tyler came along, and now the rest of you…I know my time here is running out." She crossed her arms over her chest, chuckling. "I think I just don't want to leave my family, you know? Working in the Cataclysm, I don't see them a whole lot anyways, but sometimes is better than never."

"I get that." I offered her a gentle smile. "Moving away is scary. I've been through it twice—when I moved cities in elementary school and when I moved from California to New York." I knew the state names wouldn't mean anything to her, but I shrugged it off. "We read letters Tyler's mom wrote to Thierry, which means that communication between the realms is possible. It won't be the same, but it's something. It's like how I kept in contact with my parents and friends when I left California."

Yes, all my friends except for one. That thought stayed behind a bitten tongue.

"The whole purpose of the Assembly of Six is to reunite the necklaces and make sure the realms don't clash," Savana said. She hardly looked comforted by my words. Her eyes glistened with tears in the morning light. "What'll happen when the gate closes? Could I still write to them? We won't know if not until it's too late."

She had a fair point, and it tore at my heart.

Diana rested her hand on Savana's shoulder. "That's a risk we have to take. Trust me, I don't want to leave this world, either. It's beautiful—not to mention you guys are excellent at crafting skirts."

Savana sniffed. "Fair point. I know I must do it, and I *will* do it. I just need some time to process it."

We offered murmurs of acknowledgment, letting the swirling ocean talk for us. A gull-like bird soared overhead, and as it swooped into the sea, I noticed its four, beady eyes. *Yep, gonna miss this place. This place and its...strange wildlife.*

"So, you already got one out of the three goals!" When Savana spoke again, some of her energy had returned. "We have me on-board and just need Tyler and those two necklaces."

"We need both?" Diana and I echoed in unison.

Savana tilted her head toward the cavern. "Yep. One is for the fire Mageia, and the other is for the lightning mutation—me." Her expression was thoughtful. "Surely, we can persuade Mystral to hand them over."

Diana snapped her fingers. "We can trade with her! Do any of us have shiny things we can offer? I already tore up my dress for the pearls."

I surveyed my outfit before glancing at the young women sitting before me. None of us had anything flashy. Finally, with a guilty smile, I suggested, "Vincent's glasses when you angle them correctly?"

"He'll kill us!" Diana doubled over with laughter. "But it could work! I'm gonna go ask." In a fit of giggles, she scrambled to her feet, racing back into the cavern.

Savana was on her heels, leaving me by myself.

Instead of following them, I glanced at the ocean for a final time. It was rough and miserable, like the Pacific Ocean on the rare occasion it rained. I hadn't seen such a sight in years. It'd been May when I received the acceptance letter to Indra Academy. The rain was long gone by then. Recalling it now, I wondered if the reactions of my peers had drowned out my own.

My moms had been delighted. My classmates had been confused. As for my best friend? He'd shot an arrow through my heart when I broke the news to him. His words were still fresh in my mind like it was yesterday.

"You really wanna go live in a shithole like New York City?"

"What about the sunsets, like the one we're experiencing right now?"

"Fuck you, Oliver. Fuck you."

Pushing the bitter memory away, I stood up and walked away from the cliff.

Did those magnificent sunsets still exist in California?

Chapter Twenty-Eight

CAN'T DANCE IF I'M DROWNING

Tyler

I told him I'd do it. What if he thinks I'm a liar?

How pathetic am I?

Very. It sounded like my mom's voice.

There were enough insults coursing through me to fill an ocean. But instead, they filled *me*, dragging me down.

You're wasting Thierry's time.

You got his hopes up too high.

You aren't trying hard enough.

The water wouldn't stop. The thoughts wouldn't stop. They never stopped.

Titanium will be disappointed.

Water coursed through my insides, pooling in my ankles.

You're ruining it for everyone.

You'll be punished.

That word alone made my body scream.

Pooling in my waist.

Why is Oliver bothering with someone so useless?

Pooling in my lungs.

If I drowned, would it be because I was such a bad ice mutation? Could the real ones hold their breath and survive this?

Birds in the air like fish in the water. But what happens when all you can see is the vast blue?

My mouth opened to scream for help, but all I got was more water coming in. Nothing came out. Nothing ever came out.

Chains tightened around my throat, taunting me.

Until I was submerged both outside and inside.

A forgotten stain.

I woke up drenched in cold sweat, jolting into a sitting position as I gasped for air. After that dream with Thierry, I must've dozed back off, my brain deciding to torture me itself.

My mom was crouching over my nest with her classic, unamused face, but then my vision cleared and I saw it was actually Noah. He rolled his eyes at my terrified expression. "Took you long enough. Get up."

Why did I still feel submerged? The dream was over.

The panicky ache in my chest wasn't leaving, though. I groaned and rolled over, so my back faced Noah.

"We're not here to laze around. Get up, we need to talk." Noah rested his foot on my shoulder and jostled my body.

I was upright in a heartbeat, scrambling away from him. To play it cool, I stood up, wiping away stray bits of straw and dead grass that clung to me.

Only then did I realize we were the only two in the room. Everyone else, including Titanium, was gone. Betrayal surged through my veins. *What the hell?* They were off doing something behind my back, weren't they? Maybe it was something fun. Something my presence would only ruin.

Yesterday rushed back to me, and I cringed. It made sense for the others to leave me behind.

"Jeez." Noah grabbed the sleeve of my hoodie, dragging me to the entrance. "We'll talk in the valley. I'm getting sick of caves."

I overheard quiet chatter as we slunk around the shadows of Mystral's main cavern. Her extravagant voice was rendered unintelligible by her own echo. As we slipped into the tunnel, I asked, "Do you...do you know h-how to open the trapdoor? Above the stairs?"

Noah released my sleeve, keeping his eyes ahead of us. "We should be able to push it open. You can use your ice to make holes around the door if that doesn't work."

As we passed, the ghostly bunnies paused their cleaning to watch us start our way up the spiral staircase. After a minute, they lost interest and went back to cleaning.

Climbing up was just as intimidating as going down. At least this time, I could keep my eyes on the wall and not focus on the great drop below us.

The trapdoor was easy to push, which wasn't a huge surprise. Mystral needed it light enough to be opened with a gust of wind.

Noah hauled himself into the open with ease. As I reached the entrance, he grabbed my wrist and dragged me out. It was with such force I feared he'd dislocate something.

"Alright," I finally sighed, rubbing my wrist to make sure it was fine. That was my invitation for him to talk.

"Thierry visited my dream last night after leaving yours." Noah stood with his hands on his hips, his attention on the rustling grass. "He just wanted me to make sure you're in line."

Clouds loomed over the horizon, the sky groaning like a metal machine.

I also stood, glaring at his back. "I am!"

Noah looked over his shoulder, bored. "I saw you look around for those humans on our way up here."

"Thierry and I—Thierry and I, uh, spoke about it already." I clenched and unclenched my fists. The wall in my mind was preparing to crumble and let ice shoot through.

"Then why are you fighting back?"

"I'm not!"

Noah pivoted to face me with his eyebrows knitted together. "You're being told to stay away for your own good, but I know you hate yourself enough to ignore that." His expression remained stone cold. "What's his name? Freckles? He seems to know you well. Is that red-head Dominic's fucking replacement or something?" He walked closer, his eyes widening until I saw the white around the irises. "You remember how it ended last time you hung around someone who actually cared about you, right?"

I tilted my head up, focusing on his hair rather than his eyes.

"Freckles would follow you to the edge of the world if he really wanted to!" Noah laughed with this crazed smile on his face. "He already has, hasn't he? If something happens to him or his friends, the fault will lie on your shoulders. Don't you see, mutt? You brought them here! You're going to hurt them!" He scanned me up and down like I was a juicy piece of prey. "You're so caught up in licking your wounds that you don't realize the harm you bring to others."

"I—"

"Have you seen your sister? Your mother?" Noah stomped his foot over a twig, and it snapped with ease. Was he imagining that to be my spine? "I think we all know it's your fault. All of this. Dominic's disappearance, the sadness and poverty engulfing your family, Thierry forgetting about me, all of it. So do all of us a favor and fucking toughen up. Or better yet, leave."

I stepped back, but my legs felt like they were made of jelly. None of this was new information, something I found bitterly amusing. My throat clogged, my voice coming out uncharacteristically deep and broken as I whispered, "Why now?"

Noah slumped, his energy seemingly sapped. "Because if I don't tell you, nobody else will."

I tell myself every day. Looking at the splintered twig under Noah's boot, I muttered, "I'll try harder. And—and if it doesn't work, I'll leave."

I didn't have any backup plan if that became a reality, but there were lots of places I could be alone.

"Leave to go where?" a voice from behind us whined.

We spun around to see Mystral standing a few feet away, her wings folded and head cocked like a curious puppy. Yes, a curious puppy standing at six-something feet tall with tattered clothes that'd help her win any Halloween costume contest.

"None of your business, bird lady." Noah seethed.

Mystral ignored him, instead tilting her head down. Behind her overgrown bangs, she was probably looking at me. "Savana and Titanium would be sad if you left. I would, too."

You don't know me.

Noah stepped forward so he was right at my side, as if he hadn't been lecturing me a minute ago. "He's not leaving yet. If anything, we might be able to prolong his stay!" He rubbed his elbow against my shoulder, and when I faced him, he tilted his head toward Mystral. More specifically, he was gesturing to her necklaces.

I exhaled heavily to show I understood.

"You see, as much as I hate babysitting, Tyler here is special!" Noah extended his arms in a grand gesture, shooing me to the side. "He's an ice mutation, you know?"

"Really?" Mystral's long ears perked up.

With the air Meraki's attention captured, I slowly inched to the side, creeping across the imaginary line between her and Noah.

"Yeah!" Noah continued nonchalantly. "He's the only of his kind left. Thierry took an immediate liking to him."

Oh, how I prayed that was still true. I forced myself to keep my breathing steady as I circled behind Mystral. Her feathers ruffled in the breeze. She continued facing Noah as he rambled on about how great I was. It was the most irony that'd ever left his mouth.

"He's also going to help Derngate, you know? We're taking back what's finally ours!" Noah's gaze slid past Mystral, focusing on me. "Tyler's key is the one that's been unable to be reclaimed until now."

"Key?" Mystral echoed softly.

I sprang forward with outstretched hands, reaching for the strings around her neck.

Mystral's wings spread, and a huge gust of wind blasted around her like a ripple. The force of the blow sent me crashing onto my back.

"Idiot!" Noah barked before launching himself at Mystral. His palms glowed white, smoke rising from his fingers and nostrils. "I have to do everything around here!"

I hit my palm on the ground, sending ice crystals zigzagging around Mystral. Noah jumped right at her, holding her at flame-point as he focused on the necklaces. "Nobody has to get hurt if you hand those over," he snarled.

Mystral bent her knees slightly before jumping up, her wings effortlessly pushing her into the sky. "These are mine!" she yelled over the wind she'd summoned.

Noah aimed his palm at the sky, shooting a torrent of white fire that whooshed past Mystral's wings. "Get down! This isn't a fair fight!"

"What fight?" Mystral glided right over him.

The strength of her wind sent Noah sprawling several feet away. Mystral landed, twisting around to face me. Her bangs were swept to one side, revealing a gray eye that stared right into my soul.

"Well?" she purred, daintily gesturing to her necklaces. Her words were laced with false innocence. "Don't you want them?"

I glanced at Noah like an expectant dog. He struggled into a sitting position, clearly fine, but he was looking right back at me. A challenge blazed in his eyes. It said, "Go on, you know you want to prove yourself."

You have no idea. I extended my palm, creating a long, thin icicle in my clutches. All I had to do was cut the ties of the necklaces and snatch them up.

Mystral lunged at me again, the roar of another wind attack whistling past my ears. This time, I let myself hide behind a shield of my ice, waiting for it to stop before advancing.

Hadn't I done this before with Thierry?

It seemed like Mystral need to recharge after that last attack. She stood rigid, breathing heavily. I took that opportunity to race right at her, aiming the ice's sharp edge at her neck.

Just cut the ties.

What if I miss?

Just cut the ties.

But what if—

I came to an abrupt stop as Mystral grabbed the icicle with one hand. She squeezed it until it shattered right before us.

"A little boy like you isn't developed enough for a fight." Mystral leaned down to glare at me with a frown. "It was a nice try, though."

I extended my hand toward the crystals dangling above me.

Mystral pulled back, fluttering her wings so she hovered a few feet in the air. My sweaty fist closed around nothing.

"You could've helped him," Mystral said calmly to Noah.

Noah pushed himself to his feet, glaring at me. "I wanted to see if there's actually a useful bone in his body." He rubbed his shoulder as he turned around and slowly started his way to the trapdoor. "I guess not. His confidence yesterday was only an act."

He surrendered, leaving Mystral and me in the valley. The air Meraki landed neatly, tucking the necklaces under her shirt, out of grabbing range. She turned her head toward me and said, "Your friend isn't very nice."

"Sorry." Even with Mystral's eyes hidden, I couldn't bring myself to look her in the face. Instead, I focused on her magnificent, black wings. I was worried, in spite of her excellent fighting skills, so I muttered, "You...you aren't hurt, are you?"

"If you're going to feel guilty about it, why make the effort of trying?" Mystral didn't sound bothered, surprisingly enough. "This was your second attempt, and you still came out unsuccessful."

I crossed my arms over my chest.

"Your friend said that you hurt people."

"You heard?"

Mystral inspected her nails, which were as sharp as her talons. "If you truly hurt people, then why would you ask if I'm okay? You're amusing, boy." She walked closer, crouching down to be at my eye level. "All the thoughts are scrambled in your head. You can't pick one, can you?" When I didn't reply, she giggled like a gossiping teenager. "That's why you let the emotions of others sway you. But what do *you* want?"

"The–the necklaces." My voice was hoarse.

"That's what someone else wants."

"And I want to make him happy."

Mystral didn't look convinced. "You don't want to be alone, do you? I understand. I live here by myself and would do anything to make others stay, even if that means keeping my gems to myself. They'll stay until they get them, but they never do. I have some bones for proof if you wanna see!"

Seriously? Swallowing a wave of nausea, I nodded to the strings around her neck. "They aren't yours, though."

"So? They're mine now." Mystral shrugged. "The point is, sometimes, you have to be selfish. How can you help others if you can't help yourself?"

Thinking back to Noah's words from earlier, my heart sank. The reason I was hurting others was because I couldn't take care of myself. Simply, I couldn't.

Mystral smiled at my pained expression like she'd cracked the code. "Does that make sense?"

"Maybe?"

"Ah." Mystral folded her wings, leaning back to stretch. "Well, I hope you find your answer. Catch you later, little human."

As she soared back into the air and swooped behind the cliff, I exhaled, "I hope so, too."

CHAPTER TWENTY-NINE

I PINKIE PROMISE

OLIVER

THE PUZZLE WAS ALMOST complete. Five of us sat in the bedroom, in a circle around a nest, as we brainstormed how to get Mystral's necklaces back.

Our group consisted of me, Luke, Vincent, Diana, and Savana. That was almost everyone. I wondered what Isabel and Camila would think when we returned with both Savana and Tyler. Surely, that would make up for how long we'd been away.

"I already said we're not using my glasses to trade with her!" Vincent was snapping at Diana for the fifth time in three minutes.

"Would you rather go home or be able to see?" Diana jeered.

"Both!" Vincent exclaimed. "I would love both! And as a person with good eyesight, you don't know how much these bad boys cost!" He gestured to his glasses like they were special action figurines Diana had mistaken for dolls.

Savana pointed to Vincent's necklace. "How about that?"

Vincent buried his pendant in his fist. "Absolutely not."

Luke cleared his throat. "Have we tried to reason with her?"

A short laugh came from the entrance. We turned around to see Noah leaning against the archway, watching us with a raised eyebrow. His face was all scratched and his pants were ripped at the knees. "Yeah, have fun with that. The bird lady is a real joy to be around."

Savana's ears pinned back. "Hey! Did you pick a fight with Mystral or something? She'd never attack unprovoked!"

"Hmph." Noah flopped into his nest, resting his arm over his eyes. "Sav, are you really planning to take her down with these humans? You might have the numbers, but you don't have the power."

"Yeah?" Vincent made a fist toward him. "Come here and I'll show you just how powerful I am!"

I rested a hand on Vincent's shoulder, then faced Noah. "And it didn't work for you despite having powers?"

Noah rolled onto his side so his back faced us. "Tyler's the one that fucked it up. That stupid mutt has the worst reflexes."

"He's not stupid, let alone a mutt!" I snapped back. "Watch your mouth."

"Was Tyler with you?" Diana peered at the entrance like she was waiting for Tyler to appear.

"Shut it, Freckles. And yeah, he's probably still up there with"—The echo of fluttering wings rippled through the cavern—"her. Hah, speak of the devil!"

Luke cleared his throat. "I'm gonna go into the tunnels to see if I can find anything shiny. Maybe we can trick Mystral into taking something she forgot she already had."

Savana shot to her feet. "I'll come with you!"

They left in a hurry, leaving no time for Diana, Vincent, or me to react. Noah didn't move from where he lay in his nest.

Vincent sighed and took off his glasses to clean them. "We're wasting our time. When we get the necklaces, let's just go home."

"But we came all this way for Tyler!" I protested. "You can't just give up now."

"He clearly doesn't want to go home," Vincent fired back. He scowled at his lenses before pushing the glasses back on. "How are we supposed to change his mind? I don't think shiny things will encourage him the way they do for Mystral."

Diana pouted at him. "Why can't you have a little more faith? Oliver's right. We've come so far!"

I nodded and added, "Tyler's been manipulated."

From his nest, Noah laughed. "Or have you considered that he can make his own choices?"

"And if they're the wrong choices?" Diana pressed.

Noah looked over his shoulder to glare at us. "What makes you think you guys are the heroes? Is everything you do and say correct?"

"Exactly!" Vincent barked. "Tyler's a prince who'll have a whole world to rule someday."

"Don't you *dare* start siding with *him*." Though I was talking to Vincent, I was wagging my finger at Noah. "What happened to our conversation in Ikrel?"

Vincent balled his fists. "Well, fuck this destiny! None of us asked for it! I have the right to be angry."

I turned to Diana to see if she'd defend me. She just stared back with this face, like she was balancing on a tightrope and concentrating on not falling.

Even Noah didn't have a comeback for that one.

"You're insufferable," was all I managed to say. This wasn't a fight worth pursuing.

As I started for the exit, Noah broke into quiet laughter, and I kicked his ankle. "I'll get back to all of you later," I muttered. Before leaving, though, I paused and glared at Noah. "You said Tyler was with you, right? Where is he?"

I half expected Noah to not reply, especially right after I'd kicked him. He absently waved to the entrance. "Probably still in the valley. His stupid cat went looking for him, so I'm sure they'll be back eventually."

I squirmed when I heard him call the cat stupid. She'd been nice, despite how freaky it was that she could talk. I forced a smile and said through clenched teeth, "Thanks."

Stepping outside the nest room, I followed the direction Luke and Savana had gone off in. My new goal was to speak with Mystral, get the necklaces back, and try to smooth things over as soon as possible.

In the large cavern where the main staircase rested, I found Savana and Luke piling little crystals into the crooks of their arms.

"Do you think these are enough?" Luke adjusted the crystals in his arms to give me a better look.

In the darkness, they glittered in all sorts of colors. The dusting bunnies had done a good job keeping them clean. I nodded. "I hope so."

Savana opened her mouth to reply, but she fell silent and looked over her shoulder. With her ears perked up, she called, "I know you're hiding there."

Mystral stepped out of where she was lurking behind the staircase. She played with her hands, like a guilty child who'd broken a vase or snuck downstairs after bedtime. "We have to talk, don't we?"

I tried to exhale the tension from my shoulders. With everything and everyone falling apart around me, I had to at least make this work. Still unconvinced I could hide my frustration from earlier, I turned to Savana in hopes she'd begin.

Savana blinked in surprise, running her free hand through her hair. The motion seemed to calm her slightly. "Right. Okay. Uh—"

"Ta da!" Mystral pulled something out from behind her. It was my dagger.

"How did you—" I frantically pat myself down to make sure I wasn't imagining it. My dagger was meant to be safely secured in my boot.

"I stole it while you were asleep." Mystral's feathers ruffled with pride, like all of her shame from a minute ago never existed.

Savana cleared her throat. "What does the dagger have to do with this? Uh, you know what we're here for, right?"

"The dagger comes in later. Doesn't the Cataclysm preach patience?" Mystral frowned, raising a hand toward her chest. "And you see, I don't give my jewels to simply anyone. I can't remember the last time I did such a thing." She nodded to the crystals Savana and Luke still held. "You can't fool me with those. They don't add up in value."

I forced a neutral expression. While my companions grumbled and dumped the crystals on the floor, I asked, "What exceptions do you make?"

"Exceptions? There are no exceptions. You don't get stuff through special qualifications."

"That's the thing," Luke argued weakly, "we *do* have special qualifications. We're successors to the Assembly of Six and need those necklaces."

Mystral let out a hum. "You don't have proof." Her smile showed off her fangs. "You're a mere human!"

Luke clasped his hands together, holding them over his chest as if he were praying. All he uttered was, "Ruslan."

The air behind Mystral wavered, and flaming threads formed out of nothing. They twirled and blazed into the glorious beast of Ruslan. He hovered over Mystral, and while he didn't make any moves, he stared down at her with his tongue swiping over his maw.

Mystral glanced over her shoulder and yelped to see the creature looming over her. She spread her wings over her head like a shield. "Get that thing out of here before it eats my seabunnies!"

"Still think we aren't special?" Luke asked with a scoff.

"Woah, woah, woah!" A nervous grin played on Savana's face. "I like the lion, but let's not fight over this." She turned to her old friend with a pleading look. As she spoke, she put her hand on Luke's shoulder. "Let's just talk this out, okay? Why do you want to keep the necklaces?"

"They're pretty." Surprisingly, Mystral didn't elaborate. They were pretty. That was it.

I focused on the dazzling crystals around Mystral's neck, one shining purple and the other orange. My reflection stared back at me, a face filled with awe. "They *are* pretty," I agreed after a slight pause. "You collect them, don't you? I saw a bunch of other crystals sticking out of the guest bedroom ceiling." It had been like falling asleep under the stars.

Mystral preened her feathers with her hands. Every few seconds, her gaze twitched toward Ruslan before focusing on us again. "Yes! I like them a lot."

"Listen, do you remember Thierry, the guy I work for?" Savana sounded distracted as her attention was also captured by the crystals, but as she continued, she forced herself to meet Mystral's gaze. Her next words were more grounded and present. "He wants to collect them to strengthen Indra Academy's portal. You remember that, too, right? We learned about it in school."

"That won't be good." Mystral fumbled with the necklaces like a child soothing themself. "Which means someone has to keep them from him!"

"Exactly!" Hope fluttered in my chest. "This is why Savana and I want them. We're going to make sure Thierry doesn't take them, okay? That's the duty of the Assembly of Six. You can trust us."

Mystral stepped back. "But I'm already taking care of them!"

Savana clenched and unclenched her fists. "In terms of realms, the necklaces will be further from his reach if they're with us in the human realm. Please?"

"I don't want to!" Mystral tucked the necklaces under her shirt.

Luke, who'd reverted to silence to keep Ruslan in place, sighed, "Why not?"

Mystral pouted, her head lowering and ears drooping. Through the curtain of her brown bangs, I noticed her eyes watering. "Because then you'll all leave, and I'll be by myself."

Silence.

Savana, Luke, and I exchanged a nervous look. Mystral had a point. There hadn't been signs of a significant other or any family during our stay in her home. She truly lived alone in this gloomy place.

"Hey." I tapped Mystral's arm to make her look up, and I smiled when she did. "Taking the necklaces doesn't mean the portal will close right away. I can come back and visit! We all can!" A lump formed in my throat as a backup plan came to me. "And if that's not enough, you can keep the dagger."

Mystral's jaw dropped. "Do you promise?"

I lifted her hand and hooked my pinkie around hers. "I promise."

Savana scoffed at the gesture. "Is that a human thing?"

"Pinkie promises? Yeah!"

Mystral giggled, wiping her eyes. "I like it."

Releasing her pinkie, I extended my hand with my palm facing upward. The silent invitation was an obvious one. From beside me,

Savana also held her hand out. Luke released the tension from his shoulders, and Ruslan dissolved into thin air again.

Mystral paused, her lips drawn in a thin line. She slowly pulled the necklaces out from under her shirt. Her gaze flickered from the crystals to Savana and me, and back again. After what felt like a lifetime, she sighed and took the necklaces off.

"Thank you." Savana grabbed hers, and at her touch, it glowed bright purple.

Once I saw it didn't hurt her, I carefully took the second necklace. It was so light in my hand, no heavier than a feather. To top it off, the weight of carrying a stolen dagger had been passed on to someone else.

Savana, Luke, and I left the cave in silence, and only when we emerged from it did Savana mutter, "That seemed a little too easy."

I weighed the small crystal in my hand before tightening my fist around it. "We should be grateful."

Once she'd declared she was gonna go find Diana, Savana left. Luke also made a swift exit to go calm down his brother after I described the rising tensions from earlier. Meanwhile, I escaped to the bedroom in case Mystral changed her mind and came after us.

Only Noah remained in the room. He was sitting up now, weaving little bits of straw together to form a braid. When it started to fall apart, he burned it to a crisp. Aware he had an audience, he glared over his shoulder to where I stood in the archway. More specifically, he was glaring at the necklace I still held. "Well, would you look at that, Chosen One? At least tell me Savana got the other one."

"Yeah, she did." As I spoke, I put the necklace on, hoping it would be safer to wear it than keep it in a pocket.

"Good." Noah wiped the ashes from his palms before smiling coldly at me. "Why do you look so uncomfortable? Aren't I allowed to congratulate you on not being a totally pathetic excuse for having a fire Mageia?"

"You want something," I blurted. It was a blunt response, but what else was I supposed to say? Slowly, I approached and sat on the nest across from him.

"Yeah, and so do you. What brought you here—other than that necklace? I know about your oh-so-prestigious boarding school." Noah did sarcastic jazz hands as he spoke.

My gaze slid over to Tyler's empty nest. A wrong move on my part, because from in front of me, Noah hummed as if he had a lightbulb moment.

"Just as I thought. You came for the mutt, huh? Gosh, what do you see in him?" Noah wrinkled his nose. "He's creepy and pathetic."

"Creepy?" I echoed in disbelief.

Noah let out a hollow bark of laughter. "Hell yeah, he is. He talks funny, like there's a frog in his throat, messing everything up. Nothing comes naturally to him. Everything has to be this big struggle for that brat." He crossed his arms over his chest, scowling at our shoes. "Nobody could tell why."

I clenched my fists, suddenly wishing I still had my dagger. "What gives you the right to insult him?"

"Maybe you'd be more understanding if you knew Tyler's at fault for what happened to his older brother, Dominic. He was my best friend."

Was.

It felt like a lifetime ago, but the night I met Tyler, I asked if he had any siblings at Indra Academy. He stuttered that he used to but never elaborated. It had been my assumption that the sibling had graduated, but now...My stomach cramped up, and the hairs on the back of my neck rose. "Whatever the case is, you shouldn't talk bad behind his back."

Noah scoffed. "What are you, a teacher?"

"You have the attitude of a fifth grader."

"So you'll really defend him, even after how he insulted you yesterday?"

A layer of frost spread over my lungs. "I'll give him the benefit of the doubt."

Noah's eyes blazed. "You think you know him so well? I've known him for half his life! He used up his chances a long time ago."

"What do you mean? What happened?"

After a pause, Noah sighed. "It was almost exactly three years ago, during winter break. Dominic, his brother, had disappeared a few days prior, but then, he came back all weird. He was desperate to show me and Tyler something. Tyler made us do it at Central Park. Something about feeding the ducks at the same time, and Dominic could never say no to him."

His eyes glossed over as he recalled it. "Anyways, Dominic started manipulating water in the lake like a Meraki. I think he found the portal, went to Derngate, and unlocked his Mageia all by himself." His shoulders hunched up. "Someone must've seen us, because as we were leaving, a few masked guys ambushed us. They—they took him away."

My mouth opened, but nothing came out. The anger in my chest from earlier was flickering like a dying flame, trying to stay alight. There were a million things I wanted to say and ask, but in the end, all I choked out was, "And he never came back?"

Noah glared at the floor. From the way his face scrunched up, I thought he was about to cry. He didn't, but his voice still shook when he spoke again. "Never. And it's all Tyler's fault. He made us go to the park that day. We could've gone anywhere else. But he insisted we went to the fucking park."

Maybe this explains a thing or two. The hostility Noah held toward Tyler. Tyler's jumpiness. That didn't excuse Noah's behavior, but I doubted he'd respond well to a lecture. "I'm sorry, Noah."

"Don't be. I'm just disappointed it didn't harden Tyler up. He still makes me sick." Noah pushed himself to his feet, narrowing his eyes at me. "You never answered my earlier question, though. Do you see something in him?"

I nibbled on the inside of my cheek. Considering how strong Noah was, the last thing I needed was to get back on his bad side. If I'd ever been on his good side in the first place, that was.

Did his question need much thought, though? From the moment I met Tyler, I'd wanted to protect him from the storm beyond Isabel's window. I'd wanted to shield him from the terrors of the thunder and the torrential rain. That urge to preserve the innocence he had left grew even with the divide between us. Tyler was no helpless baby bird, but he was too easily swayed to venture on his own yet.

Under my breath, I muttered, "No."

Noah studied me for a good moment without saying anything. He didn't seem to find whatever he was searching for, so he just lowered his head and started for the exit. "Good."

I watched him leave, only to recoil a moment later. Tyler was huddled against the earthy wall, staring right back at me. His eyes were wide, mouth open like he wanted to shout but had lost the words. Titanium sat perched on his shoulder, whispering something in his ear. Whatever it was she said, Tyler's expression shattered like a glass pane.

Before I could say anything, he turned around and left.

Chapter Thirty

DEER IN HEADLIGHTS

Tyler

I was done for.

How did it take me two unsuccessful attempts, while Oliver got to swoop in and take that necklace with ease? What was it he had that I didn't? Charm? Social skills? Maybe a bit of everything.

When I returned to see him having a civilized conversation with Noah, something in me snapped. Why did everything have to come so easily to him? Blind with rage, I threw Titanium off my shoulder, abandoning her, and left for the valley once more. At least I could breathe up there.

Night had fallen, but clouds blocked every star from view. Such darkness made me pause, but once I'd summoned a small glowing icicle, I continued. If anything, the tool gave me an idea.

As soon as I was on solid ground, I raised my hand and fired at it. A massive shard of ice erupted from the dirt, making everything tremble from such force.

It wasn't enough.

I kicked my leg at the earth, sending pillars of ice shooting upward. As I let my body relax, the pillars cracked and crumbled like ancient ruins. Like I was in Greece and not a realm of elemental magic.

I glared at the clumps of ice. It wasn't *enough*.

But when was enough?

With a roar I shot my hand forward, propelling sharp bullets of ice right at a large shrub. They ripped through the branches, dead leaves falling pathetically and piling on the ground.

I stared at it, but my mind was racing. With every jagged exhale, little clouds puffed out of my mouth. They felt so nice against my flushed skin. But it wasn't enough to stop my shaking. To stop the storm brewing in my aching chest.

Spinning around, I stormed to the ice shard that still jutted out of the ground, pointy and solid. I swung my foot back and kicked the base of the crystal. It didn't budge, only sending a wave of pain flooding my toes. With a cry, I hobbled backwards. My foot throbbed, but the relief of feeling something was stronger.

Too bad it couldn't last, because the sound of crunching foot-steps made me glare over my shoulder.

From the person's height, I expected it to be someone like Noah, Luke, or Mystral, but I found my tough exterior rotting in a way those people could never cause. As they stepped into the light of my crystals, it hit me like a truck.

Approaching me was Emperor Thierry, with his fiery crown in all his glory.

I stood up straight, like a soldier. My head was spinning, making the ice around us seem fuzzy. What was Thierry doing here? He was supposed to be back at the castle, waiting for us!

There was this familiar cold tugging in my stomach: that horrible feeling when you know something is wrong. It's when your limbs seize up and you're waiting for the worst, but you can't tell when it'll hit. All you know is that it will happen—maybe right when you let your guard down.

"I came for a visit, to see how things are running," Thierry explained as if he read my mind. "You, Noah, and Savana have been taking your time, after all."

"We're–we're–w..." It felt like I had cotton in my mouth. "Working on–on it. Um...weren't you—weren't you with Mm...McKenzie?"

"McKenzie isn't with the Cataclysm anymore." Thierry's voice was tight. "She ran away, like a coward."

When Thierry said she wasn't with us anymore, my mind instantly thought of death. But when he continued, my shoulders drooped in relief.

That must've been a wrong move, because Thierry's throat jumped. The flames on his crown expanded. "Do you really believe that silly little story?" He raised his brows in disbelief. "That McKenzie simply ran away?" When he cocked his head to one side, the light from the ice crystals dulled, drenching us in darkness.

The way he spoke reminded me of my mom. His voice was woven with disgust and disappointment. I shook my head vigorously. "I'm sorry. I'm sorry. I didn't mean—"

"Those Indra Academy students took her. They wanted to save their own skins. You aren't going to let them brainwash you, are you?"

Another shake of my head. Another apology.

Thierry swayed back, his dark gaze scanning my trembling body.

Even in the dark, I saw his fist swing my way.

Agony exploded in my right eye, and my teeth tore through my bottom lip. Hot blood pooled in my mouth as I landed on my side, gasping. I looked up in astonishment through blurry eyes. Thierry stood over me, breathing heavily, mouth twisted in a sick smile like he'd enjoyed that. He was nothing more than a shadowed monster.

"Have you learned your lesson?" he panted.

I nodded frantically. Before I could get up, Thierry's foot contacted my chest. He shoved me with it, pushing me onto my back. Then he stomped on my stomach, grinning as I coughed up more blood. My body convulsed. I tried rolling onto my side, gasping and hacking and trying to not drown.

"I learned my lesson!" I coughed.

A kick to the face.

"Hey!"

He stomped on my cheek.

No, no, no, no, no.

It felt like my face was about to shatter.

Not again, not again, not again.

I thrashed and screamed as he crouched and rained blows down on my face. His fist crunched against my cheek again. He rose to his feet only to kick my chin and then slam his boot onto my forehead.

Nobody would hear it. Why would anybody hear it? I might've been a world away from the shed, but those moldy walls still blocked any sound from reaching another's ears.

The next time Thierry lowered himself, I reached forward and slapped him across the face. While incapable of damage, it made a pleasant clap that mimicked thunder in the distance. My fingers raked through his stubble, and I kicked out my legs at his stomach. I started firing ice at random, miraculously hitting Thierry's ankle.

The force of my shove sent him reeling backwards. Everything spun as I struggled to my feet. Blood and saliva pooled in my mouth, now dripping from my nose as well.

"How else are you meant to learn?" The ice capturing Thierry's leg melted, and he shook the water off with impatience.

"Is this because–because McKenzie left?" I couldn't hear myself over the racing of my heart.

Thierry came closer, raising his hand again. I flinched with a cry, but all he did was stroke my hair. "Perhaps you should've kept yourself in line the way I should've with McKenzie. As soon as I focused on you, she slipped out of my grip."

"I'm sorry." I dragged my tongue over the split in my lip to mop up the blood, gagging as it returned right away. With the cease of blows, I took the chance to spin around and make my way to the cave entrance. My mom had never hurt me in front of someone other than my siblings. Surely, Thierry would be the same. If someone else was there, I'd be fine.

Thierry's hand jerked forward and grabbed me, tightening around my left arm. "You're going to listen to me," he snarled, squeezing my muscles. Smoke rose in the short distance between us, making him look like a dragon. "If you don't get your act to-gether, you'll never see those Indra Academy students or Dominic again. Hell, what's stopping me from taking them out right now? They've clouded your judgment."

A strange heat spread along my arm, but I didn't register it until pain seared my skin. I writhed and yelled, but I couldn't break away. A hole was burned into my hoodie, Thierry's fire now tearing into my flesh. "Wait–wait—*stop!*"

Thierry leaned forward, resting his other hand on my shoulder. His nose was inches away from mine. "Those people are not your friends, Tyler. They're *not* friends. Understand?" His voice was awfully sweet and almost motherly. "I thought you loved me."

I nodded frantically, too choked up to speak. Everything smelled of burning flesh.

"Good." Thierry finally pulled away, smiling cheerfully. Like I was his finished masterpiece.

A painful streak of red was burned into my arm, which I cupped my hand over to hide it. I forced myself to smile, despite how heavy I felt. "I'll fix it! I'll fix everything!" My voice sounded like a wrung towel.

"Do you promise?"

"I promise."

Chapter Thirty-One
ALL FOR YOU
OLIVER

Titanium said that I needed to knock some sense into Tyler.

Vincent said I needed to knock the lights *out* of Tyler.

Their complaints had me suffocating in guilt. It was partially my fault things got this bad. Tyler had been right the other day; if I'd kept a closer eye on him, he never would've come to Derngate. Crystal had argued a similar point the day we met. So of course, I felt responsible for cleaning up this mess.

I had been searching for Tyler through the tunnels when a voice behind me said, "You must go to the valley at once."

I spun around to see Crystal Lacey standing nearby, her white glow illuminating the gloomy passage. "Is that where Tyler is?"

The ghost's face was tight with urgency. "Yes. But please, hurry. I...I mean it this time when I say he's in danger."

"What?" My heart skipped a beat. All the worst-case scenarios threatened to flood my brain at once. I swallowed my rising panic and pushed past Crystal to find the entrance. "I'll go right now. Thank you!"

Crystal didn't follow me, but right before I turned the corner, I swore I heard her say, "Good luck and be careful."

Mystral was hanging out by the base of the staircase, examining the dagger I gave her. As I approached, she looked up and held the weapon toward me, handle first. "There's a storm above. I think you need this more than I do."

I stared at the dagger in shocked silence, only able to choke out "thank you" as I took it from her. Sheathing it in my boot, I swerved around Mystral and started up the stairs.

Fat raindrops greeted me as I hauled myself out of the entrance hole, damp earth clinging to my coat and cloak. My boots struggled to grip the slushy terrain shrouded by nighttime.

"Tyler?" I called over the rainfall. "Tyler, are you out here?"

Only silence answered. Groaning to myself, I stood up and inspected the area. Crystals and clumps of ice were littered everywhere, simple proof of Tyler's presence. My reflections peered back at me, warped by raindrops streaming down the ice crystals. There seemed to be no active sign of trouble.

"Tyler?" I tried again. *Please don't tell me he ran away again.* Panic clawed at my throat, and I started to pace back and forth, surveying the land. Before I called out again, though, a black blob in the near distance caught my eye.

It was Tyler approaching me, but something didn't seem right. His posture was falling apart, and he was hunched over like he was in pain. Black spots covered his face, sending a chill down my spine.

I fought to keep my smile from dropping. "Hey, are you oka—"

"How many times do I have to tell you?" Tyler cut me off. There was something different about his voice. It was like he was speaking through fluid. "I'm not going back."

"Why?"

Tyler blinked, then blinked again, before gritting his teeth. "Just quit already! Then you can all go home."

Home. I extended my hand toward him, a gesture of welcoming. "We want you to come with us."

"It's not you who wants me back." Tyler began to pace, a smile creeping on his lips. "It's Isabel. You–you only ever spoke to me because of her." He faced me again, laughing hollowly, "You're just a puppet! You all are!"

"I don't know who gave you that idea, but it isn't true." Regret clumped in my throat. Tyler had a point. If Isabel hadn't assigned me to look after him, I never would've known about his existence. "I know that *I* want you back."

Tyler summoned a jagged icicle in his grip, storming forward until he held it to my throat. "Why?"

The glow from Tyler's ice lit up his face. Immediately, I saw the results of the danger Crystal had mentioned. He was hauntingly pale, with blood splattered across his face and crusted over his broken lips. That explained the dark spots I couldn't identify. His right eye was swollen half shut. On his forehead was the mark of what I believed to be a footprint.

I put my hands up to show I meant no harm. Still, my heart felt like it was beating in my throat. "Who did that to you?"

"That's not important!"

"It is!" My voice raised. "You don't deserve—"

"What do you know about deserving?" Tyler seethed. With the rain streaking down his bruised face, he looked horrible. "You're only thinking of yourself. You have people who like you to go back to! Do you think anyone will care if I come back or not? You should've minded your own business." He was breathing heavily, and his next words were a fierce exhale. "We're strangers! You shouldn't care about me."

What in the world? I tensed up, shoulders raised like a threatened cat. "If I only thought about myself, you think I would've gone through all the trouble of coming here? I came this far out of my own free will and my desire to protect you!"

A shudder racked Tyler's body.

"And does it matter if we haven't known each other for long? There's nothing wrong with showing kindness to strangers. Everyone should be given a chance." Weariness seeped into my tone. Weariness from all the fighting and time spent repeating myself. "You don't have to be my friend. You don't even have to forgive me for the trouble I caused. But please, you can't stay here." *The proof is all over your face.*

Tyler looked me up and down. The icicle he held trembled in his hand. He looked so concentrated, I feared he'd slit my throat. But no, he was looking at my chest, where my fire necklace glittered in the rain.

"Give it to me."

"What?"

"Give me the necklace!"

I closed my fist over the crystal, hiding it from sight. "No."

With Tyler's free hand, he swiped at it, but I dodged him. "Just give it to me! Please! Then—and then you guys can go home, and we'll forget this ever happened!" The whites of his eyes were visible around his dual-colored irises, all harsh with desperation. "Oliver, *please*. What do I have to do? Do I...do I have to fight for it?"

"Absolutely n—"

Before I could finish, Tyler advanced again, this time with the icicle in his grip. A frigid cut to the cheek made me recoil with a yell, a thin trail of blood seeping down my face.

Is that the game he wants to play? I brought my hand away from the necklace so I could unsheathe my dagger. Warmth flooded my palms, smoke rising from my fingertips. The freckles along my arms and cheeks glowed orange, enhancing my vision in the dark night. I swiped at the air, letting a wave of fire wash over the spot right beside Tyler. It was a warning shot that the rain doused.

Tyler wasn't looking to go so easy. He jumped right into it, using his feet to direct lines of ice crystals in my direction. The triangular scars on his cheeks burst into blue light, clashing against my orange.

I weaved around his crystals with surprising ease. When Tyler tried shooting a larger chunk of ice my way, I deflected it with my blade and sent the ice shattering. Fire roared in my ears.

His attacks were choppier than I expected, especially when his attack against Ruslan had been much more coordinated. Now, he was firing at random, just trying to hit me. I dodged and sliced away every icicle without a problem. That only seemed to worsen his mood.

"Why do you even need the necklaces?" Tyler yelled as he rammed into me. We both disregarded our powers as we fought with our arms, pushing and shoving like little kids. "At least Thierry needs them for a reason! You just find them pretty! You're like Mystral!"

"There's something—ow!" I was cut off as Tyler punched under my jaw. Stumbling back, I tried again. "There's something at Indra Academy, okay? It's calling us back, and we need the necklaces. We need *you*."

At the mention of my school, Tyler's scowl deepened, and he tackled me to the ground. He sat on my stomach to pin me down, attacking my chest like a wild animal.

"What did I do?" I raised my voice as I grappled with Tyler and tried to throw him off me. The way he put all his weight on my body left me to writhe as he beat me. A part of me feared using force. "Is it about Indra Academy? If I knew keeping you there would turn out this badly, I would've helped send you elsewhere!"

"What elsewhere?" Tyler finally stopped punching. "I have nowhere else to go! *This* was my last resort, Oliver. I'm not like you! I don't have parents I call every day, or—or a mom who looks happy to hear my voice. Do you know how fucking spoiled you are?" The fire in his eyes dimmed. His shoulders drooped, like he could no longer hold the weight of the crying sky. "At least your moms wanted you. You were a wanted child."

Pattering rain filled the silence that followed. Chunks of hail started falling from the sky, too. It reminded me of the storm that engulfed New York City the night Tyler appeared at Indra Academy's doorstep.

"I curse people. My mom didn't even want me. She did it all for Thierry. And now what am I supposed to tell my dad? That I failed him, too?" Tyler put his hand to the right side of his face—the half that was all swollen. "I–I have to get this right! Failure isn't an option! It—" His words were garbled in his mouth as he dribbled a mixture of blood and saliva on my chest. "I have a—I have a chance to make it right. My parents will keep loving me. I'll get my brother back. Oliver, I can't leave!"

I studied his face, too stricken to find the words. The idea of parental love made me think back to the night Tyler and I met—the night Tyler arrived with a purple chest and bones jutting out of his form. Finally, I whispered, "I don't think that was love, Tyler."

Tyler gave me this wild, desperate look. "What? With my mom?" He started to laugh. It sounded more like a crow being tortured. "My mom would've killed me a long time ago if she didn't love me. But she keeps me alive, you know? She puts a roof over my head and keeps me in check."

"She's hurt you."

"She loves me." Tyler grabbed my necklace, but because I was lying down, he couldn't pull it over my head. He tugged at it, groaning when the chain didn't break. "Please, just give it to me!

If you won't, then at least kill me. I'm as good as dead without the necklace."

He reached for my dagger, but I tossed it several feet away.

"I'm not killing you." My voice shook.

Tyler's face contorted. His glowing marks cast weird shadows, as if he were telling campfire stories and not asking to die. He whispered, in a voice that sounded much more like himself, "Please." The glowing marks began to flicker, like a dying firefly.

"We can fix this together. I–I'm not going to kill you." I was afraid of what he might do if I didn't restrain him, but I didn't want to trigger him through touch. My body was frozen from where he sat on top of me.

"It's the necklaces or die!" Tyler's voice grew hysterical. He gripped my shirt's collar tightly. "Noah said I'm—said I only cause suffering! I mean—look at you! Look at my family! Look at me!" His breathing hitched, his markings flashing blue intermittently. Blue and off, blue and off.

I tried to move, but Tyler kept going.

"Either way, you won't see me again. It's for your own good. I'm protecting you! Please! Please, please, please..." He fluctuated from whispering pleas to screaming them, his raspy voice piercing the night.

Blue markings, on and off, on and off. I murmured words of comfort, trying to soothe the distraught boy, but he didn't seem to hear me. He had this faraway expression on his face, and he was desperately looking at me as if I were someone else.

Eventually, Tyler's grip on my collar went slack, and his begs began to slur. His markings flashed rapidly, just like how his lashes fluttered desperately, before his eyes rolled back and he fell right on top of me with a tiny *thump*. The blue glow switched off entirely, and then there was silence.

"Tyler?" My own freckles had stopped glowing, and I felt this awful chill. Tyler's heart beat against my chest, but the slowing of it didn't bring me any comfort.

I rolled Tyler off me and pushed myself into a sitting position. I frantically shook his shoulders. "Hey—that's not funny! Wake up!"

He just flopped like a rag doll.

I was about to run for help when the squelch of mud alerted me of someone approaching from behind. Looking over my shoulder, I saw it was none other than Emperor Thierry Colliss standing over us, in the flesh.

He scowled down at the unconscious kid. "At times like these, I wish Bryce had followed in my footsteps. He would've gotten that necklace from you without all this mess."

When he stepped closer, I shielded Tyler with my body. "Get away from us!"

"That's my son, you imbecile." Thierry leaned over us, looking like a monster in the dark. Lightning flashed behind him, illuminating the holes in his ears and casting a shadow over his face. Dry blood was crusted on his large hands. The light danced around his outline in what would have been an angelic silhouette but was really a scene straight from hell, complete with his devil-like crown.

I was so paralyzed in his presence, I couldn't do anything as he plucked the fire necklace from me. He put it on with a grin. "Thank you, Oliver Stylus. It turns out you were more helpful than *he* was in the end."

"You hurt him, didn't you? Before our fight?"

Thierry scoffed. "I'm an angel compared to his mother."

That wasn't comforting in the slightest.

"Now, then, why don't we get down to business?" Thierry crouched down next to me, yanking Tyler from my grip. He picked him up, and for the briefest moment, Thierry looked like an ordinary father carrying his sleepy kid from the car to the house. That was if you didn't regard Thierry's terrifying design and Tyler's horrendous state.

I stood with numb legs. Tyler's head lolled back, and I wanted to scream for Thierry to handle him with more care. But who was I to instruct this man what to do? "What business? You got your necklace already."

Thierry clicked his tongue and shook his head. "I need to collect the other one. I know Savana already has it, so this is perfect! As for you..." His gaze hardened as it focused on me. But then he smiled, and it looked genuine. "I'm inviting the rest of you to a party."

"A what?" I managed to choke out.

"A party! After all this, you deserve to indulge in Meraki culture." Thierry started toward the entrance to Mystral's cavern. "Your whole group is invited. Actually, scratch that. Why don't you all come home with us?" He paused, looking over his shoulder. "It would be rude to decline."

Emerging from the darkness behind Thierry were several of his guards, all prepared to defend the royalty standing before me. They stood in silence, their eyes boring into me.

I forced myself to smile at the emperor, despite wanting to strangle him. "I think coming with you is a great idea."

I don't remember much of what happened next. I have a vague memory of Thierry barging into Mystral's cavern and ordering his Cataclysm trainees and us Indra Academy students to come with him. Nobody said a thing, perhaps horrified by Tyler's bloody face or the fact that I stood behind Thierry with my head bowed in defeat.

The one good thing about Thierry's guards being there was that they had a few horses and wagons. Maybe that's how they'd arrived so quickly. It helped with transporting us back to the castle. My classmates and I were ushered into a wagon separate from Thierry, Noah, Savana, and Tyler's.

Luke stayed by my side the whole ride to Audun, whispering apologies for not helping sooner. He let me lean on his shoulder when my eyes drooped halfway shut from exhaustion. Diana and Vincent didn't utter a word. I noticed that up ahead, even Noah looked unsettled by Thierry's actions. He awkwardly comforting Savana, who was crying, maybe because she had to leave Mystral so suddenly. And Tyler, the boy who'd read so much about birds back at Indra Academy, never got to say goodbye to the winged young lady.

That was my last coherent thought before the rest of the night slipped into an inky puddle. My fatigue had caught up to me. I wasn't sure if I passed out or not—that remained a mystery. I just remembered becoming alert on a fluffy mattress with Diana curled up and asleep on the far edge. On another nearby mattress were Luke and Vincent. We were in a fancy room that must've been for guests, decorated with pristine furniture I could only imagine finding in a castle. Beyond the large windows, the sky was an explosion of pale pink and yellow.

The sun was rising.

Careful to not disturb the others, I stood shakily, pausing to catch my balance. Dizziness blurred my vision. My cheek was crusted with dry blood. Everything was sore, and each breath hurt. Peeking under my shirt, I grimaced when I saw purple and yellow bruises blooming along my chest.

I left the room. With my tunnel vision, I didn't pay much attention to the guards posted in the corridors. They watched me in silence. Either Thierry had ordered them to let us roam around, or these guys were about to lose their job.

After some awkward stumbling around, I peeked inside what I quickly realized was Tyler's room. I silently entered without a plan or anything to say. It didn't matter in the end. He was still out cold, spared from having to face reality for just a little longer. He looked the most peaceful I'd ever seen him. Titanium sat by the crook of his neck, watching me like a guard dog. She didn't say anything.

The room was big and fitting for a prince. But the unconscious, broken boy looked like he should be anywhere but here. *Prince Tyler.* The name didn't have a ring to it or anything.

I kneeled by Tyler's bed, pressing my forehead against his mattress. "I'm so sorry," I whispered, even though he wouldn't hear it. "It's like I failed you, but I don't know how."

Silence met my words. I looked up, watching how Tyler's chest rose and fell with each breath. He was human. He was drooling on his pillow. He was alive, and that was the reminder I needed.

"It won't happen again," I vowed quietly. I pivoted so my back rested against the bed frame, and I faced the decorative ceiling. "I swear on my life, Tyler, your parents won't touch you ever again."

I recalled what Vincent asked me just a day ago: Would I die for Tyler?

It was a question I let hang in my mind until the door creaked open. Savana poked her head in. Her tired eyes widened when they met mine. "I didn't think you'd be up yet."

I shrugged as she approached and sat next to me. "Just wanted to check he's okay."

"He'll be alright." Savana looked at Tyler briefly before focusing on me again. "And you? Everything fell apart so quickly last night...What really happened?" She licked her thumb and wiped it over my bloody cheek.

I melted into her touch. "I don't know. I...I really don't know." Weighed down by the hopeless knowledge that Thierry had our necklaces again, my head sank onto Savana's shoulder.

She didn't say anything as the tears came pouring down my face. All the noise in the universe was reduced to sniffles and hiccups that I refused to show the world.

As if my sadness was contagious, Tyler let out a weak cry in his sleep. His body twitched like he was flinching from something.

It was such a horrible sound. I wanted to extract the agony buried deep in his flesh and make sure he never felt it again. But there was no such cure. I reached my hand forward, giving his scarred fingers the slightest nudge, and he drifted off again.

It was then, through my tear-filled eyes, did I realize I was resting against a Meraki, someone from the species we'd spent all this time hiding from. I pulled away from Savana, who smiled and said, "Let's rewrite what's to come, okay?"

To that, I managed to whisper, "That sounds perfect."

Chapter Thirty-Two
DOMINIC
Tyler

IN THE DARKNESS, DOMINIC asked his favorite question: Where does it hurt?

Curled up in a ball so tight, I whispered to myself, "Everywhere."

Not one part of my body was spared. Everything felt like it was burning. It felt like my muscles were twisting and forming braids, similar to the ones girls on the playground made with their hair. As soon as the feeling registered in my mind, I wanted to roll over and sleep for a month. But when my eyes opened to slits, there wasn't a jewel-studded ceiling above me. This ceiling belonged to my bedroom in Thierry's castle.

Did I dream it all? I brought my hand to my face, only to wince. My skin felt hot and sticky and crusted all over. When I pulled my hand down, I jolted at the sight of blood under my fingernails.

It was an ordinary morning. Maybe everything was a dream, and I was in the shed. Mom would arrive any minute now with a cup of water, asking while I chugged it down, "What did we learn?"

I sat up, and the world swam in my vision. Everything was fuzzy. My movements felt weird, too. It was like I was stuck in a jar of honey.

No, this was definitely the castle. Gloomy, midday light poured in from the window, and the waterfall roared in the near distance. There were no more crashing ocean waves. I was in a bed.

The door squeaked, and I shrank away from the sound with hunched shoulders. Whoever entered squealed "Tyler!" and the voice instantly relaxed me.

It was Titanium bounding across the room, jumping onto my lap, and melting into a black blob. She took a moment to roll around and purr like an ordinary cat before she opened her white eyes. "What happened last night?" she asked. "Thierry burst in out of nowhere and he was carrying you and Oliver was right behind him...He said that we were all going home."

"What?" My throat stung, and I swallowed before trying to speak again. "I–I don't..." And then it hit me. I remembered Thierry's attack and how I tried taking the necklace from Oliver. "Where–where are...are they okay?"

"The Indra Academy students were given a different room. They're fine." Titanium balanced on her hind legs, putting her front paws on my chest. She began to lick the dry blood off my face. "Oliver said Thierry did this to you?" she mumbled between licks.

I squirmed. "We were just training. He got, um, a little rough, that's all."

Titanium paused and looked down. "Uh huh." It was a blunt response, full of doubt.

I followed her gaze and jolted. She was looking at my left arm. More specifically, the hole in my sleeve that was a window to the ugly burn Thierry had inflicted on me. "Oh no."

Titanium's eyes scrunched up comically as they lit up my sore face with their white glow. "You don't look good."

"I've been worse." I didn't remove my gaze from the hoodie, tears welling in my eyes. I'd taken care of it for three years. Sure, it'd gotten dirty and bloody, and I'd never washed it, but it had survived.

And now Thierry had put a hole through it. Somehow, that hurt more than the burn.

*Wait...*I lifted my hand to the burn, creating a fuzzy image in my mind. My palm flickered blue, but as I cast frigid air onto the wound, waves of pain and nausea rocked through me.

"You shouldn't put ice on burns," Titanium warned, blocking my view of my arm. "McKenzie told you your healing ability has limitations."

"Would've—I would've liked to rem...remember that earlier." Hunching over, I put my hand to my face instead. I kept my power to the lowest setting I could manage, partially afraid of impaling myself.

After a moment of watching, Titanium finally backed away and left the room. I watched her go, unable to find the words to call her back. Maybe she knew all the horrible things I did last night.

Thinking about it made me grimace as best as I could with split lips and a right eye that wouldn't fully open. I curled up on my side, bringing my knees to my chest, the way I always did in the shed back home to preserve space.

I tucked my chin and mouth into my hoodie, which stank of smoke and earth. How was it that a few weeks ago, it was cleaned at Indra Academy? What differentiated Oliver's love—shown by washing it—from Thierry's love—shown by burning it?

One hurt and the other didn't. One wrapped me in a blanket of warmth and the other was suffocating.

Tears stung my eyes, but I refused to let them fall. Why couldn't I have listened to Oliver sooner? He was right. He was always right. *Just stay alive, Tyler. It won't happen again.*

Dominic used to say that to me all the time. What a liar.

I didn't realize I had dozed off until the door opened again, and I heard shuffling footsteps in the back of my mind. I opened an eye, but I kinda wished I pretended to stay asleep. That ice had barely done anything for my face, and my burn throbbed.

Titanium was back, and this time, Oliver was behind her. His eyes were bloodshot from what looked like crying, and a bandage covered the cut on his cheek. He fumbled with something in his hand, and only when Titanium muttered something to him did he step into the room.

He smiled weakly and said, "Glad to see you're okay."

When he approached, I sat upright and scooted away from him until my back hit the headboard.

Oliver lifted whatever he held for me to see. It was a hand towel, dripping with water. He inched closer and carefully held it toward me, a bit like I was a stray animal.

I watched the towel dangle from his hand. Something like that could be used as a whip when wet and heavy. My heart began to skip beats. I snatched it from him to make sure he didn't use it against me. It was ice cold, and my hot skin rejoiced. I buried my face into the damp fabric like I was putting out a fire.

"Look, I just want to talk." Oliver waited until I looked up before continuing. "I know, I know—I keep saying that, and we keep going in circles, but I want you to hear me out."

I glanced at Titanium in silent hopes she'd dig me out of this hole. But she simply sat on my bed again. Lacking the strength to resist him, I nodded and pressed myself further against the headboard. Flipping the towel onto the other side, I dabbed it over my burn wound. It took everything in me to not yell aloud.

Oliver hesitantly sat on the edge of my bed, keeping his hands on his lap and in plain sight. His black nail polish from Indra Academy was all gone. "Noah told me about your brother." He paused, watching my shifting expression before continuing. "And I just thought it'd be worth—I don't know—showing that I know how you feel? Th-that I understand what it's like being unsure of where you belong."

When I didn't move, he started to scratch at his nails, probably trying to chip away some microscopic bits of leftover polish. "I don't know what it's like losing a sibling since I'm an only child, but if it counts, I lost my parents. Both—a car accident the night they were coming back from a trip. It was dark and muddy and they just...didn't come back, y'know?"

Despite the sadness of the story, a smile painted his lips. I could tell it was forced, though. That it was broken. It didn't look right on the face that was always bright and cheery or set and determined. I wanted to smack it away. But all I could do was stare, my mouth open. For some reason, it felt familiar, like I'd pieced this together before. Perhaps it had been in a dream, but I'd forgotten.

"And my best friend from California—" Oliver's voice cut off after blurting that part out, as if it had taken him, too, by surprise. He shook his head and corrected himself more slowly. "He isn't dead, similar to the way Dominic might not be, but he's still so far away, it aches. Gosh, he was even more than a best friend. He was my everything. My moon to my stars. My universe!"

The same way Dominic had been for me. He had been my gravity. Since losing him, I'd been drifting aimlessly in the dark.

"So wouldn't...wouldn't you do anything to bring him back?" I finally whispered.

Touched by the light, tears glistened in Oliver's eyes. He looked small with that bandaged cheek and glazed eyes. "I would."

The mattress shifted beneath me, creaking in a way that reminded me of my bones.

I leaned forward, wincing at the weight it put on my burned arm. "That's, uh, that's why I'm here. At the start of all this, Thierry–Thierry said he had information on Dominic. And...and if I stayed and helped him, he'd tell me about it."

Oliver's eyes widened. "So that's why you wanted the necklace so badly. Oh, Tyler, you should've mentioned that!"

"I'm sorry." Hot shame filled my throat. "The only...The only reason I did it was to–to get my brother back. My mom and sister—they know it's my fault. I thought they would forgive me if I did something good."

Oliver opened his mouth, but nothing came out. He lowered his gaze to the floral pattern of the duvet, on the first proper bed I'd ever had. His shoulders hunched up, maybe with guilt for being unable to offer me such luxurious arrangements at Indra Academy.

"Thierry sugarcoated the story he told you—the one about reuniting the human realm and Derngate. I don't know how to explain everything, but things didn't end on good terms between the two." Oliver tugged a strand of his hair. "Thierry believes he's the hero, but do you realize what consequences it'll have if he succeeds? Everything will be thrown out of balance. In the chaos, everyone will turn to Thierry as a source of knowledge since he's the emperor and has been to the human realm before. His Meraki-are-superior complex will endanger us humans. He'll have the power to shape the new world in a way we can't trust."

Oliver's gaze drifted up to my black eye. "Even if all this didn't exist, if Thierry really cared about you, he wouldn't have hurt you in such a way. He'll keep using abusive tactics to keep you close, and that's not okay."

Titanium nodded, reminding us of her presence. "I should've mentioned something sooner. I thought he'd be fine with McKenzie and Savana nearby, but..."

Oliver frowned at me.

"So, then what?" I rasped. "Thierry ex-expects me to take the throne. I'm the prince. I–I can't go home, either. I'll be a failure. A traitor. Oliver, my mom..." I couldn't comprehend what sort of living hell she'd put me through if I dared show my face.

"You're not going back to your mom." Oliver's voice was firm. "That's for certain."

The unwavering force in his voice rattled me, but not in a bad way. Oliver's devotion was a type I'd forgotten about after I lost Dominic. Oliver had gone to the edge of a different universe for me. It was so endearing, but... *What if it was all for nothing?*

I bit my lip, only to flinch. It still tasted like blood. "We're going in circles again. Didn't I say I'm out of options?"

"We want you to come back to Indra Academy. Nothing has to change! You can still sleep in the dorm with me and Bryce and hang out with us..." Oliver's voice was coaxing. "There's more to it than that, though. You remember what we told you back at the Timber Coast, right? About how your presence led to a domino effect? I...I understand how that might've turned you off, being put on a high level of importance so suddenly. But know that you aren't by yourself. I'll—*we'll* be with you every step of the way."

Me, important? I wanted to feel pride, but all that came over me was worry. Thierry had called me important, too, for being a prince and ice mutation. Yet just last night, he'd beaten me into the ground. Important, huh? I tensed up as I faced Oliver, waiting for a similar reaction, but he was still.

Shaking my head, I whispered, "I'll let you down."

Noah's words from before came rushing back, about how I didn't bring anything good to the table. He was right. Simply looking at Oliver's battered body was proof.

"I know the past isn't something we can change," Oliver said, "but we can still fix the future. Tyler, we need you back at Indra Academy for more than selfish reasons." He sounded so much like Dominic, able to soothe while being serious. "Thierry's project is going to hurt people. We have to do something about it."

"I can't. I–I might hurt you."

Oliver shook his head and smiled. "I know you'll do what's right. It's worth treating people like they deserve another chance, you know? We got more to us beneath the surface than people think. Trust is a fragile thing when you've been hurt, I understand. But we have to grow around that pain. You aren't doing this alone."

I looked to Titanium again, who purred and nodded her head. Ages ago, McKenzie had mentioned that Shadow Guards were designed to comfort, educate, and guide. And here she was. I was about to lean into the warmth of that idea when I felt something cold tug at my stomach.

Oliver must've noticed, because he asked, "Are you okay?"

"I just, uh…" I held Titanium close to my chest, letting her purrs soothe me. "I should—I should say sorry first. For last night." My lungs squeezed. "I learned to solve things through–through, um…fists. It wasn't right of me to hurt you. I turned into my mom last night."

"You're a good kid, Tyler—nothing like your mom." Oliver hesitated, kinda like he wanted to ruffle my hair or hug me reassuringly, but he didn't. Instead, he stood up from my bed and held his hand toward me. "Why don't we find you something to eat and drink? The rest of us have been talking about an escape plan, and we want you there for it. I hope you know how to dance, by the way."

I looked at his hand. It wasn't raised above me or twitching with violent urges. His fingers were a little limp, like he himself wasn't sure and wanted to withdraw it.

Carefully, I took his hand and let him lead the way.

CHAPTER THIRTY-THREE

MAY I HAVE THIS DANCE?

OLIVER

WHEN THIERRY WALKED IN on us in McKenzie's now-abandoned office, he initially stiffened before his posture relaxed and he smiled. He seemed delighted to have all us kids getting along. Well, everyone but Noah, who was sulking elsewhere.

"I'm so glad to see you've made friends with Savana and Tyler," he praised us, but his enthusiasm at this prospect, when he'd been so against us before, suggested he knew we were a threat. He was just waiting to make his move.

Thierry turned to his son. "And it relieves me to know you're okay after that awful fight with Oliver."

Tyler didn't meet Thierry's eyes. He lowered his head until his hair fell over his bruised face.

None of us responded, since we all knew I hadn't been at fault.

Don't let him further twist the story, I pleaded silently. With my fists clenched, I eyed Thierry, trying to keep my face neutral. This was my first time seeing him in proper daylight, not in a dream or under the cover of nighttime. His amber eyes, the same color as Bryce's, seemed to pierce holes in my lungs, making it hard to face him and breathe at the same time.

"Is there something we can help you with?" I managed to ask.

"Yes, actually." Thierry folded his hands in front of him primly. "I want you six to get ready. We're going shopping for tonight's party. Your attendance is required for the speech I'm giving." When Vincent opened his mouth to argue, Thierry added, "I will not take 'no' for an answer."

Luke and I shifted uncomfortably and mumbled our acceptance, whereas Diana and Savana squealed and high-fived each other. Thierry watched them for a moment, and then, with a satisfied smile, he turned and left.

When the door shut behind him, we all faced the girls.

"What?" Diana puffed out her chest. "Shopping is shopping, whether it be with your friends or the villain! Besides, our excitement eased the tension between us and Thierry, didn't it?"

We couldn't argue with that.

It felt strange visiting Audun again, especially without our cloaks. Thierry insisted that we would be fine as long as we stayed with him. He distributed little pins to put on our clothes, shaped like the fiery horns of his crown. Some Meraki looked at us funny as we passed by, and some were ready to attack on sight. But Thierry soothed them with words of reassurance, telling them that we were harmless and here to help him.

He eventually let his guard down and left to chat with some patrons outside the boutique we were in. The shop was adorned with floral decorations in vases, and a phonograph hummed with jazz melodies in the background. Other than us, the new Assembly of Six, and a few stray Meraki, the place was empty.

Thierry's disappearance was perfect, because that's when I noticed a cloaked figure with coily hair springing around the sides of their hood, checking out racks in the far corner.

"You actually ran away, huh?" I murmured, approaching the hooded figure.

She stiffened, but relaxed once she realized it was me. McKenzie lowered her hood, and while her smile was tense from days alone, her eyes were bright. "I ended up sheltering with Reed. They were understanding. I've been waiting for you guys to return, but it took a while."

I observed the puffy dresses she was perusing. "Sorry about that. Anyways, we're escaping tonight."

"Actually?"

"Yeah. Thierry is hosting a party, so it'll be perfect." My attention was captured by the dresses again. I wasn't sure if I was tempted to call Savana and Diana over to check them out or if I was tempted to take one for myself. They certainly caught my eye, but I resisted the urge to try one on. I already had an outfit picked out and didn't want to risk upsetting the emperor.

McKenzie pursed her lips. "A party, huh? Sounds fun. I'd attend, but I think Thierry is out for my head." She stifled a laugh and brought her hands away from the dresses.

I rocked on my feet as I juggled my thoughts. "Why don't you wait at the portal for us?"

McKenzie fell silent, but then her eyes widened as if an idea had struck her. "I think I know a way I can help from there. Say, how fast can you guys run?"

"Uh…I'd assume it depends on the circumstances?"

"I can work with that." McKenzie flipped her hood back on just as Thierry reentered the store. She winked at me and whispered, "Good luck" before whisking herself outside. Nobody gave her a second look.

Thanks. We'll need it.

Thierry and Noah left early, making Savana responsible for us returning to the castle on time. Vincent groaned about how we should just leave now, but I immediately shut his idea down. Thierry had the necklaces, and we weren't going anywhere without them. Anyone could tell Vincent just wanted an excuse to not show up to the party. I must admit, though, we looked pretty darn good when we finished shopping.

I had on a navy-blue suit with a matching tailcoat that went down to my shins. It reminded me of those dresses from earlier with its big ruffles that started at the waist and cascaded down. With some help from Diana, I braided the strands of my hair that didn't fit in a ponytail and clipped them above my head like a crown.

Luke hadn't been afraid to step away from the dark tones. He ended up in a white suit adorned with golden details that glimmered in the light. They matched his little blond tuft of hair.

Vincent looked like the villain or mad scientist in your average movie. He wore a dark trench coat over a black suit, so the only color in his outfit was his golden pendant. When he revealed it to us, Diana laughed, "You're like a plague doctor!" Vincent looked ready to strangle her.

Diana, of course, outshone us guys. She had a puffy dress that was made of an assortment of sage green and white fabrics, with billowy sleeves and tons of lace. Her heels were a matching pristine white, clacking against the cobblestone streets.

Savana looked like her dark twin, with a similarly cut dress consisting of deep purples, yellows, and blacks. You'd think she was dressed as a witch for Halloween. Mystral would've been proud.

Tyler, who'd clearly never been shopping for a special occasion before, went with the first outfit offered to him and left it at that. It included a formal black jacket, but he ruined it by tying his hoodie around his waist. When told to take it off, he shook his head. He was more interested in finding a bow for Titanium.

"We don't look stupid, do we?" Vincent groaned as we walked through the darkening streets in our getup. The town had quieted down at a record speed. Perhaps we scared them away with our wonderful fashion tastes.

"Not at all!" Diana slung her arm over his shoulder, making them both stagger. "I say we look fabulous." Only then did she seem to remember their tension from the other day, and she shuf-fled to the side.

I glanced over at Vincent, whose expression was a mixture of hesitation and longing. When he met my gaze, I raised an eyebrow and tilted my head in Diana's direction. If Vincent was going to shoot any sort of shot, he had to do it before things got chaotic.

My point got across to him. Vincent cleared his throat and pulled Diana aside. They were still close enough for me to hear him say, "I'm sorry for yesterday...and for what happened in Ikrel's prison. It was wrong of me to take my anger out on you."

Diana stayed silent.

"I let my own fear blind me," Vincent continued, "from recog-nizing your view on all this. But remember what you told us—that we have allies back home. You aren't alone. Let me be an...an ally."

"That could mean a lot of things." Diana looked like she was biting back a smile. "Do you mean as a fellow queer kid, as a part of the Assembly, or—"

"Everything!" Vincent interrupted with, flustered. "An ally for everything."

It was obvious that the rest of us were eavesdropping, holding our breaths while we waited for a response.

Finally, Diana started laughing. She doubled over, playfully slapping Vincent on the shoulder. "That's so sweet! I never knew you were such a softie!"

"I'm not!" Vincent's voice cracked.

"You totally are." Diana gulped for air, straightening up to catch her breath. She smiled at Vincent, her cheeks tinted red. "That means a lot, though. Thank you."

Vincent gave her one final look before frantically turning away. "Yeah, of course." He brought his necklace to his lips in a nervous gesture.

I let their banter drone on in the background as the castle came into view. Upon our arrival, the guards outside stiffened, but once they noticed Tyler and the Thierry-approved badges we wore, they let us inside.

An orchestra's melody floated out from beyond the courtyard, which we crossed with haste. Every torch in the castle was lit, creating a bubble of orange warmth against Derngate's frigid night. As we wandered through the halls, I noticed some of the guards seemed relaxed, hardly acknowledging us except for the occasional nod to Tyler. The prince blushed furiously and looked away every time.

"This is it." I wrung my hands in anticipation as I followed the music with the group. My body still ached with fatigue from yesterday, but I tamped down my urge to retreat to the cozy bedroom and sleep more. There wasn't time to relax. I had to hold on until we were home.

At the end of the hall were two large wooden doors propped open, revealing the ballroom. We paused at the entrance, taking in the boisterous scene.

No wonder the town was so dead; everyone had come to the party. On the sidelines, Meraki mingled, consuming or serving food and drinks. Everyone wore puffy dresses and suits far more extravagant than what my friends and I had on. In the center were pairs waltzing around, which we watched, dumbstruck. Tyler had his hands over his ears, cringing. He looked ready to bolt. I think he would've done so if not for Savana standing behind him.

"How are we supposed to find Thierry and Noah in this crowd?" I stood on my toes, searching for the duo in the sea of people.

"We'll be sure to spot them when the speech begins." Luke took my hand, pulling me forward. "Until then, may I have this dance?"

I was certain my face was bright red. "I—yeah!"

Luke dragged me onto the dance floor and immediately twirled me around. I stumbled with a yelp, the big ruffles of my coat threatening to trip me. After a split second of watching everyone else, we rearranged ourselves, so his free hand held my waist while I held his shoulder. My chest ached, more from the close contact with Luke than any remaining pain from Tyler's beating.

The orchestra in the corner started to play a happy, rather up-beat song as Luke and I fell into the box step, the only dance I knew. My boots clomped against the wooden floors like the hooves of a panicking horse as I fought to keep up with him. Having my dagger—which I'd managed to scoop up on our way back to the gorge—shoved down my boot didn't help.

"Have you done this before?" I asked with a nervous laugh.

"In elementary and middle school!" As the music's tempo picked up, Luke grinned. "Hang tight!"

The next thing I knew, we were spinning from one end of the dance floor to the other. Everyone else did the same. Dresses and coats opened like flowers in the candlelight. Somewhere in the distance, Vincent and Diana were laughing. Savana was flirting with nearby girls. Tyler was hiding. I hardly noticed, though. All I could think was, *how is Luke talented in so many fields?* It was a question that left me so lightheaded and giddy.

Somewhere in the blur, I caught a flash of familiar blond. I had to do a double take to make sure I wasn't seeing things. "Luke, check it out!" I forced him into another spin, so we switched spots. "Is that Reed?"

"What?" Luke's jaw dropped in amazement, his voice cracking. A huge smile spread across his face. "My gosh, it is!"

"Let's break apart, okay? Spin on over to them."

Luke's pace faltered. "What about you?"

I paused, looking around with a hum. Vincent and Diana were engaged begrudgingly in a dance of their own, leaving them out of the question. A little past them, though, at an empty table, was the hunched-over form of Tyler. He had his head down on the table, his hands still blocking his ears like it was too loud for him. To answer Luke's question, I said, "I'll be okay! We'll regroup right before the speech."

"Sounds good." And with that, Luke released me and spun off in Reed's direction.

For a split second, I caught Reed's face brightening with joy to see Luke again. The two of them began to chat away excitedly.

I smiled to myself before starting toward Tyler's table. But some guy must've had too much booze, knocking into me, and sending his drink flying.

He whirled around, glaring at me. "Human scum! Watch where you're going!" His ears pinned back, but as he took me in, they relaxed. "My apologies, ma'am."

My face felt as hot as the sun. I was about to correct him when a hand grabbed mine, twirling me away from the Meraki.

It was Emperor Thierry, with a smug expression playing on his lips. "Now I see why the fire Mageia is represented by a fox. You're cunning and able to deceive anyone with your beauty."

Somehow, that made me squirm harder than being mistaken for a girl. "Uh, thanks?" Sweat beaded in my armpits as I glanced in Tyler's direction, watching his form ebb in and out of sight.

"While I'm here, though, shall we?" Thierry grabbed my waist, and he hoisted the hand he held higher up.

Yet again, I was paralyzed, which meant "yes" in Thierry's book. This man was on a whole other level than Luke. He swept me across the room with ease, leaving no room to falter with how swift his movements were. It was like he was dancing on his own, and I was a puppet.

"You have an interesting coat. I don't recall this being a game of illusion." His gaze bore into my face. As he smiled, his fangs glinted in the candlelight.

"I just thought it was nice." It was hard to keep my voice steady. "Is this about being called a ma'am? I don't care who I'm perceived as."

Thierry's smile hardened, not so genuine anymore. This was sly, just like the fox he described me as. "I think your carelessness will get you killed."

What?

I broke away from him, freezing in place. He, too, stopped dancing. We just faced each other in the middle of the dance floor, oblivious to the partners dancing and twirling around us.

Thierry bowed again. The gleam in his eyes reminded me of who this man truly was. "Now, will you please excuse me? I have a presentation to host. *Bonne soirée, mon chaton.*"

Then, he left. I stared after him in shock. *Kitten?* Thanks to my moms, I knew the bare minimum of French, so his flirtatious farewell made sense in a horrible way. My legs threatened to give out, and I stumbled to the side of the dance floor to avoid being trampled. The noise around me dampened, making me feel like I was underwater, and my vision swam. I was disgusted with myself for not realizing it sooner: *I'd just danced with the devil.*

Chapter Thirty-Four
Achilles Heel
Tyler

"You were sitting here the whole time?" Noah laughed when he found me at the table by myself. He was sporting a fancy black suit with a blood-red rose sticking out from his pocket.

I didn't look up to face him. All I did was nod. My heart had been in my throat all night, and my arms ached from keeping them up to block my ears. This had been my first real party. Nobody had mentioned it would be so loud.

Noah's hand patted my shoulder roughly. When I flinched and straightened up, he grinned. "The speech is about to start. Come on, Thierry wants us on stage with him. It's just for protection—it's not like we'll have to do anything. Besides, you might as well try acting like royalty." He said the last part bitterly, which didn't surprise me.

"Right," I whispered. *This is it.* The thought of being on stage made my throat burn, but I couldn't back down now. As the music slowed, I followed Noah around the outskirts of the ballroom, to where the stage was set up in the back. "So, uh...what's Th-Thierry even going to do? Is it—"

"Nothing evil," Noah cut me off. "He's probably just going to talk and brag about the necklaces. Use it as proof of his power and to enhance his goals. I think those other humans are here to make him look better."

"Okay." I shook out my hands, wiping my sweaty palms on my pants. For an ice mutation, I felt awfully hot. Why was it so stuffy in here?

The crowd quieted down, the music fading before stopping completely. Everyone was facing the stage now, applauding as Thierry stepped forward. Noah herded me on after him, and we stood idly at the side. Savana joined us a minute later, beaming as she always did. All I could hear was my heart thumping. My skin crawled as eyes bored into me. I clenched my fists, digging my fingernails into the palms of my hands. If I collapsed, this whole thing would be ruined for both Indra Academy and the Cataclysm. I'd humiliate everyone. Instead of focusing on that, I examined the wooden boards below.

"People!" Thierry began. "I welcome you all on this fine evening. For months now, I've gone on about how we Meraki deserve better than this. Why are we paying the price for something that happened centuries ago?"

Everyone was watching him with wide eyes and smiles. Some were already applauding again.

"I'm going to reclaim what is rightfully mine. No, scratch that. *We* will reclaim what is rightfully ours!" Thierry didn't even need a microphone. He could hypnotize the crowd with just his voice. As his echo faded, he pulled the fire and lightning necklaces from his pocket and raised them in the air. "I've only spoken the truth to you! These gems power the portal to the human realm. This is for everyone who doubted my ability to retrieve them!"

Gasps and awed voices filled the air as people cooed like excited pigeons.

It's all lies. I watched the crystals dangle above the stage, my muscles tensing. Any second now…

Thierry began to speak again, his attention shifting away from the jewels and back to the crowd.

I raced forward, past Thierry, and jumped off the stage. As I passed him, I snatched the necklaces from his hand, sliding down a ramp of ice that went all the way to the door. The crowd screamed as they scrambled out of my way. Thierry shouted something inaudible, and I got a glimpse of him and Noah chasing after me.

The Indra Academy students, plus Savana, were right behind me as I broke into the hall. Our boots thudded against the red carpet, the exclamations of brainwashed citizens fading into the background. Every guard in sight stormed after us, but the element of surprise gave us a head start. Titanium yelled something about racing ahead to find McKenzie, and the black cat swiftly disappeared out a window.

"This is amazing!" Luke cried in delight.

"They're after us, though!" Diana glanced over her shoulder in alarm. She ditched her heels and caught up to us barefoot.

I handed the necklaces over to Oliver and Savana just before the castle shook, dust falling from the ceiling.

Spawning from thin air was a massive, sparkling yellow lion. Vaguely, I remembered fighting against it just nights ago. It put itself between us and the guards, roaring and nearly drowning out Luke's cackle of triumph. "Yeah, get 'em, Ruslan!"

There was no time to see how long the lion could stall Thierry's goons for. We made a break for the castle gates, speeding past confused partygoers and guards who hadn't been in the ballroom when I'd stolen the necklaces.

Bursting through the gates and into the night, a gasp of surprise caught in my throat. Surrounding the castle was a blaze of orange, where the forest was meant to be. "Fire!"

Vincent grinned. "McKenzie mentioned helping from a distance. Hah, she's a genius!"

A bolt of lightning lit up the sky, striking the burning forest. Thunder boomed through the air. Without a doubt, that was Savana's doing. I heard her cackle from beside me.

"Will the fire be enough to lose them?" Oliver looked behind us again. "The guards stopped"—He paled—"but Thierry and Noah are coming!"

"Doesn't matter! Keep going!" Diana shouted. As we spilled into the forest, she yelped and cursed at the twigs digging into her soles. "We're not safe until we get to the portal!"

Overwhelming amounts of smoke wafted through the trees, and a roar filled my ears. The flames welcomed us. They loomed between us and the sky, threatening to envelop us in a toasty hug.

Fumes blocked the moonlight like a thick blanket, aggravating my lungs with every inhale. Branches snapped and broke as the flames consumed them, littering the path with embers. Every few moments, Oliver and Savana paused to slash fire and lightning into the distance, feeding the inferno.

Somewhere in the chaos, a whistle played a somber melody. That most definitely wasn't from our group.

As we ran, I stole glances at the others, only to realize their features were...glowing? Oliver's freckles were emitting orange light while Luke's were yellow. Those lightning-shaped scars on Savana's cheeks were shining more purple than usual, and Diana's hair was now a beautiful blue and turquoise ombré. Glowing feathers sprouted from Vincent's cheeks.

The blue tint of my vision suggested that my scars were glowing, too. Our paces faltered as we gawked at each other in awe. The pull I felt toward the five of them was so strong it felt like gravity. No Mageia was needed to connect our vibrantly colored details. This phenomenon must've been something deeply rooted and triggered by the danger around us.

"You guys!" McKenzie's voice snapped me back to the moment. She appeared in the smoke, her sooty palms giving her away as the arsonist. "The portal is this way, hurry! Titanium is protecting it, but she can't keep it up forever."

"Was it one of you that whistled?" Oliver asked, barely audible over the chaos.

McKenzie stiffened. "No. Shit, that means we have to leave right—"

Before she finished speaking, the light around us dimmed and flickered, making me look around. Shadowy figures were weaving through the trees in a swarm, growling and chittering. They looked just like Titanium: black, with white, pupilless eyes, and in the form of many, many creatures. *Shadow Guards!*

From the way they dispersed into the fire storm with their teeth bared, it was clear they weren't on our side. A few heartbeats later, we were surrounded.

Stepping past the row of Shadow Guards were Noah and Thierry, the latter clapping slowly. "Great, now we have all the traitors," Thierry snarled, pinning me with his death glare. "I don't understand. Don't you want to change the lives of millions? To change the world? You have that power as heir to the throne." The passion in his voice was familiar, but this time, rage seemed to ooze from every part of his body.

As much as I wanted to give in and return to being his puppet, I shook my head. My palms glowed blue as I revved up the ice in my system. I created a stack of pointy icicles and handed them to Luke, Diana, and Vincent. I didn't want to assume their glowing features equated having unlocked powers. They needed some kind of weapon.

"Do you know what the human world is gonna look like if you let Meraki run around? Like this!" Diana threw her arms in the air, gesturing to the inferno surrounding us.

Noah just smiled at her. "You're the one who started it, Princess."

Vincent's features twisted in anger as Noah uttered the nickname. "And we're going to end it, too!" He launched himself at Noah, icicle at the ready.

Dozens of Shadow Guards erupted from the flames and jumped at us.

Chitters, grunts, growls, shouts, squawks, howls.

The forest was a fucking zoo.

I didn't have time to feel bad as I slashed and impaled every Shadow Guard in sight. Hopefully, Titanium would understand why we had to slaughter her kind. Was it really even a slaughter, though? Every time a Shadow Guard evaporated, it started to regenerate in the distance. I was given the terrible reminder that these creatures were immortal until their host died.

Thierry joined the attack, ruthlessly sending red blazes of fire our way. He kept to the outskirts to blast us from afar, with strength that could take us down if he wasn't playing around.

It was a dance meant to tire us out. Twist one direction to avoid being burned to a crisp. Twist the other direction to avoid being eaten alive by a living shadow. A dance we couldn't afford to lose.

McKenzie deflected Thierry's attacks while Savana and Diana fought the Shadow Guards side by side. Vincent wrestled with Noah on the ground, and Oliver protected Luke from more Shadow Guards as he knelt and touched his palm to the ground.

I grabbed a shadowy ferret clawing up my leg and flung it away, slashing it in midair. How much longer could we keep this up?

I made my way to Savana and hissed in her ear, "Take the Shadow Guards elsewhere! Use your lightning to take them all out at once!"

"What?" She looked bewildered but nodded anyway. She tore away from the group, running into the woods. Only when McKenzie, Vincent, Luke, and Diana followed did most of the Shadow Guards start chasing them. The remaining bunch retreated to where Noah and Thierry were, nipping and snarling at Oliver and me as they passed.

"What is this?" Noah wiped drops of blood off his cheek, glaring in the direction everyone retreated to. "Cowards!"

I walked right over to Thierry and stood tall as I met his gaze. Last night, he was beating me into the ground, and right now, his eyes had that same hungry look. Still, I refused to back down. "We'll hand one of them over. Just tell your Shadow Guards to back off."

"Are you out of your mind?" Oliver shielded his necklace and shrank away. He was breathing heavily, seeming to droop from the exertion of fighting.

Just do it! Then you can run! You don't have the experience with Thierry that I do. I'll fetch it myself. I couldn't dare say it out loud. I had to pray a glare would get my message across.

Thierry cocked his head to one side, his fiery crown expanding "Oh? Go on, then. Hand it over."

As his Shadow Guards slunk away, Oliver and I exchanged a look. He shook his head subtly, clutching the crystal for dear life.

All I wanted was to tell him it would be okay. Approaching him, I extended my hand and whispered, "Please trust me."

A heartbeat passed before Oliver unclasped the necklace, putting it in my hand.

"It was a feeble effort, but I applaud your bravery," Thierry mused as I returned to him.

I clutched the necklace tight. "Take it and leave."

To my surprise, Thierry didn't move. "What, without you?" He gave me his plasticky smile again. "Don't you love your dear father? Are you going to leave after everything I did for you?"

My heart broke at those questions. I'd been without a dad my whole life. And when I finally got the chance to have a father figure, he'd endangered me as much as my mom had. Luck didn't run in the family. Misfortune had captured my siblings long ago. Someone had to break that cycle.

"Yes," I answered finally.

What happened next was nothing more than a blur, a commotion. Noah blasted a wave of white fire right at me, time suddenly slowing as it inched closer.

Oliver rammed his body into mine, yelling for me to move. He slashed his dagger out in front of us, deflecting the wave of fire.

The blade exploded on impact.

Hot air slammed over the two of us, fire roaring in my ears as we went flying backwards. We landed several feet away, but bruising was the last of my worries as an anguished scream filled the air.

Oliver was laying a few feet away, writhing and tearing at the forest floor. Noah stood over him, watching with a wild grin as he spasmed and fought for air. Smoke poured from Noah's nostrils and fingers, his eyes wild and hands fiery.

The lower half of Oliver's right pantleg had been torn away, the skin beneath it a hideous assortment of blacks, whites, and reds. His leather boot was melting into the open wound of flesh, muscle, and blood. It was a burn unlike any other.

Oh no, oh no, oh no. He can't be dead. Fuck, fuck, fuck! I wanted to screech the profanity at the top of my lungs. Fighting the rational urge to run away, I raced to Oliver's side, crouching down to hide him from Noah. The necklace was long forgotten about as I slid it back in my pocket. Oliver groaned and twitched, incoherently protesting for me to leave. The orange glow on his freckles flickered like a dying candle flame.

McKenzie's lesson on healing rushed back to me, and Titanium's earlier warning about ice against burns went flying out the window; I had to at least *try*.

I leaned over Oliver's leg, trying to ignore the fragments of bone visible. Ice surged through my body, but before it could slip through, I tightened the wall in my mind. My glowing palms hovered over his leg. Frost spread over the wound.

Oliver screamed again in response, kicking and thrashing as he seized up.

"Stop it!" I leaned against Oliver's stomach to keep him in place, aware of Noah and Thierry watching in amusement.

"You're both fools." Noah yanked me back by my coat's collar. He stomped his foot on Oliver's leg, who cried before passing out. His glowing marks flashed before fading completely.

A part of me was relieved to have Oliver unconscious. I'd want to be, too, if my leg looked like that. The other half of me was shaking all over.

I pulled away from Noah, collapsing beside Oliver and using my back to shield him. "I said I'd give it to you." My voice wobbled, and I couldn't tell if it was from fear or rage. "Oliver had no part in this. You didn't have to hurt him!"

"Oh really?" Noah glanced over his shoulder to smile at Thierry. "Can I kill these two?"

Before Thierry could respond, a flaming branch hit the back of his head. He stumbled forward with a grunt, spinning around to see who'd thrown it.

Luke had come back, probably to fetch us. Though all the fight left him as he took in the scene. His face went ashen with horror when he saw Oliver's mangled leg. "What have you done?"

I couldn't tell who the question was aimed at. I could only watch as Luke raced to us, pulling Oliver into his lap and shaking him. Oliver's head just lolled back. Not a word. Not a breath. His neck hung exposed, and parted lips welcomed in the smoke.

"Come on, get up! Get up, Oliver! Please! Oliver! No, no, no…" Luke thrust his fingers against his friend's neck and sighed, which could only mean Oliver still had a pulse. His hand moved from Oliver's neck to his head to better support it. But that didn't stop Luke from looking at me with terrified eyes. He repeated, "What have you done?"

"Noah got him." My mouth was as dry as the burning forest.

Thierry stepped toward us, humming a disapproving tune. "If I remember correctly, the boy sacrificed himself to save you, did he not?"

"Too bad it was in vain, though," Noah said.

How could Noah be smiling at a time like this? He looked more alive than ever. Without a second thought, he crouched down, putting his palms to the ground. A tsunami of fire surged toward us, with all the strength of the sun.

I didn't have it in me to scream. Luke and I just threw ourselves over Oliver's body, shielding him as heat slammed over us, only to dissipate.

What?

I risked a glance up. Standing over us was Ruslan, as tall as the canopy above. His leg had shielded the attack, and he seemed unscathed and furious. Beside him was a glowing fox just as large, yipping and growling at the stunned villains.

Next to both fantastical creatures stood Titanium. She had grown, just like the lion and fox, taking on more leopard-like features. But I knew that my precious Shadow Guard was inside.

"What in the—" Noah's exclamation was cut off as the fox swatted him backwards, deeper into the forest. The massive creature chased after Noah as if he were a toy, leaving puddles of fire in every paw print.

"I made some friends!" Titanium explained with pride, watching the fox drive Noah away.

"You saved our asses!" Luke breathed out. "Ruslan, it's about time you showed up. Thank you!"

"Luke, get Oliver out of here," I said. "Titanium and I got this." Glancing at the massive cat, I searched for confirmation.

The feline purred and nodded.

Luke adjusted his grip on Oliver before carefully lifting him bridal style. The blue ruffles of his tattered coat spiraled to the ground like a waterfall. Before leaving, Luke looked at me with a mix of fear and determination on his face. "Don't get yourself killed" was all he said before turning and running as best as he could.

The massive lion followed like a bodyguard, leaving Titanium and me to face off against Thierry. It was miraculous that he hadn't gone after Oliver and Luke. My father had watched the scene go down, his smile gone, and gaze hardened once more.

I sliced my arms through the air, propelling bullets of ice forward. Thierry blasted the majority away with his fire, but one managed to cut a gash along his temple. His palms glowed orange, which could only mean he was about to start attacking. Titanium shrank to about waist-height and launched herself at Thierry.

On Thierry's other side, I fired more ice bullets, knocking him into Titanium, who bashed him back in my direction. We batted Thierry about until he backed out of our path and regained his footing. He was starting to look as bruised and scratched as I was.

"Don't worry, son. I won't kill you." Thierry wiped the sweat and blood off his forehead. "You're far too valuable to die just yet."

Deep down, something in me wanted to beam at such a comment. *Don't you see, Tyler? He thinks you're important!* But after everything he'd done and wants to do? And the measures he'd take to get there?

I raised my palms and fired a blast of ice right at him. Thierry easily swerved to one side, his face lighting up.

He lunged at me with outstretched arms as if he were going in for a bear-hug. I ducked down and rolled away, grabbing a handful of soil and ash and throwing it at his face. As he struggled to clear his eyes, Titanium jumped on him, clawing his face and dragging him to the floor.

My foot slammed against the ground, and a massive ice crystal shot up around Thierry, encasing him inside and leaving only his head free. The rest of him was frozen. I could've left it at that, but adrenaline still coursed through my veins. In one swift move, I punched him in the face. The sickening crack of Thierry's nose breaking rang through the air.

He threw his head back with a grunt, wriggling around, trying to free himself. Every time he melted some of the ice, I just created more. I could tell he was going easy on me, because if he wasn't, I'd already be dead. Defeating an emperor wasn't meant to be this easy. That was something both Thierry and I knew.

Was this merely a false victory? Would we cross paths like this again? Whatever the case was, in this moment, *I* was the last one standing.

"It's over." I glared down at him, panting as my excitement from the fight waned. In its place, exhaustion settled in my bones. The burn on my arm was throbbing like crazy. "You lost." My scars lost their glow, and my vision shifted back to normal.

"That's my precious little fighter." Thierry glared up at me, his face contorted. "I taught you well, son."

I shook my head. "Don't–don't call me your son."

Thierry narrowed his eyes. "Oh? Without me, you'd have nothing. You'd *be* nothing. Isn't this what you wanted from the start? A purpose? A family?"

In my head, I pictured the Indra Academy students. Oddly enough, homesickness tugged at my heart. I had been blind to choose blood relations over chosen ones.

"Exactly." My voice was hardly above a whisper. "And I'm going to find my family."

Titanium grew in size, bowing down to let me climb on her back. I'd never ridden a horse—or cat—before, but I had no time to worry about that. "Goodbye, Dad."

Those were two words I thought I'd never say.

Then, we were out of the clearing, past the fire, and headed back to where it all began.

CHAPTER THIRTY-FIVE

A SPECTACULAR FUCK UP

TYLER

WITH THE FIRE NECKLACE, traveling through the portal was a breeze and maybe the easiest task I'd faced all night. A crowd of faces greeted me on the other side, in Indra Academy's strange passageways. Diana, Vincent, McKenzie, and Savana were all there, as well as Camila. Luke and Isabel had gone with Oliver to the hospital.

Knowing that, we entered the library in silence. Our distraught expressions were easy to notice, even in the darkness of night. Everyone's glowing features had faded, leaving us with bloody scratches, like we were the world's most unfortunate cat toys. Us kids stood in battered, ripped formal attire. Just an hour ago, they'd been dancing, and my only concern was how loud it was.

Dead silence.

McKenzie softly suggested we get some sleep and that we'd talk in the morning, after we'd rested and recovered from the shock of the fight. She and Camila were all teary eyed from being reunited. They each looked ready to bawl at the sight of each other.

Before we could leave, Camila pulled out a first aid kit and asked if anyone else had been injured during the battle.

We glanced around at each other, grimacing at the slashes and bites we'd accumulated. Our clothes sagged and loose threads stuck out. Diana's pearly white dress was now covered in dust and soot.

Camila had us sit down so she could apply antibiotic cream to our wounds, as well as Band-Aids for those either bleeding or at risk of infection.

I thought I could get away with hiding the burn Thierry had inflicted on me. However, as we stood up to depart, my stomach plummeted, and my body tingled and went numb. My legs gave out, and I collapsed back into my chair.

All eyes turned to me.

"Tyler? Is everything alright?" Camila was by my side in an instant.

"I'm fine," I said through chattering teeth.

Camila brushed my hair out of my face, resting her hand on my forehead. Her touch seemed so far away, and I practically melted into it. The nurse quickly grabbed my shoulders to make sure I didn't fall face forward. "You're burning up."

Burning up? How could that be when chills were racking my body? With my head hanging downward, I opened my mouth to protest that I was fine. All I managed was an unconvincing groan. With a heavy hand, I pointed to my burned arm.

Camila didn't need words to understand. She turned to face McKenzie and the others. "I'm taking him to get help. Keep an eye on your breathing for signs of smoke inhalation, okay?"

Darkness greeted us outside the main building. Snowflakes pelted down from the sky like bullets, biting at my skin and sending shivers jolting through me. It felt so good against my arm, the way it feels once you've jumped in water after running barefoot on hot concrete.

I vaguely remembered Camila and McKenzie helping me across campus, and Camila asking one of the school security guards for a ride. I tried resisting, explaining I'd never been in a car before and that I couldn't do this. They ignored me, or I was simply muttering nonsense.

When Camila and I got in the car and said goodbye to McKenzie, who'd stayed behind, I huddled against the leather cushioning. As we pulled onto the main road, I wondered if the driver would stop if I claimed to feel sick.

Camila sighed from where she sat next to me. "My older brother works there, and I trust him with my life. He'll treat you well, okay?"

The nurse had a brother who worked in a hospital? Quite the sibling dynamic. I wasn't sure if I wanted to laugh or cry. Instead, I brought my knees to my chest and watched the snowflakes whip past the window, longing to be tossed somewhere far away just like that.

∞

Bumping into Isabel and Luke at the hospital wasn't a happy reunion. Luke was almost unrecognizable with his dull eyes and weak, uncertain voice. Isabel looked equally exhausted. Since Camila's brother, Dr. Alvi, was busy, we stayed with Isabel and Luke in the family lounge.

Isabel asked Camila in a hushed voice if it was wise to wait so long before treating my wound. Camila muttered something about how we couldn't trust other doctors to not report the abnormal strength of a fire Mageia burn.

Even at three in the morning, people lingered around and existed in an eerie silence. I felt like a lab rat under the fluorescent lights.

Somewhere between Luke's relentless pacing and him joining me on the couch, I dozed and dreamed of Oliver. Every time I startled awake, I glanced around in search of him, only to realize where I was and go back to sleep.

In a few hours, the rest of the world would wake up. Everything would resume as normal.

It won't, though. It never will. I squeezed my eyes shut, only to see Oliver's limp body on the forest floor, and I sat up with a sharp inhale. If only time could stand still for just a little longer. As much as I wanted to see the sunrise and end this floating feeling, what if it was to hear we were too late? To hear Oliver was gone?

Gone and off the dance floor like Dominic.

My chest squeezed and I breathed in again. No luck.

When we finally met Dr. Alvi, he spoke to me in kind tones, though it didn't matter since he had to touch me to see everything was functioning. In the mirror, I could see my collarbones and ribs. I could see my elbows and knees jutting from my arms and legs.

The shirtless boy looking back at me was just as shocked. His right eye was swollen half shut and surrounded by hideous shades of purple and blue. Welts, bruises, and scratches littered his thin body, and a deep cut split his lower lip. He looked so pale, and his hair hadn't been brushed in days. White pus oozed from the burn on his arm.

Slowly, I raised one hand. The boy in the mirror did the same. I felt as hideous as I looked.

Dr. Alvi explained everything to Camila like I didn't exist. At one point, he called me lucky. "A little more severe, and he would've needed a skin graft for that burn. A little more under-weight, and we would've admitted him here."

A little smarter, and Oliver would've been okay. I was anything but lucky.

Before giving us a list of antibiotics and care instructions, Dr. Alvi asked his sister if he should call child protective services over my non-burn related wounds. Camila immediately said no. She insisted that everything was fine, that she and Isabel would look after me until "all this is over."

Then what? I kept asking myself during the ride home.

Finally, I could untie my black hoodie from around my waist and hug it like a distraught child with their blankie.

Then what?

The sun was rising when we arrived at Indra Academy. Camila said I should return to Oliver and Bryce's dorm to rest. Without Oliver there, I almost didn't want to.

I was too tired to object.

On my way back to the dorm, I was distracted by hushed voices in the common room. It was a relatively spacious room at the end of the hall, decorated with couches, chairs, an old television, and a station to boil water for coffee or tea. Unsure of why anyone would be congregating there now, I couldn't help but check it out.

Peeking out from behind a wooden beam, I caught the dark shapes of Diana and Vincent sitting on one of the couches with their backs to me. Diana was hunched over and letting out these small, hiccupping sobs. Vincent spoke to her in a low, soothing voice I hadn't thought was possible for someone so aloof.

Vincent slowly raised his arm and put it on Diana's shoulder, bringing her closer. With another heaving wail, Diana melted into his embrace. While she cried, Vincent met my gaze before scowling elsewhere. It was a subtle gesture that sent my stomach rolling.

He didn't say anything, but his glare spoke a thousand words. I quickly escaped the scene.

Titanium was curled outside the door to Bryce and Oliver's room, having waited for me all night. She immediately jumped up and started purring, sinking into my good arm when I lifted her. Bryce answered my quiet knocks almost immediately, seeming wide awake. The pained look on his face told me he knew. Luke must've called him from the hospital.

While Bryce inflated the air mattress, I went to the bathroom to change into my old pajamas. When I returned, I wearily described our adventure.

"So, you faced off against Thierry, huh?" Bryce listened, his face clouded with anger. He absently stroked Titanium, who laid on his lap. "That damn guy. I'll kill him, I swear."

"You—you know Thierry?"

Bryce looked disgusted, maybe with himself. Rubbing his slightly pointy ears, he muttered, "He's my father."

My stomach lurched. That couldn't be possible! "But he...he's mine, too."

We made eye contact. The truth was obvious, though neither of us said it. My half-brother was staring back at me. I couldn't tell if the pain in my heart was improving or worsening. Bryce was the real heir, sitting right before my eyes.

We were two souls born from the help of an evil emperor, sitting in the consequences of rebellion. How lonely.

We couldn't dwell on that, though. Bryce broke the silence by suggesting I sleep while he went to class. His voice was choked up and tight, and he looked like a mere kid. After pulling the curtains over the windows to dim the room's light for me, he left.

Lying on the air mattress with Titanium kneading my chest, I couldn't fall asleep. It didn't matter how heavy my eyes were. Hot and cold flashes traced along my skin, intensifying the memories playing on loop in my head.

It should've been me. Oliver was supposed to be back at Indra Academy, reunited with his friends.

I could've turned onto a different road that rainy night. I could've gone home or controlled myself and not gone with Isabel. The possibilities of what might've been roared in my ears, making me dizzy.

If I'd never convinced Dominic and Noah to go to the park with me, maybe Dominic would still be here.

If I'd never been born, maybe my brother and Oliver would've led normal lives. My mother would still have the smile she wore in photographs. It wouldn't have been lost to time.

It should've been me. I'm so sorry, Oliver.

Chapter Thirty-Six
SO, ABOUT THAT LEG...
OLIVER

BLACK OCEAN WAVES RUSHED past my body with every inhale and sank back into the darkness with every exhale.

Inhale. Exhale.

Inhale. Exhale.

I just lay there on my back, focused on my breathing, feeling the water flow between my fingers. My eyes drifted shut and I enjoyed the sensation of sunlight on my skin. When was the last time I'd experienced such peace? It was just me and the roaring ocean.

And the sun, of course, which reminded me of its presence with its heat. Even after I acknowledged it, the sun kept going. Sending more and more heat through my body. It ignored my pleas to stop, and I squirmed in the sand. The warmth kept cranking up, up, and up, until a blaze surged through my right leg.

Searing pain stabbed my body, and then, the next ocean wave swallowed me. The sand below me disappeared. I was drowning again. The whole ocean roared in my ears, bubbles streaming from my mouth.

The thundering wrath suddenly came to a stop, leaving a high-pitched ringing sound. Through it, I could hear murky voices. None of it was intelligible.

I blinked, only to scrunch up my face as blinding light greeted me. It danced behind my eyelids in shades of red. There was no more black ocean lulling me to sleep, which was made evident as the voices grew clearer.

I forced my eyes to open, if only to slits. Immediately, I noticed a blurry figure dressed in blue. They looked back at me expectantly.

I shifted my gaze downward in hopes of understanding what was happening. Sluggish alarm overtook my confusion as I noticed the little wires along my arms. I shakily lifted one hand and touched them.

"They're just IVs to give you fluid. Don't worry about them," a voice said. It belonged to a woman. The figure in front of me.

The first thought that came to me was, *what the hell? Where am I?* I tried to sit up, but my body failed, and I slumped against the uncomfortable mattress. Piercing sensations rippled along my right leg at the movement.

A warm hand reached for mine and squeezed it gently. "You had quite a time last night. Just take it easy for now." The voice was cozy, and callus-hardened fingers rubbed against mine.

I glanced to the side, my heavy eyes latching on to a familiar face. It was Luke staring down at me, his expression tight with anticipation. A large Band-Aid covered his left eyebrow, his eyes bleary from an evident lack of sleep.

"Where...?" My voice grated against my throat, all sore and scratchy.

"Hospital," Luke answered with a nervous smile. "You don't remember?"

I swallowed and winced. "No."

"Anesthesia can blur your memory a bit," the woman in blue said. She was a nurse, then, confirmed by Luke's mention of a hospital. Turning to me, she added, "You were in the Post-Anesthesia Care Unit for an hour or two before this."

Me? In a recovery room? I wanted to ask why, but I just started giggling. Surely, I shouldn't have been freed from there when I couldn't even remember it! What had we talked about? What had they told me? What was wrong with me?

Another round of pain overtook my body, which was my answer. My hand, still entwined with Luke's, seized up. I faced him, focusing on the dirty white suit he wore. The realization hit me like a truck. I hadn't dreamed that dance or anything else, had I?

"Derngate," I whispered. "What happened?"

"Our roleplay campaign got too intense, and a fire broke out." Luke scratched absently at the Band-Aid over his eyebrow. Then, he looked at me softly as he murmured, "We're home. I owed you, didn't I?"

Of course Luke remembered our in-joke.

"Now then, can you please rate your pain for me?" The nurse let authority bleed through her voice, not fazed by our roleplaying fib. "On a scale of one to ten is fine, with one being little to none and ten being the worst ever."

I took a moment to listen to my body. It felt like I'd been run over on the highway. The sharp twisting in my leg could convince me it was on fire.

I struggled to count through the brain fog, wiggling my fingers to keep track, before finally putting up seven. It wasn't an ignorable pain, but even through the lethargy, I didn't want to be a hassle.

The nurse smiled and nodded, writing something on a nearby clipboard. "We'll get you some more medication for the pain. Let us know if it helps or makes it worse."

While she and Luke got into a small conversation of their own, I took the time to finally survey the room. It was a private space, the white walls decorated with a mix of painted aquatic animals and stars. A TV and armchair sat across the room, and a counter ran along the wall next to the IV pole. My room was the ocean and space merged.

I wanted to cry, not because the walls were childish and silly, but because they felt like home. To distract myself, I stared at the ceiling in a drowsy attempt to piece the rest of the puzzle together. The whole escape had been a blur of flames and smoke, but at one point, Noah had gotten a hold of my leg. Everything between then and ending up here was a mystery. *And somehow, we escaped?* I brought my hand to my chest, confused to feel bare skin. With the hand Luke still held, I squeezed his fingers to grab his attention.

I tried sitting up again, asking in a furious whisper, "What happened to everyone else? And—and the necklaces?"

"The necklaces are with Isabel. Everyone is safe and back at Indra Academy, don't worry." Luke gently laid me back down. "Focus on yourself right now, okay?"

We won? Tears sprung to my eyes, and I couldn't tell if I was hurting more inside or outside.

It wasn't long before the door clicked open, and a young man slid in. He wore a white coat and had short black hair and tan skin. His face looked a little familiar, but I couldn't put my finger on why. His eyes lit up upon meeting mine. "Glad to see you're settling in nicely! How do you feel?"

I hesitated before saying, "I think I'm okay?" The pain in my leg had dulled to a throb, which was heaven compared to earlier.

"Do you remember any of our conversation in the recovery room?"

"No. Luke said there was a fire." I grimaced at the bland explanation. "And I got hurt. That–that's all I got."

As the man pulled up a plastic chair next to Luke's and sat down, I caught a glimpse of his name tag, which read "DR. ALVI." Wasn't that Camila's last name?

"That's understandable. It's why I came by now—when you're more awake." His smile faltered for a second, maybe at the idea of repeating himself, but it was only for a moment. "I won't go into full detail, but it was one of the worst burns we've seen here in quite a while. I was shocked by the severity of it." He rested his fingers on the edge of my blanket. "Shall we?"

Even without knowing the details, a lump formed in my throat. I nodded absently. When he threw the covers off, I winced and instinctively looked away. I took a deep breath and held it, as if I were about to jump into deep water, and forced my eyes downward.

My right knee was wrapped in a mountain of bandages and gauze, but everything below that was...nothing.

Nothing.

I sat up—a sudden jolt of adrenaline coursing through me—with one hand squeezing Luke's and the other tightly gripping the bed railing. My chest constricted as I peered over, searching for the lower half of my leg. "Where's the rest?"

"Like I said, your right leg was burned. In medical terms, a third-degree burn. But you may also consider it a fifth- or sixth-degree burn, considering the damage." Dr. Alvi's smile was gone, and from next to him, Luke stared at the floor. The nurse occupied herself with paperwork.

I blinked and then blinked again as my vision swam. "Don't they...Don't they have skin grafts for that type of stuff?"

Dr. Alvi heaved a sigh. "They do, but not in this case. Infection had already set in by the time you got here. You were going into shock. It was beyond saving." He shifted in his seat and nodded to my knee. "If we kept it, you never would've fully healed. The chances of being able to walk properly again would've been slim."

"So you just sawed the whole thing off?" My voice rose to a shout. Some stupid machine behind me started to beep quicker.

Luke squeezed my hand again, resting his other on my shoulder. "Oliver, take a deep breath. There are other people here, and—"

"And *you*." I shook him away, raking my gaze over his body, which trembled just like mine. Despite the stricken look on his face, I couldn't find any traces of shock. "You knew, didn't you? Why didn't you stop them? What kind of friend are you?"

Luke shrank back a little. "Trust me, I tried!"

"Clearly, you didn't try hard enough."

His hurt expression was enough to tell me I'd taken it too far. But that was the least of my worries right now. A storm was swirling in my gut, hellfire threatening to break loose. The beeping machine was running on overdrive, just like my heart.

"Your friend is right," Dr. Alvi spoke after a moment, "Take a deep breath and—"

Before he could finish, I lurched to the side and retched.

I'd never forgotten what my best friend from California told me the night my parents died. I was sleeping over at his house when the cops arrived, bearing the news and saying a social worker would come for me in the morning. Once the officer had departed, I was left a sniffling mess on my friend's bedroom floor.

My friend had pulled me close and tilted my head to the ceiling, where he'd had those glow-in-the-dark stars scattered.

"They're with the stars now, always able to see you" was what he'd told me. It was cheesy, and we were only fifth graders, but it always stuck with me.

"There's too much light pollution for that" is what I'd sobbed back.

His smile was a bit pained, broken. "That doesn't mean the stars aren't there."

When I'd settled down with my moms, I bought a pack of those glow-in-the-dark stars for myself. I even took them to Indra Academy with me, where they resided on my half of the dorm's ceiling.

Now, I was lying in a hospital bed, and only a sliver of night sky was visible through the curtains. Still, beyond patches of gray clouds, I could see an airplane gliding by, its blinking light pulsing every few heartbeats.

Is my leg a star now, too? I wondered.

It didn't feel that way. The ankle that no longer existed itched and stung like crazy. Every time I reached forward to scratch it, my fingers swooped past empty air. Bolts of pain and twisting sensations racked my body.

It took everything in me to not cry out loud. The armchair in the room folded into a cot, and even though I'd snapped at him earlier, Luke willingly offered to be my roommate. I didn't want him to hear my distressed sounds.

I half expected him to leave earlier. He had the perfect chance to. Shortly after my fit, my aunt burst into the room with wild concern in her eyes. It turns out the hospital had contacted her while I was still out, and she'd thought it was a morbid prank. Her precious nephew was supposed to be asleep in his dorm at Indra Academy. In her panic, because the school wasn't answering the phone, she'd called Luke's dad to see what was up. Through another call to Luke himself, we were forced to tell them what happened.

Luke's dad visited earlier as well, mainly to see his son was okay and drop off a change of clothes for him. He offered Luke a ride back to Indra Academy on his way to work, and I also insisted that he go back, partly out of guilt. Of course, Luke had refused. Maybe it was because my aunt couldn't stay, as she had her own kid back home to take care of.

Though I imagined Luke was having second thoughts now, because whenever he moved, the cot squeaked and groaned. He eventually gave up on sleeping and started playing with his phone. Every other hour, a nurse came in to check my vitals, and the anticipation of them returning made relaxing impossible for both of us.

"What time is it?" I rasped into the darkness.

Luke squinted at the phone's bright light. "One in the morning. Sorry, I'm just texting Vincey. You wouldn't believe how mad he was because I didn't answer his calls earlier." He tapped the screen a few times before lowering it to look at me. "You should get some rest, though. It's been a long day."

The burning along my shin made it clear getting some sleep wouldn't be as easy as Luke made it sound. As I tried rubbing the phantom shin with my other leg, the painful sensation spread all over. I gripped the bed railings as heat swept under my skin. The sweaty feeling mingled with the reek of vomit and smoke that still clung to me. *I need to shower. I need to shower right now. And to brush my teeth and put on something more comfortable.* I needed a better mattress. I needed my leg back.

In the end, all I could say was, "I don't feel so good."

Luke sat up properly, frowning in the darkness. "Are you nauseous again? I can go find—"

"It just hurts."

Luke hesitated before heaving a sigh and approaching, sitting on the side of my bed. "Is there any way I can help?"

My bottom lip quivered as I pulled him close and buried my face into his shoulder. "No, just be here. I–I'm sorry for what I said earlier—about you being a bad friend." My voice cracked, and I drew in a shaky, deep breath before continuing. "I didn't mean it. You're an amazing friend, you really are."

"I know you didn't mean it," Luke murmured, resting one hand on the back of my head. "It's okay, don't worry."

"It's not okay. Not just for what happened earlier, but for so much more. This shouldn't have happened. How could I have been so reckless?" I knew I should've been grateful I made it out of the fire alive, but that thought only led to another, more chilling one.

We'd escaped. We had vital information about Thierry's plan to merge Derngate and the human realm. The plan that was so confidential, he and Noah tried ending our lives. My blood turned to ice as I pulled back to face Luke, gripping his arms tightly. "What if they find us? What do I do? I can't be here! They're gonna find Tyler—they're gonna kill him! And they're gonna kill *me* to get to him. Luke, I don't want to die!"

Luke shook his head and hugged me again. "You're out of there. You're safe. It's over, and you're okay. We all are."

"No, no, no..." The tears blurring my vision finally spilled free, rolling down my face like splotchy waterfalls. A sob racked my body as I wailed, "I don't want to die!"

Luke didn't say anything for a while, just cooing words of comfort and hugging me while I cried. The rest of the world fell away. We sat there for ages, and even after my tears slowed and the shaking stopped, he didn't move. As the fog of exhaustion blurred my mind, I heard him whisper, "I swear on my life, Oliver, those sick bastards will suffer for everything they've done."

I'm certain the freckles under his eyes were glowing as he said that.

CHAPTER THIRTY-SEVEN
A GHOST IN ALL OF US
OLIVER

A COLD BREEZE STIRRING the air roused me at some point in the night. Had someone opened the window? I opened my eyes, head tilting to the side, expecting to find either Luke or a nurse hovering over me. Luke was fast asleep from where he'd rearranged his cot beside my bed, his hand limply holding mine. The room was empty except for us.

So who...? I looked back in front of me, jumping a bit, when I saw Crystal sitting on the side of my bed.

Upon noticing I was awake, she smiled. It was a guilty "I'm sorry" type of smile. Starry tears were in her eyes as she whispered, "You humans amaze me."

"There was a letter for you," I croaked. "At the school..."

"Shh, I know. We'll talk later." Crystal rested her hand on my forehead as if checking my temperature. Drowsiness overcame me. "Rest now, Oliver. You did well."

I closed my eyes for only a moment, but when I opened them again, Crystal was gone. Left in her place were tiny specks of light falling to the ground like snowflakes. They melted as they landed, the room soon lapsing back into darkness. The air once occupied by her presence was cold. She had gone back to pure cosmic dust.

And so I pretended to fall back into a bed of stars, hugged by the ones I didn't get to thank before they left.

Chapter Thirty-Eight

INNER CHILD

Tyler

LUKE FINALLY TEXTED BACK. When Vincent told us at breakfast the next day, we immediately crowded around his phone as he read the message out loud.

Oliver was going to be okay, thank the stars. On the not-so-bright side, his leg didn't make it. Just like that, the energy around us pulsed from anticipation to shock.

Diana broke the silence. "He's alive, and that's what matters." From her queasy expression, I wondered if she was comforting us or herself.

But now what? I wanted to scream. My brain still clung to the fact it was because of me Oliver had ended up in this situation. If I hadn't been so stupid, so blind...

According to the calendar, Thanksgiving break was right around the corner, meaning we'd been in Derngate for a little under two weeks. Every so often, I caught Diana texting her parents, insisting she was fine after being off the radar for so long. Vincent, too, spent lots of time phoning his and Luke's dad with apologies.

Until the break started, everyone else would be in classes during the day, preparing for exams and catching up on missed work. While I felt better after lots of sleep and some antibiotics, I still wasn't in the right mindset to be around Savana's extroverted energy. My goal was to keep to myself, with one exception.

As breakfast ended and everyone departed to their first period, I chased after Vincent and tapped him on the shoulder.

"Is it okay if I, uh..." I pointed to the phone in his pocket.

Vincent narrowed his eyes. "If you what?" Like everyone else, he had Band-Aids all over his face and hands. It made him ten times scarier.

"Call...someone?"

"Who?"

"Oliver...?"

Vincent started to walk away again. "I don't have his number."

I followed, falling in step with him. *He's so fast!* "No–no, that's...Th-that's n-n-not what I meant. I, uh, I meant—can I call Luke? And...and have him talk to Oliver?"

Vincent sped up. Without even blinking, he said, "No."

I felt the familiar ache of disappointment in my chest. "Why not?" *He's mad at me, isn't he? Or maybe Luke and Oliver are mad. Of course they'd be mad. Didn't I see Luke's face back in the fire? He was furious with me.*

"Why should I? Weren't you all set on being by yourself?" Vincent stopped in his tracks, whirling around to face me. Students sidestepped us like fish swimming around an obstacle in the river.

"I—"

His lips curled downward in an angry, confused way. "Just because we came all this way for you doesn't mean you're special. Take your crown off and look around." He threw his arms wide into the air, making me flinch. "Yeah, you think *that's* scary?"

I nodded, biting down on my lip to hide its quivering.

"You wanna know what's scary?" Vincent's shaking voice rose to a yell as he continued. "You hospitalized Oliver, for fuck's sake! And my brother got roped into it all! The two of them should be here."

I knew all this already, but it still made a lump form in my throat and my eyes water. Apologies bubbled up in my throat, but I swallowed them down. Another small nod was all I could muster. My gaze darted over to the phone he still clutched in his hand, and I carefully reached for it. *Maybe I could...*

Vincent recoiled, glaring at me as if I was a roach. "Pathetic" was all he muttered as he turned away. As he stormed off, he called over his shoulder, "Get your priorities in check!"

I watched him disappear into the sea of students, unable to move my legs. I only snapped out of my trance when the tardy bell rang. The hallway was empty now. Knowing nobody would hear it, I whispered "sorry" before turning to leave.

∞

I spent the rest of the morning wandering around campus with Titanium. Her chattering was drowned out by the roaring in my head, something now caused by Vincent rather than a fever.

He was right, as bitter as the truth was. Why would everyone suddenly listen to me after I'd been so horrible?

Every time that idea came to mind, Titanium jumped before whirling around to face me. She could probably feel every negative emotion radiating from my body, something I was guiltily aware of. It was burdening her, too.

While students poured outside for lunch, I stood idly near the track, willing myself to go look for Bryce. But doing that would mean going through the crowds and making myself known again. That thought alone was terrifying, so I settled in a shady corner of the courtyard.

"You should find Bryce if you know where he sits." Titanium chased a dead leaf as she spoke, but her ears were perked up to show she was listening. "I'm sure he's lonely without Oliver and Luke."

I rolled up a ball of snow, then put it down before starting on another, smaller sphere. "He doesn't want to babysit me."

Titanium stopped jumping around to face me properly. "Is this about what Vincent said?"

Grabbing another clump of snow, I molded it into two triangles and put them atop the snowballs. To my disappointment, the snowcat looked nothing like Titanium.

"You can't deny what he said. I messed up big time. I–I don't think anyone is gonna want me on the team. They regret it. I know that for sure."

"Did Vincent tell you that, too?"

I didn't respond.

Titanium shook her head, dislodging the snow from her whiskers. "What happened was Noah's fault, not yours."

"I hurt people."

"Snap out of it! You don't!"

I rubbed the ripped fabric of my sleeve. "Oliver got hurt the moment I agreed to come back. Don't you see? I'm cursed."

"Cursed is a strong word," a voice said from nearby.

Yelping, I looked up to see McKenzie approaching. She wore one of Isabel's trench coats, looking more like a mom than the former right-hand woman of the enemy. Like Camila, she'd seen better days.

"Isabel is calling a meeting with the Assembly of Six. The...the new one. You guys." McKenzie cringed a little when she had to specify, as if she hadn't imagined this day would come. Her next words were more certain. "She sent me out here to find you. The others are waiting."

The firmness of her tone left Titanium and me no choice but to follow. As I walked away from the corner, someone's soccer ball knocked into my snowcat. The cat's head was taken clean off, beheading it unceremoniously.

McKenzie led us down the familiar halls of the main building, where we weaved around students and teachers going about their business as usual. They had no idea several of their peers had just returned from a magical dimension. They were oblivious to the war brewing in the realm behind the bookcase in the library. Oblivious to it all.

Warmth from a hidden heater blasted against my face as I followed McKenzie into the main office. Titanium jumped onto my shoulder, her fur pressing against my neck and acting like a fuzzy blanket. I felt like I was floating as McKenzie opened the door leading into the principal's office. I staggered upon seeing how crowded it was inside.

Vincent, Diana, and Savana sat in plastic chairs in front of Isabel's desk. I had to admit, I was impressed with how Savana's fluffy earmuffs hid her unusual features. The principal stood behind her desk, arms over her chest, with a fixed and serious frown. She relaxed and her expression thawed when she glanced at McKenzie.

"Looks like we have everyone here," Isabel announced as I shimmied into an empty chair next to Savana. From the way the principal's voice wavered, I could tell she was thinking about Luke and Oliver's absence, but she didn't dwell on it. Isabel clapped her hands together, fingers entwining as she faced us. "First of all, welcome back, all of you. The past few weeks were a ride, weren't they?"

We mumbled our agreement.

McKenzie moved closer to Isabel, taking a folder out of her coat's inner pocket and giving it to her. "I wrote all the information I'm aware of."

"Thanks." Isabel scanned over the papers inside, her eyes darkening as she kept going. "Thierry hasn't given up on bringing the Meraki age back, huh? It intrigues me he didn't kill Tyler for his Mageia."

I shuddered at the idea. Isabel had no idea I was Thierry's son, did she? "He–he wanted my help."

"Then it's good you're here." Isabel smiled, but it didn't reach her eyes. "If anything, we've slowed down his progress."

"Which means it'll be easier to kick his ass." Vincent leaned forward with a smug grin on his face. "We need to pay Thierry back for what he did to Oliver, after all."

Isabel wrenched her gaze away from the paper, her brows knitting together. "We can't make any moves yet, especially without Oliver and Luke."

Diana deflated a little. "We have to wait? Come on, you can't hype us up only to leave us on a cliffhanger!"

McKenzie shook her head. "Just because we have to wait doesn't mean we can't take advantage of this time. Isabel, Camila, and I can start tracking the other necklaces."

Savana and I exchanged a brief look before pulling our necklaces out. The weight lifted from my shoulders when I gave Isabel mine. I could breathe easier knowing I wasn't carrying Oliver's necklace.

"And the rest of us?" Diana whined.

Isabel looked to McKenzie, who gave her a curt nod. The principal heaved a sigh before turning toward us again. "Meraki information might be rare to come across here, but it's not impossible. I'll search for some sources you can skim over. But until Oliver and Luke are back, we can't move forward. All six of you must be present for the next step to work."

"Next step toward what?" Titanium asked from in my hood. As she jumped onto the table, her claws made little clicking sounds against the hardwood.

McKenzie bristled slightly before relaxing, like even she had to come to terms with abandoning the place that was once her home. "The next step toward taking down the Cataclysm. If the world turns to Emperor Thierry in the chaos his invasion brings, there'll be no stopping him."

Savana grimaced. In an unusually quiet voice, she asked, "Does this mean I can't go home?"

"Not for a while," McKenzie said, remorse thick in her voice. "I'm sorry, I truly am. Just remember this is a war against the Cataclysm, not the Meraki."

Nobody spoke for a moment.

Savana's eyes were a shiny ocean, and I feared, because the strength I remembered of her scream, they'd unleash a tsunami. She must've caught the way I looked at her, because she smiled at me and rubbed her eyes. "I'm okay, Tyler, don't worry." With a steady arm, she held her hand out, palm facing down. "I can stay missing for a while longer. So come on, like Vincent said, let's kick some ass!"

Diana and Vincent shoved their hands next to Savana's. Aware of their gazes on me, I hovered my hand over theirs. While our features didn't glow, some sort of strength pulsed through my arm and into my body. It tingled and tied knots in my stomach.

Maybe we really were meant to be a team.

"We've waited twelve years to see that," Isabel murmured, half to herself. "But there's time to seek vengeance later. Vincent, you're in contact with Luke, right?"

Vincent hesitated before nodding. He pulled his hand away, and when that surge of power faded, the rest of us did, too.

"Ask him when's the earliest you can visit him and Oliver." Isabel's eyes rounded with sympathy. "Tell them what we've told you. We need them on the same page as us. I know Camila plans to check up on them, but it would mean a lot if you guys spoke to them as well."

"Yeah, sure." Vincent fiddled with his pendant. "I'll wait for more updates since Luke mentioned Oliver wasn't feeling great." He paused, giving me a deathly glare before returning his eyes up front and shrugging. "I don't think it'll take long, though. I'll bet Luke will grow restless by tomorrow."

McKenzie dipped her head in understanding. "Then you'll visit when they're ready. There's still a while until your lunch break ends, so you're all excused."

As she started to quietly chat with Isabel, the rest of us filed into the hallway. It was only us in the main hallway: three teenagers, one pre-teen, and a cat. Adolescent voices in the distance buzzed in my ears. All I could focus on were the faces in front of me. And the faces that were supposed to be here. And the face that brought us together.

Diana, Vincent, and Savana started down the hall, quietly talking about grabbing a bite to eat. I stood frozen in place with

Titanium perched on my shoulder. I absently stroked her back as I watched the others leave.

"Tyler?" Isabel's voice called from the door to her office. She poked her head out, smiling at me sheepishly. "May we talk to you alone?"

It would've been rude to run away, so I ignored the temptation and shuffled back inside. McKenzie nodded at me.

I slumped in one of the chairs, noting a sewing kit atop a nearby cabinet. Pointing to it, I asked, "Can–can either of you sew?"

"Hm? Oh yes!" McKenzie grabbed the kit and sat on Isabel's desk in front of me, gesturing to my hoodie.

I sighed, taking the hoodie off before handing it to her. My shivers weren't from being cold, despite only having a T-shirt on underneath. Titanium jumped on my lap to slow my bouncing leg.

Isabel slid back into her chair, a silent invitation for her old friend to begin.

"I overheard you in the courtyard." McKenzie didn't look at me as she looped the needle and thread into my hoodie. "You feel responsible for what's happened, huh?"

She took my lack of response as an invitation to keep going.

"No soul is born cursed. I hope you know that." McKenzie worked effortless with the needle and thread as she spoke.

Isabel's stormy gaze bore into my skin. "Did your mom ever tell you she was a teacher at Indra Academy?"

"My–my s...siblings mentioned it." I furrowed my brows as I recalled it. When my mom had pulled me out of school, I overheard my sister asking if she'd homeschool me, as my mom had a degree in education. She never did.

McKenzie's eyes were glassy as she recalled it. "Your mom taught world history. Camila, Isabel, and I were all in her class together. I'll never forget how she suddenly disappeared in the second semester. We all saw she was pregnant, but then her mental and physical state declined, and..." She paused, pursing her lips as she recalled the tale. "We thought she was gone for good. But in June, just days before we graduated, she came back for one final goodbye. And you know who was in the stroller?"

She looked right at me with this bittersweet smile.

"You were the cutest baby ever, I'll admit." McKenzie ripped the leftover thread with her teeth, returning the hoodie to me. "Your mom, she..."

Had Isabel, Camila, and McKenzie witnessed my mom's negligence in person? I'd gotten so used to people ignoring it, I used to wonder if it ever happened in the first place. I hunched over and whispered, "Yeah."

Isabel focused on her desk, running her finger along the pencil drawings etched into the wood. I guess it wasn't as fancy as I thought it was. "She was teaching one final lesson and you kept crying and crying. You wanted her, but she just ignored you and kept talking."

It sounds just like her.

"Isabel finally decided she couldn't take the noise anymore and scooped you out of the stroller. While Sadie taught, Isabel bounced you on her knee until you were laughing. You stole the show after that."

Was she trying to humiliate me to death? I nodded slowly. It wasn't like I could deny something I did as a newborn.

Isabel's face was also flushed at the memory. "What we're trying to say is that we saw you when you were only weeks old. You didn't have any horns or red eyes or a forked tail. You weren't a devil or curse." While her tone was lecturing, there was this softness to it. "Do you know what I felt when you wrapped your whole hand around my finger? It wasn't an impending sense of doom. There was only happiness."

"People change," I muttered.

"People retaliate when the world bites them." McKenzie smiled wryly. "Souls are molded with time, not born a certain way. And you know what? Those wounded hearts can be mended." She nodded to me. "Deep down, you're still reaching out for a hand to hold. You've been scared away because people took advantage of you. You've been manipulated and hurt."

I looked down, tracing a finger along my scarred knuckles. "I-It's no excuse."

McKenzie sighed, hopping off the table. She gathered the sewing materials into the kit. "Maybe it's not. But treat that inner child with love. Don't hide from him." She moved toward the door, only to pause. "That goes for your problems, too. You're here now, and you're safe. Trust me, I also felt weird about coming back, but I talked to Isabel and Camila, and suddenly, it was like I never left. Confide in those you have."

"Oliver's just mad at me." My voice was a fierce whisper.

McKenzie gave me a sad smile. "You have no proof of that. If anything, Oliver's going to need your support now more than ever. There's no harm in talking to him."

Then, she left me with Isabel. It felt like a lifetime ago that I sat in this exact spot with her, hearing that my presence was bringing change.

"I...I guess I'm not–not going home, then," I finally whispered.

Isabel's eyes were full of anguish. "Oliver told me about the state you were in the night you arrived here. Tyler, if I'd known about the abuse Sadie was putting you through, I would've done something so much sooner. I always had doubts about her as a mother. I should've followed my gut. I'm so sorry for lying to you."

I looked at her reflection in the shiny lacquer of the wooden desk rather than Isabel herself. "Please don't hurt her. She's struggled enough." It tore at my heart to think of her and my sister, Mia, all alone.

"Not everything can be forgiven." Isabel stood. I hadn't noticed the tears in her eyes until the pale light hit her face. She smiled nonetheless. "What happens to Sadie is a conversation for another time. I will not call the authorities until this is over, so you may rest easy. This is my responsibility now. I don't want you to worry too much about it, okay?"

Only when I nodded did she gesture that I was excused. Titanium and I were alone once more as we stepped into the empty hallway again. Particles of dust floated around us, the silence filled by

Titanium's purring as I stroked her back. McKenzie's and Isabel's words hung in the air.

"It's worth listening to their advice," Titanium murmured eventually.

"I know." I swallowed. The truth grated my throat. "It's just hard. But I'll...I'll try."

Turning my head, I faced the window overlooking the courtyard. I listened to the chatter and delighted shouts of teenagers. Closing my eyes, I felt like I was back in elementary school. It didn't matter that this was a high school or a boarding school. No matter how old the students were, they sounded the same.

Maybe we all had an inner child scraping under our skin, screaming for freedom.

Chapter Thirty-Nine

SIX AT LAST

Oliver

THE REST OF THE week was a blur. It was a whole bunch of phone calls convincing my moms I was okay, gentle physical exercises, and wanting to smash my head into a wall twenty-four seven. I also hadn't showered in a week, which had left me a sticky mess and my hair greasier than ever.

Luke suffered alongside me. We had matching dark circles under our eyes, and we woke up exhausted no matter how long we slept for.

With my aunt unable to visit for long periods of time, I was grateful Luke stayed. He found little ways to lighten the experience by cracking jokes and giving me a hand to squeeze when the nurses changed the dressing on my stump. When he got restless, he went out for short walks and returned with board games from the lounges for us to play. We often found ourselves falling asleep mid-round. It was the only time we could relax.

My moms had trouble booking a last-minute flight to New York. I insisted they didn't have to go through the trouble, but they ignored me.

The phantom pain was worse at night, but I was jacked up on "enough medication to sedate a horse," one nurse had jokingly commented. It left me loopy yet sleep deprived. Thank goodness Luke was there to pay attention and help me with everything I spaced out on.

Dr. Alvi said my stump was healing nicely, but I couldn't say the same for the part of me that was missing. My stitches looked like a zipper leading to the inside of my body.

There was always someone to talk to at the hospital, whether it be about my vitals, my residual limb, or my rehabilitation.

Bryce visited every day after classes. He always brought our schoolwork and the takeout he got on the way to the hospital. Like the staff, he expressed his concern over Luke ditching school, but when Luke responded with a firm "I'll do the work from here," Bryce gave up. Even he looked like he'd seen better days. He said sharing a room with Tyler without me was the most awkward thing ever, especially once they'd learned they were half-brothers.

I insisted that Bryce should go easy on Tyler, and he gave me such a confused look. He couldn't believe I was defending the kid who'd put me in this situation. I told him we'd talk properly when I returned to Indra Academy. My voice was bitter when I said, "You never mentioned being a prince."

Bryce looked shattered.

Things got better as the days inched by. Or at least, kind of.

It was another morning of Luke coaxing me to try the vanilla yogurt, which tasted like toothpaste. "Come on, at least a few bites. You'll start to feel better once you have some fuel in your body." When I didn't budge, he added, "The sooner that happens, the sooner you can get out of here."

Deep down, I knew he was right, but everything I tried to eat in the hospital truly tasted like shit. Even the takeout Bryce brought us didn't appeal to me. The guilt of burdening a friend by being unable to stomach the food kept gnawing at me.

The reminder of my friends—especially Vincent, Diana, Savana, and Tyler—made my chest tighten. According to Luke, they were visiting today, mainly to discuss things we should've gone over days ago. They'd wanted to give me some time to recover, though, and Thanksgiving break had finally arrived.

The delay had also helped Tyler. I was told a burn on his arm had gotten infected, and nobody wanted to drag the injured kid around Long Island. Now that he was feeling better, the impending visit was just around the corner.

And what'll everyone say when they see you hardly functioning? It was a stinging thought that made me wince. I hesitantly licked the yogurt, only to gag. As soon as Luke looked elsewhere, I spat it into a napkin.

"It's that bad?" Luke frowned at the cup as I shoved it to the far end of the overbed table.

"It's awful."

Luke nudged the cup toward me again, chewing his lip. "Take another bite, and I'll tell Vincent to bring us takeout. I know outside food will beat this any day."

I huffed. "You'll make him bring us takeout either way." Still, I dipped the spoon back into the yogurt, licking off the contents. Right after swallowing, I grabbed the water bottle from my bedside table and chugged it down.

"Hey, good job!" Luke reached for his phone and went to text his brother.

I leaned back, studying him for a moment. The bandage over his forehead had been removed days ago, revealing a fresh scar slashing through his left eyebrow. It didn't upset him, and if anything, he thought it was cool. I'd apologized for it countless times, but this time, I had something else to apologize for.

"I realized I never said sorry for breaking that one promise." I smiled guiltily at Luke's confused face. "Remember back at Reed's library, how I said we would visit them on our way home? And then we, uh, never got to visit them?"

Luke blinked in surprise. "Oh, it's okay!"

"I know you like them."

"I do, but you know what? I got to dance with them at the party, and that was more than enough. Something tells me that wasn't a goodbye." Luke's voice didn't waver. It was steady, without doubt. "It was a great night up until everything went south. I'm also happy I got to dance with *you*."

I sank deeper into my bed, holding up the fox plushie Luke had bought me a few days ago. It stared back at me with its beady black eyes, reflecting my pale face and greasy hair. When my gaze slid past the stuffed animal, it focused on my leg under my blanket. *Will I be able to do those things again? Dancing and running?* I bit my tongue to keep myself from tearing up.

After a minute, I sighed. "I'm happy I danced with you, too."

The next hour was an agonizing waiting game. There wasn't much I could do other than watch Luke pace back and forth, which didn't last long as he soon offered to find board games for us. Thinking about being left in the room alone made me queasy, but Luke's legs kept bouncing and twitching.

I caved, and he practically bolted out of the room. It was only fair since he'd been cooped up with me for almost a week now. Of course, I hadn't forced him to stay, but he saw how I gave the hallway untrusting looks and knew I'd feel better with him nearby. Usually, he only left the room when I had other company or was sleeping, when thoughts couldn't overwhelm my brain.

Come on, Oliver. Thierry isn't going to waltz inside any second now. Still, my shoulders refused to loosen. I leaned back, holding the fox plushie close to my chest as I looked to the window. The curtains were open, revealing the first blue, sunny sky I'd seen since Derngate. It was dazzling and made my eyes prick, a gorgeous sight. Maybe, just maybe, it meant things were clearing up.

My tentative smile fell as my gaze traveled downward, to the crutches propped against the wall. How could things be clearing up if I could barely use those? Dr. Alvi had given them to me a few days ago, encouraging me to stay active and keep the blood flowing. I could only hobble a few steps before getting dizzy to the point I needed to stop. *So suck that, Dr. Alvi.*

Excited voices from down the hall came into earshot, grabbing my attention. At first, my stomach cramped up, my body preparing to lurch away from unwanted nurses. But to my delight, it was Diana who skidded into the room, her eyes wide upon meeting mine.

"Oliver!" She raced to my side in a flash, grabbing my shoulders and pulling me into a hug. "You scared us half to death! Gosh, I would've killed you if you died. How are you? Are you well?"

I laughed, partially because I couldn't find any words to answer with at first. "I'm sorry—I never meant to scare you. It's great to see you again!" I pulled away in time to see everyone else file into the room more slowly. "It's great to see *all* of you again."

Vincent, Savana, and Tyler were lingering by the entrance. Seeing them in the flesh made my heart ache so much it took my breath away. They looked as bittersweet as I felt.

"Hey, don't crowd the door like that! Come on, make yourselves comfortable." Luke's voice piped up as he wrestled his way past Tyler and Vincent to reenter the room. He balanced a stack of board games in his arms that he carefully placed on my bed.

Savana joined Diana by my side, waving around a paper bag. She wore a fluffy hat that hid her ears, making her look as human as the rest of us. "We got you bagels!"

I took them from her. My mouth watered when I felt the packet was still hot. "You guys are saints!" A stack of bagels sat inside. They smelled fresh from the bakery. "Come sit and share. I can't eat these by myself."

Luke dragged his cot closer to the bed, which he and Tyler then sat on. The others disregarded that and piled onto the sides of my bed. Why wasn't Vincent sitting with his brother? The glare Vincent shot Tyler's way was my answer. *What happened?*

Tyler looked out of it, only shaking his head when Luke offered him some food. Diana mentioned they had to leave Titanium at Indra Academy, so no wonder Tyler looked a little lost. Maybe he was still under the weather. While the swelling had gone down on his face, he still had the remnants of a black eye.

Whatever was going on with Tyler, he seemed upset. He kept glancing at me with this twisted expression, like he wanted to scream but had forgotten how to.

In fact, *everyone* looked at me a little guiltily.

"What's up?" I set my half-eaten bagel down.

Vincent's chuckle was strained. "It's just...weird facing reality and knowing how differently things could've ended. If we'd had a more organized plan..."

"If I hadn't helped Noah with such gruesome fighting moves in the past..." Savana continued.

"If we'd just *been* there"—Diana threw her arms out to gesture to everyone—"we could've done something before it was too late."

Something in me wanted to agree because they were telling the truth. Things might've been different if we'd all made different choices. But none of them deserved to drown in shame. I smiled, despite how my chest tightened and I longed to cry. "Please don't blame yourselves. I got reckless and wasn't watching where my feet were going, that's all." They didn't look convinced, so I added with more strength, "I'll be okay, you guys."

Nobody spoke again right away. Their smiles and nods didn't match their troubled eyes.

"Enough about me, though. How are things at Indra Academy? Have you guys been okay?" Without my phone, I'd been relying on Luke for updates on what happened around the place.

Savana's expression brightened, just a little. "The human realm is cute! You guys got funny vehicles and the butterflies are awfully small. I haven't seen any Shadow Guards, either."

"We call those pets here," Luke said lightly. "They don't talk, unfortunately. Well, other than some birds, I guess."

Savana nodded intensely. "Then I will find myself a bird!"

We laughed, and Savana didn't seem to understand, but she giggled with us.

"And the whole Meraki deal? What did Isabel say?" It was a question I'd been dreading. We'd succeeded, yes, but at the cost of my leg.

"Isabel was surprised we came back with Savana, but relieved! She said it saved us the trouble of searching even more." Diana grinned, nudging Savana's shoulder playfully. "The necklaces are safe with Isabel, too, so we don't have to worry about those anymore."

Vincent nodded wearily. "Isabel and Camila said our main goal is to collect all six necklaces. Now, with all of us united, we can move onto that."

We exchanged glances with each other. Vincent was right, the realization hitting me like a blow. All six of us were together. It was a strange, yet welcome, feeling.

"Obviously, not right away," Luke said to his brother after a moment. "Oliver still needs to heal."

I frowned. "You guys can keep going without me. I don't want to hold anyone back."

Savana shook her head. "We're a team. Nobody gets left behind." Her lip quivered, and after unsuccessfully attempting to hold herself back, she pulled me into a tight embrace.

The others quickly followed suit, smushing me in a suffocating group hug. Only Tyler didn't join, watching from a distance with the tiniest smile.

"I love you guys so much. I–I'm sorry for all of this." The words came out as a choked whimper as my throat closed. "I never meant for everything to become such a mess."

"It's not your fault, Oliver." Luke pulled away to smile at me. It was warm and genuine. "And we love you, too."

∞

For the next hour, we tried to play Monopoly, but we eventually gave up and started breaking the rules, making our own along the way. It was the loudest the room had been during my time occupying it, and the difference was startling. For a moment, it felt like I was back in Indra Academy's common room, goofing off with my classmates.

Tyler still sat on the cot, picking at his nails and staring at the floor. When a nurse came in and said we should start to wrap the visit up, he wilted in relief.

We'd already gone overtime for the visit, so our goodbyes were rather rushed. It was mainly me convincing everyone I would be okay on my own since Luke decided to go home for Thanksgiving break. He promised to visit as often as he could. My moms were landing in New York the next day, so I wouldn't be alone for long.

Still, my hands shook, and I resisted the urge to scream out, *Please don't leave me here by myself!* But I put on a smile for everyone, and only after they filed outside and disappeared into the hallway did it vanish.

Right when I fell back to unwind from the visit, the door creaked open. Tyler stood at the entrance, his eyes wide and lips in a thin line.

"Hey, did you forget something?" I looked around the room for whatever called him back here.

Tyler opened his mouth, jaw twitching, before he shut his mouth again. He shook his head and staggered to the side of my bed, digging his hands into his pockets. He pulled out a crumpled piece of paper and briefly scanned it before holding it toward me. "I–I...I w-wrote it down."

I took it from him. My eyes were greeted by a swarm of sloppy letters on the page. It took a moment for my vision to clear. "Want me to spare us the awkward silence and read it out loud?"

Tyler hesitated before nodding. Like a child at story time, he sat on the side of my bed and hugged himself tightly.

"Okay." I began to read aloud.

Hi Oliver,

I'm writing this to tell you I'm sorry. Not just for what happened to your leg, but for everything that happened beforehand. I treated you so badly when you only approached me out of kindness. You tried so hard, and I shot down your efforts every time. I should've given you a second chance, like how you said everyone deserves. You just wanted the best for me, and I fucked that up. There's no excuse for it and no denying it. I've acknowledged what I've done, and I'm fully prepared to make it up to you, however you see fit. I'm sorry. I'm so sorry, and I'll keep saying it until it's okay. You have a smile just like my brother's, and I nearly lost it a second time.

Please don't forgive me right away, because I hurt you on a scale beyond fixing. I just wanted you to hear I'm sorry, and I mean it with all my heart.

Feel better soon,

Tyler

The letter blurred before me, rendering me speechless. I looked over at Tyler to see his reaction, jumping a little when I saw fat tears rolling down his cheeks. He had one hand clamped over his mouth, his face was scrunched up, and his whole body was shaking. His hiccups and whimpers slid past the cracks of his fingers.

"Hey," I murmured. When he looked at me, I smiled. "It's alright. I hear you, Tyler. I hear you." He nodded but cried even harder. *I gave this kid the fright of a lifetime, huh?*

If it weren't for the tears rolling off his chin, I would've thought Tyler was frozen in time. He sat unmoving, like he was deep in thought, before slowly pulling his hand away from his face.

And then, he leaned forward and hugged me.

My jaw dropped, my breath catching in my throat as he squeezed me. "I—"

"I'm so sorry," Tyler cut me off. "I'm sorry. I'm so sorry!"

"Woah, it's okay!"

"It's not!" Tyler began to sob again. "I was so stupid. I–I..." A shudder racked his body.

My arms twitched as they hovered in the air. "Would you like a hug back?"

Tyler nodded, and I carefully put my hands on his shoulders. For once, he didn't jump at the contact. "I walked away because–because I didn't want to hurt you! A-and that just made it worse. I was so selfish."

I shook my head, even though he couldn't see it with his face buried. "From what I remember of the fight, Noah was aiming that fire blast at you. I pushed you out of the way because I wanted to save you." If saving him had nearly killed me, I didn't want to imagine what would've happened to Tyler if I hadn't. "Even if there was no magical 'chosen one' business, I'd do it again."

Tyler didn't look up. "Would you?"

"I would. I was starting to see you as a little brother, you know? A part of Indra Academy." I put all my strength into my voice. "And I couldn't lose you the way I lost my real family."

Tyler whimpered. He took in a shaky breath before pulling away, rubbing his arms like he was cold or scratching away the physical contact. "I'll–I'll make it up t...to you. Somehow."

"You don't have to," I protested.

Tyler stood up. "I want to."

I sighed, folding his letter and offering it to him. When he shook his head, I put it on my bedside table. "Only if you want to," I repeated. "But honestly, just you being at Indra Academy is enough."

A smile pulled on Tyler's lips to hear he was wanted. That was all he'd been looking for. He wiped his eyes and started for the door, only to hesitate. "I'll, um, I'll tell Titanium y-you said hi? Uh...and I'll see you back at Indra Academy."

And with that, he was gone. I glanced at the window once more, where a little sparrow pecked at stray twigs that'd been carried to the sill by the wind. It sang a quiet tune to itself, pausing once it became aware it had an audience. We stared at each other, and the bird took off while continuing to sing.

A soft feather fluttered from the bird's wing, spinning on its way down. It came in through the open window and landed on the foot of my bed. I leaned forward and picked it up, examining the gentle, brown hues before looking to the window again.

The bird was gone, and all that remained was the beautiful blue sky.

EPILOGUE

LOVE AND POWER WERE foolish concepts. If they killed so many people, why would anyone devote their life to searching for them?

Humans just enjoyed fixating on something.

Sadie Lynn had fallen prey to that infatuation. Her tattered flats didn't make a sound as they carried her through the dark, empty streets of Manhattan. Her coat was frayed and thin from being worn so much over time and did little to protect her. Little clouds puffed around her weary face with every exhale. Her eyelids drooped from the exhaustion of endlessly searching for someone, each attempt unsuccessful.

This night was different, though.

She navigated toward a familiar alleyway, and as her shadow cast along the stretch of concrete, a nearby rat scurried into the trash. It didn't faze her as she headed straight for the dark outline of a man.

"So it wasn't a lie," she said, her voice a rumble.

"Why would I ever lie to you?" The man stepped into the moonlight. Even wearing humble street clothes and a hat to cover his ears, he was no stranger. "Do you know why I called you here, dearest Sadie?" A smile played on his lips as he extended a hand toward the woman's cheek.

She caught his wrist before he could touch her, with a cutting glare. "There are many reasons, Thierry. I hope at least one of them is to apologize."

Thierry lowered his arm with a scoff. "Apologize for what?"

Sadie's throat jumped with rage. She shoved Thierry, and a nearby puddle shot upward and dangled right over his head. "For never coming back! Do you know how hard it is to raise three little kids in an apartment you can hardly afford? You're a heartless man."

"Lower the water. You don't see me wielding fire on the street, now do you?" Thierry spoke nonchalantly, not batting an eye at the scornful woman. He smoothed down the hair poking out of his hat with a smile on his face. "I'm here to make up for that. How would you like to help me?"

"You made that offer twelve years ago." Sadie relaxed her shoulders. The water trickled back into the puddle. "And like I said before, I have a daughter to take care of."

Thierry cocked his head to one side. "Oh? What happened to your little son?"

Sadie searched Thierry over, her eyebrows knitting together. "Who? Your little ice mutation? The damn fool ran away weeks ago. I didn't think he'd stay away so long." A realization struck her, and she stiffened. "You know something, don't you?"

"That's what I want your help with, darling." Thierry held back a laugh. "Tyler *was* under my supervision the last few weeks, but he left me, too. You raised an agile kid." He ran his finger along his nose, and only then did Sadie realize it was crooked. "You can help me find him again."

Sadie pursed her lips. "Why should I?"

Thierry began to circle her, humming a light tune. "Because if you do, you won't have to stay in that horrible apartment anymore. Your daughter can grow up happy, and your son will grow up to be powerful." He stopped just a little behind Sadie, leaning down to whisper in her ear. "And I know you want your plaything back. He wants you too, you know? I've seen his dreams. They're always about you and some dark, horrid, cramped place." Thierry chuckled. "Tyler loves and misses you."

"Does he?"

"He does. Tell me, though, do you love *him*?"

Sadie ground her teeth. "He's my son for fuck's sake. Of course, I love him." Her words were hollow and sounded as worn as the bottoms of her shoes.

Thierry looked doubtful.

"Give me my son back!" Sadie's voice rose. "It's all thanks to him we're in this situation. Allowing him to run free is dangerous."

"You still have that flame inside of you. How admirable." Thierry gave her a teasing look before pushing past her and out of the alley.

When he stopped on the sidewalk, Sadie slowly followed. A nearby streetlight flickered on and off, contorting both of their shadows every few seconds.

"Where do we begin?" she asked into the silence.

Thierry turned, facing east. There was more than a sunrise coming from that direction. They both knew Long Island was also that way. Grinning, Thierry rumbled, "I know where he is."

BONUS MATERIAL UP AHEAD!

Oliver Stylus!

Tyler Lynn!

Savana Taylor
Vincent Ferris
Diana Divata
Luke Ferris

Acknowledgements

I was twelve years old when I decided I wanted to be an author. Even back then, as a bright-eyed and clueless sixth grader, I knew I wanted to share Tyler's and Oliver's story with the world. I told everyone I could about it. My friends. My classmates. My family. My babysitters from whenever my parents would travel for work. This went on for years as I countlessly rewrote and edited the book. People entered and left my life in the time it took to fulfill my promise of publishing *Indra Academy: Reborn*. And here it is.

I've been drafting this moment in my head since I was twelve, but even now, I'm at a loss for words. It's unreal to believe my silly story is now a reality. I couldn't have accomplished this without some amazing people.

To Kayla, my beloved younger sister and best friend, thank you for your endless support. Thank you for being my first fan and for always cheering me on. I appreciate your brutal honesty that made me rewrite this book twice. You saved it, and for that, I'm eternally grateful. *Indra Academy* wouldn't be what it is today without you.

Thank you for having so much faith in my craft and letting me be the one who inspired you to start writing your own stories.

To Dad, thank you for your unwavering dedication to help bring this book to life, and for letting me read every manuscript out loud to you. I will forever cherish those nights of hearing you suggest sinister plots and theories. Thank you for always playing heavy metal music in the car, saying, "This song reminds me of your book!" You taught me to be brave with my writing, that *Indra Academy* could be bigger than I imagined. And thank you to Mom as well, for always listening to my rambles and allowing me to organize my thoughts with you. Thank you both for encouraging me to make something memorable with my writing skills.

To my editors, Hannah and Sarah, thank you for your endless wisdom and helping me polish *Indra Academy: Reborn*. The writing sprints we did together in late 2020 and early 2021 pulled me out of the worst writer's block of my life. You guys showed me how powerful being in a writing community is. Your sharp eyes and open minds helped me notice and align ideas I didn't know were possible. Thank you for helping me navigate this daunting world of publishing. I'm grateful I didn't have to take these baby steps alone.

To my fourth grade teacher, Steve Reifman, thank you for seeing the potential in me before I saw it in myself. Thank you for reading my short stories about Crystal Lacey and sitting with me at lunch to discuss them. You were the first person to ever settle down with my writing and treat it as something worth reading.

Thank you for the praise and encouragement that moved me to keep creating stories after I left your class.

To my fifth grade teacher, Lindsay Light, thank you for always believing in me. Thank you for donating that annotated copy of *A Writer's Notebook* by Ralph Fletcher to me, with the message inside saying you can't wait to read my first book. This was months before I started *Indra Academy's* first draft. You had full confidence I would continue to write stories after elementary school. I'll never forget your kindness.

To my wonderful beta readers, Ella, Parker, Avery, Caroline, and Isabella, thank you for being *Indra Academy's* first true audience outside of my family. It was an honor to let you into my little world and share my love for these characters with you all. Thank you for accepting *Indra Academy* with all its quirks and bumps in the road. I couldn't have asked for a better team.

My gratitude extends beyond the people listed here. Thank you to those who have followed my journey since day one, and to those who stuck around out of curiosity. Thank you to those who doubted me and inspired me to prove them wrong. And thank you to everyone who gave me a chance, regardless of whether or not they remained in my life. I couldn't have done it without you.

ABOUT THE AUTHOR

Nurit Noik was born and raised in Southern California, with her love for art and reading developing at an early age. She dedicated her adolescence to writing stories, cheered on by her family and Penguino, her trusty penguin plushie. When she isn't working on her novels, she's usually drawing, going horseback riding, or scouring the neighborhood for cats to cross paths with. *Indra Academy: Reborn* is her debut novel.

www.ingramcontent.com/pod-product-compliance
Lightning Source LLC
Chambersburg PA
CBHW051207130726
47988CB00001B/11